The Weird Tales of Tanith Lee

Dedication

This one's for Mavis Haut. A magically wonderful friend and astonishing digger in the roots of all of Tanith's subconscious jungles. With deepest love from us both. xxx

John Kaiine, April 2017

The Weird Tales of Tanith Lee

Introduction by Mike Ashley

IMMANION PRESS
Stafford England

Cover Art by John Kaiine
Interior layout by Storm Constantine

Set in Garamond

ISBN 978-1-907737-79-4

IP0130

Author Site:
Daughter of the Night: An Annotated Tanith Lee Bibliography:
http://www.daughterofthenight.com/

An Immanion Press Edition
http://www.immanion–press.com
info@immanion–press.com

Books by Tanith Lee

A Selection

The Birthgrave Trilogy (The Birthgrave; Vazkor, son of Vazkor, Quest for the White Witch)

The Vis Trilogy (The Storm Lord; Anackire; The White Serpent)

The Flat Earth Opus (Night's Master; Death's Master; Delusion's Master; Delirium's Mistress; Night's Sorceries)

Don't Bite the Sun

Drinking Sapphire Wine

Volkhavaar

The Paradys Quartet (The Book of the Damned; The Book of the Beast; The Book of the Dead; The Book of the Mad)

The Venus Quartet (Faces Under Water; Saint Fire; A Bed of Earth; Venus Preserved)

Kill the Dead

Electric Forest

Days of Grass

Sung in Shadow

A Heroine of the World

Sabella

Lycanthia

The Scarabae Blood Opera (Dark Dance; Personal Darkness; Darkness, I)

The Blood of Roses

When the Lights Go Out

Heart-Beast

Elephantasm

Eva Fairdeath

Reigning Cats and Dogs

Vivia

The Unicorn Trilogy (Black Unicorn; Gold Unicorn; Red Unicorn)

The Claidi Journals (Law of the Wolf Tower; Wolf Star Rise, Queen of the Wolves, Wolf Wing)

The Piratica Novels (Piratica 1; Piratica 2; Piratica 3)

The Silver Metal Lover

Metallic Love

Death of the Day

The Gods Are Thirsty

Mortal Suns
The Lionwolf Trilogy (Cast a Bright Shadow, Here in Cold Hell,
No Flame but Mine)

Collections

Nightshades
Dreams of Dark and Light
Women as Demons
Red as Blood – Tales from the Sisters Grimmer
Tamastara, or the Indian Nights
The Gorgon
Tempting the Gods
Hunting the Shadows
Sounds and Furies
Dancing in the Fire
Colder Greyer Stones
Space is Just a Starry Night
Phantasya
Blood 20

Also Published by Immanion Press

The Colouring Book Series
Greyglass
To Indigo
L'Amber
Killing Violets
Ivoria
Cruel Pink
Turquoiselle

Ghosteria Volume 1: The Stories
Ghosteria Volume 2: The Novel: Zircons May Be Mistaken
A Different City
Legenda Maris
Animate Objects

Contents

An Awareness of Worlds

Mike Ashley

We were treated to Tanith Lee's writing for nearly fifty years, and it will continue to treat readers for centuries, for it is timeless. You can dip into any of her books at any time during her career and you will find her distinctive voice, unchanging, unique, eternal.

There was always something about Tanith and her work. Although she wrote fantasies, fairy tales, vampire stories, science fiction, just like hundreds of other writers, she was something apart. She never was "just like" other writers. A story by Tanith Lee unveils a voice alone, a true Scheherazade, someone with a distinctive vision of the world and who explored that world, or those worlds to be accurate, with a highly perceptive and mindful set of eyes. It was as if she was recording, or "channelling" as she called it, a real, but alternate landscape.

Her publisher, the late Donald A. Wollheim, once said to me, (in a letter in 1988), "Tanith Lee is undoubtedly the finest fantasy writer in the English language today." He felt she deserved the Grand Master Award, despite her comparative youth. She was eventually named the World Horror Grandmaster in 2009, and won the World Fantasy Lifetime Achievement Award in 2013, and the Bram Stoker Lifetime Achievement Award in 2015. I still don't feel she received enough awards, but then to paraphrase the title of one of her books, reading anything by Tanith is like drinking sapphire wine. It is intoxicating, and you have to ration yourself, but I suspect too many people rationed themselves too much. She was so prolific that I wonder just how many people have been able to read everything. I confess that I haven't – but I know it's there and, from time to time, I can partake further of the Tanith wine and lose myself in its opulent texture and bouquet.

There is a special bouquet about the stories in this collection as they are distilled from a very distinctive grape, from the vineyard of *Weird Tales*. Known as "the unique magazine", *Weird Tales* was the legendary American pulp, which originally ran from 1923 to 1954 and has been revived several times since. The original incarnation is best known for having published the works of H. P. Lovecraft, Robert E. Howard and Clark Ashton Smith, as well as stories by Ray Bradbury, Robert Bloch and Manly Wade Wellman, but we should not forget that it also published much highly original work by women: C. L. Moore, Mary Elizabeth Counselman, Everil Worrell, Greye La Spina, G. G. Pendarves and plenty more.

Weird Tales was revived first in 1973 and again in 1980. It was in this second revival, edited by Lin Carter, that Tanith appeared with "When the Clock Strikes", her dark, mysterious and infinitely superior retelling of the Cinderella story. It was later included in her collection *Red as Blood*, as one of the "Tales of the Sisters Grimmer", but perhaps more significantly Jack Zipes selected it for his showcase anthology of the best fairy tales, ancient and modern, in the western tradition, *Spells of Enchantment* (1991). That helped cement Tanith's already acknowledged position as one of the great storytellers of her age.

Weird Tales continued to publish her regularly. Lin Carter ran another story, "The Sombrus Tower", in the second volume of his *Weird Tales*, (issued simultaneously with the first), but after two more volumes Carter's licence on the magazine expired. After another brief change of publisher, it was revived again in Spring 1988 by George Scithers, Darrell Schweitzer and John Betancourt as a beautiful neo-pulp, the first issue strikingly illustrated by George Barr.

Tanith was present in that first issue with "Death Dances", and more significantly in the second number, Summer 1988, which was labelled a "Special Tanith Lee issue". Alongside stories by Morgan Llywelyn, Brian Lumley, Nancy Springer, Harry Turtledove and others, were two new stories by Tanith, an interview, a bibliography and a profile, by Donald Wollheim, in which he called her the "Empress of Dreams". The whole issue was stunningly illustrated by Stephen Fabian. The story that opened the issue was "The Unrequited Glove", a clever title for what is, for Tanith, a comparatively straightforward but nevertheless ingenious reworking of the "The Beast with Five Fingers" motif. Her other story closed the issue, "The Kingdoms of the Air", a wonderfully Arthurianesque Grail story, which I reprinted in my anthology *Chronicles of the Holy Grail* in 1996. The stories show two facets of Tanith's work: the unsettling strange story in a seemingly respectful setting and the historical fantasy in an exotic and remote setting.

Of special interest was the interview with Tanith conducted by Darrell Schweitzer. She revealed how she had always wanted to be a writer as it came as easy to her as breathing. But she also remarked "One's whole life is an apprenticeship. You never learn your trade fully. You can always learn some more. I'm an apprentice now. I just happen to be a professional apprentice."

Tanith appeared regularly in *Weird Tales* with 28 stories in total, all reprinted here, including one story published only in a special electronic preview edition of the magazine for the 2011 World Fantasy Convention. There were two more in the magazine's brief reincarnation as *Worlds of Fantasy & Horror*, when the publisher briefly lost the licence to the title. She became the first writer to have a second special issue dedicated to her work in 1994. Schweitzer gave no apology for this, saying that, "...the lady is one of the literary dynamos of our time, enormously prolific in the novel, the short story and all lengths in between; but, quite unlike most hyper-prolific writers of the past, she has maintained an astonishingly high level of quality throughout her career."

That's because she was always learning, always exploring, always experimenting with the unpredictable. There is a good example in that issue with her opening story, "The Persecution Machine", dedicated to Edward Gorey. Voted the most popular story in the issue, this haunting piece, classified as steampunk by some, is an exploration of madness, or more accurately paranoia manifested by a machine. The magic of the story is in how the narrator also starts to hear and then see what drives his uncle to madness. And it reminds me of something Tanith said the first time we met.

Back in 1981, Tanith and I took part in a book programme for Tyne Tees Television, in Newcastle, called *A Better Read*. We had corresponded on and off before then, but had not met in person. Both Tanith and I had separately taken the train up from London, but I had not realised Tanith was on the train until near the end. I stood up to stretch my legs and see if I could get a drink and only then discovered that Tanith was on the seat one back from me, on the other side of the aisle. She was looking out of the window, somewhat wistfully I thought. I hesitated a second or two and she must have noticed and looked up at me, so I felt I ought to introduce myself. She was pleasant and welcoming, but at the outset I had a feeling I had interrupted a train of thought, and that phrase is very relevant. I sat opposite her and it wasn't long before she said (and I can't recall the exact words after all these years, but this is the gist): "Trains are rather like our thoughts, our imagination. From them we can see the countryside fly past and we're not really part of that world, and yet it's part of us." She paused and I was about to say something when she added: "I wonder how much each world is aware of the other."

It's a lovely thought, and we got into a rather philosophical discussion about the nature of reality and how much the past might impress itself upon the landscape, and before we knew it we were in Newcastle, but that single sentence of hers stayed with me, because it's part and parcel of what fantasy and fiction is all about. Two worlds intermingling in our minds, where for a while fantasy and reality overlap.

Tanith Lee brought that merger to an art form at a very high level. Tanith's stories impress themselves upon our mind as if they were always a part of our world which we had somehow forgotten. They are enjoyed at their best when we accept them in the same way that she believed in her worlds. Those worlds are there, just beyond the window, but if we speed past too fast we may lose them. So savour these stories and relish the awareness of other worlds. They will soon be part of your world.

When the Clock Strikes

Yes, the great ballroom is filled only with dust now. The slender columns of white marble and the slender columns of rose-red marble are woven together by cobwebs. The vivid frescoes, on which the Duke's treasury spent so much, are dimmed by the dust; the faces of the painted goddesses look grey. And the velvet curtains – touch them, they will crumble. Two hundred years now, since anyone danced in this place on the sea-green floor in the candle-gleam. Two hundred years since the wonderful clock struck for the very last time.

I thought you might care to examine the clock. It was considered exceptional in its day. The pedestal is ebony and the face fine porcelain. And these figures, which are of silver, would pass slowly about the circlet of the face. Each figure represents, you understand, an hour. And as the appropriate hours came level with this golden bell, they would strike it the correct number of times. All the figures are unique, as you see. Beginning at the first hour, they are, in this order, a girl-child, a dwarf, a maiden, a youth, a lady and a knight. And here, notice, the figures grow older as the day declines: a queen and king for the seventh and eighth hours, and after these, an abbess and a magician and next to last, a hag. But the very last is strangest of all. The twelfth figure; do you recognise him? It is Death. Yes, a most curious clock. It was reckoned a marvellous thing then. But it has not struck for two hundred years. Possibly you have been told the story? No? Oh, but I am certain that you have heard it, in another form, perhaps.

However, as you have some while to wait for your carriage, I will recount the tale, if you wish.

I will start with what was said of the clock. In those years, this city was prosperous, a stronghold – not as you see it today. Much was made in the city that was ornamental and unusual. But the clock, on which the twelfth hour was Death, caused something of a stir. It was thought unlucky, foolhardy, to have such a clock. It began to be murmured, jokingly by some, by others in earnest, that one night when the clock struck the twelfth hour, Death would truly strike with it.

Now life has always been a chancy business, and it was more so then. The Great Plague had come but twenty years before and was not yet forgotten. Besides, in the Duke's court there was much intrigue, while enemies might be supposed to plot beyond the city walls, as happens even in our present age. But there was another thing.

It was rumoured that the Duke had obtained both his title and the city treacherously. Rumour declared that he had systematically destroyed those who had stood in line before him, the members of the princely house that formerly ruled here. He had accomplished the task slyly, hiring assassins talented with poisons and daggers. But rumour also declared that the Duke had not been sufficiently thorough. For though he had meant to rid himself of all that rival house, a single descendant remained, so obscure he had not traced her – for it was a woman.

Of course, such matters were not spoken of openly. Like the prophecy of the clock, it was a subject for the dark.

Nevertheless, I will tell you at once, there was such a descendant he had missed in his bloody work. And she was a woman. Royal and proud she was, and seething with bitter spite and a hunger for vengeance, and as bloody as the Duke, had he known it, in her own way.

For her safety and disguise, she had long ago wed a wealthy merchant in the city, and presently bore the man a daughter. The merchant, a dealer in silks, was respected, a good fellow but not wise. He rejoiced in his handsome and aristocratic wife. He never dreamed what she might be about when he was not with her. In fact, she had sworn allegiance to Satanas. In the dead of night, she would go up into an old tower adjoining the merchant's house, and there she would say portions of the Black Mass, offer sacrifice, and thereafter practice witchcraft against the Duke. This witchery took a common form, the creation of a wax image and the maiming of the image that, by sympathy, the injuries inflicted on the wax be passed on to the living body of the victim. The woman was capable in what she did. The Duke fell sick. He lost the use of his limbs and was racked by excruciating pains from which he could get no relief. Thinking himself on the brink of death, the Duke named his sixteen-year-old son his heir. This son was dear to the Duke, as everyone knew, and be sure the woman knew it too. She intended sorcerously to murder the young man in his turn, preferably in his father's sight. Thus, she let the Duke linger in his agony, and commenced planning the fate of the prince.

Now all this while she had not been toiling alone. She had one helper. It was her own daughter, a maid of fourteen, who she had recruited to her service nearly as soon as the infant could walk. At six or seven, the child had been lisping the Satanic rite along with her mother. At fourteen, you may imagine, the girl was well-versed in the

Black Arts, though she did not have her mother's natural genius for them.

Perhaps you would like me to describe the daughter at this point. It has a bearing on the story, for the girl was astonishingly beautiful. Her hair was the rich dark red of antique burnished copper, her eyes were the hue of the reddish-golden amber that traders bring from the East. When she walked, you would say she was dancing. But when she danced, a gate seemed to open in the world, and bright fire spangled inside it, but she was the fire.

The girl and her mother were close as gloves in a box. Their games in the old tower bound them closer. No doubt the woman believed herself clever to have got such a helpmate, but it proved her undoing.

It was in this manner. The silk merchant, who had never suspected his wife for an instant of anything, began to mistrust the daughter. She was not like other girls. Despite her great beauty, she professed no interest in marriage, and none in clothes or jewels. She preferred to read in the garden at the foot of the tower. Her mother had taught the girl her letters, though the merchant himself could read but poorly. And often the father peered at the books his daughter read, unable to make head or tail of them, yet somehow not liking them. One night very late, the silk merchant came home from a guild dinner in the city, and he saw a slim pale shadow gliding up the steps of the old tower, and he knew it for his child. On impulse, he followed her, but quietly. He had not considered any evil so far, and did not want to alarm her. At an angle of the stair, the lighted room above, he paused to spy and listen. He had something of a shock when he heard his wife's voice rise up in glad welcome. But what came next drained the blood from his heart. He crept away and went to his cellar for wine to stay himself. After the third glass, he ran for neighbours and for the watch.

The woman and her daughter heard the shouts below and saw the torches in the garden. It was no use dissembling. The tower was littered with evidence of vile deeds, besides what the woman kept in a chest beneath her unknowing husband's bed. She understood it was all up with her, and she understood too how witchcraft was punished hereabouts. She snatched a knife from the altar.

The girl shrieked when she realised what her mother was at. The woman caught the girl by her red hair and shook her.

"Listen to me, my daughter," she cried, "and listen carefully, for the minutes are short. If you do as I tell you, you can escape their wrath and only I need die. And if you live, I am satisfied, for you can carry on my labour after me. My vengeance I shall leave you, and my witchcraft to exact it by. Indeed, I promise you stronger powers than mine. I will beg my lord Satanas for it, and he will not deny me, for he is just, in his fashion, and I have served him well. Now, will you attend?"

"I will," said the girl.

So the woman advised her, and swore her to the fellowship of Hell. And then the woman forced the knife into her own heart and dropped dead on the floor of the tower.

When the men burst in with their swords and staves and their torches and their madness, the girl was ready for them.

She stood blank-faced, blank-eyed, with her arms hanging at her sides. When one touched her, she dropped down at his feet.

"Surely, she is innocent," this man said. She was lovely enough that it was hard to accuse her. Then her father went to her and took her hand and lifted her. At that the girl opened her eyes and she said, as if terrified: "How did I come here? I was in my chamber and sleeping..."

"The woman has bewitched her," her father said.

He desired very much that this be so. And when the girl clung to his hand and wept, he was certain of it. They showed her the body with the knife in it. The girl screamed and seemed to lose her senses totally.

She was put to bed. In the morning, a priest came and questioned her. She answered steadfastly. She remembered nothing, not even of the great books she had been observed reading. When they told her what was in them, she screamed again and apparently would have thrown herself from the narrow window, only the priest stopped her.

Finally, they brought her the holy cross in order that she might kiss it and prove herself blameless.

Then she knelt, and whispered softly, that nobody should hear but one – "Lord Satanas, protect thy handmaid." And either that gentleman has more power than he is credited with or else the symbols of God are only as holy as the men who deal in them, for she embraced the cross and it left her unscathed.

At that, the whole household thanked God. The whole household saving, of course, the woman's daughter. She had another to thank.

The woman's body was burnt, and the ashes put into unconsecrated ground beyond the city gates. Though they had discovered her to be a witch, they had not discovered the direction her witchcraft had selected. Nor did they find the wax image with its limbs all twisted and stuck through with needles. The girl had taken that up and concealed it. The Duke continued in his distress, but he did not die. Sometimes, in the dead of night, the girl would unearth the image from under a loose brick by the hearth, and gloat over it, but she did nothing else. Not yet. She was fourteen and the cloud of her mother's acts still hovered over her. She knew what she must do next.

The period of mourning ended.

"Daughter," said the silk merchant to her, "why do you not remove your black? The woman was malign and led you into wickedness. How long will you mourn her, who deserves no mourning?"

"Oh, my father," she said, "never think I regret my wretched mother. It is my own unwitting sin I mourn." And she grasped his hand and spilled her tears on it. "I would rather live in a convent," said she, "than mingle with proper folk. And I would seek a convent too, if it were not that I cannot bear to be parted from you."

Do you suppose she smiled secretly as she said this? One might suppose it. Presently she donned a robe of sackcloth and poured ashes over her red-copper hair. "It is my penance," she said, "I am glad to atone for my sins."

People forgot her beauty. She was at pains to obscure it. She slunk about like an aged woman, a rag pulled over her head, dirt smeared on her cheeks and brow. She elected to sleep in a cold cramped attic and sat all day by a smoky hearth in the kitchens. When someone came to her and begged her to wash her face, and put on suitable clothes, and sit in the rooms of the house, she smiled modestly, drawing the rag or a piece of hair over her face. "I swear," she said, "I am glad to be humble before God and men."

They reckoned her pious and they reckoned her simple. Two years passed. They mislaid her beauty altogether, and reckoned her ugly. They found it hard to call to mind who she was exactly, as she sat in the ashes, or shuffled unattended about the streets like a crone.

At the end of the second year, the silk merchant married again. It was inevitable, for he was not a man who liked to live alone.

On this occasion, his choice was a harmless widow. She already had two daughters, pretty in an unremarkable style. Perhaps the merchant hoped they would comfort him for what had gone before, this normal cheery wife and the two sweet, rather silly daughters, whose chief interests were clothes and weddings. Perhaps he hoped also that his deranged daughter might be drawn out by company. But that hope foundered. Not that the new mother did not try to be pleasant to the girl. And the new sisters, their hearts grieved by her condition, went to great lengths to enlist her friendship. They begged her to come from the kitchens or the attic. Failing in that, they sometimes ventured to join her, their fine silk dresses trailing on the greasy floor. They combed her hair, exclaiming, when some of the ash

17

and dirt were removed, on its colour. But no sooner had they turned away, than the girl gathered up handfuls of soot and ash and rubbed them into her hair again. Now and then, the sisters attempted to interest their bizarre relative in a bracelet or a gown or a current song. They spoke to her of the young men they had seen at the suppers or the balls, which were then given regularly by the rich families of the city. The girl ignored it all. If she ever said anything it was to do with penance and humility. At last, as must happen, the sisters wearied of her, and left her alone. They had no cares and did not want to share in hers. They came to resent her moping greyness, as indeed the merchant's second wife had already done.

"Can you do nothing with the girl?" she demanded of her husband. "People will say that I and my daughters are responsible for her condition and that I ill-treat the maid from jealousy of her dead mother."

"Now, how could anyone say that?" protested the merchant, "when you are famous as the epitome of generosity and kindness."

Another year passed, and saw no huge difference in the household.

A difference there was, but not visible.

The girl who slouched in the corner of the hearth was seventeen. Under the filth and grime, she was, impossibly, more beautiful, although no one could see it.

And there was one other invisible item – her power, (which, all this time she had nurtured, saying her prayers to Satanas in the black of midnight), her power was rising like a dark moon in her soul.

Three days after her seventeenth birthday, the girl straggled about the streets as she frequently did. A few noted her and muttered it was the merchant's ugly simple daughter and paid no more attention. Most did not know her at all. She had made herself appear one with the scores of impoverished flotsam, which constantly roamed the city, beggars and starvelings. Just outside the city gates, these persons congregated in large numbers, slumped around fires of burning refuse or else wandering to and fro in search of edible seeds, scraps, the miracle of a dropped coin. Here the girl now came, and began to wander about as they did. Dusk gathered and the shadows thickened. The girl sank to her knees in a patch of earth as if she had found something. Two or three of the beggars sneaked over to see if it were worth snatching from her – but the girl was only scrabbling in the empty soil. The beggars, making signs to each other that she was touched by God – mad – left her alone. But, very far from mad, the girl presently dug up a stoppered clay urn. In this urn were the ashes and charred bones of her mother. She had got a clue as to the location of the urn by devious questioning here and there. Her occult power had helped her to be sure of it.

In the twilight, padding along through the narrow streets and alleys of the city, the girl brought the urn homewards. In the garden at the foot of the old tower, gloom-wrapped, unwitnessed, she unstoppered the urn and buried the ashes freshly. She muttered certain unholy magics over the grave. Then she snapped off the sprig of a young hazel tree, and planted it in the newly-turned ground.

I hazard you have begun to recognise the story by now. I see you suppose I tell it wrongly. Believe me, this is the truth of the matter. But if you would rather I left off the tale... No doubt your carriage will soon be here... No? Very well. I shall continue.

I think I should speak of the Duke's son at this juncture. The prince was nineteen, able, intelligent, and of noble bearing. He was of that rather swarthy type of looks one finds here in the north, but tall and slim and clear-eyed. There is an ancient square where you may see a statue of him, but much eroded by two centuries, and the elements. After the city was sacked, no care was lavished on it.

The Duke treasured his son. He had constant delight in the sight of the young man and what he said and did. It was the only happiness the invalid had.

Then, one night, the Duke screamed out in his bed. Servants came running with candles. The Duke moaned that a sword was transfixing his heart, an inch at a time. The prince hurried into the chamber, but in that instant the Duke spasmed horribly and died. No mark was on his body. There had never been a mark to show what ailed him.

The prince wept. They were genuine tears. He had nothing to reproach his father with, everything to thank him for. Nevertheless, they brought the young man the seal ring of the city, and he put it on.

It was winter, a cold blue-white weather, with snow in the streets and countryside, and a hard wizened sun that drove thin sharp blades of light through the sky, but gave no warmth. The Duke's funeral cortege passed slowly across the snow, the broad open chariots draped with black and silver, the black-plumed horses, the chanting priests with their glittering robes, their jewelled crucifixes and golden censers. Crowds lined the roadways to watch the spectacle. Among the beggar women stood a girl. No one noticed her.

They did not glimpse the expression she veiled in her ragged scarf. She gazed at the bier pitilessly. As the young prince rode by in his sables, the seal ring on his hand, the eyes of the girl burned through her ashy hair, like a red fox through grasses.

The Duke was buried in the mausoleum you can visit to this day, on the east side of the city. Several months elapsed. The prince put his grief from him, and took up the business of the city competently. Wise and courteous he was, but he rarely smiled. At nineteen, his spirit seemed worn. You might think he guessed the destiny that hung over him.

The winter was a hard one, too. The snow had come, and having come was loath to withdraw. When at last the spring returned, flushing the hills with colour, it was no longer sensible to be sad.

The prince's name day fell about this time. A great banquet was planned, a ball. There had been neither in the palace for nigh on three years, not since the Duke's fatal illness first claimed him. Now the royal doors were to be thrown open to all men of influence and their families. The prince was liberal, charming and clever even in this. Aristocrat and rich trader were to mingle in the beautiful dining room, and in this very chamber, among the frescoes, the marbles and the candelabra. Even a merchant's daughter, if the merchant were notable in the city, would get to dance on the sea-green floor, under the white eye of the fearful clock.

The clock. There was some renewed controversy about the clock. They did not dare speak to the young prince. He was a sceptic, as his father had been. But had not a death already occurred? Was the clock not a flying in the jaws of fate? For those disturbed by it, there was a dim writing in their minds, in the dust of the street or the pattern of blossoms. *When the clock strikes...* But people do not positively heed these warnings. Man is afraid of his fears. He ignores the shadow of the wolf thrown on the paving before him, saying: it is only a shadow.

The silk merchant received his invitation to the palace, and to be sure, thought nothing of the clock. His house had been thrown into uproar. The most luscious silks of his workshop were carried into the house and laid before the wife and her two daughters, who chirruped and squealed with excitement. The merchant stood smugly by, above it all yet pleased at being appreciated.

"Oh, father!" cried the two sisters, "may I have this one with the gold piping?"

"Oh, father, this one with the design of pineapples?"

Later, a jeweller arrived and set out his trays. The merchant was generous. He wanted his women to look their best. It might be the night of their lives. Yet all the while, at the back of his mind, a little dark spot, itching, aching. He tried to ignore the spot, not scratch at it. His true daughter, the mad one. Nobody bothered to tell her about the invitation to the palace. They knew how she would react, mumbling in her hair about her sin and her penance, paddling her hands in the greasy ash to smear her face. Even the servants avoided her, as if she were just the cat seated by the fire. Less than the cat, for the cat saw to the mice... Just a block of stone. And yet, how fair she might have looked, decked in the pick of the merchant's wares, jewels at her throat. The prince himself could not have been unaware of her. And though marriage was impossible, other less holy, though equally honourable contracts, might have been arranged to the benefit of all concerned. The merchant sighed. He had scratched the darkness after all. He attempted to comfort himself by watching the two sisters exult over their apparel. He refused to admit that the finery would somehow make them seem but more ordinary than they were by contrast.

The evening of the banquet arrived. The family set off. Most of the servants sidled after. The prince had distributed largesse in the city; oxen roasted in the squares and the wine was free by royal order.

The house grew sombre. In the deserted kitchen, the fire went out.

By the hearth, a segment of gloom rose up.

The girl glanced around her, and she laughed softly and shook out her filthy hair. Of course, she knew as much as anyone, and more than most. This was to be her night, too.

A few minutes later she was in the garden beneath the old tower, standing over the young hazel tree, which thrust up from the earth. It had become strong, the tree, despite the harsh winter. Now the girl nodded to it. She chanted under her breath. At length, a pale light began to glow, far down near where the roots of the tree held to the ground. Out of the pale glow flew a thin black bird, which perched on the girl's shoulder. Together, the girl and the bird passed into the old tower. High up, a fire blazed that no one had lit. A tub steamed with scented water that no one had drawn. Shapes that were not real and barely seen flitted about. Rare perfumes, the rustle of garments, the glint of gems as yet invisible filled and did not fill the restless air.

Need I describe further? No. You will have seen paintings, which depict the attendance upon a witch of her familiar demons. How one bathes her, another anoints her, another brings clothes and ornaments. Perhaps you do not credit such things, in any case. Never mind that. I will tell you what happened in the courtyard before the palace.

Many carriages and chariots had driven through the square, avoiding the roasting oxen, the barrels of wine, the cheering drunken citizens, and so through the gates into the courtyard. Just before ten o'clock, (the hour, if you recall the clock, of the magician), a solitary carriage drove through the square and into the court. The people in the square gawped at the carriage and pressed forward to see who would step out of it, this latecomer. It was a remarkable vehicle that looked to be fashioned of solid gold, all but the domed roof that was transparent flashing crystal. Six black horses drew it. The coachman and postilions were clad in crimson, and strangely masked as curious beasts and reptiles. One of these beast-men now hopped down and opened the door of the carriage. Out came a woman's figure in a cloak of white fur, and glided up the palace stair and in at the doors.

There was dancing in the ballroom. The whole chamber was bright and clamorous with music and the voices of men and women. There, between those two pillars, the prince sat in his chair, dark, courteous, seldom smiling. Here the musicians played, the deep-throated viol, the lively mandolin. And there the dancers moved up and down on the sea-green floor.

But the music and the dancers had just paused. The figures on the clock were themselves in motion. The hour of the magician was about to strike.

As it struck, through the doorway came the figure in the fur cloak. And, as if they must, every eye turned to her.

For an instant she stood there, all white, as though she had brought the winter snow back with her. And then she loosed the cloak from her shoulders; it slipped away, and she was all fire.

She wore a gown of apricot brocade embroidered thickly with gold. Her sleeves and the bodice of her gown were slashed over ivory satin sewn with large rosy pearls. Pearls, too, were wound in her hair that was the shade of antique burnished copper. She was so beautiful that when the clock was still, nobody spoke. She was so beautiful it was hard to look at her for very long.

The prince got up from his chair. He did not know he had. Now he started out across the floor, between the dancers, who parted silently to let him through. He went toward the girl in the doorway as if she drew him by a chain.

The prince had hardly ever acted without considering first what he did. Now he did not consider. He bowed to the girl.

"Madam," he said. "You are welcome. Madam," he said, "tell me who you are."

She smiled.

"My rank," she said. "Would you know that, my lord? It is similar to yours, or would be were I now mistress in my dead mother's palace. But, unfortunately, an unscrupulous man caused the downfall of our house."

"Misfortune indeed," said the prince. "Tell me your name. Let me right the wrong done you."

"You shall," said the girl. "Trust me, you shall. For my name, I would rather keep it secret for the present. But you may call me, if you will, a pet name I have given myself – Ashella."

"Ashella... But I see no ash about you," said the prince, dazzled by her gleam, laughing a little, stiffly, for laughter was not his habit.

"Ash and cinders from a cold and bitter hearth," said she. But she smiled again. "Now everyone is staring at us, my lord, and the musicians are impatient to begin again. Out of all these ladies, can it be you will lead me in the dance?"

"As long as you will dance," he said, "you shall dance with me.

And that is how it was.

There were many dances, slow and fast, whirling measures and gentle ones. And here and there, the prince and the maiden were parted. Always then he looked eagerly after her, sparing no regard for the other girls whose hands lay in his. It was not like him, he was usually so careful. But the other young men who danced on that floor, who clasped her fingers or her narrow waist in the dance, also gazed after her when she was gone. She danced, as she appeared, like fire. Though if you had asked those young men whether they would rather tie her to themselves, as the prince did, they would have been at a loss. For it is not easy to keep pace with fire.

The hour of the hag struck on the clock.

The prince grew weary of dancing with the girl and losing her in the dance to others and refinding her and losing her again.

Behind the curtains, there is a tall window in the east wall that opens on the terrace above the garden. He drew her out there, into the spring night. He gave an order, and small tables were brought with delicacies and sweets and wine. He sat by her, watching every gesture she made, as if he would paint her portrait afterward.

In the ballroom, here, under the clock, the people murmured. But it was not quite the murmur you would expect, the scandalous murmur about a woman come from nowhere, who the prince had made so much of. At the periphery of the ballroom, the silk merchant sat, pale as a ghost, thinking of a ghost, the living ghost of his true daughter. No one else recognised her. Only he. Some trick of the heart had enabled him to know her. He said nothing of it. As the step-sisters and wife gossiped with other wives and sisters, an awful foreboding weighed him down, sent him cold and dumb.

And now it is almost midnight, the moment when the page of the night turns over into day. Almost midnight, the hour when the figure of Death strikes the golden bell of the clock. And what will happen when the clock strikes? Your face announces that you know. Be patient; let us see if you do.

"I am being foolish," said the prince to Ashella on the terrace. "But perhaps I am entitled to be foolish, just once in my life. What are you saying?" For the girl was speaking low beside him, and he could not catch her words.

"I am saying a spell to bind you to me," she said.

"But I am already bound."

"Be bound then. Never go free."

"I do not wish it," he said. He kissed her hands and he said, "I do not know you, but I will wed you. Is that proof your spell has worked? I will wed you, and get back for you the rights you have lost."

"If it were only so simple," said Ashella, smiling, smiling. "But the debt is too cruel. Justice requires a harsher payment."

And then, in the ballroom, Death struck the first note on the golden bell.

The girl smiled and she said:

"I curse you in my mother's name."

The second stroke.

"I curse you in my own name."

The third stroke.

"And in the name of those that your father slew."

The fourth stroke.

"And in the name of my Master, who rules the world."

As the fifth, the sixth, the seventh strokes pealed out, the prince stood nonplussed. At the eighth and the ninth strokes, the strength of the malediction seemed to curdle his blood. He shivered and his brain writhed. At the tenth stroke, he saw a change in the loveliness before him. She grew thinner, taller. At the eleventh stroke, he beheld a thing in a ragged black cowl and robe. It grinned at *him*. It was all grin below a triangle of sockets of nose and eyes. At the twelfth stroke, the prince saw Death and knew him.

In the ballroom, a hideous grinding noise, as the gears of the clock failed. Followed by a hollow booming, as the mechanism stopped entirely.

The conjuration of Death vanished from the terrace.

Only one thing was left behind. A woman's shoe. A shoe no woman could ever have danced in. It was made of glass.

Did you intend to protest about the shoe? Shall I finish the story, or would you rather I did not? It is not the ending you are familiar with. Yes, I perceive you understand that, now.

I will go quickly, then, for your carriage must soon be here. And there is not a great deal more to relate.

The prince lost his mind. Partly from what he had seen, partly from the spells the young witch had netted him in. He could think of nothing but the girl who had named herself Ashella. He raved that Death had borne her away, but he would recover her from Death. She had left the glass shoe as token of her love. He must discover her with the aid of the shoe. Whomsoever the shoe fitted would be Ashella. For there was this added complication, that Death might hide her actual appearance. None had seen the girl before. She had disappeared like smoke. The one infallible test was the shoe. That was why she had left it for him.

His ministers would have reasoned with the prince, but he was past reason. His intellect had collapsed as totally as only a profound intellect can. A lunatic, he rode about the city. He struck out at those who argued with him. On a particular occasion, drawing a dagger, he killed, not apparently noticing what he did. His demand was explicit. Every woman, young or old, maid or married, must come forth from her home, must put her foot into the shoe of glass. They came. They had no choice. Some approached in terror, some weeping. Even the aged beggar women obliged, and they cackled, enjoying the sight of royalty gone mad. One alone did not come.

Now it is not illogical that out of the hundreds of women whose feet were put into the shoe, a single woman might have been found that the shoe fitted. But this did not happen. Nor did the situation alter, despite a lurid fable that some, tickled by the idea of wedding the prince, cut off their toes that the shoe might fit them. And if they did, it was to no avail, for still the shoe did not.

Is it really surprising? The shoe was sorcerous. It constantly changed itself, its shape, its size, in order that no foot, save one, could ever be got into it.

Summer spread across the land. The city took on its golden summer glaze, its fetid summer smell.

What had been a whisper of intrigue, swelled into a steady distant thunder. Plots were being hatched.

One day, the silk merchant was brought, trembling and grey of face, to the prince. The merchant's dumbness had broken. He had unburdened himself of his fear at confession, but the priest had not proved honest. In the dawn, men had knocked on the door of the merchant's house. Now he stumbled to the chair of the prince.

Both looked twice their years, but, if anything, the prince looked the elder. He did not lift his eyes. Over and over in his hands he turned the glass shoe.

The merchant, stumbling too in his speech, told the tale of his first wife and his daughter. He told everything, leaving out no detail. He did not even omit the end: that since the night of the banquet the girl had been absent from his house, taking nothing with her – save a young hazel from the garden beneath the tower.

The prince leapt from his chair.

His clothes were filthy and unkempt. His face was smeared with sweat and dust... it resembled, momentarily, another face.

Without guard or attendant, the prince ran through the city toward the merchant's house, and on the road, the intriguers waylaid and slew him. As he fell, the glass shoe dropped from his hands, and shattered in a thousand fragments.

There is little else worth mentioning.

Those who usurped the city were villains and not merely that, but fools. Within a year, external enemies were at the gates. A year more, and the city had been sacked, half burnt out, ruined. The manner in which you find it now, is somewhat better than it was then. And it is not now anything for a man to be proud of. As you were quick to note, many here earn a miserable existence by conducting visitors about the streets, the palace, showing them the dregs of the city's past.

Which was not a request, in fact, for you to give me money. Throw some from your carriage window if your conscience bothers you. My own wants are few.

No, I have no further news of the girl, Ashella, the witch. A devotee of Satanas, she has doubtless worked plentiful woe in the world. And a witch is long-lived. Even so, she will die eventually. None escapes Death. Then you may pity her, if you like. Those who serve the gentleman below – who can guess what their final lot will be? But I am very sorry the story did not please you. It is not, maybe, a happy choice before a journey.

And there is your carriage at last.

What? Ah, no, I shall stay here in the ballroom where you came on me. I have often paused here through the years. It is the clock. It has a certain – what shall I call it – power, to draw me back.

I am not trying to unnerve you. Why should you suppose that? Because of my knowledge of the city, of the story? You think that I am implying that I myself am Death? Now you laugh. Yes, it is absurd. Observe the twelfth figure on the clock. Is he not as you have always heard Death described? And am I in the least like that twelfth figure?

Although, of course, the story was not as you have heard it, either.

The Sombrus Tower

Vesontane rode into the Southern Waste. The frigid sunshine became a blue fire reflected in his coal-black armour; the wind unrolled his umber hair.

The fertile lovely land of Krennok was far behind him, and his king's house, and the warrior brotherhood in which he had won his place with spear and sword. Two beautiful women were left behind him also, each wondrous in her own way, pale, and melanine, slender as a flower stalk, lush as a rose. Even his name was, to all effect, left behind him, for in Krennok, most had heard of Vesontane, but here, in the dead country, few men travelled, and less news, and fame died like the grass.

But the five sisters had heard it, those five shadowy witches who had come to Krennok-dol five months ago. They had wailed a prophecy like death, for five men, allegedly all heroes, and certainly among them was Golbrant, reckoned by most the truest of all the king's warriors, the bravest, the most honourable, the best. He had been making music with the gold harp, which he lifted like a bird from his shoulder. It had a woman's face, the harp, and when the sisters spoke in the king's hall, among the marble pillar-trees, some had said the woman on the harp wept acidulous green tears, like the sea. Four times the witches had spoken. And then they spoke a name Vesontane knew better than any other, for it was his own.

"Vesontane, Vesontane," they moaned, five reeds sounding as one, "Beware the dark genius of the Sombrus Tower, which stands in the desert on the sun's left hand."

Each prophecy they gave sank in the breast like an iron shaft. No man who heard them quite kept his colour. Of the five named, none quite kept his soul. Some part of it seemed blown away. And presently, the five men, too, were blown, like autumn leaves, from the house of the king, from the land of Krennok, away into the wastelands, under the ivory sky. Golbrant rode towards the coast, towards the steel shelves of the sea, the spot where his warning lay in wait for him. But others rode far and wide to shun the warnings that had been given them, to dry hills where the sisters had spoken of a low-lying swamp, into withered forests to avoid the prediction of treeless spaces, to the spreadings of misty low-land lakes to escape the vision of a pointed mountain. But Vesontane, blown like the rest, restless, from the hold of Krennok-dol, sought, as Golbrant did, the scene the women had cursed upon him. The southward land on the left hand of the sun. And on the way, word had reached him, how he was not sure, by a dream, or the voice of a bird calling, that Golbrant had died. It was not without a dreadful irony, for, having hunted his fate along the coast and not found it, Golbrant had turned back towards Krennok, but missed the road, regained the sea, and come on a tall white tower. And in the tower was a blood-haired death...

In the dawn, Vesontane had built a cairn of stones. He had kneeled and prayed for Golbrant's spirit. In the hard rays of the sun, Vesontane took the amber cross from about his neck and laid it under the topmost shard, a thing of sacrifice for the memory of a brother. There was another to avenge Golbrant, and many to pray for him. Vesontane possessed even another cross, of polished slaty corundum. But there is sometimes a need of superfluous show and meaningless gesture. Vesontane had such a need.

Rising from the cairn, he left it alone at the brink of the day, and rode on.

The Southern Waste was the palest brown, the shade of winter acorns. All such lands tended to assume a particular tonal value, and to depart little from it. Here and there, a desiccated plant seemed to balance the sky on its prongs. Stacks of nutmeg-tinted rock evolved, floating like enormous ships, their bases lost in a tidal haze of dust. And it was cold. Primrose clouds let fall a thin dull hail in the west, which rattled over the plain. The sun shone bitterly.

On the third night after he had made the cairn, Vesontane dreamed that a girl was watching him. Her face was muffled by her hair, or a veil, but she bent near, and he felt her eyes. All night he dreamed it, dreamed a girl watched him, and when he woke at sunrise, he found it was so.

She stood some paces away, but leaning forward. He had slept armoured here, like a mythical insect, his horse, blue-grey as smoke, tethered nearby, and a fire, which had died on the ground between them. The girl had established herself, as if to make the fourth corner or ray of a star formed otherwise by fire, horse and man. She was not veiled, as in the dream, and her powdery hair was bound about her head. Vesontane returned her look, and saw that, though she was very young, she was ugly. He got to his feet, and bowed his head to her for courtesy. She was a woman, and had come to him alone in the wilderness. It was the habit of the warriors of Krennok-dol to honour women, whatever their station or their face.

"Childlady," Vesontane said to her, "what is it you want of me?"

"Your help," whispered the young and ugly girl.

"Tell me how?"

"A year gone, I wandered by a certain place, and a certain creature seized on me and took me prisoner. Now I languish in that jail it made, and there I'll rot if no brave man can set me free."

Vesontane touched the blue cross at his throat. "But, childlady, you're frankly here, standing by me in the waste. How also can you be imprisoned elsewhere?"

"Regard what I am," said the girl. "I am youthful but hideous. In reality, I am a woman, and beautiful, but the creature keeps my beauty and my years to itself. These things it imprisons. Only what is left of me is at liberty to wander the plain. Don't abandon me to my anguish."

Vesontane crossed himself, and thereafter he saw the sunlight shining faintly through her. He heard the crunching tread of fate in the dust behind him, but could not turn aside.

"Show me the place where this being imprisons you," he said.

She raised her arm and pointed. The end of her pointing fixed the fifth ray of the star she had made with him, his dead fire and the horse. At her finger's end, on the edge of the horizon, there was a slim tower, the colour of a shadow.

"In God's grace," said Vesontane quietly, "how is it known, or if nameless, speak the title of the plain, as you call it hereabouts."

"Land or tower have no name," she said. "But a creature dwells there and I am its captive. Fight for me, but let me go."

"Go then," he said, and she vanished.

Though nameless, he knew which tower it was that stood before him.

He ate bread and drank wine. He fed the horse and saddled it. He prayed. His face was white, and implacable. He mounted the horse, and rode towards the dark tower on the horizon.

The cold sun climbed, touched the apex and descended. The land flowed, an unrolled carpet of stone, superficially changeable, ultimately changeless. Vesontane saw cliffs march at the corners of his eyes, rising up and sinking down. He saw defiles and chill ravines. At noon, he passed through a wood whose trees were thin as poles, their lower branches lopped to little knobs by a past snow. The leaves on their upper ribs – the boughs curved up there like rib cages of skeleton beasts – were also thin and sallow. It was easy to keep the dim tower in sight between them. Two hours after he had left the sallow wood, he came on another. It held a clear dark pool, at which he allowed the horse to drink. They emerged from the second wood in the last hour of the sun. The tower looked no nearer.

When the sun went out, which truly it seemed to do in the waste, as if pinched suddenly between earth and air, Vesontane dismounted. He prayed, broke his fast and slept.

In the morning, he repeated the process, mounted, rode on.

By noon, the tower looked no nearer.

An acrid wind blew, and it hailed again. The stones struck his armour like spent arrows in battle.

When the hail stopped, he saw, between himself and the distant tower, long-winged birds circling in the sky. Presently he came to a gallows. A man had been hanged there months before and had been eaten by the birds. Pickings were so scarce, they still congregated in the spot, hopefully but without hope. Vesontane glanced at the bones, and they spoke to him.

"Warrior, are you riding to the Tower Sombrus?"

Vesontane reined in the horse, which sidled with fear. Vesontane drew his sword, and held the cross-shaped hilt before him. "So I believe. Why do you speak to me?"

"Why not? Few pass this way. If you reach the tower, you'll find a part of me there."

"You will tell me," said Vesontane, "that in the tower lie your skin, your flesh and your blood."

"I will."

Vesontane laughed shortly. His hands were numb. "Tell me, too, how you know the tower's name?"

"I forget," said the bones of the dead man. "Ask my flesh, when you find it."

A bird swooped and flew in Vesontane's face, its beak greedy for his eyes. He slashed with the sword, and the bird fell in two pieces on the ground.

Vesontane rode away. The other birds did not follow him. The bones harped in the wind.

As the sun was setting, he rode through a gully and came out on the shore of a mere. The water was smooth as a mirror but, as if the surface had been breathed on, it reflected nothing. A pavilion stood on the shore by the mere, like an upended flower-bell, of a shade so subtle as to be unrecognisable. The sun gave a last red flash and was gone, and the pavilion opened. A small retinue appeared, who set out chairs and a table and a canopy. Candles were lit into colourless bloom and a woman walked from the pavilion.

She resembled both the women Vesontane had left in Krennok. She had the voluptuous form of Marguin, with whom he lay, and the moon-pale elf face of Liliest, the virgin to whom he made songs. But her headdress, her hair and her gown were a shadow and her eyes were shadow.

"Welcome, warrior," she said. "Dine with me."

He knew the food and the wine would be shadows, too, but he dismounted from the horse and tethered it, and went to her table by the lake.

It was as he had foreseen. Meat and drink, bread and fruit, all ghosts. Even the water in his cup was ghostly, though it had a taste of bruised herbs. They made conversation, but the woman asked him nothing relevant. She said: "How do you find the waste; does it compare favourably with other wastes?" He told her that it did. She spoke of the tedium of sun and moon, passing forever over and over the sky, and he agreed with her that it was hard on them, but worse for the stars, forever fixed. She had one of her shadows bring him a shadowy harp. Vesontane plucked shadows from it. He sang her a song he had fashioned to Liliest, but added words he had spoken in the joy of her bed to Marguin. His voice rang pure and sound across the silences of the night, and he thought of Golbrant, and the woman-faced harp, strummed now only by the currents of the sea. The woman rose and took Vesontane's hand and led him into the pavilion. Her touch was real, and when he drew her into his arms the rest of her was real and she seemed to burn him with the heat of her blood. A shameful excitement overwhelmed him, for in her he might possess two women together, the timid innocent and the sweetly and profanely knowing. But the tower was shadow, the tower of lust must be a shadow too. At an unbearable instant she stayed him, and whispered in his ear: "I am sealed. Not as a maiden, but worse, more closely. Pierce me? Never, I'll promise you." And when he groaned, she said, "The Sombrus Tower divides. The maiden leaves her maidenhood, the known woman is robbed another way. The tower divides us from ourselves."

Just then the cross about his throat brushed the tip of her breast and she was gone. The whole pavilion lifted up over Vesontane's head. It became an enormous bird and flew away across the mere and he saw its solitary reflection as if in burnished steam.

The crimson moon hung overhead and he perceived the tower, far off, miles away. The pain of his loins seemed to recede as the tower had receded.

With his sword, he wrote in the dust of the shore:
WHY HAVE THEY NAMED YOU SOMBRUS?
The wind blew the letters away.

He kneeled and prayed until he slept. He dreamed he stood by a cairn of stones. He had raped a girl-child and had come to do penance under the scourges of the priests. But there were no priests, only a bird sitting on the cairn, which said to him: "Men name a thing because they fear it, to make it less. The tower has no name. Nor you."

Vesontane woke. The lake had disappeared and he could not, for almost an hour, remember his name.

He rode three further days across the waste, towards the tower occasionally called Sombrus. Always, it stood clear before him, and was never obstructed. Where stacks crossed the way, there would be a gap exactly adjacent to the shape of the tower, so that he could see it. When the hail fell, between each stone, the tower stood straight as a long needle. In the darkness he saw it, though it was almost the tone of the dark. But never did it come nearer. Never did he reach it.

By day, there were strange events. He came to a ruin whose chimney smoked, though there was no fire. He beheld a snake changing its skin, but it was the skin which slithered away. At night, stranger. A barge, draped by gauzes, dripping lights, sailed by through the air, and stretching up his sword to the length of his raised arm, he scratched its keel with a rasping noise.

He rode for two more days. He saw a place like a field, but it was a field of skulls, where staked heads had been placed on poles. The skulls did not speak, and he was now so conditioned that he expected them to, listening as he went by.

His food was gone. The horse grubbed dry burned grasses, crisp with morning frost. Now and then, there was a stream, but not all of them were real, or drinkable.

The tower stood always before Vesontane, over slopes, across ravines, beyond rocks, subsidences, dust-bowls. But never did it come nearer. Never did he reach it.

He thought: *Eventually I must break free of the Southern waste, and cross the boundary of some other land. What then? Has it power to persist outside this waste?* He came to know the tedium of the sun and the moon, forced forever to crawl over and over the sky. The whole wilderness was enchanted, tainted by the tower, and he might never reach the limit of it, as he might never reach the tower itself.

One morning, dizzy with hunger, he woke and asked himself what he was doing. He had been warned of a doom, and he had diligently pursued it. But the doom ran from him. He stared towards the slim dark needle on the horizon, no nearer than it had been on the day the ugly child-girl had pointed to it. Was there dishonour in abandoning an enemy who would not stay and give battle? Or in forsaking a quest it was beyond his means to accomplish? Perhaps the answer was before him in the very elusiveness of the phantom. In seeking to confront his fate, he had averted it. His heart lightened, but doubt wailed at his elbow. A quest incomplete was solely that, a vow unkept, a broken thing. And who turned from a fleeing foe had sometimes earned a blade between his shoulders.

Vesontane waited until the sun was three handspans above the rocks, then he set a fire. There were many sides to his nature, and somewhere inside him was a pagan, also. As he had built the cairn for Golbrant, now he built the fire. Every morning and every dusk he had prayed to God, and now he offered to the gods of the waste, cutting a lock of his hair and burning it in the fire, throwing in also a ring of dull gold from his middle finger. With his sword, he made a small clean cut in his arm and offered them his blood; he spat, offering the water of his mouth. Lastly, he kneeled again, and performed upon himself the deed supposed a sin since it wasted the procreative force, with a sick and cringing pleasure spilling his seed, shivering, into the pagan fire.

For a while he lay on his side, looking for a sign, either of anger or of absolution, even perhaps of compromise. No sign was vouchsafed him, and at length the fire perished. He thought of the green dol hill, and Krennok's saffron skies, of the fruits and vines, the hunting, of song, of love. He thought of some priest, stern, wise and gentle as a father, the washing away of error, and a white rosebud once seen in Liliest's hair, and Marguin's smooth nails combing his arms.

He saddled the horse and mounted it, and turned its head and his own away from the phantom of the Sombrus Tower, away from the south, towards the north, the border over which he had ridden some seventeen days ago, following death.

Everything at once looked new to him, and he gazed at it, swaying slightly with fatigue and disorientation. The brown earth was studded by glassy pebbles, the rocks veined by quartzes, marbles, carbons. The sky was violently still, choked by cloud, which had been immobilised, though somewhere a narrow wind blew, compressed by its passage between tall stones and through mean hollows. Having lowered his eyes, next raised his eyes, he now centred them on the horizon before him, with a wild craving for the empty vista which he would see.

Continually focusing on the tower had become for him like the continual ache of an unhealing wound.

Above, the sky, below, the waste ground, directly before him, two knife-cut ridges. And framed between them far, far away, the dark tower.

Vesontane gave a cry. It struck the stillness and shattered. He held the horse motionless, and stared at the tower before him. Then, slowly, he turned only his head, and looked back the way he had been travelling.

There, about a hundred paces off over the plain behind him, a rider rode a blue-grey horse southward, towards a distant shadow-coloured tower. His armour was coal-black, the wind unrolled his umber hair. He did not look behind him, as Vesontane was doing, yet suddenly he too cried aloud. He too was Vesontane.

Oh, God deliver me, though I forsook the road of my destiny and am unworthy. Oh God, whose arm is mightier than the gate of hell!

A rider rode into the south towards a distant tower. In the north stood a distant tower. Vesontane had only to ride towards it...

He turned the horse briskly eastward. He drove it to a heavy lumbering gallop. He did not look ahead, nor behind him.

After half an hour, the horse stumbled and he reined it in. Vesontane crossed himself. He prayed. He imagined the pure prayers of Liliest, uttered for his sake, and Marguin's scalding tears. He looked up and saw a distant tower in the east. Looking behind him, he saw three riders; each rode towards a distant tower. One rode south, and one north, and one rode west. While his purpose had been single, he had known tedium and banality, no more. Once his purpose had been split, two purposes, the sorcery of the tower had claimed him. Divided. Divided him from himself. And again. But he did not learn, nor did it matter. He rode this way, and now that. To the points of the compass he rode, quartering, and quartering the quarters. For each digression, his twin appeared at his back, riding opposingly, and when he turned, he saw them...

He shouted after them, and none answered. He looked away from them and a vast shout of many many voices, all his own, stunned the waste. Thereafter he was quiet.

Up in the air, as a bird flies, save there are no birds here. Behold the great circle of men, forever riding away from each other towards those slight, far distant towers. Forever riding away, yet drawing no farther from each other than some hundred paces, forever riding, yet drawing no nearer to those distant towers. Yet forever riding, forever riding, forever, forever, away, away, away.

Death Dances

Death came to Idradrud at suns' rise. She had appointments to keep.

The city lay along the banks of its river, a river green as jade and thick as soup, sprinkled with garbage, rotting hulks, and slave-powered quinqueremes like floating towers. The tiered towers on the banks kept still, save in the occasional spring earthquakes, which revived religion in the city as only the plague could do otherwise. Domes and minarets and steeples stood against the Great Sun and the Sun-Star on the yellow-green sky. But closer to the earth, the slums that were the truth of Idradrud, and the cut-throat alleys which bisected them, huddled in the warming sludge and muck. Diseased-looking steps piled into the water. There were those who got their living from the river in an immemorial way. Not by plying goods or hauling sail, not by catching the slightly-poisonous fish or the now-and-then-lethal oysters, but by detaining the corpses to be found in the water, stripping them of valuables, clothes, bones, and hair even – to be sold later for wigs. This trade was carried on by boat, or sometimes it was performed by those who, holding their breath a long while, swam deep down into the jade broth, down to the bottom, and searched about there in the smoking mud.

Along among the quays, there was a gaudy stretch or two. Tenements dressed with balconies, awnings, birdcages, and evil exotic flowers. Here was a narrow house with its skirt in the river, pink plaster and ornate scrolling – all battered and peeling from sun and wet.

Bitza, as she gazed forth from a window, saw all those other buildings, hers and the rest, upside down in the water, one with a young woman gazing out of a window, and an eel snaking by through her hair. *But she is free,* thought Bitza on reflection, of her reflection.

Bitza, the Harlot in the Pink House, was not beautiful, but she had learned to give the impression of enormous and indefinable beauty, and was much desired. Even lords came to her slum palace to visit her. She might have been rich, but was not entirely honest. Certain enemies of her youth had died in mysterious circumstances. But she was concerned for the poor and gave most of her fortune away in the interests of caring for them – namelessly. Once, she had been poor herself, and dreaded the idea of it. Now her fine dark hair was curled and streaked with gilt. Her large eyes were perfectly shaped, the primeval colour of the river, but crystal clean as the river never was. Her body was strong and graceful, honey's hue in summer.

As she was putting loops of gold through her charming ears, Bitza's maid came fleeting in.

"Madam, a messenger-runner brought this."

Bitza took the slip of parchment. It had an unfamiliar look and texture, and a strong smell of incense. The wax was black, without a seal. Bitza imagined one of the more-than-usually eccentric lords of Idradrud was about to seek her out. (Her clients, to a man, exacerbated her.) There was one who liked to be chained and whipped by a Bitza masked like a silver eagle, and another who liked to make love while semi-drowning in a bath of wine... But Bitza broke the wax and opened the parchment, and it said: "As arranged, tonight I will be with you. *Death.*"

In one of the blacker alleys, in an overhanging storey that seemed, with every creak of winter winds and capricious shift of spring quakes, ever more likely to fall smack in the six-foot-wide street below, Kreet was lying late abed, having kicked out his boy companion several hours before. Kreet of the dark soul and the light fingers, popularly called Golden Hands – Kreet the Thief.

He had stolen monumental treasures, they said. Then been robbed of them by others, whom he had later paid by various means, without recovering the prize, or else he used the loot to bribe the city authorities to be obliging, or he had gambled the proceeds away. Then, too, despite the squalor of his lodging, he was said to own the whole alley and half the streets and crumbling edifices around. While in the apartment of dirty, nasty rooms were there not chests full of money guarded by his ruffians, and bed-curtains sewn with rubies over a bed whose sheets were seldom changed? There were.

Kreet, the Thief with Golden Hands, was not a kind man. Swarthy of skin, foxy of face and eyes – though without a fox's good-looks – his bush of long black hair was washed once a year, while his beard bathed daily in his meals. All this had become a trademark. On the back of rivals he sometimes personally tattooed these words: *Kreet dislikes me.* And others, discovering the phrase, tended to shun the bearer of it.

But Kreet loved no one, not the fair boys he misused in his bed, not his gang of robbers, who admired him. Not even the chests of ill-gettings. Kreet stole because he was good at stealing. He liked the thrill of *taking,* and the violence... Then, the skeins of jewels in his golden mitts, Kreet scowled, dissatisfied. While the violence had repercussions that were beginning to worry him.

Yet, one thing Kreet did love and like, and now he summoned it to him off the bedpost. "Come, my tatty joy!"

And down flapped a brown chicken, and nested in his arms, crooning peaceably and pecking scraps of grain from his hand that only last night had barbered a couple of noses, while Kreet crooned back in perfect communion.

But there was a scratch on the door. One of Kreet's gang came sidling in. "A messenger-runner left this at the tavern."

Kreet looked at the parchment and the black wax seal. He squinted at his robberling and instructed, "Open and recite."

The robber, who had his letters as Kreet did not, obeyed. In an incredulous and quavering croak, therefore, he presently read out these words: "As arranged, tonight I will be with you. *Death.*"

Where the bank rose away from the river, up terraces, up a hill, a domed temple stood, lifting its stone head clear of the slums. Between the temple's pillars, cool shapes went drifting, and the murmur of chants came and went, continually, and the purr of doves. The wings of these doves were clipped, for fear they should fly too far and meet the river gulls, which would tear them in pieces. But the priests and priestesses passed in and out carelessly, protected by their pale azure robes. The slums were superstitious. Idradrud did not rob or murder its priesthoods.

High up in the temple, just under the dome, was a round chamber with an altar of marble. From the altar ascended a hollow silver cup, in which there burned eternally a pastel blue flame. This flame, or Flame, was the spirit of the temple. Even in the earth-shocks, though it had faltered and smouldered, it had not gone out. It was said to be the result of a pulse of subterranean gas, which had breached the ground before the city's birth. Later, holy men saw in the gas – which could be made to catch bluely alight – a manifestation of the Infinite. So the temple was built, and the gas channelled up via pipes from cellar to altar and so into the hollow cup, where the flash of flint and tinder brought it alive once and for all.

There was always, it went without saying, a guardian for the Flame. It was the task of a year. With every new year, a new guardian was elected. To the esoteric creatures of the temple, this task, which shut them more or less all one year in the round chamber and its adjacent annexe and gallery, was considered a wonderful privilege.

Sume had now tended the Flame for seven months, and had

therefore seven further months of the Idradrudian year to tend it. White and slender as a wand, from aesthetics, incarceration, dedication, Sume wore the azure robes of her order, the sapphire rings, and her hair was bleached and tinted faintest blue, as was the hair of all the priests and priestesses. Sume, as she glided about her duties, at prayer, feeding the doves, moving along the gallery like a ghost, Sume was no different from every other inhabitant of that place. She seemed, as they all seemed, to have no life but the expression of the temple.

Yet, to such as drew close and glanced at her directly, there might come a check of surprise. For Sume's narrow delicate face hinted a curious passion that had nothing to do with solitude or the Infinite, and her dark eyes burned in a way that did not speak of sacred fire. The less reverent who had noticed this had said, *Here's one ripe for something.* But they were unsure what – mischief, mayhem, or only sensuality and sexual fall.

Now Sume poised before the Flame, straight and slim and upright, the Flame itself in human female guise. She had been repeating the morning orison, but as she concluded, a bell sounded outside at the annexe door. Someone wished to speak to her, or to bring her some news. Sume, who had no family but the temple, having been left an orphan on its steps, went quietly and without alarm to receive the visitor.

A young novice bowed low to Sume, the Priestess of the Flame. He held out a piece of parchment sealed in black. "The High Priest sent me to you with this. A messenger-runner brought it to the porch."

Sume took the parchment with a slight astonishment. Once or twice, men of the congregation had importuned her, having seen her at her offices and become infatuated with her spirituality – or her promise of the spiritually profane. Was this another such note?

It was not. It read: "As arranged, tonight I will be with you. *Death.*"

It was now midmorning, and the two suns shone high above the city, putting gold-leaf on every crease of the river and every slate of every lurching roof. While along the spires and parapets of fine mansions and palaces, the suns unctuously poured, in dazzling bad taste.

Uphill, in a high-class inn on one of the nicer streets, a young army captain, raising his eyes, was promptly blinded by three golden statues positioned atop some lord's house across the way. So that, looking back at what he had been writing, he saw only their three black after-images stuck there over his words.

It was tradition among the lower circles of the upper echelons of Idradrud, that third sons enter the army. Here they soared as fame, war, cash, and influence permitted. In seasons of conflict, they fought the battles of Idradrud, or, as now, in peace, they strutted, idled, or slothed away the time at home. Mhiglay, a captain of three companies – sixty men – a soldier, but also a scholar, had eschewed both barracks and family and put up at the inn. Poet also, he had been employed all night with that. He could not sleep, felt he would never sleep again. He had seen too much of friends who died, and enemies he did not hate yet must kill. And recently, a man who was very nearly his brother in everything but blood, had turned out to be a traitor, and it had fallen to Mhiglay to attend the military scaffold. Plead for mercy for this man as Mhiglay had done, mercy had been omitted. The near-brother had spat on him and died in agony, screaming. A scene often recaptured in dreams, which caused Mhiglay to turn slumber out of the room whenever possible.

Though duty-bound to be a clever and able soldier, and dutifully being all the role demanded, it did not fit him. He had always half suspected, and now was sure. Blond of hair, handsome, and thoroughly haggard and hollow-eyed from lack of sleep, and sleep's scourge when he accepted it, he looked the poet and scholar he surely was, and also somewhat the haunted murderer he seemed to himself to be. None would or could console him. Least of all his family of puffed uncles and irksome brothers.

No hope, no help, Mhiglay, the Captain of Three Twenties, had written on the page. *No cure, for the sickness is my life.*

And just then, even as the after-images of the statues faded out of his sad, distraught, and sleepless eyes, someone rapped on the door. An inn-girl entered, flirtatiously, (he did not see), to tell him a messenger-runner had brought something, and to hand him a leaf of parchment sealed in black.

Mhiglay opened and read the parchment. He gave a contemptuous laugh.

"As arranged, tonight I will be with you. *Death.*"

There is a saying in Idradrud of the green river, *Life will dance with some, and some Life will refuse. Yet Death dances with every man.*

When Bitza, the Harlot in the Pink House, read the message, she said, boldly, "Some kink-full suitor is playing a trick. I had better get ready."

When Kreet, the Thief with Golden Hands, read the message, he said, nervously, "Some filth-laden foe is after my hide. I had better get ready."

But when Sume, the Priestess of the Flame, read the message, she said, stilly, "Can this be so? Well, I am here."

And when Mhiglay, the Captain of Three Twenties, read the message, he said, coldly, "Then let her arrive. I am waiting."

It was suns' set. First the Great Sun sank down behind the western bank of the river, in a murky glory of red, russet, and amber. The Sun-Star followed like a lover. The sky turned to walnut brown, resembling an expanse of highly-polished table, then went black. The stars appeared, in complex patterns, such as the Sphynx, the Lion, the Lyre. The most intricate of all was that of the Winged Woman, which stretched for a quarter of the night across most of the eastern horizon, and was easily discernible, even by a child – body, limbs, wings, hair, drawn in blots of diamond. The air over Idradrud was thickly crusted with stars. So many that, even lacking a moon, which it always did, night was always also very nearly bright as day, except if there should be overcast.

Darkness being present then, punctually Death knocked at Bitza's door.

Bitza reclined in or upon a black couch like a coffin. The room was hung with black cerements and had generally been made to imitate a tomb. Bitza herself wore a translucent shroud, and bone combs in her hair.

"It is a woman," hissed Bitza's maid.

Bitza raised her brows. "Very well."

And so Death was shown up to the tomb-room, and Bitza looked at her with disfavour.

"I do not as a rule deal with women," said Bitza. "But if you will meet my price, I will consider your desires."

Death smiled. When she did so, Bitza realised she had been mistaken. "Then," she said, "it is a fact?"

Death nodded.

Soon after, Death approached the door of Kreet's lodging.

A hundred butcheroos stood ready with drawn knives, but Death naturally walked through the knives and came to Kreet's door, and the bars and bolts crumbled at her touch.

"Kill me, would you!" yelled Kreet, standing on his unclean bed. The chicken flapped his feathers and tried to take a peck at Death, but Death said, "Hush," and the chicken went to Kreet and sat on his boot. And then Kreet himself said, after a medley of oaths and cries, "Spare me! Spare me! Or at least, you damnable fiend, spare this innocent chicken…"

"The chicken," said Death, "is not inevitably my business."

Not long after, Death met Sume as she glided along the gallery of the Flame-chamber.

Sume paused. "Is it you?" she asked.

Death waited.

Sume meekly bowed her head in assent, though her dark eyes flamed more fiercely than the Flame.

And next Death came through the door of Mhiglay's room at the inn, which door had been left open, and Mhiglay seized Death in his arms and kissed her passionately on the lips.

As everyone understands, Death too plies a Boat along a River. Small shock then to behold the slim sable craft, with its sickle of sail, going like a sombre thought between the two-banked landscape of the city and its lights, and the lighted stars in the air, with only one lamp at the prow to let down a glistening green tail into the water. Now and then, one of the afloat tower-tiers of a quinquereme is passed, at rest for the hours of night, and going up twenty-nine feet, rigging folded and oars drawn in, and slaves lying in swoon-sleep, and masters getting drunk. Or some other river thing goes by, and perhaps hails the dark boat, getting no answer. Death herself stands for'ard, guiding the vessel, remote. There has never been, and is not now, any requirement to describe Death. Who cannot picture and has not pictured her? All know her and how she seems.

But amidships the four passengers sit. Fascinating Bitza is twisting her necklaces, trying to fashion some trick. Ugly Kreet scowls, and sweats, wondering if Death is bribable. And on his shoulder the chicken broods, having refused to leave him. Fey Sume is immaculate, eyes cast down. And handsome Mhiglay, his head thrown back, is bitterly enjoying the wretched romance of it all, glad to be going away.

Finally Kreet erupts.

"I complain!" he shouts, and the chicken applauds. "I complain at the bloody and stenchful injustice. Who is in charge here?"

No one replies, though Bitza looks at him and Sume ignores him, and Mhiglay laughs ironically and insultingly. Kreet lapses into invective.

At that, "Do not offend her," cautions Bitza. And bites her manicured nails.

Sume whispers, "What is life? I have had no life." Her eyes burn holes in the night.

Mhiglay says, "Be thankful."

At this point, however, all four perceive a new area of darkness on the dark, a sort of archway rising up out of the river, higher even than the quinqueremes, the distant towers on the banks: the entry to some chasm. It was never on the river before, this chasm, this tall black arch. And Bitza screams, and Kreet curses and grovels – and the chicken hides in his collar – and Sume again lowers her gaze, and Mhiglay sighs.

And the boat of Death creeps nearer and nearer toward the massive black hump where no lights show and no stars are. Only the green tail in the water flickers before them, and against it, the remote figure of Death, who suddenly speaks.

"Remember," says Death, to each and to all, "that my message to you read *as arranged*." (Then there is a silence, as the four in the boat consider, reject, revile, puzzle on, these words, not essentially in that order, while the black archway comes closer and fills the world and is surely about to swallow them.) "I am," Death then announces, "myself. Not necessarily what you think me." (And they are, surely, swallowed whole.)

It was from the most peculiar dream that the Harlot woke. In the dream, there was a boat, which had passed around a wide dark loop inside some cavern, and come out at length on the spangled lime-jade water of Idradrud's river. At which the Harlot opened his eyes and looked about him, and found the familiar cosy coarse splendour of his Pink House. Soon, joking off the dream, he rose, called his maid, and toyed with her in a luxuriating bath. She washed his hair, streaked it with gilt at his somewhat coy request, and shaved him. When once he was clothed, (in elegant leathers), his eyes drawn round with kohl, and the gold rings in his ears, the Harlot took breakfast. Then he called, "Come, my tatty angel!" and a brown chicken jumped into his lap, and they clucked pleasantly to one another.

The Thief, meanwhile, had woken from a similar dream, up in a dirty flea- tip, and at once, in a cruel clear voice that was not to be denied, exclaimed that linen must instantly be changed, floors scrubbed, and an unaccountable quantity of chicken feathers removed from the hangings.

Ruffians and knife-boys leapt to obey with alacrity. One crouched fawningly at the Thief's blue slippers. He asked if he was needed to read her anything.

"Read?" she kicked him flying. Her pale face was flushed, and her black eyes shone with relaxed malevolence. "I can read quite well for myself, you damnable ant. Was I not temple-trained?"

The kicked cut-throat beat a retreat. How could he have been so aberrant? The whole slum quarter sang of her learning, yearningly.

While the Priest who guarded the Flame had been writing poetry to it all night, adrift in intellectual space. Or so it seemed he had, only once contrastingly drifting into a peculiar dream, doubtless of vast psychic import, when he could be bothered to interpret it – but he had cast it aside on waking with a rather military shrug.

Now, standing over it, he regarded the sacred Flame, just immortalised in his verse, with eyes that matched the fire and blond hair, which did not. Eventually, leaning forward, he blew the Flame out.

"Yes," said the Priest, with gentle satisfaction. "And *there* you have it." And striking flint and tinder, he lit the Flame again, nodded at it, and walked from the chamber.

Outside, he found a novice on duty, waiting to take up the poet-Priest's guardianship, whenever he felt inclined to abscond. This often happened, as the novice would explain. This one Priest was noted for such behaviour. And for other actions. For example, exactly today, striding to the temple treasury with an idle yet undeniable salute at its sentries, he flung open the coffers. Going out on the street he began to distribute largesse to the deserving, (and sometimes, to the beautiful).

"Every temple, even ours, should have its oddity, its wayward matter," the High Priestess had declared, in glowing defence of the poet. "We are admired for our tolerance. Besides, his writings and verses are nonpareil." They were rather captivated, too, by his lack of guilt over anything.

And last of all, the Captainess of Three Twenties, which she already had some plans to increase to Six Twenties before high summer, had left her inn and gone home. Home to that family of hers so rich it was ludicrous. They were somewhat in awe of her. It was not very usual to have one's daughter enlist in the armies of Idradrud, and then to become celebrated and successful there. But she had a way with men, the Captainess. Riding into battle, with her dark hair under helmet and war-plumes, her green eyes feral, and her sword-hand rock steady, she had inspired an exceptional sort of fright in many an adversary.

Her kindred welcomed her this morning with uneasy open arms, almost as if they had expected someone else, and were bruised by the medals clanking on her delightful breast. (It was said, the last enemy general she had whipped across seven hills.) But now she only seemed inclined to push her brothers in the lily-pond. And there they went, splish-splash.

Those who got their living in an immemorial way along the river of Idradrud, these had had a busy night. What a catch – gems, cutlasses, military insigniae... and – *chicken feathers?*

It would appear a harlot had been murdered by a mad client and pushed in the water from her balcony. It turned out a thief had been attacked by rivals and dumped there, with a hole in his back, and a little fowl clinging to his collar. It seemed a priestess had grown insane and run from her temple to suicide in the unsavoury depths. It transpired an army captain had done likewise.

And yet, is there not something not quite right with the bodies the traders in death have fished from the river? Brought in by net and oar alongside the narrow boat, or raised up by the hair through panting divers bursting the surface, muddy from the river's bottom, and with shells in their beards – cadavers, such as one expects, but skins unsolid, faces washed *too* expressionless – "Just take the jewels, the coins and knives, the rings, the medals, and sword – Why philosophise? Why quibble? The river does that to corpses. But quick – strip them quick – before they melt away altogether and are gone."

And over there in the Pink House, Kreet bangs open the door and roars at his visitor: "Late again, you dog of a lord!" And thrashes a truly grisly whip, (to loud approving cackles from somewhere), and the lord – in startled, horrified misgiving and ecstasy – flops on his face to get his money's worth – and never did he recall such *enthusiasm* in his treatment formerly...

And along there, in an alley two feet wide, Sume, who has recently tattooed on the ankle of an enemy: *Sume* likes *me*, Sume picks the pockets of sozzled merchants as she asks them the hour, or the way to the blue temple of the Flame, to which she has no intention of going. And presently points out an exquisite boy, who blushes, at which Sume says to her loving homicides: "Bring me that one, for later," and smiles, oh-so-softly-eyed...

And up there, in the blue temple a moment ago mentioned, Mhiglay is sitting with his feet on the High Priest's inlaid table, oblivious to duty, the table, and the High Priest, writing nonpareil poetry on an orange skin, proudly and fondly watched on every side...

And in the topmost lower mansion of Idradrud, where gold statuary crowds the roofs, Bitza is having a 'mock' duel with an opinionated uncle, and he is in grave fear of his life…

And it is of no use asking what goes on. Asking what arrangement, precisely, led to this. Or if perhaps we are not all involved in it and simply do not recollect, or have been, or will be…

Ask Death. There she is, down in the groves just beyond the city, where the myrtles grow with snakes around their boughs. Death, pretty as a picture, in between the wild white trees. Look, you can see what she does. Death dances, with her shadow – and why should she not have one? – and all the stars in her hair.

The Kingdoms of the Air

– Who is he, that Knight riding by?

   – His name is Cedrevir. He has been Questing.

   – Pale as death, and his eyes looked blind. I thought, a good thing the horse knows its way. I thought, there is one wounded by unseen arrows.

   – They are an ancient Fellowship, these Knights. It is in their vows to invite the Quest, whatever it may be, whatever its peril or strangeness. But many return home as you have seen.

   – This Cedrevir: What Quest then was his? Do you know it?

   – Yes, and I will tell it you.

At the Midsummer Feast they met, as it is usual for them to do, this Fellowship of Knights, up there in the Castle of Towers.

In the Castle's heart, there is a great hidden hall, the entrances to which are known only to an Initiate. The hall is built as a perfect circle, its floor and walls paved with blocks of polished stone. From the high dome of the roof hang down the thousand swords and shields, banners and devices, of all the Knights who are and have been of the Fellowship. High on the walls the torches burn in iron cages of curious shape, so they resemble the heads of serpents and monsters which breathe fire. In the floor is set, in fine mosaic, a huge round sun-disc, and on the rayed rim of it stand the Knights, repeating the circle of power a third time, in flesh and steel.

For each man comes to that place fully armed and in mail, though each surcote is of undyed and unembroidered linen, and the visor of each helm lowered, and though every man carries in his gauntleted hand a sword, it has no mark.

(There are ways of knowing a man, even under these circumstances. From his height and build, his voice, his manner, or by some expression in his eyes.)

There they stood, then; at this Midsummer near to midnight, in the dark light of the dragon-torches. They performed their rites and reaffirmed their vows. In turn they confessed any of their transgressions against God, Man, or the Fellowship. They told, in turn, of their feats, and furnished proofs, which might be anything, from a lady's scarf to the severed hand of an enemy.

46

There is one further property in that hall. On a tall stand to the east is a clock, in the form of a golden sword and a marble heart on water. As the liquid drips down through the basin, the weights go up, and all morning the golden sword lifts slowly, until, at noon, it strikes a golden chiming apple in the summit of the clock. Then, as the water gradually refills the basin, the weights sink, the marble heart floats up and the sword descends, until at midnight its yellow blade pierces through the heart, which gives out a long singing note.

Shortly before midnight at Midsummer, when the sword is just grazing the marble, an Invocation is spoken by all the Knights of the circle. There are those that say a certain wine is then drunk, a wafer eaten and an incense burned. Every man bows his head and awaits what will come to him.

Then the sword enters the marble heart, and the heart sweetly cries.

Cedrevir heard the note of the heart, as he had previously heard it, twelve times in all, for he had been six years a Knight of the circle. At first, he had been strung, expectant and eager, but year by year these emotions dulled to patience. He had undertaken betweenwhiles many adventures, all successful. As a warrior he was valiant and accomplished, and as a priest – for the Initiate of the Fellowship is both – he was equally, chaste, and passionate. He had done no wrong, he had fought with honour and skill, but yet nothing had come to him at midnight of Midsummer, or in the dark Midwinter either.

Now however, as the note faded from the water-clock, Cedrevir began to hear another sound so like, that for a moment he thought the heart cried out a second time. Then he became aware that what he heard was the voice of a maiden, singing. Her tones were pure and thin as beaten silver, and her words were these:

Primo dolens lancea est
Corona dolor de Dominus
Est secundo et tertio
Gradalis cruenta fulgero

The voice rang all round the hollow chamber, and in the hollows of helm and skull it rang.

Cedrevir raised his head, sure that every other Knight did in like fashion, and looked with wide grey eyes. There at the centre of the mosaic sunburst, a column of light so sheer and bright it dimmed the torches, rose up from floor to roof. Even as Cedrevir stared into this radiance, half dazzled, uncannily half not, he began to make out objects moving, there within the column. For a moment, he did not know what these things were. Then, though never before having seen them, he recognised each, and a low faint groan burst from him. He fell to his knees, and wild bells began to ring, and mildly, terribly, the aching voices sang: *Primo dolens lancea est corona dolor de Dominus est secundo et tertio gradalis cruenta fulgero.* And down the pillar of white fire came drifting like a cobweb a spear of silver with a burning tip that shone even more fiercely than the light, and from it fell ceaselessly petals of crimson that became butterflies as they faded. And after the burning bleeding spear, a garland of fiery thorns, which also bled, and as the drops burst from it they changed to roses of gold that opened on hearts like the moon and stars themselves. Lastly, there weightlessly fell a chalice of a deep clear flaming green, a colour whose depths seemed bottomless as the sea. And from the lip of the chalice there ran a stream of blood, but the blood was like liquid gold and it blazed brighter than the sun.

Then, another voice spoke at the Knight1s right shoulder. It seemed to him it was the voice of a man, but before them, on the ground, a glowing shadow showed with folded wings. "Seek then these things, Cedrevir. The Lance of Pain, the Sorrowing Crown, the Cup of the Life's Blood. That is your Quest, and may you be true to it."

After that came darkness on the wide grey eyes of Cedrevir.

Cedrevir knew well enough what he had had revealed to him in the vision. And when he came to himself in the Castle of Towers, and recounted what he had seen – for no other but himself had been made witness to it – no man of the fellowship was in ignorance.

In the great light had passed the three holy relics of the Sacrifice of Christ: the Spear that had pierced His side, the Thorn-Crown that had garlanded His brows, the Chalice in which had been shared the sacred blood-wine of the Last Supper, and in which the true blood of His wounds had subsequently been caught.

These articles, long reverenced as aspects of the Martyrdom, are, we say, supposed to have remained on earth. Indeed, their whereabouts, as you may hear, are known, though not by situation. A fortress, called the Castle of the Jewel of Goodness, (which is, *Carba Bonem*), that is where they are lodged, and tended there by mysterious guardians. All about *Carba Bonem* stretches a vast waste that has no seasons in it, save only heat or cold, but that is named, for its looks and barrenness, the Winterlands. And in the waste is a dead forest, as old as the world, which is named the Wood of the Savage Hart. But the way to it, the forest, the wasteland, the secret Castle of the Jewel of Goodness, they lie off the edge of any map, beyond the memory of any traveller. It is not possible to come to them either by accident or by design. And so the quiet priests told Cedrevir as he kneeled before them, with his dark head bowed and beautiful hands upon the hilt of the sword which bore his device, a couched *sarpafex*.

For many days then he fasted and watched, and kept by himself or with these learned ones from whom he sought counsel. All this while, the images of the vision stayed clear before him, as if he had seen them only a moment ago, and in his ears the voices sang *Dolens lancea. Corona dolor. Gradalis cruenta fulgero.* And the last voice told him, waking and sleeping and watching, *This is your Quest. Be true to it.*

Then at last there came an hour just before sunrise, when the birds piped over the meadows, and the sky was pale as a shell. And Cedrevir came from the Castle of Towers.

He rode as if to a battle, sword, shield and lance at their stations, clad in mail of steel. Both he and the blond horse were trapped and clad in his colour, the blue-grey of distances. And worked on the saddle-cloth, and enamelled on the shield and sword-hilt, the snake-lynx of his blazon, silver and blue and gilt.

In the fields, where the women and boys were labouring, they raised their heads among the tall corn, to watch Cedrevir go by. *There is a Knight of the fellowship*, they said, *he goes Questing.* For the look of setting forth is, though unlike, as unmistakable as that other look with which, often, they return.

So he rode across the Near Lands, towards the north, for north lies the House of Winter, and in the north there are mountains, the high places. And that was all the guide he had to find a spot that is of the earth but not on the earth; a spot that some wise men say is a myth, although also a certain truth.

Beyond the Near Lands lie others less known, but all were wrapped in the late richness of summer, and it may be supposed that human tasks went on there much as they do everywhere. In the orchards, vineyards and fields, they would be making ready for harvest, toiling on into evening under the wide golden skies. At the streams and wells, the women gathered with their washing and their buckets, and by the rivers they cut reeds. Where the castles stood up on the hills, or some massive tower thrust from the woods, the sentries would remark a riding Knight. Some challenge or greeting might be offered him. And now and then, at a lonely chapel, the priest would render lodging, blessing, bread and wine, most frequently in silence.

Perhaps two months Cedrevir travelled, going always northwards, questioning on the way those he met, where it seemed the sign of knowledge was on them, here a hermit in his cell, there an old peasant woman, or a little child even, with a freckle like a star on its forehead. Otherwise, sometimes, the Knight himself would be petitioned for his help, and so would fight, a champion against some wrong. And then again, there were those who sought to tempt him aside, to view a wonder, which might be a mysterious flower that grew in a ruined pagan temple, a thing which would work miracles, or a fountain that gushed from a rock at the striking of his fist. Or there were, from time to time, those who desired to corrupt, such as a white-shouldered woman in a red gown, who leaned from her window so her long hair, scented with strange spice, brushed the face of Cedrevir as he rode by. But her he did not stay for.

One dusk, when the light still hung like a dome of crystal high up in the vault of heaven though all the landscape darkened, Cedrevir came on a broken tower beside a lake. Through the windows of the tower the shining afterglow ran like spears, and the lake itself lay like a great pool of sky fallen on the earth. Not a breeze stirred and not a cloud marred the surface of air or water. Then the stars began to dew and daisy out, and one lit more brightly than the rest upon the strand against the lake. It was a torch that burned in a cage of bronze before a pavilion. And as Cedrevir rode close, other lights bloomed in the pavilion's heart, and turned it to a bulb of softest fire.

Presently two Knights stepped from the pavilion. They were of another fellowship, and on the shield of one was the device of a falcon, and on the other a white bull with wings.

"Where are you going, Knight-at-Arms?" said he of the falcon-shield.

"Northward," replied Cedrevir. "It is a Vowed Journey."

There is not a fellowship, they say, that does not honour the Quest, or the bond of it.

The two Knights nodded. He of the bull-shield spoke next. "We guard here the Lady Marismë, our sister."

"I do not challenge that, nor offer any threat to her."

"No. But she is a seeress, trained in the Luminous Arts," said the falcon-shield Knight.

"If you would confer with this lady, our sister, I believe she will do her best to help you," said the bull-shield Knight. "Only this morning, by her art, she descried you, and said, 'Here we will linger and await a traveller from the south. He seeks a key to his Quest, which I maybe shall find for him'."

Now the two Knights stood in shadow beyond the torch, and their faces were hidden under their glistening and dark helms. It came to Cedrevir that he did not credit all that they had said to him, and yet they had spoken no lie. It was the deep shadow of occult things on them, but not of wickedness, as it was only night had darkened the lake.

Just then, the draperies of the pavilion parted with a flutter, and a woman came out. On her the torch shone full, and she was young, and fair, with clear wild eyes. Her white gown was bordered with gems like water-drops, and on her dim hair drifted a net like silver spray.

She said nothing to Cedrevir, and her eyes looked into him and through him. It was a terrible gaze, for she seemed to see his very birth and death, and all other matters that might come between. Then she beckoned, only once, and drew back into the pavilion.

"Follow her," said the falcon-shield Knight. "She is honourable, as are you. And if you were not, she is well able to protect herself. Besides, we are here."

So Cedrevir, in a sort of trance, for her eyes had curiously affected him, dismounted and entered the tent after the lady.

There was a woven carpet on the ground within the tent, and the lamps hung in clusters from posts of bronze. But the lady stood in the centre of the pavilion where there was a pedestal of carved wood. And on the pedestal before her, a golden bowl filled with water.

"Come here and see," said the Lady Marismë.

Cedrevir went to the pedestal, and looked down with her into the bowl.

At first there was only the clarity of the water over the gold. Then there came a turbulence that was in the water and not in it, and a veil seemed to be torn away. There in the bowl, as if miles off, a great host was fighting in the sky. It was a gorgeous and a fearsome battle, for a setting sun, and also bolts of lightning, flashed upon the gems and metals of the warriors, caught upon swords that blazed with inlay, and catching the crests and banners showed devices so mystic and so strange they were not at once understandable. But the sun was going down and the clouds, amethyst and purple and scarlet as the trappings of the Knights, began to lower and smother the scene. Then a trumpet sounded, unheard – but perfectly to be viewed – a long line of fire as from some comet. At the signal, through the cloud-mass, there came riding two mighty lords, and all the host drew back away from them to give them room. And this was very dreadful, for it was plain at once that these two Knights were brothers. Each was golden, each as cleanly beautiful and as sparkling as something made of the sun itself, and as hard to look on. But one was clad all in gold and white, and on his helm was a crest like stars, and on his shield a device for which there was no name at all, it might not be expressed or written, yet Cedrevir, glimpsing it, was filled by joy and terror. The other Knight was arrayed in the colours of heat and fire, and in his crest burned a green jewel so marvellous the eye seemed to drink at it. His shield had no device, but on his banner, that one bore behind him, were embroidered the words: *Non Servian.*

They met with a clash, these two, that shook the sky, their lances splintered and the pieces rained down like blood and lava on the world. Each sword came from its scabbard like a lightning stroke that lit all heaven. And as they dashed once more upon each other, the last of the red sun fell, and on a cloth of gold, dead black yet shining bright, they fought, on and on, as the moon rose under their chargers' feet.

There was no telling how long the combat lasted, time had no meaning there. Cedrevir watched with awe and misgiving, in pity and dread and triumph. It was the First Battle, when the angels of God had fought together. The golden Knight was the Archangel Michael. He clothed like fire, whose banner proclaimed his rebellion – *I will not serve* – Lucifer, before his fall.

When the final blow sang home, ever expected, ever impossible, needful and terrible for all that, the sky seemed to crack from end to end. Cedrevir did not behold the fall of him, Prince Lucifer, yet he saw filing out from the clouds a green shooting-star. It smoked and flamed, tearing downward to the earth. Over hills and heights it ripped its path, and there the ocean spread, glittering and unresting in the moon's sway. And here, in the sea, the emerald meteor went down, hissing. It was the jewel from the helm of Lucifer, the Prince of Hell, quenched in water.

But it was only the clear water in the seeress' bowl that Cedrevir now saw, and the Lady Marismë standing the other side of it, who spoke to him. "That spiritual jewel was the green ruby, his pride and pleasure. It lay in the sea, lost to him, as all else had been lost, until, with the centuries, it was washed ashore. Men, seeing it a stone beyond price, fashioned therefrom a chalice. So to the lords of the earth it passed, after the fire, the air and the water. Solomon the Wise drank from it. And through a line of kings it entered the possession of the Prince of All, Jesus, the Christ. You are seeking His Grail. In the world or out of the world."

"Lady, I am. And have always wondered at the tale, that the ornament of Satan, the Evil One, should become the holy Cup of the Christ."

"But is He not," said Marismë, "called the Redeemer?"

Cedrevir bowed his head. "But," he said, "do you know the road to *Carba Bonem?*"

"I shall tell you its name," she said. "This road is called *I will.*"

Cedrevir sighed. Then, surprised a little, he saw the lamps had burned away and that the soft light in the tent was dawn coming in from without. The moments of the magical revelation had consumed an entire night.'

"If you wish," said the Lady Marismë, "you may now accompany us to our kingdom."

Then she spoke a word, and the whole pavilion lifted as a ball of thistledown lifts. It blew up into the air, and all its appurtenances and furnishings with it, and vanished quite. There they were, then, on the strand of the lake, and nearby the lady's Knights leaning on their shields, while on the hill-slope under the old tower the blond horse cropped the grasses.

At this minute the sun rose between two eastern hills, and threw down its rosy sword point foremost straight across the lake. And out of the sun's glory, there might be seen a slender raft with a transparent sail coming slowly towards them, guided by no agency that Cedrevir could discern.

As Cedrevir stood pondering, the Knight of the winged-bull approached him and said, "Your horse is safely penned within an ancient wall, no longer visible, for this was the stronghold of magicians, and power remains. Come now with us, if you will."

Then the raft drew against the shore. The lady stepped on it, and after her the two Knight-brothers, and the three stayed, waiting courteously. So Cedrevir went after them, onto the raft, which hardly looked stout enough to uphold the lady alone. But when he was on it, it began to move again, its sail turning to the morning breeze, and went back the way it had come.

The lady was foremost of the craft, with the sunlight on her, and she said to Cedrevir, "You must know, that in time past we dwelled on shore, where the tower leans, which is all that remains of a great castle. One season, the waters of the lake rose and overwhelmed the land. We, swept away, outlasted the catastrophe. And now, live there."

"Where is that, lady?"

"Beneath your feet, bold Knight. Under the water."

The raft had reached the middle of the lake, and suddenly it stopped, with only its swan-white wake fading behind it.

Then Marismë laughed, and she went out, onto the very water, and after her, her two brothers. And the liquid of the lake buoyantly held them up, and then gently drew them in. And as she slowly sank,

Marismë called to Cedrevir. "Bold Knight, will you make bold to follow? We are your protectors in this. I, by the Arts called Luminous, Will ensure you against harm. But you must be trustful, fearless, and swift. Follow now or do not follow."

Then Cedrevir also laughed aloud. "Say then I will," said he. (But his eyes, by turns were black or blazing.)

Blithely as they, or so it seemed, he stepped onto the water, which held him upright with only a little motion, just such as the raft had had done, then gradually began to take him in, in company with the other three. Thus they sank together under the mirror of the lake.

This was the curious property either of the lake, or of the lady's magic, that there was no sensation of wetness, only of a silken levity, and that Cedrevir found himself enabled, as did his hosts, freely to breathe the water. Also, that he might hear and see, touch and taste, and in every other way respond and act as if he were above the surface on dry land.

Yet everything was, too, transmuted, and different. All speech, for example, now sounded to him like the sweetest singing. (And he heard besides the songs of the fish, which darted here and there like linnets, as he descended.) As for vision, a dark radiance hung over all things, and proceeding through the kingdom beneath the lake, every movement was swathed in the sleeves, robes and veil of silver eddies.

Under the water was a land that, in many ways, resembled the country of the earth. There was a road there, which led to a castle on a hill, but the road was paved with great round pebbles, washed smooth and lucent as glass, and above, the castle glimmered green as peridot. All about the road were orchards and groves, where fruit grew shining, like apples of milky gold.

The fish sat singing in the branches of the trees, whose foliage was fine and etoliate as strands of a girl's hair. Under the castle clustered a town of stone, and sometimes men and women passed to and fro. Seeing the Lady Marismë, these persons bowed to her. There was also something shadow-like about them, and it seemed to Cedrevir that here, too, though nothing was hidden, yet all was not shown.

As they neared the castle, the doors of the building opened and a Knight rode forth. He was clad in black, even to the plumes of his helm's high crest. The horse he sat was black and thin, but it was armoured all over, and its legs braced by black iron. And when they climbed and came up with the Black Knight, he turned his head to look at them, and he had no face, only a skull.

"It is Death," said Marismë, and she saluted him, and her brothers with her.

Death nodded, and made to pass on. Then, apparently noting Cedrevir, he spoke to him. "I shall meet again with you, in another place," said Death. "But that is many years hence."

Cedrevir crossed himself. But he would not be shamed, and looked long on Death, and it began to seem to him that behind the skull, there was a man's face, and two sombre eyes that regarded him. No sooner did he think this, than the apparition raised his hand and lowered the black visor of his helm. Death rode away down the hill on the iron horse.

"Do not be concerned," said Marismë. "Our kind, though we live, are also numbered with the drowned. He has some rights over us, being in part our king." And in the open doorway of the citadel castle, she turned to Cedrevir and said, "There are three mighty citadels of Powers. The Powers of the water, which are inconstant and eternal. The Powers of earth and fire, which mingle, and are of the passions, and by which most wrong-doing is invoked. The Powers of the air, whereof there are many kingdoms, for they lie closest to God – not in that they are in the sky, but in their permeation of everything, and their invisibility like breath, and life itself."

When she had said this, she went forward into the castle, entering a huge hall there that had looked empty and dark before, but lit up at her coming.

Presently, as it would happen in a sort of dream, Cedrevir found himself seated on a dais at the lady's right hand, before a board draped with damask. On this, every delicacy that might be got from the dry world, or that might be found in fresh water, was displayed on dishes of gold and silver, while servers processed ceaselessly through the hall, bearing jewelled trenchers and longnecked ewers of wine. And in that ambience of water, not a morsel of food was lost, or a drop of liquor spilled out or mixed in the currents of the lake, but flowed from beaker to cup, from cup to lip. Down from the roof hung gilded wheels, each with a score of flaming candles in them, and in the walls torches burned, and not a fire was quenched, though the smokes wove endless patterns through the water.

In the body of the hall, not a place was vacant at the long tables. A full company of Knights and ladies dined together. And while they dined, proud dogs with collars of pearls lay by the tables or prowled about for scraps. The servers carved and the pages hastened on their errands, and the minstrels woke their harps. And on everything lay the iridescence of the lake. But under everything there lay a dimness and a shadow.

Perhaps several hours passed at the feasting. After this time, a

trumpet was sounded and a silence fell. Up the hall there walked a
page clothed in black, pale as a plant of the deep woods, and carrying
a dish of horn and onyx. On the dish lay a fruit from the aqueous
orchards below the castle. Coming to Cedrevir, but no other, the boy
kneeled: "Will you eat of this fruit, Knight?"

And Cedrevir hesitated. "Do you not come from Death?"

"If I do, it is not himself he sends you."

"What, then?"

"The fruit, which is not forbidden yet which is a fruit of
knowledge. Perhaps a warning, perhaps a prophecy, perhaps a symbol
or a test of heart or brain. Take the fruit, and see."

Then Cedrevir took the fruit, and at once the boy vanished.
Cedrevir gazed long at the apple's satin skin, as he had outstared Death
himself. And in the core of the fruit the Knight thought he saw a fire,
but it was not impure or poisoned. So he put it before him and cut it
open with his dagger.

Cedrevir started back in horror. For from the apple came a scaled
worm, a serpent, which his knife had severed. Yet, it did not bleed,
and both parts of it ended in a head, each having cold sad eyes that
looked at him.

"You have wounded me," said the snake.

"Pardon me for that," the Knight answered, "I did not do it
knowingly."

"You lie," said the snake.

"Not so."

"Do you not recognise me, then? I am the Serpent, that creature
cursed of God and man. I am the Beguiler. I am Satan, your Enemy.
Say now you do not wound me knowingly."

"If you are he," said Cedrevir, "then, knowingly, I would cut you
from me, mind and body and soul, a hundred times over."

"It has been easy for you, this once," said the snake.

And then it shrank and shrivelled, until it was no wider than a
thread, and the thread went to ashes and crumbled, and was gone.

"What is the message of this, lady?" asked Cedrevir of Marismë.

"That you are already on your road. For no tempter would come
to you if you had not entered the sphere of his sight."

Then she rose to her feet and the great hall grew vague and silent,
as if a huge cloak had been thrown over it, and every light was
smoored.

But at her side her brothers waited.

Marismë took Cedrevir by the hand, and led him out of the hall,
and up a curving flight of marble stairs, into the well of a tower. At its

summit was a chamber, in which the windows were pillared by stone, but the casements were water where the fish swam in and out as they pleased. The two Knights took their stance, as at the pavilion, one either side the door, which then closed fast of itself.

"Now Cedrevir," said the Lady Marismë. "You are young and you are thralled in my spell. You are here with me, and blameless, and who is to see us?"

And she showed him a bed, scented with flowers and soft as snow, and hung with heavy curtains of silver stuff. Next, she threw off her gown, and stood in her shift, as translucent as the lake itself. But when she had done this, he saw through her, through shift and skin and flesh and hair, and she was made of bones, as the face of Death had been.

"Lady," he said, "I will lie beside you, but in no other way."

She nodded, as Death had done, and drawing back the covers of the bed, she revealed to him that a barrier of upturned blades ran down the middle of it, a palisade of steel. Marismë stretched herself one side of this, and he the other, the blades between them. And all at once Cedrevir slept, in that bed of swords, and in his sleep the fence grew higher and touched the roof of the chamber, which caught alight and fell down on him, and at that he woke.

He lay beside the lake, on the shore in the sunrise, and up the slope, where the ruin was, the patient horse cropped the grasses.

There was no sign of any other thing, for his hair and garments had no trace of wet. He was hungry and thirsty. The feast under the lake had not sustained him.

Yet, on opening his right hand, he found lying in the palm a little coal-black shell, and there fell from it one water drop, like a single tear.

The Knight of the Fellowship of the Circle rode northwards another month or more, and the summer waned from the land. He came among places of sterility, where the trees were thin as famine, a burned country. In the valleys they had long since stripped the white corn, and the sun had withered off the grass and leaves.

Only crows stood sentinel on the bald hill-tops. In the north, miles distant, were clouds that did not move, and these Cedrevir took for the mountains.

One noon, when the barren heat was very great, Cedrevir saw a church below him in the downlands, by a stream. The banks were shaded by walnut trees, and the water was fresh. The fruits on the walnuts were like stones, however, and when he smote on the church door it sagged wide. No one was there but lizards that rushed away like the scorched leaves over the floor. A window shaped as a wheel hung in the east wall; before it an antique banner dipped from a rafter, dark red, the fringes rusty. The altar was singular, a block of quartz, and in the depths of it might imperfectly be seen a war-axe, though how it had come there, there was no telling.

Cedrevir, going out again, tethered his horse, and stretched himself among the trees to rest through the heat of the day.

No sooner had he closed his eyes than he heard a weird, wild pagan chanting, and shouts, and the tramp of feet coming toward him along the valley.

Cedrevir started up – and as he did so, the noises died on the air. Only the stream lilted in its narrow bed, and the horse whispered to the plants under the wall's shade.

Cedrevir sat down again, and leaned his head on his hand and shut his eyes. Instantly, he heard the chanting and the outcry, as before but louder still. Now he did not stir, but only waited, and presently shadows began to flicker and dance over his eyelids, as if a company of people passed.

Cedrevir opened his eyes a second time, and wide and grey they gazed on nothing but the arid afternoon.

A third time he withdrew his sight, and past him the people trampled, and bells rang and women shrilled. Now Marismë, the lady in the lake, had said to him: The name of your road is *I will*. So then Cedrevir said softly to himself, "It is to be seen if it is to be heard, and I will see this thine and what it is."

And as he had smitten on the church door, so he smote open his own eyes with the thought.

Then he saw this: across the valley floor, following the course of the stream, came a band of men and women. They were summer-tanned, lean and ragged, but they had garlanded their heads with twisted briars. The women rang bells and the men brandished staves. In the midst was a cart, which they pulled violently along, and in the cart was bound a young maiden, wan as if near death, though in her dark hair too was caught a crown, of vine-leaves and poppies. Plainly, she was to be a sacrifice.

Cedrevir got to his feet and loosened the sword in its sheath. It transpired that, as he had formerly not seen these people, they could not even now see him; he was invisible. Unhindered then he trod behind them, and when they mounted a nearby hill, kept after.

There, among the stubble, was a ring of lifeless trees, from which the carrion birds rose at their arrival like flung, screaking stones. The ground under the trees, where they had been feeding, was littered by bones and bits of rotted meat. The spot smelled of death. As the men lifted the girl from their cart, she began to weep, but she did not beg for any mercy, judging it, seemingly, beyond them. They tied her fast to one of the trunks. She drooped there like a dying lily on a black branch. The maddened crowd ran about the tree, wailing and calling, and then an ancient man, cackling at the curtailment of youth, crept round the ring, sprinkling from a censer on the ground. It contained blood, which smoked and stank, and the crows, which had returned to the upper boughs, clapped their wings in greed.

When the ancient had completed his ritual, the people plunged together and swirled suddenly away. They went by Cedrevir, where he waited at the tree-ring's edge, without a look, and some even stumbled against him, but paid no heed to it. Their noise, which now had something more of fear than celebration, diminished and was gone. A vast silence settled on the hill. At this, the girl raised her drenched eyes and looked all about her. Her tears fell and she shook with terror, but nor did she make any sound.

Then there came a rumbling in the earth, under their very feet, and Cedrevir unslung from his shoulder the shield fronted with the sarpafex, and drew his sword.

In another second, the ground bulged and split, and out of it there burst, flaming like a molten thing, a huge lizard, a dragon.

It was the colour of brass, and in size half the height again of a man. It bore up with it a fearful smell of sulphur and decayed matter, and as it grubbed and pawed, discarding the soil, searching for the accustomed offering, from its jaws ran a venomous breath tinctured with fire.

Cedrevir stepped forward, and lifting his shield against the exhalation, called to it.

The dragon turned at once, and its orbs of eyes, that looked blind with unthinking malice, yet appeared to take him in.

"Before her, first you must be done with me, Devil-spawn," said the Knight. "Now God be at my side, in Christ's Name." And he went forward straight at the dragon, but, as he did so, covered his head and breast with the shield. A wave of the filthiness and heat seared Cedrevir like a furnace blast. Yet he came on, and struck with his sword, upward, against the underside of the ribs.

But the sword crashed on the scales of the beast, and under the scales the cage of ribs was a monumental thing. He bruised it, for the monster roared, and in the trees the waiting crows exclaimed and took flight. But no more than that he did.

Cedrevir fell back now, for the awful breath and fire of the dragon were greatly weakening.

It slunk after him, and raking at him with its forefeet continuously, inflicted instead horrid wounds in the earth, for he was too quick for it.

Then again, he struck at the beast, at its jaw that weaved above him, and one of the huge teeth in its mouth was broken at the blow.

Down the hill they passaged, the dragon sweeping with its claws and pouring out its bane-breath, Cedrevir avoiding its attack as he could – and here and there a tree stump or a boulder sprang alight in lieu of him, or cracked in pieces.

But it was in the thoughts of the Knight that he would lead it down, away from the damsel, to the stream below the church. The dragon's element was fire, but there lay water.

Among the walnut trees they passed, and Cedrevir stepped back into the stream and felt, through his mail, its blessed lesser warmth like coolness. The dragon baulked. It would not come on. It snarled, and the small stones of the walnuts might be heard popping and snapping.

"Is it water you spurn, or the holy church above?"

Then the dragon spoke to Cedrevir. "You have wounded me. Is that not enough? Let me return to the maiden who is meant for me. I would not slay you. I honour your valour. You did not mean to wound me."

"Is it you?" said Cedrevir. "You were before a little snake."

"I? Who knows me, or what I have been, or may be?" said the dragon. The words came from its mouth, in a pure voice, shining like an organ-note in the flaxen air. The words came from it, yet no men could be sure it was the dragon which uttered them.

Cedrevir answered: "You are the creature of Satan, let him protect you. I call upon my Lord. You are the weapon of the Enemy. Oh God!" cried out Cedrevir, "send me a weapon here to meet this foe."

At that, the ground quaked, even as it had when the dragon erupted out of it. Above the stream, where the church stood, there came a sound of rending, and up into the air shot a beam of light. Cedrevir did not turn, he held his eyes on the dragon, and covered himself over with his shield. But also he let fall his sword, and raising his right arm high, opened his hand. And into it there came a heavy rounded haft, and at the haft's end a wedge of brightness like a jewel. It was the axe he had seen bedded in the altar.

"I will," repeated Cedrevir. He lifted up the axe and whirled it.

The dragon coughed out a spurt of livid fire, which enveloped Cedrevir, and seemed to touch his heart and shatter it. But yet still he let the revolving axe fling free, and even as he sank down, he saw the axe-head meet the dragon's skull, and cleave it and become embedded in it. And he saw too that the skull seemed made of a substance like quartz.

The cool water laved the mail, the hair and flesh of Cedrevir. He lay under the stream, dreaming of the dragon's death. But he could not breathe the water of the stream as in the lake he had. He must rise up again and shake it from him.

He climbed the hill wearily, and the crows berated him high above. (The dragon's corpse would be difficult eating.) Going to the dead tree, he cut the ropes which bound the maiden. She saw him clearly, as she had seen the battle for her life. She dropped at his feet. She clasped his ankles, and the garland of poppies slid from her shadowy hair.

"You are at liberty," he said.

"Yes, and I thank and bless you for it. But do not leave me here, for those savages of the region will themselves kill me. They have worshipped the dragon all the years of their lives." And she looked at him with the blackest eyes, and her mouth was red as the poppies. "I am called Melasind. A great lord is kin to me. Take me only to his kingdom. It lies northward. It is not far."

Cedrevir set the girl before him on the horse. She was slender and silent, no trouble to them, but for her beauty – which did trouble the Knight. For her beauty was of a subtle and uneasy sort, like smoke.

She gave no direction to the home of her kindred, the kingdom of that lord she had not named. Northward, she had said, northward they rode, and she was content. She did not question Cedrevir on any matter.

At night, they slept upon the ground, and gentle Melasind made no complaint. She wrapped herself in her mantle and lay down, her cheek pillowed in her hand. Her slumber was discreet, but her hair strayed as she slept, it coiled and shimmered on the earth. She had been the dragon's bride, and her power over desire came from that, her virginity burned under her skin.

By day the sky was brazen. The landscape became a desert, flat-tabled plains where drifts of minerals sparkled. Not a tree grew. Water, where it was to be had, lay still in the cups of stone and tasted of metal, granite, or cinders.

Then, as an evening came on after the sunset, the girl said to the Knight, "Do not pause now. For another hour's riding will bring us to the kingdom I told you of."

Cedrevir looked before them, to the north. He saw dim, folded plateaux and the vault of night. There was no sign of any road, any wall or tower.

"There, lady?"

"There," she said. "Where the stars are coming clear."

Then Cedrevir beheld a strangeness in the sky. On the height of it some stars were flashing out, a whole constellation, but it had a form which he had never seen before in any land, or place, nor ever heard spoken of.

It was like a spear or sword, but winged, the clustered stars thick like diamonds at its centre, raying away to glinting dust at the huge pinion-points, and the whole dazzling more fiercely than any other star of the sky, or the full moon even.

Cedrevir said nothing else to the maiden, and she nothing more to him. They rode on towards the winged sword of stars. And an hour passed, as she had said it must, but with no feature of the plain altering. Then, "Draw rein," said she. And when he had done so, she leaned forward and cried in a high voice thin as a wire:

"Ex orio per Nomine."

That done, she bowed her head meekly and clasped her hands. But on the plain a mighty wind rose up. It seemed to lift the very corners of the world up after it, shards and dusts flew into the air, and in the welter of these things, soundless as an opening flower, Cedrevir saw a castle rising out of the earth. Its battlements and towers were pierced with lights, and banners curled about the tops of it. All was stillness as the wind died down. Then from the castle's walks the trumpets clamoured.

"Do not delay, we are expected," said Melasind.

So they rode forward, and as they went, the starburst of the winged sword was eclipsed behind the stoneworks, its point seeming to stab slowly to the castle's heart.

There was a gate, with torched turrets either side. The portals of this now began to open, and a Knight rode out. In the torches' light he was dressed in red. his mail red as new copper, and he was mounted on a red horse.

"You are welcome," he said courteously, and to the Lady Melasind he bowed.

With great surprise, Cedrevir heard her give a shrill merry laugh, and felt her shrink away between his arms. He looked, and saw that as the torches found her now, Melasind was a slender girl-child, some seven or eight years of age. She turned to him her laughing face and said, "In the world, I am wise. But here, in the house of my kin, I am as a child. Help me get down, Sir Knight."

So Cedrevir dismounted and lifted her down.

With misgiving, yet ever with the purpose of the Quest, he followed her under the great gate, into the castle which had risen from the earth.

A night and a day, Cedrevir remained, the guest of an unknown host, in the Castle of Earth and Fire. And so it was. For by day, only the slightest sunlight entered through the embrasures, that were closed besides by panes of thick glass tinted with cinnabar. Constantly the lamps and torches and candles burned there. It was a place of great heat, and of leaping fire-cast shadows.

The servants of the Castle waited on Cedrevir, as, in the mansions of his own land, he was wont to be waited on. There seemed nothing uncommon in it, though they did not speak to him of anything, nor did he interrogate them. At the ending of that first day, sunset filled the windows, and the Knight in red mail came to Cedrevir, greeted him with all proper forms, and asked him to descend the Castle to a hall of feasting.

Together they went down countless wide stairs of burnished basalt, by passages and chambers red with sunset and fire, and going always lower, until Cedrevir believed they had now passed under the ground. But he made no remark upon this fact, nor did the Red Knight speak of it.

At length, the last stair ended at a door, which opened itself at their approach. Beyond lay a garden, most unusual and enigmatic in its looks. No daylight ever came there, it was far beneath the earth, but in the midst of it was a pool of ebony water from which proceeded a sourceless glowing light. On the water the whitest lilies rested, and sometimes, in the lighted dark, the gold fin of a fish would blink. The walks of the garden were laid with opals and other pallid fiery gems. Herbs and flowers stood in the beds, but they had no hue nor perfume. All across the garden, nevertheless, a tall rose tree had spread itself, and every rose on the tree was crimson. But when they came near to it, Cedrevir saw that these roses were made of rubies, garnets and spinels.

Beyond the tree was another door, and through the door a hall.

They left the garden and entered the hall, and stood on its threshold. A million candles were burning there, above tables covered with cloth-of-gold, and against hangings that ran with gold, on cups of sheerest crystal and platters trimmed with precious stones. But none sat down there, and presently Cedrevir perceived that the dust of years had gathered over everything. And, as the fish had winked in the pool, now and then a black rat would flicker under the draperies.

At the room's far end, the child Melasind sat on the flagstones. She wore now a gown of yellow scarlet, and her hair was crowned with the colourless flowers of the garden. In her lap she held an agate bowl and a knife of bone, and she wept.

Cedrevir went to her and kneeled down before her. "Lady," said he, "why are you crying so bitterly?"

"The lord, my kindred, is sick," said Melasind. "Only this bowl, brimmed by the blood of a virgin, can revive him at such times. See, I have been nerving myself to it, but am afraid."

Cedrevir frowned.

The Red Knight stood at his left shoulder and said, "It is as she tells you. For long ago my lord, who is the lord of this kingdom, received a grievous wound. It does not heal. Only virgin blood can make him well, and that only for a little while."

"I do not ask the nature of the wound, nor how he came to it," Cedrevir replied. "The voice of fate, shouting or murmuring, is always to be heard on such a journey as mine. My vow is also of chastity. I have never joined with a woman, or committed any carnal act. I am as virgin as this child, and far stronger. Therefore, I offer your lord instead my blood, without fear. For my soul is in profound safekeeping."

The lord's Knight, hearing this, bowed very low. "He will receive your gift with thanks," said he. And he withdrew from the hall. But the child-girl only stared at Cedrevir.

"You must attend me," he said. "When it is done, take your scarf and bind the cut tightly. Now give me the bowl, and if you wish, look away from what I do."

So Cedrevir opened a vein in his left arm with the bone knife, and filled the agate bowl with his blood. When the deed was finished, the child-girl ran to him and bound his arm tightly, not looking at the cut. But then, she dipped her finger in the blood.

"You shall take him this yourself," said Melasind. "I will guide you to my lord's chamber."

Cedrevir felt a little weakness from the loss of the blood, and he remembered how he had lain down in the stream after the dragon's death, and heard the water singing in his ears, but not as it had sung under the lake.

"Where does your lord lie?" asked Cedrevir. "In one of the great towers of the Castle?"

"No. He is below us, here."

Cedrevir followed her, as she bore the bowl of bright blood, and her steps were quick and light, his slower and less gladsome.

She took him through a narrow door, and beyond the passage sloped and widened, lit only by the raw torches in its walls. Till suddenly Cedrevir could see they were entering among huge hollow caves underground. Soon enough, the lighted corridor fell behind them, and on all sides unfurled the shining dark, like eternal night. Yet nevertheless he could tell their path, for a hot radiance beamed out from the agate bowl.

Shortly, Melasind led him over a bridge of flint, under which, miles down, an unseen river clashed its furious way. On the other side of the bridge was a front of granite, in which a tall door of dull metal stood weirdly ajar. Through this slit went the maiden-child with her bloody lamp, and Cedrevir after her.

At once, he seemed struck nearly blind. For though no light came out from the place beyond the door, yet light blazed there within. The means of the light Cedrevir could not discern, but the cause of its power he could barely miss. For the cavern that plunged away before him was piled with such treasure it would seem to beggar the richest kings of the world above.

"Come, follow still," said Melasind, and she led him on now up hills and along mountainsides of piled gold, made all of coins and chains and casks, crowns and swords and rings, and furnishings of every type. And through the gold ran streams of silver, and down its slopes rattled slips of jewels that their feet had disturbed. Until, coming over a ridge of this colossal wealth, Cedrevir looked upon a lake of sapphires, emeralds and rubies, so blue, so green, so bloodmost red, it seemed to boil and to flash lightnings. But in the centre of the lake, as the dragon lies upon its hoard, lay stretched a man on cushions of silk. And he was a giant, clad in black armour, his face turned away, so his locks of hair, that outshone the gold, flowed on the silk like fire.

Then Melasind gave a cry, and she ran down into the lake of jewels, and over it, and came to the giant and leaned above him. After a moment, she called to Cedrevir again: "Come, Sir knight."

So Cedrevir walked out across all the jewels and when he reached the giant, gazed in his face. It was a countenance of such hideousness that none could look at it unmoved, nor without shrinking. For it was not the ugliness of any fleshly deformity, its horror stemmed from some inner twisting and torture. Then the eyes opened, and filled the face instead with an appalling beauty, but it was the endless beauty of agony that never ends.

"So you behold me, Knight," said the fallen one, and at his voice, no more than a sigh, stone and metal, skin and bone, heart and mind, were ravished and trembled and grew shamed and sick. "See what I possess," said the Lord of the Castle of Earth and Fire, "see what is mine. And see what I am brought to, that a child must fetch me gruel. I thank you for your charity, Sir Knight. Say now, may I drink?"

"Drink," said Cedrevir, but he must turn away, and leaning on a mace of silver that protruded from the lake of jewels, he hid his eyes with his hand.

After a moment, though, the wondrous horror of the voice whispered again. "Your gift does me good. There is great vitality in you. Whom then, do you serve?"

"Only my Fellowship," answered Cedrevir. "And God."

The fallen giant drank again. The bowl was drained. He said: "I serve none. I will not serve, and so may never be free. Do you think my punishment has lasted sufficiently long? No, I am not punished. I need cry out humbly only once *Ut Libet*. But will not do it. It is my pride, not your *God*, that binds me. *Ut libet. Nunquam. Ut qui libentam.*"

Cedrevir, unable to prevent himself, had gazed once more into that awful face of a fallen dragon, and in the deeps of the golden eyes he saw printed those words – *Ut qui libentam*. (Seeing that *I will*.)

"Go now," said the mouth that had drunk his blood. "Go, take your reward with this damsel. For I would not see this special virtue of yours wasted on another after I have had benefit from it.'

"Lord," Cedrevir replied, "you know I may not take any pleasure with her in that way."

"That is to be seen."

And then there came up in the golden eyes a redness, like two dead suns that rose underground, and over the mouth, and all the features, went a ghastly flaring, as if wax melted in flame, and the being roared, and all the cavern seemed to break apart and the jewels rushed up over their heads like a storm of water.

Melasind took to her heels, and catching at his hand, she pulled Cedrevir after her. And in his terror, which was like no other fear in the world, he allowed her to do it. Together they escaped the cavern of riches, and ran over the unillumined bridge above the unseen river, and up the slopes of stone into the passage, and so back into the banquet hall, with all its places laid and not a single guest. And beyond that they ran, to the subterranean garden, and here both the doors slammed on them, and cold silence fell.

Cedrevir felt a longing for water, and leaning to the lily-pool, he raised some to his face and lips. As the rings settled in the pool, he saw reflected, between the white chalices of the flowers, Melasind, and she was no longer a child, but a damsel again, with sweet high breasts and a rosy mouth, and hair that poured to her hips.

Then Cedrevir drew his sword and smote that image in the pool so it smashed in pieces.

The damsel laughed. "But did he not give me to you?" said she, "And here I am, and we are prisoners in this garden. Who is to see?"

"I should see it," replied Cedrevir. "I am both warrior and priest. I will not break the vows I made. They have fashioned me, in water and fire, on the anvil, as this sword was fashioned. Though I desire you, lady, which you, and he, both know too well, I have another duty, and a better lust than for your love."

"Alas," said Melasind, and she hurried to him, swift and sinuous as a snake, and threw her arms about him and sought his lips with hers. But he remembered her, how she had been a child, sexless and innocent, who cried at the notion of a wound. And desire left him, and he put her away, though the heat of her body burned him through. Lifting his voice, he cried out then, as she herself had done on the night plain: "*Ex orio per Nomine!*"

But the Name invoked was now Another's, and all the power and passion of Cedrevir, which that place had stirred, turned otherwise, tore wide the enchantment.

With a screeching and thunder, the Castle of Earth and Fire seemed to burst, and up from the garden rushed the whirlwind, and taking Cedrevir in its grasp, hurled him through disintegrated stone and iron, glass and fire, onto the surface of the tindered land.

And as he lay on the breast of the world, the ground shook, and on the horizon a fiery crack, the shape of a serpent and two or three miles in length, healed itself, and thereafter everything was darkest night, without a beacon or a star.

But transfixing his palm, even through the steel of the gauntlet, was a blood-red thorn. And plucking it out, it left no mark on him. (And the cut from which he had filled the agate bowl had also vanished, leaving only a scar, a broken circle like the sickle moon.)

In a dream, then, he heard the voices sing:

First the Sword of Paining,
Second the Sorrow's crowning,
Third the Blood-Grail shining.

As in the Castle of Towers they had sung, dulcet as silver bells.

And after these, he heard the seeress Lady Marismë, who said, "Water inconstant and eternal, earth and fire that mingle, and the many kingdoms of the air."

When he wakened, the land was changed, as if swept by a mighty broom that had tumbled boulders, and the sky of earliest day showed the strokes of the broom in long riven skeins of cloud.

But northward, now, he saw the mountains sharp and clear as swords. Partially transparent they seemed, and hard as forged steel. Yet before the mountains was a vast forest lying on the land like the smoke of an old burning.

Now, this might be that forest called the Wood of the Savage Hart, and since he looked on it and found it there, Cedrevir so named it. Mounting his horse, which wandered docile on the plain, he rode north again, and in a few hours entered under the tangled branches.

In the stories, the trees of that forest were all dead, but the towering trees of the forest Cedrevir had entered, though leafless and often leaning with half their clawed roots from the soil – which was itself only of dust and stones – yet they seemed to pulse and throb with liveness, as if with the very beat of hearts. And even those trees which had fallen seemed quickened by a strange force, and here and there the roots had driven back into the unnourishing ground.

There were no birds, nor any truly living thing which Cedrevir might see, or hunt for food. But, as a Knight of a fellowship he was accustomed to fasting. As the noiseless days and silent nights went by, his thoughts grew only flawless and crystalline, and for the horse, it survived by sometimes chewing on a kind of mastic that exuded from the trees. Of water there was no scarcity, for the nights were chill and brought a frost which, in the sunrise, melted in quantities, dripping off the boughs and gathered in the stones until midday.

The only flowers of that forest were the sun and the moon. There was too an overcast, which hid the stars, and also that constellation of the winged sword. But probably this had been, in any case, a sorcery.

One dawn he woke from a deep sleep, in which the bell-voices chimed. Not the length of a spear away, a creature was drinking at one of the water-puddles in the stones. It was a hart, cold white, but between the forked horns of it a gold blossom seemed stamped upon its forehead.

It appeared to Cedrevir that this was a magical beast, the genius of the wood, and so he rose and began to go towards it, but at that the hart tossed its head and ran away. Yet it ran only to a clearing some score of trees distant, and there again it stood, flickering in its whiteness like a candle-flame, as if awaiting him.

Accordingly, Cedrevir untethered and mounted his horse, and rode slowly after the hart, which seeing him come on began to trot before him.

In this manner, the morning and the noon passed, the Knight following and the white hart dancing before him. If Cedrevir should spur his horse, then the hart would run, so fleet the man seemed likely to lose it. However, if Cedrevir should lag or pause, the hart too stayed itself, browsing on the dark mastic of the tree as the horse did.

When the afternoon came down into the forest, still the hart went on and Knight rode after. It was a cheerless day, the season was no longer summer, nor anything, cool and dry, and without kindness.

There seemed no change in the woods, but for the natural alteration of the light. Later, a pale amber westering glow flowed through the trees. Later yet, the dusk began.

Where did the creature lead him? In the crystal thoughts of Cedrevir, from which the fast too had sloughed most of the need for sleep or rest, the motive of the pursuit of the hart shone indivisible and immaculate. On a Vowed Journey, such things had all a reason.

Night won the land.

They had reached another of the hollow clearings, and now the hart stopped of its own accord and turned to face its pursuer. It gleamed dimly, even in the utter dark, and between its horned brows the golden flower was like a lingering speck of day. Then, a fearful metamorphosis occurred. The hart leapt abruptly high into the air, so its feet no longer touched the earth, and as it did this, it seemed to leap out of its own skin, which pleated away into nothing behind it. From the skin of the hart there emerged a huge white lion, with a grey hoary mane like the spun frost, and eyes of flame. And in mid-air it sprang at Cedrevir, for his throat, and for his soul too it seemed.

The horse neighed in terror and plunged aside. The lion-beast, meeting the horse's flanks in its spring, ripped with huge talons, but only the cloth and leather of the caparison were breached. The lion hung then from this vantage, glaring in the face of the Knight. And in the black silence of the forest, the hatred and blood-craving of the lion were like a torch. But Cedrevir had by now freed his sword. He swung it over and thrust it down, into the lion's jaws, until the hilt, where was engraved the sigil of the *sarpafex* grated on the fangs. And the eyes of the lion turned to blackened coals. It fell away, and lay on the earth, still faintly shining, so Cedrevir beheld it was now only a flaccid pelt, without sinews, flesh or bones.

Cedrevir did not marvel, for he had come into a state of the marvellous, where nothing surprised him. But he bowed his head and gave customary thanks to God. Lifting his eyes again, he saw glow-worms in the wood, and then that they were not glow-worms, but the lit tapers of a procession of men and women, which wandered through the trees into the glade. As they drew closer, he noted also that they were garbed, the men as priests, the women as nuns. Reaching the spot where the skin of the lion sprawled, two of the priests raised it and bore it off. They spared no glance to Cedrevir, but passed him, chanting softly some litany he could not recognise.

Cedrevir leaned from his horse. He caught at the mantle of one of the nuns. "Where is it that your mysterious company goes?"

She answered, "The earth is fading. The sky will fall. You may follow us, if you wish."

"But where, holy lady?"

"It is true, all places are as one in the world's death."

And with no more reply than that, (though that perhaps reply enough), she slipped from him. And all of them had left him, the lion's skin carried in their midst.

Cedrevir dismounted and, leading the horse, went after.

Soon the way ascended. They climbed, the religious procession, and behind it Cedrevir. The trees thinned. The Knight looked about him, and saw they had emerged on a range of cliffs, which might be at the foot of the northern mountains, although these he could not make out. Though the forest had been stricken and non-verdurous, these cliffs were bare of everything but the rock itself. Presently, however, he might see the destination of the travellers. It was a skeletal chapel, roofless and wrecked.

A curious light came down. At first, Cedrevir took it for the glow-worm sheen of the tapers. But then, thinking over the words the nun had spoken, he looked up to heaven. And there was a strange sight, and one which filled him with a deep and sorrowing fear.

The night above had become a canopy, opaque and impenetrable, empty of moon or stars. Yet it was a canopy wonderfully adorned. Across the whole length of it, which stretched to the twelve quarters, ran scrolls and frettings of gold and silver, not in motion but still, as if painted there. And as Cedrevir gazed at this, the whole of it seemed always sinking a little nearer, so that indeed the sky, or this entity of the sky, was falling, by slow inches on the earth below. And from it nothing alive could fly away, but must be crushed beneath. Yet so beautifully fashioned it was, the great black coffin-lid of heaven, that now he saw gems of exquisite lucidity set into the metal, lilies of pearl and asphodel of the clearest topaz, and hyacinths of such purple corundum he could hardly bear to look at them. In his heart, Cedrevir wept. God, dismayed by the unrelenting wickedness of Man, let down the sky to end His creation. Yet, too, he honoured it with beauty. Not cruel water nor ravening fire, would be the quietus of mankind, but black air flowered with jewels. Yes, Cedrevir's heart wept, and overflowed with pity for the Creator, and love and an anguish of fear, and resignation, also.

And so he followed the company into the chapel, and here they doused their lights, and were illumined only by the falling slow lights of the sky.

But where they had laid the lion's skin, suddenly there was also a fire on the earth. The pelt blazed up, and the flames divided. Out of them came daintily stepping a little snowy fawn, with a golden cross between its brows. For a moment it was clearly visible, and then it vanished, and the glittering ashes of the fire snuffed out to nothing.

A wind blew through the chapel, among the silent watchers there. It was fierce yet strengthless, all the winds of the world flattened under the lid of the sky. After the wind had passed, dew or rain fell, but it died to dust even as it touched the ground.

Looking up again, through roofless walls, Cedrevir saw the canopy had come so close that every flower and decoration might be measured by the eye, huge in dimension, with gems set within gems. Then again, he bowed his head. And heaven fell.

There was neither heat nor cold, nor sound nor vision nor thought. There was no pain or smothering. A vast *un-ness* covered all, and all was absorbed in it.

After the darkness, there was light. After the death of sleep, a second awakening. The Knight Cedrevir was as you have yourself seen him, well-made, and fair to look on, and he stood as formerly, clad in mail and fully armed, but alone, upon a mountain-side. The world lay far beneath, or it was gone entirely to a ring of palest most insubstantial brightness, like the sea.

The sky was all around, roseate blue with dawn, and clouds passed below and on all sides, moving leisurely as swans on a morning lake. And the sky too was full of golden flowers and silver flowers, like those which had fretted the lid of the Annihilation. But these flowers hung, as if woven in a tapestry, and as he began again to climb, now and then they brushed his face or shoulders, and they had only the touch of flowers, but they did not break or fall.

Above there was a castle, which grew up from the mountain, and as it grew it changed to gold, so it was a thing of fire like the sun, and he could not keep his eyes on it. There was a road also under his feet, and it was laid with lapis-lazuli and sapphire. While, at the roadside, trees sprang out of the mountain, and their boughs were all blossom, yet fruit hung from them that shone like mirrors and gave off a perfume like no fruit or bloom of the earth.

By accident or by design it is not possible to come there, but by faith and will, sometimes, it is.

For Cedrevir had entered a kingdom of the Kingdoms of the Air, and before him rose *Carba Bonem*, blinding him with its glory.

As he approached the gate, a horn blew within the Castle, a long and liquid note, and the doors of the gate opened without a sound.

Within lay a court. It was paved with marble, and on every side the towers went up blazing, and one tower above the others like a shaft of flame, whose head was not to be distinguished.

At the centre of the court stood a tawny willow, the curved trunk of which was braced with silver. From its boughs depended the helms and swords, spears and shields and colours, of many scores of Knights, marked with their various devices, so it was a gaudy object, this brown tree. Under it, there waited a maiden dressed in sackcloth. Her hair was white as salt, and her eyes the pallid green-azure grey of glass, but she was thin and twisted, and her face beautiless.

"Stay, Knight," said she. "You must leave your weapons and your colours here."

"As others have," said Cedrevir, "and not reclaimed them."

"Not all reclaim them, it is true," said the maiden.

"But you have entered the *Azori Mundi Regna*, the Kingdoms of the Air, and must obey their laws."

Cedrevir unsheathed his sword, and unslung the shield from his shoulder. These he gave her, with his war-helm. And she raised the items, as if they were no weight at all, and hung them on the tree.

"Who guards you, lady?" he asked her then, "are you alone, and still make this harsh demand of any man that comes here?"

"There is protection, though invisible. I am Morgainor, and it is I myself who guards this place, and its treasures, which you seek."

"So I do," he answered very low.

"Enter the tower then, the tallest of all, and go up the stair."

At these words, Cedrevir went pale, and his heart thundered. He said, "Is there no other preparation?"

"What is to be can only be."

So he left the maiden, who had called herself Morgainor, and crossed the court, and the door of that tallest of the towers opened for him. He saw beyond a stair ascending. It was of polished ebony, inlaid with ivory. And in the tower too, the flowers of gold and silver hung in the air, brushing his face and shoulders as again he climbed upward. And he was filled by feverish lightness, and tears stood in his eyes.

Now as he climbed the stair of ebony and ivory, it did begin to suggest itself to the Knight that, aside from the flowers, which he might see and feel, the air thickened with unseen presences and sometimes they too brushed him, as if with draperies or wings. Where the stair curled about itself, as it did very often, it seemed to him he detected voices also, soft and melodious, but they spoke in a tongue he had never heard.

At last, he saw the light of the sky again before him, but, as he stepped off from the stair, he found the way was closed with a palisade the height of three men, and made from the bones of men, and the day streamed through them and through the eyeless skulls, which were very white and pure, as if fashioned of alabaster, but they were not.

This door would not open for Cedrevir. He paced before it, and saw dimly through its eyelets radiant day beyond.

Then a shadow moved in an inner corner of the door, and there was a stooped, gross woman there, dressed in sackcloth, her pale hair matted and her face very ugly, though her eyes were the eyes of the maiden in the court.

"You must give me a gift," said she, "or I may not open the way for you."

"What would you have? For I have nothing."

"Give me," she said, "a coal-black shell and a blood-red thorn."

Then he considered how he had remained true to himself, and to his vows, at the castle in the lake and the Castle of Earth and Fire, and how, waking, he had on both occasions found tokens left him, the shell and the thorn. So he took them from his belt and placed them on the ugly woman's palm.

At that she smiled, and she shook her head, and closed her hand upon the things. "I am Morgainor," she said. "Do you recollect? You have met me before."

"If you are Morgainor, then you are she. I have given you what you asked."

"Yours is a heart that has no stain, nor any occlusion," she said. "I see through it, therefore. Alas, did you never question what you have been given, to give it up so easily in turn?"

"A shell," he said, "a thorn."

"Knight, I will render you one thing in exchange, and then will open the door of bone." And she held out to him her other hand, the right, and on the palm lay a golden needle. Cedrevir took this, and as he did so the door broke at its centre and folded wide for him to pass.

Beyond, the day was itself standing open, like a flower; it dazzled him, that upper sunshine.

The atmosphere was rare, thin as silk, and fragrant, and cold. The place was by the turret of the tower, its topmost roof, and so high a place the Castle itself had now vanished in the cloud below. A pavement stretched on every side, a round space without a wall, and at the centre of the pavement was a ring of white stones, each about half the height of a man. That was all, and the sun's rays smote on the stones, the pavement, and the gold turret, so everything was caught in a brilliant haze.

Then, from the brilliancy, forms began to shape themselves. Cedrevir stood immobile, and next he kneeled, for these creatures, though never wholly seen, yet appeared like angels, gleaming, and clad in robes of samite, with great wings, and having every one a nimbus about its head. And these strange ethereal beings went to and fro in the air itself, not treading the pavement. (But they did not go inside the ring of stones.)

Cedrevir knelt and prayed then, for the dazzle of the sun and of the angel-beings had brought him all at once to a leaden weariness. As he prayed, too, every slight transgression, every weakness of his life, came into his mind, and he was ashamed. He began to believe that, like those others whose weapons and colours remained on the willow tree, he too would shrivel in this bath of light, and die. Flawed as man and as priest-warrior, he partly longed to leave the height, he could not bear the peerlessness he sensed hovering over him.

Then he heard the chime of bells, and startled, looked up. In the sky to the east he saw a sight.

A glistening barge came floating down the air. It had a sail that shone like red bronze, and the prow was carved like an eagle. A band of Knights rowed the barge through the ether with gilded oars, and young girls stood in the stern and rang bells in their white hands, and chanted dolefully.

Down and down the barge descended; it slipped over the ring of stones and landed weightless on the tower beneath the turret. When that was done, the Knights put up their oars. One, who was clothed in white, came from the barge, and with him an old, crippled hag-like woman, dressed in sackcloth, who hid her face behind a veil. These two approached, and while the White Knight stood aside, the hag addressed Cedrevir.

"I am Morgainor. We meet a third time. Will you give me back now the golden needle, for if you do, I will then instruct you in the mystery."

Cedrevir rose from his knees. He looked at the White Knight, whose face was as splendid as sunrise and as unearthly. Cedrevir looked at the hag, who peeped hideously from her veil with faded azure-green grey eyes.

"Lady, before, you seemed to warn me that I had given up to you too easily the shell and the thorn. Shall I relinquish as easily this needle?"

"You must. And since you must, you shall."

"I believe I have begun to guess the riddle," said Cedrevir He lowered his eyes and said, "The shell was symbol of the Blood Cup, and the thorn symbol of the Sorrow Crown. The needle is the Lance of Pain. I am unworthy of the vision which was sent me and so, unwittingly, but at the design of God, resigned the key to these sacred relics. Nevertheless, this needle I still hold, and if I do not part with it, perhaps I shall be granted one further sight of the Lance. Or, I shall be granted clean death upon the lance of a Knight more worthy than I, maybe such a one as he that stands before me now."

Then the hag said this: "Cedrevir, you must not presume. If God has chosen you, how do you dare to judge yourself unworthy? What is your knowledge beside the knowledge of Him? You see into your heart, but He sees much more. It is your soul He sees. Whatever is said to you, whatever you gain or lose, what do such things matter? Did the Christ not promise Heaven to a wretched thief?"

Cedrevir sighed deeply. He said, "I am in God's hand." And he gave the hag Morgainor back her needle.

She took it. She said, "Go to the barge. That is the mystery and the last test. There is no more to say."

Cedrevir went towards the barge, and as he walked, the White Knight with the archangel's face, fell into step with him. And the White Knight said, "in the barge lies one under a curse, and you may free her from it." But his voice was remote, like distant music.

"What curse is that?" inquired Cedrevir, expressionless, and his heart ached within him, at the words of the hag Morgainor, at doubt, and *because* of doubt. He was not uplifted or comforted. His eagerness lay spent.

"That you shall see, the nature of the cursing. But to break it is, of itself, most simple. One lies within the barge. Embrace her, and kiss her, on the lips. All shall be well."

"That I may not do," Cedrevir replied, dully. "All and every intimate connection with women is forbidden me."

But now they had reached the barge. The beaked prow craned above, and the sail had netted the sun. At the stern, the young girls stood with folded hands, bowed heads. The Knights were motionless. A ladder led into the midships of the vessel, and Cedrevir mounted it and stepped down into the barge. There lay a canopied bier, the hangings of which were blue silk.

"It is not to be, I can do nothing," said Cedrevir to the White Knight.

But, "Look on her. Perhaps you will pity her enough to do it."

Then, impelled, Cedrevir crossed to the bier and lifted aside its hangings. At the view, he recoiled, unable to repress a groan of darkest loathing.

Then again, disbelieving, he stared, and could not take his gaze away.

On the bier there spilled a faintly-stirring mass. If it was a female, it was the more terrible for that, for it was also reptile. The ripplings of its curded flesh, shapeless under a swathe of silk, gave way at the upper limbs to the little clutching arms of lizards, sheathed in lustreless metallic scales. And from the waist its lower part was a serpent, oozing in a slime. And round the whole slithered hair that lived, fatted worms, the snake-hair of a gorgon. The face grew from the torso – that had no scales. It was in truth a woman's face, but old as a mummy, all fissured and crinkled, lipless and having no teeth but the four long fangs of its serpent side, these broken and discoloured. An evil stink arose from it, as it laboured there at life, half-torpid and half-awake. And finally Cedrevir, sick with horror, dragged away his stare from it, but just then it spoke.

"You are wounded by the sight," said the voice, "But I by the existence."

And it was the voice of a lost child, that tore his heart.

"That is undeniable, lady," he answered.

"But you, if you would, with one kiss, might set me free. How long does a brief kiss last? How long my life?"

Then Cedrevir looked again on the monster. His gorge rose, but now for the first he saw her eyes. They had no colour and seemed mostly blind, yet in the windows of them shone the well of the world's tears. A hundred centuries of direst misery. Perhaps a hundred more if he should stint compassion.

To kiss her was not lust or longing, to kiss her was a kind of fearful death, and never sin.

So Cedrevir, keeping wide his eyes on hers, leaned down into the stench, and shimmering shadow. He put his hand under her head, among the hair of worms, and he put his face to her face, and his lips upon her serpent mouth, and kissed her the kiss of all the love-desire in him that never once had he bestowed.

It was as if he had grasped lightning or the rushing sea. He opened his eyes yet wider, and lifted his head, and saw there in his grasp a maiden so lovely and so fair that not even the wonders of the Castle could outshine her. Her hair, flowing over his hands, was like spring sunshine on wild flax, her eyes were like marine turquoise, her lips were red and her clear-water skin as white as may. And all of her was slim and sweet and human, but quite perfect, so her gentle fingers that touched his brow fell there like petals, and with her perfumed breath she said to him, "Kiss me again. And in that moment he could not stay himself, and he did kiss her, in her beauty and in his great irreconcilable lust.

"I too am Morgainor," he heard her murmur then, as the earth and sky wheeled about him. "And now you have given up to me all."

There was no thunderclap or shaking of the stones, but the light entirely perished. Everything was gone. The tower, the sky, the angel forms, the Knights and maidens, and the barge. Morgainor too, melted like water from between his hands. And Cedrevir was left in anguish and the dark.

But not for long. For presently, a new lamp was kindled. It was like the intimation of sunrise under storm.

Cedrevir, in his despair, looked yearningly towards it, and held himself ready, nearly gladly, for chastisement.

Next, through the smokes of the cloud, he beheld a searing hint of gold, and then of silver, of crimson, and of a depthless ruby green. Up in the air, anchorless, they wafted. He saw them hang in space, as if a thousand miles away – the Spear, the Thorn Crown, and the Grail. And Cedrevir, in his agony, covered his face and wept aloud, for he knew very well that now the culmination of his Quest was denied him. Even as he thought it, and other things more bitter, a burning wind passed by and colours stained against his tight-closed lids. After which the dark returned, without, within.

From the dark a voice spoke at last, at his right shoulder, and it seemed to Cedrevir that he had already heard it once, at the coming of the vision on Midsummer Midnight. But nothing now was to be seen.

"Cedrevir, were you not warned, and did not heed? It is your presumption that has denied you the final prize."

"Lord," Cedrevir replied, "it is my sin which has kept it from me."

"Who are you, before God, to judge yourself or how you sin? Know this. In the moment of the second embrace, you had not lost the Quest, You lost it in the moment that you deemed yourself one fallen, and damned yourself,"

"Fallen and damned I was. My vows were broken."

"And who are you to say you will never sin? Are you not a human man? Or are you a god, who is above sin?"

"I am a man. A sinner, and cast from grace."

"Since you must be perfect in your own eyes, Knight, perfect as God, it is your own grace that you have fallen from. It is not for you to know how God has judged you, blameless or to blame. But be assured of this, even the King of All cannot grant you what you stubbornly refuse to take. Go then, Knight. Go down again to the world. Believe this, your fault is forgiven, for a man has only to say *Forgive me* for his sins to be stripped from him. But you are proud. You say in your heart to God, Oh God, forgive me. But to yourself you say, *I* cannot forgive myself. *I will not.*

After that, the voice was silent, and a wan twilight came, and in the twilight Cedrevir stumbled down from the high place, over the stair of ebony and ivory, perhaps for many hours, and came at length into the court, the darkness gone, and another lesser darkness come, for already night had shut its wings.

There the willow cascaded to the ground, and on its ghostly weft the trophies of the Knights eerily spangled and swung. No figure was near, but three times round the trunk of the tree was coiled a silvery snake, which hissed at him. When the snake did this, the shield and helm and sword of Cedrevir dropped to the marble. He went and took them up, and in heavy grief turned from the Castle and descended the mountains.

A night and a day he travelled, scarcely knowing what he did, and eventually he lost his way and his wits, and wandered some while. In a valley of the world, kindly people found him, restored him as best they might, and brought to him a horse that was his own lean and sad, which they had come on similarly wandering the valley a month before.

Of the Forest of the Savage Hart there was no sign, and the valley was set in verdant hills, flowered with fields and orchard-land, though now the winter came on them.

Cedrevir rode south before the snow, which pressed behind him and covered the earth with its white cloak. So, turning his head, he could yet see the snowy northern mountain-tops for several days, shining up in the sky like shed pieces of the winter moon.

He saw, however, no unusual sights, and no uncommon adventures befell him.

Cedrevir returned, as you yourself have noted. And as he seemed, so he is. The Quest is more often resolved in such failure than in death. For now he knows the colours and the weapons on the willow tree remained of those who journeyed on to some explicit bliss he is denied. Or that he has, as the angel told him, denied for ever to himself.

– But tell me, then, since you have told so much, how do you know it all? His journey and his grief and loss.

– How do I know? How could it be, but that I too, long, long ago, have gone Questing. I too have striven and failed and fallen. I too have heard those awful words and known – not in heart and mind, but in my soul – the truth of them. God it is not, who is cruel. But we ourselves. *Mea culpa. Mea maxima culpa.* I, too.

The Latin used in this story is the Mediaeval 'cat' Latin of the Imperii Quattuorviri.

The Unrequited Glove

Jason Drinkwood had many advantages. He was both young enough and old enough, and good-looking enough, and well enough off, that nothing very much need lie very much out of reach for very long. During the Amerenglish season along the coast, he was generally known by sight, and by name, for at that time, 'Jason' was an uncommon appellation, particularly augmented by such dark wavy hair, bright blue eyes, expensive garments and ice-cream-coloured car. His code of conduct, nonetheless, was quite decorous. He did not belong to the artist or poet caste, whose seasons sometimes ran in tandem with the Amerenglish one. He was seen to drink, but never drunk, to gamble a little, but never recklessly. He would dance, and he would dine, but with the air of one only performing a natural duty naturally well. Though the ice-cream car might sometimes be spotted swimming home along the palm-lined roads in the dusk of dawn, it was never anything but tidily driven. In other words, Mr. Jason Drinkwood was not a man of passions. And so, though there had at first been some speculation in the caravanserai of the colony as to what his intentions and inclinations might be, they were, when noted, of a very ordinary and discreet kind, and in the order of three: female, sophisticated, *brief.*

It was something of a surprise therefore, when Jason Drinkwood was sighted with Alys Ashlin.

Miss Ashlin was a painter, partly American it was believed, and rather more than partly something else, something fey and foreign, which had afforded her a slender and unreal quality, two large and gazing eyes, and wispy ash-blonde hair. That she should be an artist was no more than one would expect, that she had some money also was, admittedly, an oddity, but since she did not 'mix' very much, it was supposed she might go on as she wished. There had, of course, been some curious rumours now and then, but it was the age of the rational, and one had only to look at the girl to know her for a hopeless romantic, who would probably drink herself to death on cocktails before she was thirty-five.

Certainly, she was not Mr. Drinkwood's type, not at all. Presumably he had met her at some gallery. Presumably her moth-like attractions had for some reason piqued a jaded palate. Whatever the cause, the colony observed that they lunched together and took picnics to the hills in the pale car, and drank white *fine* and Russian Blushes at Co's, and danced at The Balconies, and all other fashionable spots.

Then, quite as suddenly as it had begun, the affair ended. A dark lady was seen to occupy the ice-cream chariot, and a dark lady was seen to be dining with Mr. Drinkwood at Piccaletta's. No one was in the least surprised, nor expected any more of the matter, except perhaps news of Miss Ashlin's abrupt illness in the morning gazette.

The sigh which escaped the chiselled lips of Jason Drinkwood had nothing to do with the seraphic and cloudless day, the cuisine of a just-completed breakfast, or any of the prospects before him, save only one. Putting down the small blonde card, he said, "Very well. You can bring her up here."

Thereafter Jason rose to his feet, and prepared to put another cup of coffee into his lean and graceful frame.

It was, he believed, inevitable, that this final confrontation would have to come. Unfortunately, that was the trouble with these unusual women. Though they might be entertaining for a while, they soon became merely irritating, and then, when one wanted to finish it, they simply did not know how to behave. Had he not, he now asked himself, done everything perfectly and with utter good manners? He had cancelled their last meeting, giving plenty of notice, and using the most courteous and apologetic address, with just the hint of terminus he had felt necessary in Alys's case. And had he not sent her a box of white roses, three dozen of the things? What more did she want from him? But he knew only too well. She wanted a *Scene*. That was what all her tribe required.

It was true, he had met her at a gallery, her own to be precise. She had been looking very chic that day, and he had mistaken her for an idler come to buy. Something in her quality had given him an urge to investigate her, and by the time he had invited her to lunch and she had accepted, it was too late to back out when he realised she was The Alys of the paintings. He knew nothing about art, had never had much time for it. He cared for pictures and ornaments as he cared for fine weather, for he liked and appreciated pleasant surroundings. Her feelings, on the subject, which began to be displayed almost as soon as the *entrée* was brought to the table, were both alien and unalluring. However, Miss Ashlin, (all those A's, S's, and I-Y's seemed quite overdone), was shy. She preferred not to talk about herself, but liked to listen to him. He therefore set out to amuse her, poor little thing.

Her vulnerability did rather appeal to him, even while he knew it was a mistake to like it. He could not bear stupid women, but had a deep distrust of clever ones. Alys did not fit either of these niches, though she was destined to represent both to him by the time he sloughed the liaison. Her trust and her simplicity in the matter of the male initially filled him with a desire to protect her. Later, of course, every frailty demanded of him that he pierce the weak place with a honed stiletto. Though he would not so have qualified it to himself, he was drawn to Alys Ashlin by the instincts of the tiger for the tethered lamb. Perhaps the tiger too has moments of enjoying the lamb's charm and the music of its bleat. Perhaps, if not too terribly hungry, the tiger also will delay the ultimate seconds when he falls on his prey and tears out its entrails.

When he had caused enough damage to her, and she, trying equally to protect herself and appease him, had lain at his feet gasping 'but what have I *done*?', Jason had sensibly withdrawn, cancelled the next meeting – there was no fun in killing a dead sheep – and sent a box of a dozen or so white roses to mask the stench of spilled blood.

However, now, incredibly, the lamb – having already written to him on three occasions in the most aggravatingly mild of terms – had arrived at his lair. To have it out with him, he concluded with dread. To make her *Scene*.

The door opened, and she entered the sunlit room, a wisp of ashes and fainting blonde violets.

"Oh. Hallo," said Jason, with slight astonishment, as if he had been expecting anyone but she. "Will you have some coffee?"

"Thank you. I don't think so."

"Do. It's very good."

Previously, she had always done exactly as he told her. But now she said again, "I don't think coffee is appropriate."

"Really? Why ever not?"

"Jason – I may still call you that?"

"Don't be so absurd," he said, harshly.

She lowered her wild eyes – they truly were wild, as if she had come straight from the hills and the old pagan altars there, instead, plainly, from off the manicurist's couch.

"Jason... I'm very obtuse about these things. I'm afraid I don't understand at all. Is it that you're finished with me?"

He poured some more coffee and tried to check a not unpleasurable surge of rage. "Well. What an ultimatum. When do the tanks arrive, and the air-cover?"

"Please, be serious, Jason. I should like to know."

"Oh, should you? Like to? I don't think so. Or you'd be quite well aware of the facts already."

"I see. I think I see."

"Good. Splendid." He shot her a look as he lit a cigarette. She did not smoke, she had said it affected her eyes. Certainly, something had done so. They were larger than ever, and though not exactly reddened, the pre-dawn greyness of their depths was bluer and more saline. "You know really, young woman, you're making an awfully big issue out of this, aren't you? I mean..."

"What do you mean?" she inquired softly.

He saw with dismay that she was pulling off her mauve gloves, a signal of intended temporary permanence. "For God's sake," he said, "we spent some time together. An interlude. It was delightful, Alice. Thank you so *very* much. But now. What can I say? I hope you won't force me to be rude."

"You mean that it is over, absolutely over. Between us."

"'It.' What is there supposed to have been? Over? Obviously."

"Yes, obviously."

"For heaven's sake, Alice," (he had always insisted on pronouncing her name in a straightforward way, none of that *Aleez* ridiculousness), "for heaven's sake. You're acting as though we've been Romeo and Juliet. Good God, woman. Try to grow up."

"But," she said, "I love you."

He turned his back on her at once. Oh Christ, much worse than he had thought. Of course, he knew, but even she, surely, should have had the tact not to use this idiocy. After a moment he mastered himself and said, "I'm very sorry." Then, when there was only a silence, he added, "Look, I have to be over the other side of the bay in about ten minutes' time. You'll have to excuse me. I must go." He had visions of her weeping or swooning on the sofa, being unable to rid the room of her – but when he flung round, to his genuine surprise on this occasion, he saw she was silently gone. All that remained was one of the faint violet gloves, the left one, lying *évanouissement* by the coffee pot. He fired a look of hatred at it, for she might use it as a pretext to come back. He would have to send it to her, bloody woman. But *later*. For now, he was getting out.

He ran down the villa stair with a feeling of release and exultation, as if he had just won some sort of race. And for once he drove the car rather fast along the coast road.

In the small hours of the following day, when he returned, Jason noticed, vaguely, that the glove too had gone. He put this down to the tidiness of his domestics, or to a miraculous display of common sense by Miss Ashlin, in returning to retrieve her property during his absence.

About a week after these events, Gerard Caul, an intermittent friend of Jason Drinkwood's since their first meeting in the caravanserai, received a message at his hotel. Responding to it, he called Drinkwood's villa. The conversation was short. "Caul? Thank God. I'm glad. Can you come over? No, I mean now. Come to lunch. Well as soon as. Five o'clock? All right. But you'll he there. Wrong? Oh... Probably nothing. No, nothing's wrong at all. Five o'clock. Till then."

Gerard, a prosaic but easy-going man, not without wealth or influence, arrived at the proper station which was, in the current parlance of colony etiquette, five minutes late. Driving up to the villa, he was rather startled to see that something was slightly amiss with its facade. His first thought was of birds, or geckos, but when next he came across the famous car, drawn up between the flower-beds and an old fountain, Gerard rejected the notion. The peculiar marks had a symmetrical nastiness about them that suggested manic human rather than faunal activity.

Presently, meeting Jason on the lower of the two terraces, Gerard waited until the drinks had been served and they were alone to remark, "Well, and who have you fallen foul of, my boy?"

At which Jason started, spilled some of his drink, and retorted with a careless laugh, "What on earth do you mean?"

"*Absit omen*," said Gerard, and refilled Jason's glass himself. Even if he had not by now been searching for signs, he might have noticed that Jason's face appeared rather dirty, rather colourless, and that his hands had developed a nervous tremor. "Someone, patently," said Gerard, "has it in for you. The car, for example."

"That was very unfortunate," mumbled Jason. "It seems to have found a supply of something in the kitchen, I'm not sure what, some kind of molasses, or glue. Very difficult, you know, to get off. I apologise for my face. That's simply writing ink. I'd forgotten how damned resistant it is to soap and water."

"Ah, yes," said Gerard. He opened his cigarette base and offered Jason the beautiful snow-white cigarettes. And watched Jason take and try to light one with his tremulous hands. "But who is this ingenious enemy, and why haven't you gone to the police? I know they can be difficult. Is that the problem?"

Jason laughed again. Dropping the cigarette, he lowered his ink-stained face into his hands and shuddered.

"My dear fellow," said Gerard, immovable.

"I'm quite all right. I shall be splendid in a moment. It's just the – frankly, the bloody hopelessness of it. I don't know what to do. At first, when it only ran about, and moved things, I tried to laugh it off. Then I thought I was going mad. But I'm not the only one to see – that boy ran off, you know. Scared to death. I think the woman's caught a glimpse, too, but she just accepts it. Well, she knows *she's* safe enough. But the worst of it is, I feel such a fool. I mean, look at me. I tell you I'm afraid to go to sleep. The days are bad enough. All I can do is move out, but – I did try sleeping at – well, somewhere else, you understand. But somehow, and this is the positively horrible part, *somehow* it followed me. It must have got into the car – I don't know how, I'd been so careful – but in the morning I woke up – in this state, *patterned*, you could say, But much worse. My – companion was rather put out. One could hardly blame her. There was ink all over the sheets. She thought it was some schoolboy prank of mine."

"Yes," said Gerard. He extinguished the stub of his cigarette, folded his arms, and gazed upwards at the line of balconies above. The sun was beginning to touch them now to a languid mellowness, while the green of the oleanders shone like torches as the light drove through. It was an exquisite hour, made strangely, like the chill first dawn, always for strange revelations.

Suddenly Gerard found Jason almost at his feet, gripping him and whimpering, "You have to help me, Gerard, you have to help me..."

It was just at this moment that Gerard became aware of a different note of colour in the vine that grew about the balconies. It seemed to him the leaves contained a flower of palest mauve, or perhaps even a mauve bird, for surely it had only just appeared – but his attention was now distracted.

"Drinkwood, I'm quite prepared to do all I can. But you must tell me first..."

A large ball of mud-clay, about the consistency of setting tempera, hurtled down from the direction of the balconies. It landed on the drinks tray, splattering the soda siphon and sending Jason's glass flying. Jason gave an uncharacteristic shriek and leapt to his feet. At that instant, a second mud-ball, rather larger and rather more glutinous, struck him squarely in the chest.

Instinctively, the eyes of Gerard Caul had risen once more to the vine. He had the impression of a capricious nymph, casting missiles from a slender hand gloved in softest mauve. At the same time, Gerard realised and comprehended no flesh and blood nymph, however svelte or small, could hang there in the tenuous foliage. And then, *then*, he caught sight of something, something definitely mauve and capricious and definitely operating entirely alone, scrambling lightly away, up the creeper, over the balustrade and into the house.

"Whatever was that?" inquired Gerard, with the disarming fascination of a man who knows that all things have a reasonable explanation.

Jason Drinkwood, sitting in his chair with the face of ink-stained death, told him.

"Oh, come now," said Gerard.

An hour and a half later, Gerard Caul took his leave. He had offered to do a great many things, but most of them had involve the summoning of doctors. Since Jason insisted, with ever-increasing hysteria, that no human agency was at work against him, Gerard was forced to concur that at least no *external* human agency was. Which left only Jason himself as the psychopathic culprit. Gerard had no desire to be included in such a fiasco, even on behalf of a friend. Besides, the atmosphere of the house was beginning to bother him. It felt positively booby-trapped. After he had explained to Jason for the twentieth time that mud might be come at near to the roof, and that birds had been known to drop portions of it in the past on undeserving persons below, enervation began to steal a march. The last straw was then presented to him as Jason, now drunk, postulated a search of the house culminating in the laying of ambushes. At this juncture, Gerard rose to his feet. In a weak moment, he had offered Jason sanctuary at the hotel, but this had only resulted in Jason's frantic mirth and avowals that he would be 'followed.' Gerard left the villa. Like every true realist, he knew that in certain areas of life, all one could do for a friend was to desert him.

That Mr. Drinkwood seemed to be suffering from some form or illness of mania was quickly the talk of the colony. As the days of liquid honey spilled themselves over and over into each other, as the blue seas poured ceaselessly to and fro and the blue skies answered them with their equally ceaseless immobility, the talk rose and fell along the boulevards, over the cafe tables, and in the fashionable shops of the Monte d'Oro. Even at the Casino, they might sometimes be heard to remark that Drinkwood was never seen there now, and the great dinner parties that splatter the turn of season with champagne corks and fireworks, also deplored his absence. It was a fact, he had been a social asset. He was so eligible and so unobtainable, so dashing, and so completely safe. What a pity it was, they said, whatever it was. But what was it, precisely? He had taken to the drink after all, they said. Or someone had thrown him over that he had cared for – no, not anyone here, some mysterious one in

London, or Boston, or New York, or Paris… Or it was some hereditary ailment. Or he had lost all his money. Yes, that seemed the most likely. Some kind of financial crash. These things happened constantly, even to the young and the beautiful.

Of Miss Ashlin, nobody thought to ask, or to whisper. They had all forgotten her quite. As far as anybody knew she was painting somewhere, and running her petite gallery, as she had done for years. Now and then, even, a picture, might be bought from her. But she did not figure in the drama of Jason Drinkwood. She had never been suited to him, wan, wispy little thing in her dilute purples and blondes. Pressed against his bronze, his vivid eyes, his white teeth and suits and car, she had been seared to cinders. But one never saw his car now, did one? There had been some sort of an accident, one thought. Those who had applied to Gerard Caul had formed the impression that Mr. Jason Drinkwood was suffering from hallucinations, and had been strongly advised to seek medical aid. Mr. Caul did not visit Mr. Drinkwood. They were not seen together in the bar at Co's, or on the tennis court at The Balconies.

It must be fairly serious, if such old friends now avoided contact. It must be rather unsavoury.

Night had fallen, and the villa lay plastered in a black stucco of darkness. At its heart sat Jason Drinkwood, drinking gin to keep awake, and to keep fear at bay. His servants had been sent forth days ago, since they had become mere witnesses to his humiliations. Besides, they facilitated disasters by those things they brought into the house in the way of foodstuffs and cleaning fluids, long after his ban on more dangerous substances. It was true, had it wanted to, his foe might already have murdered him, with one of a selection of knives, with some heavy object pushed onto his head, by fire or poison. Even the time in the car when the mauve silk hand, weightless and bodiless yet firm as flesh, had flown up at him, it was not his throat it had gone for, or even the wheel. No, it had merely perched there, on the dash, gentle and elegant, and he had stared at it, stared at every line and angle of it, every little crease in the material of its gloved life, every little stain and mark that it had acquired in the processes of its hounding him. And, staring, he had run the car – in some ghastly evocation of a pun – off the road and into a palm. When he came to, dazed and groaning, the glove had hidden itself again. It was always shy when it had had its way with him. It would conceal itself, in a closet or a drawer, or behind a curtain. Sometimes he caught it peeping at him around a piece of furniture.

Several times, before the incident with the car, he had attempted to destroy the glove. Once he had almost got hold of it, but as he struggled to retain his grasp, it seemed to go all to nothing, not even to cloth but to air – and then he had lost it. He had lain on the polished floor where he had that time fallen, and watched it hurry upstairs, running on its finger-tips.

He had even allowed Gerard Caul's doctors to look him remove him over. Jocund and reassuring, they had nevertheless wanted to remove him from the villa to costly nursing establishments in which they took an interest. But by then he had realised the glove would follow him wherever he took refuge. Even as they tested his heart, and shone lights into his eyes, he had been aware of the glove sidling round the room, now and then pausing behind the physician's back, as if to examine something, a plant or an ashtray. It was very careful with all the doctors, the glove. It never once played at revealing itself, as in the case of Gerard it had. Gerard, naturally, had refused to believe that any such thing was possible; it had been safe to flirt with him. Even he, Jason Drinkwood, did not properly believe in the glove's animation and life, and perhaps that was what gave it its power over him. He constantly expected them to stop, the silly endless puerile awful tortures. He would constantly be thinking, on some level, that it was all nonsense, such things did not happen. And all the while the glove would be scuttling about behind the chairs, coming down from the picture-rail to tweak his hair, to upset salt into his food and dash his wine glass to the ground, to break and to despoil, or merely to flutter, sweetly as a butterfly, about him, until he broke down himself and cried like a child.

After the car, he gave up all hope.

Now he sat, with his broken wrist arrested across his chest, idly tapping the gin glass over and over against his teeth, looking sightless on darkness.

He knew the glove was near. It always was. He knew also that, if he should get up, it would pursue him. He made an experimental shift in his chair, and heard, in the huge cricket-sewn rhythm of the villa's silence, a dim slim rustle, over near the windows.

"I'll tell you what I'll do," said Jason Drinkwood coldly to the mauve glove that haunted him, "I'm going to go out now. I'm going to go out and walk across to the Monte. I'm going to go along to the gallery. Yes. Her gallery. I'm going to go straight up and knock on her door. That's what I'll do."

He wondered if the glove could actually understand words, if, as it were, it spoke English. And if that should be so, he puzzled a moment, would it try to stop him? When he got up, he flinched as he heard it lisp across the floor. But there was no assault, and by the time he stepped out onto the plains of night, he sensed that it was only going to shadow him, weaving independently along in the blue-black, avoiding the lamps, keeping under the trees, probably disappearing just before he reached his destination, the gallery on the Monte, where Alys Ashlin had her being, and painted her pictures, and worked her febrile magics of the night.

When he arrived at the gallery, which located itself on the oldest side of a picturesque small square, it was almost three in the morning. Yet, looking up from the street, he perceived there was a soft light in the upper storey. By using a tiny courtyard at the back and climbing the outer stair, he attained her studio door and jangled the bell. There was usually a porter, but he might be in bed by now. In fact, it was she who answered, appearing not at the door but on the balcony, and he gazed up at her in dismay, wondering how he could have allowed himself to be so foolish as to come here. For she was so slight a thing, so irrelevant to him, surely he had imagined it all? But then the veiled glow of the summer moon, sailing high above the hill, caught in her eyes. They were like opals, colourless, changeable, unlucky.

"Will you let me in?" he said.

"It depends what you want," she said.

"You know that," he said. He no longer felt foolish, only desperate, looking up into those cold moon-opal eyes. "I've come to tell you, to ask you – to make it – stop."

"What are you talking about?" she said.

Was she enjoying it, this power, or afraid of what he might do, maddened by all the tricks? She sounded only very tired.

He pointed to the sling which contained his wrist. He did not bother to show off his decoratively soiled clothing, the tiny holes sliced in its fabrics. "Do you see this?"

She nodded, he thought, but he was not sure. Her eyes flashed oddly as she lowered them to his arm.

"That's enough, isn't it?" he asked. "Isn't it?"

"I'm afraid I don't understand."

He found he could not speak about it directly, just as it seemed she refused to. He said lamely, "It's a bit unfair, you know. What did I do? I hardly wronged you, you know. For God's sake. I've had enough."

She sighed then. The sigh was like a leaf, sweetly fluttering down. The moonlight touched her hair, her white face and her slender white hands on the balustrade, above the pots of vermilion dorisa, black by night as old blood.

"Mr. Drinkwood," she said slowly, looking past him across the roofs of the Monte to the implication of the distant bay, "I can only tell you this. Our first duty is to ourselves. To protect ourselves. There are things I must do, and obligations I must fulfil. I can't let you get in the way,"

"For Christ's sake," he exploded, "what are you saying?"

"I told you once that I loved you. My emotion was very strong. You don't understand about such things, it would be fruitless to explain. But you hurt me very much, very deliberately, and there were only two things I could do. Either let the hurt eat into and perhaps destroy me, or to turn it away. Turn it back. The gift of pain you gave me, I don't want it, Mr. Drinkwood. Return to sender. If it was to be you or me, it must be you,"

"You're mad," he said. He felt quite sick, and cold sweat had broken out all over him. In avalanching terror he added, in a withered, dying voice, "If I – do you want me to come back to you?"

"No thank you," she said. And then, "I'm very sorry. Good night."

"Wait, you bloody bitch!" he screamed, and a door opened sonorously in the storey below. Out into the moonlit yard stepped the porter, a large, faceless, obsidian shape, staring up at him. Jason was a moment stupefied, looking down at this apparition, as the balcony doors were drawn to above him. *Romeo and Juliet*. Well, he had said that.

He came down the stair unsteadily, and the porter towered in his path.

"Get out of my way," Jason mumbled.

The porter obeyed him, without haste, but when Jason had negotiated the courtyard gate, he heard it being locked behind him.

He stood deflated in the alley, tears streaming down his face, in rage, in fear, in utter embarrassment and futility. As he did so, there came a soft rustling close by, like a small mauve sigh blowing through the shadows.

The letter, which was delivered by hand to Mr. Gerard Caul's suite at the Hotel Fleuris, did not especially delight him. It was in a version of Jason Drinkwood's formerly entirely readable, if slap-dash, hand-writing. It began, '*Dear Caul, You can still help me, if you will. I take this opportunity, since at the moment I'm not being observed, rather I do the observing, for I can see it sitting in a strawberry tree outside the window. It keeps watch on me, and I on it. Of course, how can it read? But maybe it can, by some peculiar means, do so. I can't take the chance. So, when I lose sight of it, I shall hide this letter on my person, next to my very skin.'*

Getting so far, Gerard Caul was inclined to throw down the letter, but, since the remainder was brief, he resolved to finish it.

'My plan is to get out of the place – not just the villa, the whole country. The first steamer to the first homeward port. Spells don't travel over water. I remember hearing that. It may not be correct, but it's the only hope I've got. And no luggage, nothing it can stow away in. Just the garments I happen to be standing up in, and whatever essential cash and documents. And – it mustn't know what I'm up to. This is where you come in, Gerard, if you'll see me through. I won't waste your time with obvious details. You've got all the pull that's necessary. Use my funds, you know how to get at them. Just simply book me on the first boat out, with some kind of reference of your own – it may be needed. Say I've been ill, under a strain, am really quite a decent fellow, etc. I rely on you. I'm at your mercy. If you won't, I tell you I'm through, I'm lost.

Yours. J.D.

P.S. If you can see your way to doing this, don't telephone me. Write me just one word: YES. And then, later, date and time, only the numbers. Oh Gerard, for God's sake, do it.'

Gerard Caul was offended by the whole project, but, in default of anything else, old stranglehold-ties of friendship presently forced him to pick up a pen, and write, aloofly, in a firm hand: *'Yes. G.C.'*

About the middle of July, a curious occurrence overtook the passenger steamer *La Sebastienne*, as she was *en route* for open water.

The majority of the passengers had dispersed from their departure posts along the ship's rail, and were heading for their cabins, or the saloon. A few still at large on the landward decks were engaged to see a young man, who was in the process of removing his shoes and socks. These he then hurled away into the kohl-blue water, in the manner of offerings. They were shortly joined there by a shirt, a tie and a jacket.

The acute had already noticed that the dress of this individual young man, while of excellent material and cut, had nonetheless undergone some weird farewell rituals, prior to embarkation. These were felt, however, to be insufficient grounds for dispensing altogether with social dictates in the matter of modesty. As bit by bit, piece by – and by now intimate – piece of apparel was jettisoned, the volume of comment on the decks increased to a roar. Presently assistance was applied for. The ladies either turned their heads, or did not turn their heads, as a bevy of ship's personnel swarmed over the madman and bore him off. He was by this time completely naked, his face a study in triumph and anguish. Though generally it was not his mood which drew most attention.

By the cocktail hour, it was reported that the mad passenger lay sedated in his cabin, to which replacement clothing had been taken in the spirit of encouragement. It transpired that he had been rather ill, under rather a strain, that he was very sorry for his outburst, that everything was taken care of. For the remainder of the trip he was not seen again, though frequently looked for. At landfall he was smuggled ashore. The air resounded to the twang of pulled strings.

Thereafter, the occurrence merely entered the lists of those travellers' anecdotes, which are seldom believed and yet which tend to become the myths of other places, any places where one has never ventured, the lands of Unreal, the islands of Elsewhere.

For the sea, it swallowed Jason Drinkwood's clothes and presumably anything else that might have attached itself to them. And when the wake of *La Sebastienne* faded from the water, nothing at all was revealed there, but the sunlit currents and the ghostly, palmate shapes of fish.

For his part, Gerard Caul – to whom the ship-board episode had filtered – would have been happy to hear no more of the subject, which signed itself J.D. Gerard was of that estimable order of men who are able to leave behind all waste items, among them wasted friendships, with only the neat arm movement normally required in such disposals.

However, in the ensuing months, a letter arrived, a letter warm with gratitude, acidulous with proper self-mockery, and bright, ah so very bright, with relief. A letter, that is to say, from Jason Drinkwood, who, from his flat near Kensington Gardens, in the ancient city known to itself as London, now revealed that business was as usual. Indeed the letter, for all its warmth, acidity and brightness, cautiously skimmed the past, cautiously *hinted* at what would seem to have been an era of sickness, some bad dreams, an involvement with a silly and unstable female person, a revolt against summer heat and foreign climes. Only the postscript seemed a trifle odd. It requested that Mr. Caul would please omit to reply. Nothing, it turned out, that came from Mr. Caul's present part of the world, was being permitted access to Mr Drinkwood's London life.

Gerard, who had not a wish on earth to reply, was gratified by obliging.

It happened a week later, that Gerard saw Alys Ashlin, as he was driving up across the Monte d'Oro. It was the swiftest viewing, a vague momentary sight, recognisable only because of Jason's agonies of description. She was standing outside one of the *patisseries*, buying flowers from a woman who sat there under her sunshade on the pavement. Pale violet flowers they were, the whole image a pastel, the whites, blues and lavenders of the merchandise, the dry old woman, the mild amber shade above, the contrasting blonde of the girl's hair and the little hat, the cool hands taking the clear wild mauve of the spray in a stream of blanching sun. Ah, yes, not at all displeasing. Gerard thought Miss Ashlin rather charming, a type of woman somewhat neglected now, like certain kinds of art, out of her time, delicate, fragile and too easily crushed, a gauzy thing. Then she was gone from his vision and his awareness. At no other hour of his life did he ever see her, and seldom heard of her again, and that only in the way of her work.

But it was less than a year before he heard something else of Jason Drinkwood.

"But surely, surely he must have loved her quite terribly. Oh, I do wish you'd tell me who she was."

Gerard who, if he had needed it, had used the interruption of lighting a cigarette to mask any shock he felt at the news of Jason's suicide, now answered, "My dear Cecilia. So far as I know, there was no one at all. That was just a foolish piece of gossip."

"But you're so wrong," said Mrs. Cecilia Hanson.

"Well, that may occasionally happen."

They were seated in the Long Room at Co's, overlooking the lawns, the bougainvillaea, and the bay. The summer had come back, as if it had never been gone, the distressing fire-wind of the early months was over, everything was set for another colonial season. Mrs. Hanson, whose husband had for years had business dealings with Gerard, and who, intermittently had had her own dealings with him, now continued silkily, "Of course, I know you and Jason Drinkwood lost touch – of course, you had *heard* he was dead?"

"Oh, naturally," lied Gerard.

"From the window," said Mrs. Hanson, in such a way that he suspected her of testing him. "Six floors. And the railings," added Mrs. Hanson. "Simply awful. I can never understand it. I mean, I can understand a man might feel driven to take his own life. But the method. An impulse, it must have been. He was so *sunny* the day before, quite himself. Not that I knew him well, ever." Her voice sharpened a little, grated a fraction, before she smoothed it over. "But Harry had just had lunch with him, at the London place, that good one. For heaven's sakes. But there you are. Brooding over this mystery woman you tell me never existed. And suddenly, unable to bear it any longer. So, the window. I blame the oranges myself."

"The oranges?" said Gerard, wondering, rather more than what she was talking about, how soon he could slip away. A vicious woman, he did not want to antagonise her unduly, but it was too hot for seduction, as it was too hot for Cecilia Hanson's toiling complexion.

"Harry ordered oranges at lunch. They came from the hills here. He told me, Jason seemed quite distrait about it for a minute or two, then just broke out laughing, and ate two of them. But I can only conclude it was a sad reminder. Good lord. Three hours after he flings himself from a sixth storey window."

Something tugged gently at Gerard's memory. It said: *'Don't write, my boy. Nothing from your neck of the woods, not for a while.'*

"Oranges," said Gerard. He stubbed out his cigarette.

Cecilia Hanson sensuously licked the olive from her drink, a habit he disliked. There was a gleam in her eye he did not care for, and this harping on lost love... Well, in the interests of fair trading with Harry, after all, he might have to take her along the coast to that dreary little shack of an hotel, chase her through the frothy waves as she giggled girlishly, overpower her in the dark room thick with scent and mosquitoes. Good manners. It did not do to offend such women.

"Now Gerard, you will tell me, won't you? Or am I going to have to do something reckless to get it out of you? What would you like?"

"Ah, Cecci. You shouldn't tempt me this way."

She snuggled closer. She wore a new perfume he liked better than the previous one, although probably, by the end of the endless afternoon, he would have come to loathe it utterly.

"Well, who was she?"

"Now, Cecci, I've said I have no idea. There was no one."

"Yes, there was. Or why would he have kept her glove?"

To a man as prosaic, as easy-going, as influential, as efficient and modern and jaundiced as Gerard, his own reaction to this statement was an unwelcome, threatening thing. He turned cold, as if a wave had rushed up on him, from his feet to his skull, a cold cold icy comber from the depths of some unremembered, non-existent sea.

"What do you mean her glove?"

"Well, don't snap at me, for goodness sakes. I only know what Harry told me – you know they called him and he had to – well, he said there was a glove, a woman's glove, lying there on the – right by Jason's body, under his hand. He must have been clutching it when he – as he... And Harry said it was such a pathetic little glove, all worn and torn, almost colourless, all wrinkled – it looked as if it had been through just about everything, and he must have been always wringing it in his hands or something."

Gerard's mind slipped suddenly away from Mrs. Hanson. It slipped away and saw a pale mauve fish swimming, and a pale mauve spider crawling, and then a pale mauve five-fingered wisp of silk scrambling, running on tip-toe, up rocks, over stones, thorough bush, thorough brier, over park, over pale, through flood, through fire... And finally falling, fainting, from a crate of oranges. Dragging itself, poor crushed, sodden, rent and ruined fragile tinsel thing, through all the by-ways of London, and up the steps, under the door...

"Why Gerard," said Mrs Hanson, "Gerard? Oh Gerard, I truly have missed you so."

The Winter Ghosts

Winter is a ghost that haunts the world. You know it by its grey transparencies, its crystalline white comings and goings.

It was early in the winter that I went to the town to see about some business for my Father, and was told I must call in on my Aunt. I resisted. "She has been good to you, young man," they said. She had paid for my education, and other things. My life was full of obligations, it seemed to me, and nowhere was I free to do what I wanted. I had been the slave of my school, and now was my Father's, working in his shop, where I did not want to be, and trapped in the village of my birth. I had seen and done nothing. But there again, what would I have chosen to do? I had no great driving talents. I liked to read and to lie a-bed, for either of which occupations there was now slight time. Every day I was up at dawn, for on Sunday I must go to church to show my respect to God. At night, I ate my supper and fell between my sheets exhausted. What a life. The town and the prospect of visiting it had cheered me a little, despite the winter road and the stubborn old horse, the wayside packed by forest, starving beggars who seemed to signal from every glassy bush, according to rumour, and the first waves of wolves that I hated and feared along with everyone else. But now my sojourn in the town was to be divided between my Father's commission and my Aunt's fancy. It was *decided; I was* not to stay overnight at the inn, but at my Aunt's house. My heart sank into the floor, it stayed there, and I left it behind.

The ride was not too bad. A faint flurry of snow disturbed the horse, who for a mile kept stopping and shaking his head distractedly. I saw no beggars, and no wolves, though once I heard one howling. I arrived at the town gates before the sun set on a grey thick sky. I should proceed at once to the Aunt's, attending to my Father's wants in the morning.

I had not seen either the town or the Aunt since childhood. Both had been different then, more interesting to me. I had half anticipated some sense of purpose or festivity in the town, and there was none I could perceive; the shops blinkered, the populace running homeward before the cold. Hardly a soul on the streets. The inn looked welcoming with its gold and red sign, but now I was not going there.

What did I remember of the Aunt?

She had been slender and excitable, with a high hot colour in her cheeks. Her dark hair was drawn up with combs, and curled. She wore a dark red gown and was dancing, for it had been a festival – hence my anticipations – memories – of the town.

As a child I had liked her, but she had paid me very slight attention. Her own father was alive then, and had she not been engaged to be married? There was some tragedy or scandal never spoken of to me. Her money had come to her with the town house, at my Grandfather's death; my Father benefited in other ways. My Aunt was then alone in the world. Having no one on whom to squander the excess of her small riches, she made provision for me and my two sisters. In me, a less grateful wretch she could not have hoped to find. Far better I had liked the little drummer doll with his bells, the first gift she gave me indifferently at the festival. That was fifteen years ago. She would be old now, for she was not young then.

I reached her house, which stood to the side just off from the square. Ancient black trees, already edged with snow, occluded its walls. The shutters were fastened, and not a light showed. The house might have been deserted, the impression it gave. I dismounted, secured my horse, and tried the cumbersome knocker.

I had knocked some six or seven times before I got any answer. And then to my surprise it was the Aunt who had come to the door and opened it.

"Old Ermine died," said she, standing in the dim hall, which just barely fluttered at her lamp. "Now I'm my own maid. My own housekeeper, too. You mustn't expect too much," she added, as if we had been speaking for an hour.

It seemed she knew me, for who else but the looked-for nephew would call on her? Nevertheless I introduced myself politely, and then she extended her dry powdered cheek for my kiss. She was indeed as aged as I had feared, a skinny old woman in a wrinkled reddish dress, with eardrops of dull pearl, which perhaps she had put on to honour my advent. She wore no rings, but her hands had been mutilated by rheumatism. She led me in.

It transpired there was still an antiquated man, Pers, she called him, who would see to my horse, as he saw to the fire in the parlour, and other manly work. I caught a glimpse of him, about a hundred he looked, but the horse was getting on too, they would be patient with each other.

The parlour was like home: Crowded by slabs of the furniture, which was all I knew, and that spelled affluence, and entrapment, had I given them names. Crystal and china, perhaps never used, bulged upon a wooden mountain, dully catching the firelight through their dust. The fire was a poor one – what else could you expect of Pers?

"Will you take some tea?"

I doubted there was a drop of spirit in the house, and felt a very real and unjust anger at her, my Aunt, forcing me here to this cage, uncomfortably not equipped to please me in the least.

We had tea, and some thin jam, and she told me I should not smoke, not in the rooms. I had guessed and not tried – truth to tell, I was not much of a smoker, though it was expected in a man, a sort of condoned vice.

By now it was night, these unshuttered back windows very black beyond the rusty curtains. In the town a few panes were alight, but they looked dim and parsimonious. My Aunt had lit two lamps, these windows of hers would have that look.

I forget properly what we spoke of. There were long silences; what could she expect? She asked me of my work, which I disliked, of my school, which she had provided and I hated. She asked of my uninteresting family, and my sisters, one of whom was now married to a fat bumpkin very suitable to her.

Finally, in a sort of sneering pity, I said, "I remember you dancing in a red dress. You gave me a doll with bells. I was very young."

"Ah, that was another time." She added, obscurely. "Another woman."

Later we went into the dining room. And I had my first shock.

The long old table was hung with a lace cloth over mulberry velvet, and meticulously laid with china and a silver service. There were ten places, each fully set.

"I thought we dined alone, Aunt?"

"I never dine alone. But then again, you will see no one besides me. I, of course... I see them all. In my imagination, you understand."

Pers brought in the dishes, there were only three; they had come from an obliging cook shop, heated up in the kitchen below, but not sufficiently. Water was served with the meal. Very proper.

I was interested to see Pers pass every plate from the eight other settings. On to each was placed by my Aunt a tiny portion of the frugal meal. Pers filled each goblet from the water jug. I looked on, and tried to picture ghostly fingers raising the glasses, invisible hands plying the knives and forks. Pers left us.

"Who is here, Aunt? Won't you tell me?" I inquired, because I was so very bored, a leadenness had stayed with me compounded of snow, tiredness, inertia. Besides how could her secret guests be a hidden matter when she paraded them?

But she was reticent.

"People of my past."

"Is Grandfather there?"

"Grandfather? Of course. It is a family table. He is at the table's head."

"Your fiancé, too?"

But she lowered her scaly eyes and would not answer. I had been indecorous, probably.

"Why did you never marry, Aunt?" I demanded brutally

"It was a long time ago."

"I recall everything well. I recall the man –" I did not – "dancing with you downstairs."

"No, no," she said.

But I was irked enough I did not allow her any rights to pain. She had interfered in my life, it seemed to me, and made things worse. She had forced me here when I might have drunk brandy at the inn. "Surely you can tell me? I've only heard stories of it –"

"What stories?"

"That he jilted you. Left you almost at the altar –"

"Oh the liars! Who said this?" She was inflamed now, surprising me a little.

"Servants – an old nurse I had –"

"None of it is true. He died. He wasn't young. His health wasn't good. The excitement... He took a chill and was dead in a week."

There was the longest silence yet.

"But you see him here tonight?" I even shocked myself at my grossness. Perhaps the water had made me drunk, I was used to a glass of wine at home.

At last she spoke to me. "Yes. I see them all. I invite them here. Why shouldn't you know? My father, my betrothed. My mother takes her place. And my mother's two sisters. Then there is my girlhood friend I see, there. She died so young. She is the youngest among us. And there is my tutor, whom I feared and loved, and who darts me terrible stern glances, because he thinks I have forgotten my lessons. And he's right in that, for I have. And old Ermine is with us too, now. I included her a month after her death, for she required her rest before that..."

A nasty but interesting idea came over me that I could see them after all. The Grandfather as I recalled him with his fob watch and high collar, the invented mother I had never myself witnessed, and her aged crone sisters in their black and lace and old-fashioned hair. The young friend caught fast for ever – perhaps she did not mind – I put her in an antique gown. The mature bridegroom, coughing a touch at his handkerchief. The elderly tutor. And old Ermine, who once or twice I had really seen, for she had been mercilessly sent to the village on my Aunt's errands when only a trace younger. I guessed Ermine was content, to sit at last at her mistress' table, even to the tepid meat and water.

"Pray don't let me prevent you," I said, "conversing with them all, if that's how you usually go on."

"You think me very eccentric," said my Aunt. "But those who are dear to me – those for whom I have a responsibility. What else should I do?"

As she had put me through the school, just so she kept these by her, these withered flowers, her ghostly dinner guests. For ever, or until her death, and – why not? – maybe beyond her death, they would sit nightly at this drab table, eat the unpalatable food – I was becoming as foolish as she.

"Well you must do as you think fit, Aunt. And now I thank you for this meal, but ask you to excuse me if I go presently to bed. The long ride tired me greatly, I'm up so early, and must be off early tomorrow, I fear, on my Father's commission."

She was startled a moment, then she settled down. The old are early to bed also, she told me, she did not keep late hours. But I must take a cup of tea with her in the parlour, to cheer me for my couch. Out of the kindness of my unkind heart I consented. I spent one further hour with her before escaping to the dusty dark room aloft. There in the great bed, by the poor light of one thin candle, I had meant to read a smuggled book.

But my own bane of tiredness came in on me. Soon the lines swam and I blew out the candle and yawned myself to oblivion.

There I dreamed of being a prisoner in my Aunt's house. I could not get out, and was in the act of bribing Pers to open a tiny door in the cellar for me – I think it did not in real life exist – when I woke. It was a milky dawn, and the fine snow blowing, and I had my Father's business to transact before I could start out on my ride home.

My Aunt was not yet risen, so I left my message of gratitude and farewell, with Pers.

The business took up half the morning, and when it was done, I gathered myself to the inn and there on top of the bread and stale tea of my hasty breakfast, I put in three brandies against the rigours of the ride home, which truth to tell I was now dreading. I had a sort of presentiment of ill luck, which drinking the brandy, rather than dispel it, had brought closer.

Shortly after midday, though it looked more like dusk, I left the town, and the staid old horse and I went down the road, and in among the great stands of the forest.

The snow had stopped, and a freezing was coming on, you felt it approach like a stealthy noise. Now and then a branch cracked in the forest at the cold, but there was no other sound save for the plodding of the horse. A faint smoke hung once in the distance from some charcoal burners. Otherwise there was no hint of any human creature. I might have been alone in the woods at the world's edge out of a legend. And this thought oppressed me, even as I began to have a quite incompatible fear of robbers.

Robbers there were, but not of the mortal type. About an hour after I had got beyond the town, when my home in my Father's house, so despised, had begun to seem to me the dearest place on earth, a small pack of wolves started to follow me.

Despite all that is said, and agreed, on wolves, they are in fact not so much of a foe to a mounted man. But I feared them and disliked them in company with anyone I could think of. My childhood had been spiced by the tales of other children the wolves had carried off and eaten, and only a dead wolf was a pleasure to see, as occasionally I had.

Their eyes were the worst, for their shapes, loping along a few yards behind me, were almost lost in the trees. But out of the afternoon dusk now and then would come a green flash, or I would see an actual eye, fastened on me with a malevolent unique intensity.

I tried a sharp shout or two, which gave them doubts, but then on they loped again. I was the only moving thing of any size for miles. They were curious, and they were hungry.

How I longed for a joint of raw meat I might have bought and thrown to them, how I longed to have drunk more, or less. Or that the old horse might have been pricked to a gallop. But my attempts to hurry him presently confused him – he did not like the wolves either, but was inclined more to congeal to stasis and shiver than to hasten off.

Perhaps they would get tired of me, and let me be.

They did not.

About mid-afternoon, when I had been followed a good hour, the old horse managed a brief canter, hit us into a low-slung bough that brought snow down on me, and stumbled. Between the bough and the stumble I went out of the saddle and slithered to the ground. As I lay there stunned, the horse, relieved of my slowing weight, gave a bright whinny and fled along the road.

I sat up before I was ready, and my head rang. Then I tried to get to my feet and slipped full length again. And then the wolves, there were five of them, came out of the trees and on to the road.

They stood looking at me, and vividly do I recollect their lean black shapes against the snow, each one exactly resembling the model of the others, as if all had been cast from a single mould of wickedness. Their eyes were like the eyes of cruel men, intent and hypnotic, yellow as flames. Was any one less than the others? An entity they were, one thing, and all gazing upon me. I despaired.

In that moment I imagined myself at the gate of death. And this is what I saw: First the terrible rending agony of being eaten alive, and then the mildewed pit of the dead, from which a faint drear voice was calling me. "Come, dear nephew," it said, "sit down. I've laid a place for you."

And out of the teeth of wolves and shadows of the grave I emerged into that cold dining room with its table of mulberry and lace, and sat myself before a setting of dusty china and silver. To my right was an ugly young girl in an outdated gown, and to my left a balding scholar in a shabby coat. All around were old ladies with piled up fake curls, and a coughing man of sixty, and my Grandfather consulting his watch, for I had come late and kept them waiting. And there, opposite his place, sat my Aunt in her red dress and eardrops, nodding and smiling at me, as she helped me to a bobble of cold steamed food, and Pers filled my glass with water –

"*No!*" I cried. "You shan't!"

And I flung myself forward at the wolves. I was shouting and roaring, and out of my pocket I had taken my wooden matches, which I struck in panic and nearly set myself alight.

Perhaps it was these brief gusts of fire, or the awful noises I made, and which I myself heard as if from a great distance, but the foremost wolf backed off. As I rushed screaming down at them, all five turned sideways into the bushes, and bolted suddenly away from me between the trees.

They were gone.

For some minutes I remained, yelling and stamping, jumping up and down in the snow, while burnt matches stuck to my burnt fingers and the hole I had fired in my sleeve.

I recall I howled I would not go, I would not be caught for ever, for eternity, in that smothering. No, not I.

When I came back to my wits, no hint of the wolves lingered. A vast emptiness was there, and I was blazing hot inside the great orb of the cold. I went down the road for something to do, and found the horse loitering at the wayside a quarter mile off.

I mounted him in silence, and he walked on.

Who would believe me? I have heard since of men frightening off wolf packs with loud cries and curious behaviour, but that was in other lands, and at another time. For then I knew only I had not been brave and had best keep quiet. More than their eyes and teeth I had feared the dinner table of my Aunt, I did not want to be another of her winter ghosts. It was that cowardice which made me turn against the wolves, and, seven months later, the same cowardice which made me run away for good to another less safe, stranger, and more ordinary life.

The Lily Garden

There is a wisdom to youth, which later gives way to a different wisdom, of age. To have one usually precludes the other. Both are valid, and both in their manner, sad.

When Camillo was young, and a student at the great university of Ravenval, he took a room which overlooked, as it happened none of the other apartments in that building did, an ancient garden belonging to an impressive but ruinous house of very ill-repute. I do not mean it was a brothel, nothing so simple. No, a magician was said to live there, who name was known but seldom spoken. For general purposes, he was called The Alchemist, and his dwelling The Alchemist's House.

At first Camillo was only interested in the garden, which was overgrown by oaks, ilex and a great pine, because it represented to his imagination, straying from his books, a wild forest. Late at night, when he had blown out his candle, he would stare upon the moon caught fast in the pine tree. If a dog howled from some neighbouring tenement, he would think of wolves treading the trackless undergrowth beneath the high wall. Sometimes, strange sounds came from the garden itself. Doubtless owls, bats, rats and hedgehogs caused them, but to Camillo, who had never left the city, they were the noises of a wilderness. He liked the garden very much, and if he had been four years younger, he would have found a way at once to get over into it. But now he was a student, a young man. Already responsibility had laid hold of him.

The Alchemist was reportedly never seen. But he had an elderly servant. One day Camillo saw this servant on the street leading from the marketplace, and recognised him from description. Accordingly, he followed the servant, discreetly, and not unaptly, since he himself lived close by, back to the House. Sure enough, the servant came to the building, but ignoring the great door fronting the street, went around to a smaller door set into the garden wall. This he managed with a key. As the door opened, Camillo was afforded a tantalising glimpse into the garden's forest: vast trees of darkest green and coppery black, some rotted statuary.

Thereafter Camillo, when free from his studies, would loiter between the market and The Alchemist's House – there was a convenient inn.

Came an afternoon when the elderly servant, returning, dropped in the street a great package of some unguessable nature. Camillo hastened to his side. "Good sir, pray let me assist you."

"That is very kind," said the old servant, who was hunched in the back. Camillo retrieved the package – which felt pliable in a most unpleasant way, perhaps being a portion of a body purchased from some graveyard dealer for alchemical experiment.

They came to the door in the wall.

"Allow me to carry this inside for you."

"Alas, young sir, I must return a churlish response to your courtesy. My master – you may have heard of him…" – and here the servant spoke the forbidden name - "does not permit any but myself to enter here."

"At least let me bear your burden up on to that terrace there. Who will know?"

"My master," replied the servant simply. He spoke without fear, but it was the fearlessness of one who needs not fear as never does he trespass.

So Camillo was once again shut out. By now, of course, he was mad as the snake to enter the garden. On this occasion, he had seen the terrace, mossy steps, a fountain of naked nymphs – and all about this clearing the enormous ravenous trees.

Someday, I shall make myself rich. Such a garden, such land will be mine.

But he knew even then in his heart that these riches were unlikely, and here he was quite right.

Camillo began to brood on how he could get into the garden of The Alchemist.

He was not afraid of The Alchemist, this being an aspect of the wisdom of his youth. Yet also it was a figment of the *unworldliness* of his youth. There might have been much to tremble at. But Camillo discounted the dread name. He troubled only not to fall foul of the city's laws regarding property. And this meant that he must find a way to open the garden door by stealth, unseen, unknown, and doubtless by night.

Camillo therefore contrived to steal the key of the elderly servant. He did this by distracting the fellow at the wall with the gift of a pomegranate – a wicked deception, for the old man's eyes actually filled with tears at the supposed gift. The key was then removed from the door by Camillo, the old man ushered inside, already forgetting he had not retrieved it.

Camillo then took himself to a place where keys were copied, and had this service done for him.

Returning at dusk he cast up the original over the wall so it should land on the grass beyond - he had prudently locked up behind the servant – as if it had been dropped there.

Thereafter Camillo impatiently waited for one whole night and one whole day before daring his enterprise of invasion.

It was true that now and then a few dim lights might burn high up in The Alchemist's House, and on this night too they did so. Only when the last light, a very high and dim one in a narrow tower, was put out, did Camillo creep down through the lodgings and cross the street to the garden wall. It was by now three in the morning and from the old cathedral the wonderful clock with its figures of knights and maidens, imps and angels, was striking the dull dark hour. Camillo was not sleepy, he was wide awake, alert with a light supper and a little wine. And with his fiendish curiosity, his actual *lust* to enter.

The key proved difficult. It had not been very well made, or else some extra bar was on the door. If so ultimately it failed, and Camillo finally pushed wide the barrier, closed it soundlessly, and was alone in the moonlit garden of the magician.

The trees towered like steeples, and the house was all but lost in them, and any way silent as death itself. But the terrace glowed under the moon, and the fountain of the nymphs with their grey-green night girdles of ivy.

Camillo crossed the terrace with caution, keeping to its shadow side. Something squeaked in the undergrowth, and Camillo did cross himself. But there again, though this was the wisdom of youth it was also a foolishness, for if any demons had been left on guard, what use that single lapsed gesture of a strong young mortal hand?

Then, besides, he jibed at himself. Only some little hog of the shrubberies was passing. And lo and behold up in the tall pine had begun to sing a golden nightingale. She was pleased to have a visitor, he had not heard her previously.

The garden had a night scent on it, but also now the perfume of flowers.

When he descended from the terrace, he found a new wall of yew, and in the wall presently an arch. Beyond lay a formal garden, as unlike the wild of the outer place as could be. It was a bower of flowers, of every sort of night-blooming lily known on earth, and perhaps the lilies too of Mercury and Venus and Saturn, so strange and fragrant was the odour of them.

In the middle of the inner garden was a patch of turf, with a sun dial, now a dial of the moon, and beyond this, under an awning of lilies, all of which were opened wide, sat a figure. Was it a statue – that of a young girl deftly tinted by paint, a faint rosiness to the lips discernible even in moonlight, a darkness to brows and lashes, and on the long and flowing locks, part plaited and part free, the faintest blondest hint of a colour almost pink? The robe of the being was fashioned like a dress, which gave proper evidence of all the feminine sweetnesses, yet slender and virginal. And indeed the robe flowed like the hair, down over the ground, decorously. The face was young and pure – Camillo thought – as that of an especially beautiful Madonna in the church.

Camillo stared some while, from behind the curtain of the yew hedge. He stared long enough that he expected no change, had come to the complete conclusion that the image was indeed a statue – when it moved. It moved actually very little. It raised one hand, and touched a lock of its own hair – no more, you might say, than the stirring of a petal. But Camillo jumped in his skin.

It must be remarked, there was something to the beautiful girl that was supernatural. Or so it seemed. After all, Camillo must have succumbed, in some form, to the idea of The Alchemist's House. He remembered now strange tales, most of them from books. The wizard in his tower. And in the bower, stolen forth by night, his daughter, or some princess in his thrall, who held the secrets of her slave-master's power.

Now, what should he do? In the story, the hero stepped forth to confront the fair damsel. They were at once in love and in league. Camillo was not ready for either state. He therefore quickly, quietly, and, in later years he admitted, most cowardly, stepped away instead.

Camillo left the lily plot, hurried over the terrace, and let himself out into the street. Here he locked up the door of the whole garden again.

No sooner was he back safe in his room across the street than a band of drunken carousers went down the way below, as if he and The Alchemist's House were of no import. *Let that be a lesson*, he thought. For the idea that all over the wall was not worldly had fastened on him. His was this world, of stones, and drunks, ink and paper, bread and warts and human things.

Thereby he sealed himself to the lily garden of the magician as Eve did to the Apple Tree, when first warned it was not for her.

Some days and nights then passed, and Camillo did not think of the garden. That is, he would not allow thoughts of the garden to remain.

But thoughts of the girl did stick to him. What had she been? What? And some book-memory of a life-size doll, or statue enabled by magic to move, began slowly and insidiously to obsess him.

It was no use. He must return, and look for her, and see of what sort she was.

Probably, thought he, some pretty servant of the house, perhaps the magician's secret mistress, who mooned herself by night for fear of the prying eyes of day.

So Camillo took the key from where he had hidden it from himself, which was up the chimney, and on a night of no moon at all he went down, a little cool and unsettled, hearing the cathedral clock strike only for two, but all the lights out, as it seemed not only in the two houses, but everywhere in the city.

Oh, it was like a night of the dead. Such utter blackness. And Camillo commended his own bravery, and opened the door to the forbidden garden.

The key went more easily on this occasion, as if now it were familiar with the lock.

Beyond was a darkness that might have been black space itself, if space were filled by leaves, and spotted only here and there with the blue-white specks of stars. Nor did the nightingale sing. Nor did anything squeak in the undergrowth. The garden too had been put to bed.

But Camillo resolutely crossed the sombre terrace, glad of its concealment and uneasy at it, and came down on the black prickles of the yew hedge.

In the faint starlight, scent alone might have guided him. How glorious, how overwhelming, how almost rotten the exquisite perfumes of the lilies were. They were like a fermenting wine no mortal would dare drink – nectar.

And there among the pale forms of the flowers, the pale shape of the sun dial. And there, in her arbour, as before, *the girl*.

He saw her lighted as if by holy rays and almost cried out. Until it came to him that a little lamp was burning on a hook in the arbour wall just behind her head. And by this glimmer, she was sewing a piece of white cloth with purples and rose and red. He caught the flash of her needle. It was so ordinary – a thing he had seen women at since he could recall – and yet, how strange.

And then, she looked it seemed straight at him. The look, although not she herself said: *I know you are there. Come forth, or do you wish to frighten me?*

No! Never, thought Camillo, and got into the archway as fast as he might, for he was afraid in that moment she might scream and summon what help he could only guess at.

She must indeed have seen or sensed him, for now she did not start. Her large eyes, blue-grey as irises, gazed up at him.

"You must pardon me," said Camillo. But she was young too, it would be best to try her mercy. "I should not be here. But – curiosity. I saw you once before. Forgive me if I offend."

"No," said the girl, "you do not offend."

Her voice was very strange. It was as if she seldom used it, husky, dusky, a whisper, a shadow. But then she said, "How did you come in?"

"Oh, I have a key to the door." This bluff pleased him. If he had a key, as a visitor he was legitimate. But then, she did not seem to mind that he was here by night.

"Do you seek him?" she asked simply.

"Your – The Alchemist?"

"My master," she said.

A slave then, a *slave*. Just like the fearful, foolish, and fascinating books.

"I would not dare," confided Camillo. And thought himself a fine fellow, fit enough to dazzle her, and so perhaps he was. "I came here for another glimpse of you."

"Well you have it now."

"So I do." Camillo was at a loss. Honesty was a new game. He said finally, "But why are you out here in the garden by night? Does he allow you no freedom by day? "

"I am always free," she said. "At any hour after dusk you may seek me here. But," she hesitated, she was modest, "by day I sleep."

"I must change my habits," said Camillo.

"But you too are awake by night. And I have heard others in the streets. And there is a great clock. He told me of it. It wakes all night and strikes the hours."

"But the clock is not alive."

"But it has men and angels on it."

"They are clockwork," said Camillo. A shiver of cold ran down his back. He thought, *Truly, like knows like. She is The Alchemist's doll.*

Just then a moon rose up in a tree. It was arched in shape and high up it had a pane of ochre glass: A window come alight.

The girl looked away at it. "He has woken too," she said.

Camillo said passionately, "If he finds me, he may punish me. I must leave you at once."

She seemed dismayed. He was pulled back and forth between panic and pleasure.

He left her with a pledge of return. "Tell him *nothing*."

"If he asks, I must," she said. "But he will not ask."

Camillo fled, imagining all the while the sounds of footsteps behind him, slow, onerous, and sure. A bramble snagged his sleeve and almost he shouted. He escaped the garden a second time, unscathed, except perhaps by Cupid's arrow, the worst scratch of all.

Camillo sought the worst help he could find, that of strong drink and old volumes.

For three days and three nights he did not venture to invade the garden, and all this absence fed his senses, as the wine and the books did. Soon he was in love with the mysterious maiden, the magician's doll; lost. For he was in the story now, and what else might happen? I can make no further excuses for him. He was young, and life had not been unkind. Those are two weak schools in which to learn the first reality.

On the third night, Camillo returned to the garden, and his plan was made. He would seduce the affection of the maiden – already he suspected her enamoured of him – and then he would induce her to flight. How he should shelter her, God knew; he did not. What would become of them, likewise. Some instinct told him that if only he could get her out of the garden, vengeful pursuit would not travel beyond the wall. In this he was partly correct.

It was now a night of new moon, a slender silken light, like thin water.

The key turned with ease, the garden opened. There was no nightingale, but as he descended from the terrace Camillo saw all the lights of the house were out for sure, and the lamp in the arbour lighted.

The girl sat reading from a great book. He was impressed and pleased she had been lessoned in the wise arts. Probably she too had powers.

"Lady," he said at once, "I'm here to entreat you. To come away with me. My heart is yours!" (Oh, did he not even once tremble at the fulsomeness of those special words? – No, he did not.) You must leave this place of your captivity."

"I cannot," said the maiden.

"Yes, if I am your protector. Fear nothing. The holy church is stronger than any dark gambit of *his*."

"But all I need is here," replied the obstinate girl, turning another page idly. "Here I first saw the light, and grew, and here I live."

"His slave."

"Perhaps. I do not mind it."

"Mind it! You must. We are made free by God. Only trust in His name." (He meant in the name of Camillo, which he had not even told her.) "Trust, and I can take you from this loathsome spot."

This too was a lie. Never had the lily garden seemed so mystically fair or smelled so lovely.

The girl looked sad. She put the book aside and clasped her hands.

"Tell me of the world beyond the garden."

Camillo then became the book. He told her of the world – or all he could, for he too had never left the walls of the city.

He spoke of the streets and houses, the mansions of the rich, the churches with their goldwork and the great cathedral. He spoke of the university of Ravenval, its courts and chambers and the library. He spoke of hunting on the hills, which he had never done, the racing of horses and sailing of hawks. He went further. He described vast blue seas with ships on them, and dusty tracks, and deserts where one tree marks a well, and of the caravans of the Road of Spice, and the distant East, where obelisks tower, lamps are rubbed to produce demons, girls dance with their faces veiled but otherwise naked, and carpets fly through the air. He spoke of lands where men are black and men are golden, and where men are blue and carry their heads under their shoulders. For Camillo had read what he had not done.

And when he had finished, the maiden sat enraptured, and he thought it was as much with him as with his tales. In the pine the nightingale did not sing, but a vast planet, silver-green, had come between the oaks and stared on them like the eye of a cat.

"These are the dreams of day," said the maiden.

"You will learn to endure the day," said Camillo. "Only the evil things of night fear sunlight, and you are pure and good."

"No, the day is not my time. I do not think that I could bear the sun. It is a ball of molten matter about which the earth spins."

"No, no," Camillo hastened to reassure her, "the sun moves about the earth, passing over, and under us during the darkness."

"I must shield myself from day. I must cover up my head and sleep."

"Then so you shall," decided Camillo magnanimously. "I will guard you. And by night I will show you the world."

"It is not to be," said the girl sorrowfully.

And as if summoned by her words, a second planet, small and dully red, lit in the wall of The Alchemist's House.

"*Damnation.*" Camillo moved rapidly towards his prey. "I shall be discovered. Come now. Am I to live life without you? I offer you my heart, I offer you holy marriage."

"What is that?"

Disbelieving, Camillo reached her and raised her gently to her feet, and her long gown spilled upon his shoes, and he thrilled at the touch of it, even as at the touch of his hands upon hers. How smooth and douce was. No doll, surely, though magical.

"Trust me and trust in God. We must fly at once."

"I cannot."

"Yes!"

"No, it is impossible."

"In love, all things may be," cried Camillo softly, between fright and dominance. And he moved his hands to her waist meaning to lift her straight up in the air and off the spot, meaning to carry her if needful.

But when he lifted her he heard the oddest sound.

It was a sort of snapping, like the noise a vegetable makes when it is broken. And then the girl gave such a dreadful scream, a scream of such horrible agony, that only once had he heard anything like it, and then from a square where an execution had been taking place.

Camillo let her go. And for a moment he forgot what her scream might bring upon him, for he saw something that made all his organs change to ice.

From below her gown, long streams of thick blood were running out.

Then she fell, directly down, like a branch, and her gown tore open. And he saw that she was a maiden to the knees, and from beneath that juncture she grew together and she was a stem, a stem like that of a lily, greenish and furred, and where the stem went into the ground below the arbour were the roots of her, and like entrails they had been torn up. They writhed there, ripped in half, dying, and the blood ran from them.

And in the house other lights lighted.

But Camillo saw the face of the girl, and it was white and empty and already dead.

He spewed once, and then he choked himself to contain it, and he turned and rushed away.

Nothing did he afterwards remember of his journey through the garden, save that he must have left wide the door in the wall. Nothing did he remember of the streets he ran through. Not until he heard the great voice chime above him for five in the morning, the hour before the dawn. And looking up he saw the iron angels pass over his head with their swords upraised, and the iron knight upon his iron unicorn. And then Camillo hammered on the penitents' door of the cathedral, and after many years it seemed they let him in, and he fell in a sort of swoon under the altar of the Virgin.

For a month, Camillo lay very sick in his sister's house. But he told no one, beyond the first priest, anything of why, or of what he had done, or seen. His sickness was the war in him between revulsion and guilt, and not understanding either, he was ill for longer than a wiser man would have been.

Then, when he had recovered a little, he went to his lodging to take back his few possessions, and when he passed the wall of The Alchemist's garden, he grew so faint that a passerby helped him into the lodging house.

There he recovered, drank some wine with the landlord, and for the first time said to himself, *I must not think of this anymore.*

Then Camillo hurried to put together his books and papers and the other items that had been kept for him in his room. While he did this, up came the landlord again.

"Young sir, there is a priest below who wishes to speak to you."

"Yes, send him up then, if you will," said Camillo, thinking the church had come to collect its fee for a kindness to him, and glad enough to pay, for the payment of dues seemed a part of his healing.

Presently then into Camillo's room, which overlooked as the other apartments did not the tall trees of the wild garden, there came a robed and hooded figure, that Camillo might also have taken for a priest or friar, except that there suddenly looked out on him, as if from behind a mask, a face entirely remarkable. It was a face centuries old, yet unlined. It was a face young as morning, with the no-eyes of a skull. It was cruel, and compassionate. It was like, Camillo dared to think long, long after, the face of God – or the Devil. It was the face of The Alchemist.

"Camillo," said The Alchemist, and Camillo did not wonder how his name was known, "I am not here to rebuke you. What was mine you wantonly destroyed, and took from it also its own life, which I had given it, but which it valued for itself. This you realise, I believe. I only ask you that in future you do not meddle. Do you suppose that you have learned a lesson?"

And in Camillo's mind there was a sort of shudder, or crash, quite mild and painless, but as if all the jumbled pieces of his doubts and fears had fallen home into their proper places. And suddenly he wept, but without shame, eight burning tears. And he said: "Yes."

113

"Then I am content," said The Alchemist

And with no more than that, he left him

I am old today, and can write of Camillo who was my younger self, now as unlike me as a summer tree to a winter stick, with distance and perhaps with fortitude.

He is almost a stranger, and it is easy to speak of he and *him*, of *Camillo*, as though truly he were another. But the lesson has remained of the venture in the garden. And even now my old body would weep, if it had moisture left enough, at the wrong it did, in total innocence, as so many wrongs are done. But there is no more to say.

Antonius Bequeathed

Silvesta was late for the funeral. She wore a black costume. Long, black hair, and pale violet gloves.

The old chateau lay in a forest and was not quite simple to reach. A private plane had deposited Silvesta at the forest's edge. From here she had had to continue on foot along a winding and in spots rather overgrown track. The forest was nearly black, dense with pine and larch and hung with ivy. Sometimes the faces of wolves might peer out at Silvesta, or a hare bound away. Birds sang in the trees and frogs croaked at hidden pools. Otherwise Silvesta saw no life for two hours, until she reached the gates of the chateau, an impressive building of stone, with round, turreted towers and galleries of windows.

An elderly servant admitted Silvesta and led her up into a wide hall on the second floor. Here the other mourners were assembled. The priest had already addressed them, and they had begun to follow him out of the room. Silvesta joined the end of the procession. She knew nobody there. Everyone wore black and a stern expression, but none were in tears. The corpse, which was that of an aunt of Silvesta's she had never met, was borne, on a bier draped in purple, by four tall young men in black top-hats, and wearing masks, of an owl, a fox, a locust and a crocodile.

The party went up many flights of stone stairs, with griffons carved on the banisters, and eventually emerged onto the broad flat roof of a tower. Here the chateau dead had been buried for years.

All around were long granite vases, some six feet high or more, from the top of which spilled varieties of prolific flowers. In the centre of each flower bush might generally be discerned a brown human skull in different stages of decay.

The priest took up his station by a flowerless vase five and a half feet in height. As he spoke the words of the service, two gardeners shovelled some rich black soil into the empty vase. Then the four top-hatted, masked young men drew Silvesta's dead aunt from her bier, and lifting her high in her lace frock, let her down slowly into the jar until only her head showed above the rim. The gardeners quickly filled in the vase with soil; and packed it tightly around the dead woman's neck, until even the pearls in which she had been buried had disappeared.

The priest concluded his words and folded his hands. A hunchback appeared and went to the vase. From a bag, he took some white seeds, like grains of rice, and climbing up a small step-ladder, put them carefully into the mouth of the dead aunt. The chief mourner, a gaunt woman with beautiful false teeth, tipped the hunchback a little bouquet of notes.

Everyone went to the dead aunt, and sprinkled about her head some fertiliser from a crystal scoop. Most had to ascend the step-ladder to do so, and the more decrepit ones had to be assisted up and down, making feeble anxious sounds.

When this ceremony was over, the mourners moved below again into the house. A light rain had begun to fall on the forest. Silvesta paused to look at the vase of a more recent death, whose head had not yet completely rotted. From its greenish dough, a myrtle had started to grow strongly. This was perhaps the remains of her uncle, who, the previous year while out shooting, had been killed by pigeons.

In the hall of the chateau, the funeral guests were given cakes and wine, and then the will was read by the chief mourner.

Silvesta paid little attention to the will. She had no expectations of it. Instead, she gazed at the stained-glass pictures in the tops of the windows, which showed scenes of violence and murder from the Bible.

"And to my niece, Silvesta," said the chief mourner suddenly, with a snap of her beautiful teeth, "for her special care and protection, I leave Antonius."

All the other mourners raised their heads and stared at Silvesta.

Silvesta said: "What's that?"

"It is being brought," said the chief mourner.

Just then the door opened and in came two of the servants, propelling a large silver cage on wheels. As the cage rumbled nearer, it was possible to see inside an armchair, in which sat a very ancient, slender, white and almost transparent old man.

The servants opened the door of the cage and the ancient old man got up from his chair and came out. He stood beside Silvesta.

"This," said the chief mourner, "is Antonius. He is now yours."

"But what am I to do with him?" exclaimed Silvesta. None of them answered, and so she turned to the old man himself. "What am I to do with you? Surely you belong here?"

"I am yours," said the ancient man in a voice like a thin shaving of steel.

"This is ridiculous," said Silvesta. "I don't accept you."

"It was your aunt's dying wish," said the chief mourner.

Silvesta smoothed her gloves, and left the room. She descended the chateau and let herself out of the door. As she walked towards the gates, in the fine rain, she was aware of a narrow white shadow at her heels. The ancient man was following her.

Silvesta re-entered the forest. The canopy of the trees was so thick no rain fell through, and very little light. The ancient man glimmered behind her.

Silvesta turned. "It's a long walk. You'd better go back."

"I am yours," said the ancient man, "Silver Star."

Silvesta quickened her pace. Surely, he could not keep up with her for two hours?

But the ancient man, Antonius, did so. Now and then, the wolves looked out of the pines, but Silvesta barely saw them, she was so disturbed. She hurried until finally she was running, but Antonius trotted after her; his ankles might have rested on springs.

At last she came to the edge of the forest and saw her plane waiting on the meadow.

"You must go back now," said Silvesta firmly.

"I am yours. I shall go with you."

"There's no room," said Silvesta.

She walked to the plane and got in, and the ancient man climbed in after her. She tried to push him out, but he was both resilient and adamant, and somehow he had arrived in the seat behind her.

Presently the plane took off, with Silvesta and Antonius aboard, and flew back to the city.

Silvesta lived in a marble block overlooking the river. She was a designer of unusual clockwork animals, whose creations were very popular. Even the Mayor was often seen with a furry orange flamingo with two heads, which Silvesta had designed for him.

The apartment had a studio, a bedroom, a garden room, a bathroom and a kitchen. It was full of plants, masks, weapons, statues, small trees, architectural finds, books, jigsaws, games, dolls, and furniture. Now there was also Antonius.

Antonius sat down in Silvesta's peacock chair and switched on the television. He dialled the sound up very loud. Once the television had been put on like this, it was never off, except for a few brief moments when Silvesta turned it off. Then Antonius would turn it on again.

Antonius did not sleep, so the television was also on all night.

Because he had no teeth, Antonius did not eat anything solid. He would therefore go to the kitchen and put everything he could find into the blender, whole oranges, cashew nuts, cold chicken, zucchini.

He made these gruels several times a day, and often during the night.

Occasionally, he would go about and inspect Silvesta's rooms. He would take down swords and spears and leave them lying in a tree, or the bath, or books, which he hid in cupboards. He put a doll into the washing-machine and started it.

When Silvesta left the apartment, Antonius would follow her. Sometimes, she would rush across busy intersections, but somehow he always kept up. She could not lose him in the most crowded store.

He spent two hours every morning in the bathroom and two hours every evening.

He wore Silvesta's clothes, without asking her. They fitted but did not suit him, and he spilt orange and cashew gruel on them.

"I want you to go," shouted Silvesta.

"I am yours," said Antonius.

One morning, after her normal sleepless night, Silvesta went out, and as always Antonius followed her.

She led him to the centre of a savage park, where half-wild tigers were allowed to roam, and most visitors stayed in their cars.

"Do you like this tree, Antonius? I hope you do." And so saying, Silvesta handcuffed Antonius to a low bough.

Then she went for the day to the sea.

That evening, when she returned, two florid kind people were waiting at her apartment door with Antonius.

"We found him for you in the park," they said, beaming. "How worried you must have been."

"He was handcuffed to a tree," added the florid man. "The things these old fellows do." And he winked at Antonius, who was wearing Silvesta's golden skirt and four-inch heels.

"One of those naughty tigers was licking his feet," put in the florid woman. "I gave it a Choco-Bite."

After a month, Silvesta brought some of her acquaintances to the apartment and showed them Antonius.

"What a wonderful old man," they said.

They told Silvesta how exquisite Antonius was, added things to his gruel, turned the television up even louder for him, and soon went away.

Silvesta did not sleep and could not work. In her studio, she could hear the television even over the blasting music she played, and the sounds of the blender breaking again on a meat bone. In the city shops Antonius came after her like a ghost. In the elevator mirrors she saw his white image, behind her left shoulder.

Exhaustedly, she conducted him to an antique tea party, and two lovely, cobwebby old women took a fancy to Antonius. But as they presently informed her, "He says he belongs to you."

Silvesta packed a bag by stealth. She left her possessions and her apartment, evaded Antonius, and flew to another city. On the third day, a police escort howled into the street beneath her hotel, and next Antonius was brought up to her room.

"Here you are," they said. "How worried you must have been."

In the second month, Silvesta remembered something. She went to a firm of specialists who twelve days later delivered an amazing cage. It had a remarkable bathroom cubicle that required no maintenance, and in the open area was a comfortable armchair. It was quite difficult to get Antonius into the cage, but the burly men managed it, glaring at Silvesta afterwards and mutely accepting her large tip. Through the bars Silvesta slipped tiny earphones into Antonius' ears, and then turned on the television picture for him.

A blessed silence filled the apartment.

Silvesta worked in her studio all day on a blue, feathered buffalo that sang Strauss. In the evening, she made Antonius a gruel of roses, onions and Mozzarella cheese – one of his favourites.

Antonius did not eat the gruel. He sat staring at the silent television that only he could hear, and large silver tears slipped down his white pure ancient face

"Why?" said Silvesta. "What more do you want? Do you want to drive me mad?"

That night in the silence she could not sleep. At dawn she let Antonius from his cage. He went at once to the apartment bathroom where he remained two hours. Then he came out, splattered the kitchen with avocado and halibut, turned up the television to gargantuan pitch, and concealed a Samurai sword in the arbutus.

Antonius followed Silvesta to a dark glass building in the lower area of the city.

Seated on one side of a desk, with Antonius standing at her left shoulder, she detailed what had occurred.

When she had finished, she signed a paper, and a vast volume of notes changed hands.

Then two gigantic men came in. They wore snow white and looked impossibly wholesome. They lifted Antonius between them, and carried him away. He did not protest.

Silvesta said, "But he'll be well treated? Loud television, and his gruels..."

"Of course."

When Silvesta emerged from the building of dark glass, she went up in a helicopter to a high place. She sat there for hours surrounded by cedars and syringa.

When she got back to her apartment, she was tense and wary, but no one was waiting. No one came.

Some days passed, and some nights. The silence was profound. It grew and blossomed. Silvesta had a firm of professional cleaners in to see to the kitchen. When they had gone every trace of Antonius was obliterated. A last crossbow surfaced from the humidifier. All was calm.

Silvesta had dreams of a white figure riding after her on the back of the blue buffalo. She drank heavily for a month, until she no longer saw Antonius behind her shoulder in the mirrors of elevators.

After that, she made the Mayor a yellow lemur with three tails, the earth turned, and Silvesta re-became herself. She donated Antonius' cage to a famous aviary.

Some new apartments had gone up in the middle of the river. In the topmost of one of these, the party was to be held. Silvesta, in a long white gown, joined some of the guests, who were gazing down from the balcony at a brown jade slice of river lapping the base of the building eighty feet below.

One of the guests had a striped parrot on his shoulder, which was a design of Silvesta's. The parrot went through its tricks, and the guests questioned Silvesta about her work and her success. She was a celebrity, and they treated her with astonishment and great respect, so a transparent wall seemed to form all about her, isolating her from everyone.

It was the mode to drink a mauve wine that tasted like cold iron, and Silvesta did not drain her goblet.

Presently, she was persuaded to an ornamental table in the middle of the expensively bare and bony apartment.

On the table was a pot, out of which a pretty miniature tree was growing. The tree bore fruit the shape of tiny lemons and the colour of pomegranate hearts. In a dish lay a heap of the fruit already plucked. The hosts invited the guests to sample it.

"This is my aunt," said the hostess, pointing at the small fruiting thing. "It's the latest method. They shrink the cadaver and pop it in a pot. Then they plant one of these little trees. A lovely memorial. And the dearly departed can always be with you."

She petted the tree, and went on to confide she made a jam from the fruit and, leading them to an enormous fish tank peopled with fat black finny ovals, she demonstrated the feeding of the jam to the fish. The fish plainly relished it.

"They're carnivorous," said the hostess. "I suppose the jam…"

Some of the guests did not seem pleased that they had chewed and swallowed fruits nourished on an aunt's corpse.

But Silvesta sank into a reverie, remembering all those years ago, when she had attended the burial of her own aunt in the vase. As she was doing this, the other bright guests leaving her alone inside her walls of transparency, Silvesta passed before a tall skeletal mirror. She stopped in surprise. In the mirror was a very old woman in a long white dress and long white hair, and wrinkled ashen skin. It was Silvesta. Seventy years had gone by since the funeral at the chateau. How quickly and playfully they had gone, changing her one iota at a time, and now suddenly here she was. Silvesta studied herself with interest. At her back a few of the guests spoke of her complacently, knowing her as well as an heirloom. She was extremely deaf now and could not hear what they said.

Silvesta turned from the mirror and moved towards the door of the apartment. The host and hostess regarded her exit benignly, for an old and eccentric celebrity was permitted to behave as she wished.

Out on the street, Silvesta summoned a helicopter. She noticed how streamlined and shiny it was, an unfamiliar model. The helicopter rose into the peachbloom sky, and bore her away to the building of dark glass which, over seventy years, had added further angular terraces to its heights.

She was driven by a strange compunction, perhaps of guilt or sorrow, she did not know.

When she had reached the inner chambers of the building and explained her case, she had to wait more than an hour while computers sorted through the institution's records. Finally, a man with a beaded scalp entered the room and opened a file before her, which Silvesta could no longer read. He read aloud to her solicitously.

"No," said Silvesta, "you've made a mistake. I've only come for the remains. He was an old man then. It's been seventy years."

"Yes, yes," said the beaded man, soothingly. "But you see, we have it here. A room with a bath and television. Gruels ten times a day. Money has been extracted automatically from your account."

Silvesta had made so much money she had not missed these payments, evidently. "If it's true," said Silvesta.

"But it is."

"Then I should like to see him at once."

"Someone shall take you to his apartment."

Silvesta said that she would prefer that the unbelievably elderly person be brought to meet her here.

The beaded man set off to see to this, and another half hour went by. Silvesta sat still on a couch, watching a moving news mosaic on the wall about countries she had never heard of. Then an ancient man, pale as ice, was guided into the room.

Silvesta stood up. She was utterly astounded. He had not changed as she had done. He was just the same.

She went towards him hesitantly.

"Antonius?" she asked, in her reedy voice.

"I am yours," said Antonius, "Silver Star."

Silvesta took him in her arms.

Since she no longer slept, Silvesta and Antonius would sit up all night, watching television with the sound very loud. Sometimes they played games, and now and then one of them would take something from its place in the nine-roomed apartment, and hide it somewhere for the other to find. Although Silvesta had kept all her teeth through the wonders of modern dentistry, they were very fragile, and she was happy to eat the exciting gruels she or Antonius prepared in the unbreakable blender. For two or three hours in the morning and the evening, they companionably bathed together in the bathroom. They had no secrets from each other. They talked and talked, about everything. He never called her Silvesta, but always Silver Star.

Quite often they went out, and wandered the city hand in hand. In the park, they fed the tigers; these beasts were now quite tame, although they occasionally attacked cars. As Silvesta and Antonius rose together in the elevators of stores, Silvesta would point to Antonius in the mirror. "There you are."

Antonius smiled.

One day they visited a display of mechanical washers, wearing each other's clothes, and put a bag of oranges into the works. Juice and pulp sprayed the audience. Silvesta and Antonius hurried away before they were caught.

In secret, Silvesta left Antonius in her will to the daughter of the Mayor. Then she hid the will in a lacquer box, and went to watch Antonius watching television.

Mirror, Mirror

In the early winter a vampire began to call at our house.

What made it so terrible was that my mother, who was wise and lovely and perfect, was infatuated with her. Inside a week, she was calling the vampire 'Miriam', and they would sit overcast afternoons face to face, on the long backless couch, which caused them to lean together like two dark tulips in a vase.

Both wore black, my mother because she was still in mourning for my father, though he had died five years before. The vampire because, presumably, she favoured sombreness, just as she liked the night and the winter days when the sun was hidden in a cloud. Miriam the vampire's dresses were long, with tight boned waists and flounces. She wore black hats with veils fixed to her hair with an enormous ruby pin. When she came in the house she would draw out the pin and take off the hat. She would then play with the pin as if with a red berry or a drop of frozen blood.

She was eccentric, and did not put up her hair as my mother did. Miriam's hair hung to her waist like the black cloud that kept the sun in. She was extremely beautiful, in an awful way, her face so white and smooth without a single line, so it was like the face of a child turned to marble. Her eyes were black and rather dull but large enough they must be called beautiful too. Her lips were the pale pink of a faded sugared almond kept in the dark.

All the children on the block knew that Miriam was a vampire. The moment we saw her we knew. The way she came from nowhere as soon as the sun was obscured, and vanished again if it chanced to escape. The way she walked in her black clothes, and now and then looked at us with soft hatred, as if we were flowers she would uproot. Adults passed Miriam often with a second look, but without an inkling of what she was. We were aware, sadly, we too would move eventually into that realm, where we would be half-blind and half-deaf. It was the fee that must be paid for losing our half-dumbness. So soon as we had learned to speak fully, to control language, our other senses would be mutilated.

But for now, we saw the vampire and we recognised her. We understood it was only a question of time. And then, as in a horrible game, it was my gate she approached, and our narrow, patterned steps she ascended. On my mother's door, she knocked, and my mother fell in love with her at once and let her in.

I have no idea what excuse Miriam made for coming to the house. Perhaps that she was looking for some lost relative. It did not matter really. Within minutes, seconds, she had won. And I, returning from play, found her there on the long couch, her hat beside her, the pin twirling in her fingers, and her other hand uplifting a smoking cigarette in a long holder of bone.

My mother introduced her by some foreign name I could not assimilate and have forgotten. In any case, soon it was 'Miriam'.

Soon, too, I came to know the particular grey afternoons, like dusks, when I would enter the house and find my lovely mother in the thrall of the vampire, on the long couch, with the long windows and long ruched blinds behind them.

"Look, here's Miriam."

And the table would be piled with dainty cakes and jugs of homemade lemonade, and the matte lacquer teapot, none of which Miriam, of course, could ever be persuaded to sample, although my mother would beg her: "You're so slight Miriam. And with the winter coming... I must try to fatten you up a little, darling."

When Miriam's leaden eyes would go over me, there would come the soft flicker of hatred once again. How easy I would be to pluck. When Miriam gazed at my mother her look was quite unreadable and dense. Yet in it my mother seemed to find irresistible magic. My mother had once stared into my eyes like that, but no more.

There was another reason too why the vampire had come to our house, beyond my mother's loving and marvellous nature.

Just as she must avoid the sun, and all holy things, sacred wine and bread, the cross, Miriam must avoid a looking-glass. And in our house, there were none. The night my father had died of pneumonia, my mother had veiled all the mirrors, and later she had sent them away, like wicked servants who had stood by and coldly watched her husband's final struggle and defeat. In rather the same way, maybe, she had locked up a drawer in the bureau which contained all his treasures, things I did not know about, as if no-one must be permitted to look.

For Miriam, naturally, a house without mirrors, which would refuse to reflect her and so would give her away, was a wonderful piece of luck. How had she known? But then, everything about her was mysterious and foul. Where, for example, did she come from and return to out of the twilight? Probably a graveyard, but none of us had dared to follow. The very swish of her skirt warned us we must not.

"Oh, Miriam," said my mother adoringly, "do try a little of this raspberry cake. I baked it just this morning."

But Miriam did not touch the cake, only smoking her pale cigarettes in the ivory holder, and fiddling with the strange fruit of the ruby pin.

How long would it be before she could delay no more, before the exquisite foreplay could no longer be drawn out, and she pulled my mother into her rustling embrace and pierced my mother's human neck, and drank her blood?

Every night, when I kissed my mother good-bye before the journey into sleep, I examined her throat closely. Once she had scratched herself with a little brooch she sometimes wore, and my heart stopped. But it was not the mark of teeth.

I had never tried to *tell* her the truth, for I knew infallibly that despite her wisdom, because of the blindness and deafness of her adult state, she either would not hear or could not grasp what I would say. And if she found that I was Miriam's enemy, she might keep us apart. Probably my presence in the room, or the possibility of my arrival there, were part of the reason Miriam had held off from her deadly kiss.

In the monosyllables of our dumbness and lack of language, I conferred with other children. What could I do?

"If only there were a mirror," said Dorothy.

Then Dorothy hung her head and made her confession. "The vampire came to our house once. I saw her in the hall. There's granny's old green mirror there like a pond. And my mother saw in it. I couldn't see in the mirror, only my mother did, but she blinked, two or three times, as if something had got into her eyes. And then she said to the vampire, 'No, I can't help you.' And she shut the door."

Dorothy and I realised that Dorothy's, mother, being partly blind, did not comprehend what she had glimpsed "Miriam's invisibility in a reflecting surface. But nevertheless some preserving instinct had been activated.

It seemed to me that, since my mother was special, she, seeing or not seeing Miriam in a mirror, would know the truth fully. For my mother had beheld a fairy woman once in the park when she was all of seventeen. She had told me solemnly, about the tinsel antennae and the tiny wings. So she had more sight left than most adults. It was only that Miriam had put a spell on her.

How then to bring Miriam to a mirror and to let my mother see.

In a way, it might be easy, for when Miriam was in the house, my mother paid me scarcely any attention. I could have eaten all the cakes on the table. Then again, Miriam was subtly conscious of me, as one would be of an animal one did not like prowling in the room.

Dorothy ran up to me in her big old garden. It was a sunny wintry morning, but by two o'clock the cloud in the east would have swallowed up the sun, turning it from gold to smothered silver.

In Dorothy's hand, a misty foretaste of that silver sun.

"My shell mirror," said Dorothy. "It's all I've got."

We considered the mirror, staring down into each of our faces, puzzled to see ourselves so different from what we knew we were.

"There's a little loop," I said.

"Yes, I hang it on the wall. Then when I sit my doll on the chest, she can watch her face."

Dorothy and her doll were making a sacrifice for my sake, and I took the mirror carefully. It was the size of a small pumpkin, and the shells which decorated its edge hardly hid any of the surface. Yet it was light too, and would hang from the loop.

I took it home quickly. My mother was busy in the kitchen, sifting flour and stoning summer damsons, sensing of course that darkness was coming, and so, Miriam.

I wandered about the room where Miriam would sit, looking for a spot to set the mirror. Normally Miriam would surely detect such a thing at once, but I sensed that she was by now so involved with my mother, the clean scent of her, cologne and brushed hair, my mother's delicate skin with the tiny fairy antennae lines about the mouth and eyes, that Miriam's vampire cleverness was slightly dimmed. If I could only find a place that she avoided, perhaps she would not realise.

Ultimately it was simple. The area of the room which Miriam intuitively did not care for was, not unnaturally, the two long windows. She would seat herself on the backless couch, turned away from them, and would not look in that direction, even if my mother went through this part of the room. My mother also had taken to pampering Miriam's aversion. When she guessed that Miriam would be coming, my mother let down the ruched yellow blinds, and today, already, they were in place.

Going upstairs, I took a large safety pin from my mother's pottery bowl. Returning with it below, I stood on a chair and attached the loop of the mirror to the yellow ruched blind of the second window. Something useful occurred. The reflected yellow folds of the blind shone into the mirror, like a buttercup under the chin. It was not easy to see. I got down, crossed the room and stood in my usual position, just beyond the table where the cakes and tea were laid. It seemed to me that Miriam, sitting on the right of the couch as she always did, would now be reflected from the back into the mirror. Except there would be nothing to show.

As the sun moved low over the sky, and the cloud rose after it like a bank of fog, the light died from the windows and the mirror too turned dull.

A glorious smell of baking drifted from the kitchen. But I felt sick with hope and rage.

At two o'clock, as the cakes were lifted from the oven, cloud absorbed the sun and all down the block grey dusk breathed out into the day. The sun was pale at first as a lemon, and then it melted entirely. And as I glared out from my bedroom window, I saw the black figure of the vampire walking up the street. About her slender ankles her black skirts bounded like little dogs, and in her hat the red pin smouldered like a coal.

I ran downstairs, and as I stationed myself behind the table, our front door was knocked upon.

My mother came, washed and powdered and sweet, with combs in her hair.

"Oh, Miriam," she sighed, "oh, Miriam. How good to see you."

The vampire glided into the room as she had so often done, and as so often over me her dead eyes glimmered, and with her colourless tongue she licked her lip, thinking, I suppose, of when she could pull me up and throw me on the compost. How aggravating for her that I was always here, always about. How she would have liked to cut off my head and be done with me. Her hatred was so vast, so cushiony, she could not catch sight of mine, nor of my excitement.

She drew out the ruby pin and let fall her ghastly hat. She lit a cigarette in the bone holder. But she did not sit down.

I would not let my eyes go to the blind. Not yet. She must not have a hint. I squinted instead at her black buckled shoes and her nasty flounced yipping dog of a skirt. My mother entered with golden cakes and the steaming teapot. Putting them on the table, she added the frosted decanter of sherry.

"Something to warm you, Miriam?"

But Miriam gently shook her head. What could warm her after all, but one thing only?

"It seems so long since I saw you, darling," said my mother, and she sat down on the long couch, to the left. I would not glance at the mirror on the blind. I stared at Miriam's ruby pin spinning in one set of her fingers, and the other set with the smoking bone of the cigarette holder.

She gazed at my mother, and seduced, Miriam also sat.

Then I looked straight up into the mirror.

What I saw was so ludicrous, so terrifying, that it produced a spontaneous and unforeseen reaction.

I had forgotten, or never thought, that while Miriam would not be caught in any reflective surface, her clothes were still corporeal.

And so I beheld a corseted black dress sitting upright on the couch, straight as a rod, and in the air there flashed a turning jewel, and then, floating some four inches free of the black cuff, an ivory holder and a cigarette, which born higher up into the headless space where the collar of the dress ended, sparkled with sudden life, and out of nothing came a gush of smoke like a cloud.

Never before or since have I known the sensation, but at that instant my blood ran cold. Cold as liquid ice beneath a river at midnight.

And I screamed.

From the corner of vision, I noticed my mother's head jerk up. What Miriam did I could not see, but in the looking- glass her clothing did not shift.

My mother spoke to me sharply, but I was beyond response. My eyes were wide and fixed, glued to the image in the mirror, the headless dress of the invisible smoking woman.

And then my mother was beside me. I felt her kneeling, staring into my face. I wanted to shriek that she must turn round, look there, *there* – but no further noise would come out of me and I could not seem to move.

My mother stood up abruptly.

"How foolish children are," she said, quietly.

These terrible words loosened all my limbs, and I flopped down on the floor. I was able to look about now, and saw my mother go over to the bureau. She was unlocking the drawer with my father's treasures in it.

"But then," said my mother, slipping in her hand and taking something out, "here's a thing I'd like to show you, darling."

From my mother's hand depended a golden crucifix, which shone and burned brighter than either the coal of the ruby or the cigarette.

The vampire started up. She snatched on her hat and drove the pin into it, as it seemed right through her skull.

"Oh, must you be going? What a shame."

My mother saw Miriam to the door. Miriam opened and slipped round it like a puff of smoke, already perhaps vanishing.

My mother shut the door. She held the crucifix in her hand, and slowly her gaze settled on me. "Silly child, not to have told me. Did you think I wouldn't believe you?"

I stammered something.

"Or did you only suddenly see?" asked my mother.

"The mirror!" I cried.

"What mirror?" inquired my mother.

I babbled that surely she must understand, she must have seen into the mirror on the blind – though how? – for why else had she fathomed what Miriam was?

"Oh, yes," said my mother calmly, "of course I saw. Her dress without anyone in it. But not in a mirror." I gaped at her miraculousness. She smiled, and said, her voice trembling slightly, "I saw the reflection in your eyes."

One for Sorrow

With thanks to John Kaiine

1st Feather

Daisy saw the dress the way you see a light come on in a darkened window – sudden, surprising, to be expected.

She had been in the new flat a week, and was dutifully exploring the area, finding the supermarket and the green-grocers, the library and the off-licence, then branching out into the back lanes of curio shops and antique dealers. Here she found a rewarding shop, which sold china masks, and finally *Vanities*. *Vanities* sold clothes, not the kind for normal wear, but what you wanted as a little girl when you were dressing up. Creations of silk and satin, crushed velvet and lace, beads and sequins, buttons, hooks and eyes.

Daisy quickly located a pair of purple shoes that might have been made for her. As she was paying for them, she saw the dress.

It hung in a row of other dresses in incredible colours and shapes, and some careless hand or side had dislodged it, so it had, in a way, stepped out from among the rest. It was black and white, the thinnest silk, and marked just a little, just a little tarnished, by old age.

Daisy left her shoes and went to the dress slowly.

She could see at a glance there was no way on earth she could ever have squeezed into it, for although she was slim, the dress had been fashioned for a figure that was a wand. And it was fragile, too; to force oneself upon or into it would be to rend.

A long tight white underskirt fell to an invisible ankle, and over that a waisted tunic of black, cut in a gracefully jagged way, dropped to a vanished knee. A V-neck, with a tiny glimpse of white there too, and three-quarter-length sleeves, with white slashes, somehow described the absent body of the nymph for whom it had been formed. It was a magpie dress. And sure enough, above the right breast of the bodice flew a tiny embroidered magpie.

"It's an absolute curse," the fat woman said from the counter.

"I'm sorry?"

"That dress. The black and white. I'll swear it moves about. Half the time it's on the floor, or else it gets over into the hats."

"It's – beautiful," said Daisy, although she was not sure that beauty was quite the word.

"Like to buy it? I'll tell you now, only an anorexic schoolgirl could squash into that," said the fat woman. "I measured the waist – eighteen inches. And an anorexic schoolgirl couldn't afford it. It's two hundred pounds."

"Neither can I," said Daisy.

Outside she put on the comfortable purple shoes, but after she had walked a hundred yards, they had begun to hurt after all.

Daisy thought the magpie dress was dateable about 1912, which made it almost eighty years of age. Then again, it could have been a later copy.

She thought about the dress, actually, a lot. It was like someone she had met.

Who had worn it?

Daisy put aside her commissioned art-work, and made a drawing of the dress, and then a drawing trying to put a woman *into* the dress. But it would not come out in the right way.

As she was going to sleep in the new south-facing position of her bed, she thought: *With that cheque coming, I could probably afford it.* She had been going to have a long weekend at the seaside, and if she made it just two nights, instead of three, she could buy the dress.

But why should she buy the dress?

On the edge of oblivion, she saw a magpie flying round her bedroom. Fascinating birds. She had never minded only seeing one, although it was supposed to be, was it not, unlucky? What did they say? *One for sorrow...*

There was something about the dress, but it was not sorrow.

The next afternoon Daisy went back into *Vanities*.

"I bought a pair of shoes here yesterday, but they hurt a bit. I don't suppose you could recommend anything?"

"You should have tried them on," said the fat woman.

Daisy gave a mental shrug. She turned and went over to the dresses.

The magpie dress was not there.

"Oh – has someone bought it?"

"Bought what?"

"The black and white dress with the magpie."

"Oh *that*. No. Look, it's got up there."

Daisy looked where the woman pointed, and there the dress was, hanging up on a high rail, with its white tube of skirt depending, and the black tunic fluttering a little, like feathers, in some random breeze.

"God knows how it got there," said the woman resentfully. "*I* didn't put it there."

"Does it have a history?" Daisy asked, still looking up. The breeze must be selective, for none of the other dresses were fluttering, but then the magpie dress was very thin.

"I expect so. You'd have had to ask Mrs Taylor, but she's retired."

"I can't, then, can I," said Daisy.

"I don't know anything about it. I don't know anything about any of them. That's the only one causes trouble."

"Perhaps it flew up there," said Daisy.

But the woman only frowned.

Most afternoons, Daisy would walk to the shops, to give her body a change of movement from standing up before the drawing-board or crouching over it on the table. The illustrations had hit an unseen rock. She was having trouble with them she had not anticipated. She brooded on them as she shopped. She did not turn down the lane towards *Vanities* but on the fourth day she went into the mask shop for a present for Agatha Soames. And when that was seen to, there was *Vanities*, and Daisy walked in.

The fat woman was not in evidence, instead a young fat girl was sorting through a pile of hats with speckled veils.

The magpie dress lay crumpled on the floor.

Daisy had an urge to run to it and pick it up, to comfort it, poor helpless thing.

"You'll never get into that," said Young Fatty, with vicious pleasure.

"No, I'm sure I shouldn't."

"They was smaller then," said Young Fatty, with slight fear.

Two cheques came in next morning's post, one for some drawings Daisy had done for a magazine which had folded. They had honourably and amazingly paid her for her work, although unable to publish.

Daisy examined the cheque, cautiously. It was for three hundred pounds.

"What would I do with it?" she asked the flat, to which she talked off and on, getting it used to her. "Hang it on the wall...like a carpet? It's stupid. I don't collect old dresses."

At two-thirty she went out and walked to *Vanities* where, with her Barclaycard, she bought the magpie dress.

"I tell you what," said Old Fatty, "I think you've got a bargain. I think they underpriced this. A real antique. Present, is it?"

"Yes," said Daisy, "for my anorexic niece."

The dress hung from a picture nail in the wall of the bedroom. It seemed composed and calmed. Being black and white it went with everything and nothing. Daisy kept coming in from her work, to touch it, look at it.

One for sorrow, two for joy...

What made for joy, though? What made you happy? Well, to be able to work at what you were good at, and to get paid for it; to have a few good friends. Maybe, one day, to meet a man she could have more than just a fleeting relationship with, but then he would have to understand her, how she worked... And anyway, she did not mean herself, not Daisy.

"What made you joyful, Magpie Dress?"

And what brought you sorrow?

2nd Feather

Daisy was at a party, and she was sure she should not have come. Perhaps she had not been invited. Everyone wore wonderful clothes, even the men, for their evening wear was dated and ornate, starched shirt-fronts, tiny embroideries... And the women were like flowers from a show, hot-house lilies and roses of fire.

Before she could look down nervously to see what she had put on herself for this auspicious fancy-dress occasion, Daisy's eyes were attracted by a flicker of something up in the air. A magpie was flying round the room, round the quaint gas-fitments with their golden glow. But no. It was not a magpie. It was a woman on a wide stair.

She stood there, with her hand on the gilded bannister, looking down. To Daisy, the artist, she was the most beautiful thing, apart from an animal, that Daisy had ever seen. Her face was exquisite, and just touched by rays of colour and the gold of the lamps. And her hair was like white gold, the utterly pure shade of nature, and coiled back from the perfect triangle of her face into a gleaming shell on her long neck. And from her hair rose a black and white feather, and on her slender perfect body was the black and white dress.

I'll have to tell her I've got it, Daisy thought. But of course, the woman was wearing the dress. How odd.

The woman was descending the stair now, without hurry. Some of the guests had looked up, and seen her. She greeted them coldly, indifferently, and their faces were false. A few good friends – no friends were here.

I care for nobody, no not I, if no one cares for me.

Surely they would, if she let them. She was so lovely – but then, beauty frightened a lot of people, a threat to a man, a slap to a woman.

Daisy could not hear what any of them were saying and she realised she was dreaming, and now she wanted to wake up before the Magpie – for she *was* the Magpie – came to her. Because what could Daisy do, confronted by this dream creature? Would she have to explain herself? How could she, when there was no sound-track?

The woman moved nearer, through the crowd. Her eyes were dark. Her beauty was almost painful. She had the strangest look – as if she anticipated nothing, ever. As if she were old and dry and blind.

No wonder they hated her. To meet those gorgeous eyes and see noting in them, nothing at all.

Daisy woke.

In the half-lit dark of the city night, she saw a little, enough to register the dress had fallen off its nail, leaving the hanger on the wall.

The dress lay on the bed, with its magpie sleeves wing-spread, as if to fly.

"No, I don't want you to do this," said Daisy. "Get off." And wildly she kicked with her feet through the duvet, and the dress slid away onto the floor. "Sorry," said Daisy, "but the carpet's quite soft. Don't spook me. We have to be nice if we're going to live together."

The following morning, one of Daisy's posters leapt off the living room wall with a flapping electric noise, making her jump, so she splashed paint where she had not meant it to go.

She thought nothing much of this, however, for she was no handy-woman, and even hanging up posters was sometimes outside her range of skills.

Then she found the bathroom light was on. And later, the fire in the living room had switched on too, making the room very hot.

"Great," said Daisy.

She went and looked at the dress, and it lay there on its hanger, silent, still.

"I'm doing it," said Daisy. "Dotty Daisy."

Something went crash in the kitchen. She ran to see, and found a saucepan had come off the stacked washing-up and landed on the work surface across the room.

"Don't panic," said Daisy. She moved back into the bedroom and took hold of the tunic of the dress firmly. "Listen, lady, if this goes on, you go *out*. Maybe you're used to that, if you are what I dreamed you were. But I won't play games. I mean it."

The rest of the afternoon passed peacefully. No lights or fires, nothing falling.

Daisy finished work for the day. She had not been shopping, working through, with salad in the fridge for supper. She opened a bottle of white wine, and went cautiously to look at the dress.

"You've been good. Don't think I don't appreciate it."

If I'd met her, she'd have hated me, like she did everyone else. But then she didn't hate them, she just — didn't care.

Daisy sat on the floor before the open balcony window, looking out over geraniums and avocados to the long street, the big trees and on and off traffic.

What would it be like — not to have no one to love, but to love no one? *No one. Nothing.*

The wine had gone to her head and when she heard the smash, Daisy only got up gravely and went to look. In the bedroom, a china cat her dead mother had given her was in four pieces on the carpet up against the wall.

"You bitch," Daisy said to the dress. And she threw the last of the wine in her glass across the front of it.

It swallowed the pale fluid. The mark was barely visible. How many times had they struck at the Magpie? Not physically, for it seemed she was a lady, a society woman, protected, and yet certainly the blows had come in some schematic form, for she would incite them.

"I loved my mother. Fine, you didn't love yours."

Daisy pulled the Magpie off its hook, rolled it up — it was so slender it went to the thinnest, most flimsy coil — and put it into the built-in wardrobe under a box of shoes.

She slept with the light on. But nothing moved.

There were no dreams.

"Oh, this is just wonderful," Agatha cried. And she bore the white-beaked mask before her like an offering. "What's in the other bag?"

"Chocolates."

"Evil, wicked weasel."

"And she's brought wine," said Tony.

"Also this." Daisy handed Tony the fourth bag. "I'm sorry, but I know you're brilliant at fixing things."

"It's Lettuce," he said. "Oh, poor old Lettuce. Did you drop her?"

"No. I've got a poltergeist and it threw her at the wall."

As they sat in the large room full of books and plants and statues of Egyptian gods, Daisy told them of the Magpie, and its deeds.

"It couldn't just be a coincidence?" asked Agatha. "The flat settling, or something."

"What and turning on the fire?" said Tony. "No, she's got a nasty there all right. I think, love, you'll have to take the damn dress back to the shop."

"But how can she?" cried Agatha. "She's dreamed about the woman who wore it."

"Does that mean she owes her something?"

"She was so beautiful," said Daisy, "and so – awful."

"You've heard the expression," said Tony, "bored to death? It can happen. Sounds as if it was, to her."

He drank some more wine, and then said, "I don't know if I ought to tell you. But you're getting there any way."

"Tell me what?"

"You've never heard of the Magpie Fashion?"

"No," said Daisy. The hair rose sharply on her scalp and made her shiver. "Tell me now."

"About 1910, 1911. There was a vogue for black and white dresses for women, sometimes with feathers or feather effects. And little black hats with a feather sticking straight up. And magpie brooches. It was actually to do with the start of the cinema – everything in black and white.

"Why not pandas then," demanded Agatha, "or cats?"

"Magpies can fly. It was the element of flying in black and white."

Daisy mused. "I see. In the dream, she was the only one wearing a dress like that."

"Fashions come and go," said Agatha.

"That fashion didn't just go," said Tony. He looked uneasy and refilled their glasses and his own.

"Well?" said Agatha.

"Well," Tony said, "that particular fashion was *advised* to a stop."

"Advised – what do you mean?"

"The police advised that women, especially young, blonde women, should give it up."

There was a silence.

Daisy felt strangeness. She said, "Why?"

"You've heard of Jack the Ripper," said Tony. "Have you heard of the Magpie Hunter?"

"Oh, you're making this up," said Agatha, with some pride.

Tony shook his head. "No. In the summer of 1912, there was a guy who used to go around a certain area of London, slashing to bits blonde women in magpie dresses."

"I feel weird," said Daisy.

"*Tony.*"

"No," said Daisy, "tell me some more."

"Not a lot to tell. He did it. Murdered about eight girls. Unlike the Ripper, his victims were from all walks of life. Shop-assistants, housemaids, a couple of so-called ladies straying out on their own. And then, the murders stopped. I can't remember if they caught him. I think – no, I just can't recall."

"But you do think she – I mean, the Magpie…?"

Daisy took a gulp of wine. "She was blonde all right. And you said – bored to death."

They sat in silence again, looking at nothing.

Then Agatha got up. "I'm going to inappropriately baste the chicken."

When she had left the room, Tony said, "Sorry. I didn't mean to make it worse."

"You haven't. But what do I do?"

"Take the dress back."

"Will that be enough? Maybe they won't accept it."

"Just dump it in between a couple of others when they're not looking."

"But what does it mean?"

"I don't know," said Tony. "But there is one thing."

"Yes?"

"She can't have been wearing it – I mean, not *that* particular dress. Not if he did get her. He used a knife, you see, and – sorry – just slashed. They, and their dresses, were in ribbons."

Daisy felt inured now. She sat demurely and said, "How odd."

Agatha returned with another bottle.

It had obviously been a relief to go out. Coming back at two in the morning, pleasantly tiddly and nicely tired, Daisy knew a slight sensation of fear.

The driver of the hired car watched her to her door, then drove off, and Daisy let herself into the sleeping house.

When she opened the door of her home, and switched on the light, she had only the violent first impression that she had entered the wrong flat. Then she knew that she had not.

The worst thing had happened. Burglars had got in. The foulest type of burglar. They had thrown her ornaments and plants about the room – even thrown over her drawing-board and squirted coloured paint up the wall…

And then she realised it was not burglars.

For, no longer rolled up in the wardrobe, but on the carpet, neatly spread out with its wings unfolded, lay the Magpie Dress, the one quiet, seemly object in the ruined space.

Daisy ran to the bathroom and lost Agatha's excellent dinner.

3rd Feather

When she was a child, Daisy could remember, it had usually been very quiet in libraries, but now there were constant comings and goings, soft and not so soft conversations, the buzz of electronic gadgets. Nevertheless, she sat there doggedly at the long table, from ten in the morning until four-thirty, and read the book they had found for her. She went out once and bought a sandwich, and ate it on the bench on the forecourt. All the time, the dress stayed coiled in her bag.

She had not slept the night before, and her eyes were gritty. But even so, she read all the book. *The Magpie Killings* it was called.

At five in the morning, when she had finished as much of the cleaning-up as she could manage, Daisy had spoken to the dress.

"I'm going to presume you want something. It isn't just spite. I'm giving you that chance."

The dress had lain quiescent where she had thrown it. It had not moved and it caused no further damage. It let her roll it up again and push it down in the bag, and take it out to the library.

At first, they had said they had nothing on the subject Daisy wanted. And then someone had discovered the old book in their reserve stock. "I'm afraid all the plates are missing. Dreadful vandalism."

She was too stunned to care about the plates. She just wanted to know some facts.

Basically, the book was a list of the murderer's eight victims. There was a chapter on each one, how and why she had been in the notorious Faithways area, which the author, with inappropriate wit, had quickly re-christened the Black Whitechapel of the Magpie Ripper.

Of the murderer himself there was no proper information. He had been variously sighted and randomly described, sometimes as tall, dark and gliding, and sometimes as stocky, squat and creeping. He was alternatively a shadow, a ghost, a preying tiger, a lurching toad. Those who claimed to have caught glimpses never concurred. And so perhaps none of them had ever spotted the true murderer. What had become of him too was as much a mystery as his identity. As with Saucy Jack, the slayings had abruptly come to an end. The reason for his massacre was equally or more obscure. The author did not put forward any theories. Indeed, he smugly asserted that he had resisted them in the face of lack of evidence.

His concern was with the victims.

Daisy read the chapters with a slight sickness and a dim apprehension. The eight lives were very different, only similarly tragic because of their inevitable plunge onto the Magpie Hunter's knife – for, in each case, it really did seem as if they had been drawn to him, had almost sought him out. But was this one the owner of the Magpie Dress – or this one? It was impossible, horribly and frustratingly impossible, to tell.

And of course the plates could have – might have – answered the question at once. For evidently, judging by the table at the beginning of the book, there was a picture, although now and then only a sketch, of each of the dead women. Plus, certain other drawings and photographs, labelled *The Fatal Alley*, *A Wedding at All Saints Church*, *Faithways*, *Twilight in Faithways Square*, and so on. The missing frontispiece bore the note: *A glamorous example of a fashion which killed.*

At four-thirty, when Daisy had completed the book and her pocket mirror told her her eyes were inflamed, she felt dissatisfied and uncomfortably anxious. She seemed to have learnt nothing, or nothing that might reflect on the enigma of the violent and evil dress. And conversely, Daisy had been swimming in blood, the blood of eight blonde girls, slashed from throat to groin, silk and muslin, cotton and voile, skin and arteries; bone.

"Excuse me," a plump and pretty and blonde young woman stood, almost perversely, at Daisy's side.

"Oh, are you closing? Sorry."

"No, not for another two hours, worse luck. But look. The van came over, and I was able to get hold of another copy of your book. This one's got *all* the plates."

Daisy felt a wave of nausea. The last thing she wanted now was to see – to *see* the whole forms of those women hacked to ribbons in the alleys and squares, in the very church porch, of charmingly named Faithways.

But the assistant had been diligent and kind, and it would be rotten and rude not to respond.

"Oh, thank you. That was good of you. I'll – just take that one, then."

And so Daisy checked out and put the second copy of *The Magpie Killings* into her bag with the Magpie Dress, and went back to her flat.

The acrylic mark would not leave the wall unless she repainted. The red splotch on the curtain was never going to go either. Like a splash, of course, of blood.

Daisy tried to drink a glass of wine, could not, a cup of tea, could not, looked at her provisions of smoked fish and new potatoes with sadness. They were not going to be eaten.

Eventually she sat down, next to her bag, and withdrew the book.

Meticulously she turned to the first picture, the frontispiece. It was a dense black and white photograph, and it drained the vitality from her heart, which began to beat in slow loud strokes.

For the frontispiece – *A glamorous example of a fashion which killed* – showed a slender, exquisitely beautiful girl on a stairway. Her hair was coiled shell-like on her neck, and a feather rose from it. She wore the Magpie Dress Daisy had bought from *Vanities*. And she was the girl from Daisy's dream.

"All right," Daisy said aloud. "All right. I do believe it. Just – give me a minute."

Then she read the rest of the caption, under the photograph:

'Margaret Shawn, a society hostess of the era, and said to be one of the most beautiful women of her day, dressed in an elegant version of the so-called Magpie Fashion, even to a feather in her hair. Margaret Shawn, although she defied police advice against such garments, was not one of the murderer's victims.'

Daisy spread the dress out on her bed. She addressed it.

"Let's try. I'll trust you. But no tricks, Margaret Shawn. Or I'll burn you. And if that lets your demon out, then I'll find a priest. I'll stop you. Understand?"

Daisy rolled the Magpie up and put it under her pillow.

Then she drank some very hot tea with a little gin in it and swallowed two herbal sleeping tablets.

Would they work, against this sort of stress?

Or Margaret Shawn might prove unhelpful. Margaret Shawn might pick up the bed and throw it through the window, and Daisy with it.

But no. That was not the way for Margaret Shawn to get what she wanted, whatever the hell that was.

Margaret... it meant the same as Daisy, did it not... Pearl.

The room floated, and Daisy felt the dress stir under her neck, like a snake. But it was too late now...

She was wearing pale green tonight, *eau de nil*: Nile Water.

The man across the table from her, across the candles and the pyramid of fruit, the crystal and the wine, looked at her, could not take his eyes off her.

"Maggie, can we...? It's been a long time."

"If you like."

"No, no, I'm sorry. I shouldn't have said anything."

He had been asking permission to make love to her, that was clear, and she had not refused, yet she had put him off. How could you make love to that beauty, anyway, with those agates of eyes watching.

Then servants, came in, the ubiquitous dummy creatures of the big houses, always there, eyes and ears, and suddenly Margaret Shawn had got up.

The male port had arrived. Was that it?

Whatever it was, she was making some gracious, uncaring, flinty excuse, and leaving the room.

Up a stair, gas-lamps, a tapestry hanging, and smart pictures of long, long people with long long dogs. Now a bedroom. Hers.

Margaret Shawn was sitting before her mirror in a lacy flounced gown, and one of the maids was brushing over and over that undone stream of lemon gold hair.

"Tell me about it," said Margaret Shawn.

"Oh Madam – I can't. The Master said…"

"Never mind what the Master said. He knows I see the newspapers. He knows everyone is talking of it. I want to hear."

"But Madam… It's horrible."

"Yes, it is. Horrible and fascinating."

"They say he does it because of the black and white dresses."

"I know. Lady Pane told me. But someone saw him, didn't they?"

"Oh, Madam."

"I shall be angry," said Margaret Shawn.

The maid flinched. And Daisy knew, as she had known about the refusal to have sex, that Margaret Shawn did not punish physically, but through the psyche.

"It was – it was Liza, Madam. Liza Meadows."

"You know her?"

"Yes, Madam. Sometimes on my afternoon she and I – well, she thinks she saw him. I mean, the murderer."

"Tell me," said Margaret Shawn. "No. Stop brushing my hair. That's enough."

And she got up, and walked to the long window, and there she stood looking down onto some interruptions of great trees, and beyond a square that had a garden.

The maid spoke. She said her friend, Liza Meadows, had had to go over to Faithways, to see her aunt. Unlike Red Riding Hood, Liza had not strayed from the path, but even so, in the onset of darkness, she had beheld before her a tallish figure swathed in the coming of night.

"He was dressed like a gentleman," said Margaret's maid, "only he hadn't a hat on his head."

This was strange to Liza, and made her check. And then she realised that she had put on her only good dress and jacket, which gave the effect, in twilight, of black and white. But she thought to herself, *Why should it be me?* And she went on gamely.

There was a streetlamp which had been lit, and under it, he was.

"She said he was like a prince, Madam. I mean, from a fairy tale."

Liza, and Margaret's maid, did not have the words for it, yet it grew like a flower, out of the compost of dull sentences.

He was beautiful. So beautiful that when he looked at you – you were trapped. His hair was blonde, too, like the hair of the victims. His eyes a pale sere blue that gleamed. He seemed to hold Liza by a rope of fire, and she was drawn towards him now helplessly. And then she was under the lamp also, and he must have seen – her clothes were chocolate and pale green. Not black and white at all. And suddenly, as if the light itself went out, he turned his flame from her. And he was gone.

"Liza felt faint, Madam. She had to lean on a wall.

"Has she been to the police?"

"Oh, *no*, Madam. She had no business being there. Her Missus had warned her to keep away."

Margaret Shawn stood looking out on the busy square. A few cars came and went, like handsome insects. People walked. There too the gas-lamps had been lighted.

"It's all right, you can go," said Margaret Shawn, and her maid slunk out.

Margaret Shawn held the velvet drapes in both her hands as if she clutched at something, drowning. Yet her face was calm. Only her lips slightly parted. And her eyes rapt, wide.

Her husband looked at her like that, when he asked her to sleep with him.

But she wanted the murderer. She wanted the murderer of women. She wanted death. *That* death. The phallic knife, the orgasmic scream...

It was in every line of her immaculate, frigid body. Blonde Virgo. For whom the magpie is a special bird...

And she asked the maid for news, the way the schoolgirl asks for stories, anecdotes, about the boy she has a crush on.

Out there, out there he is.

And Margaret Shawn let her curtains fall and turned to stare at her bedroom.

She wanted nothing, disliked everything. Lusting for one thing only. Hair and eyes, the shadow, the hand and the knife.

I want to wake up.

Daisy shifted and half felt her flat about her, and then she was down again, in the dark, with beautiful Margaret.

It was another place. A long street, which Daisy knew at once, from the plates in the book that she had forced herself to see. Linden Avenue. Tall houses in the dark, *and* between, the greenish cat's eye glow of gas lights. And a turning – the alley. The Fatal Alley.

And Margaret Shawn walked into it.

She wore her black and white dress. No feather in her hair, just the pristine coiling. And she moved like a swan, the swan in the evening – over the lake.

Her face was avid, like the face of a Madonna, which works miracles if you go to it with pain and blood and tears,

Margaret Shawn walked through the alley, and back again.

It was a summer night. And nothing stirred.

How often had she come? Did she arrive by cab, perhaps, making the excuse to her ineffectual husband that she visited some non-existent friend, for friends she did not have. Only one potential friend – Him.

Margaret Shawn walked exquisitely along the alley again, and so across the avenue, and the square, where a great church brooded. Were there no police? She must have eluded them, or else the watch had flagged and she had taken advantage of that.

Death and the Maiden. She had gone out to find him. But he did not come to her. *Coitus interruptus.* Yes, her face was like that now, the lips a little slack, disappointed, a thin line between the brows.

How terrible. She had dressed for him, bathed and scented herself. And he had stood her up.

A blot appeared on the pavement. The lamps sizzled. Rain had fallen. Overhead, a rumble of thunder. Daisy heard, as she had heard the conversation in the bedroom.

How often had she come here, Margaret Shawn, searching in vain, refused by death. In heat and in rain, fire and water. Jilted.

4th Feather

The phone was ringing.

Daisy woke. It was ten o'clock.

"Yes?"

She felt hung-over, which did not come from a single gin in tea and two herbal tablets. But she had been dreaming. What...?

"It's me."

Tony.

"Tony?"

"Are you okay? You sound odd."

"Overslept."

"Damn. Sorry to wake you. Only…"

"Yes?"

"I wondered if everything was all right? I mean, the dress."

"No. And yes. I suppose so. I suppose it has something to say. Can I call you back in five minutes?"

"No," he said. "I'll call you in ten."

Daisy stumbled to the bathroom, relieved herself, cleaned her teeth and splashed water on her face. She came out and put on the kettle for Assam tea.

While it was brewing, Tony rang back.

"Sorry about that," said Daisy. "I have a contact with Margaret Shawn."

"My God," he said, "she's in the book. Was it hers?"

"The dress – definitely."

"The thing is," Tony said, "I got intrigued. You know Martin over at Streatham? Well, I phoned him up, and he had a book in the shop – "

"Not *The Magpie Killings*," said Daisy. "I've read it."

"No, this is older. Very small. About eighty pages. But you see, I sent it off to you. And now Agatha says I shouldn't have. Are you going to be okay?"

"Oh yes," said Daisy firmly, pouring and sipping the Assam, clenching her toes. Under the pillow she could see the edge of black and white. "I'm going to be fine."

"It'll probably arrive in your second post."

"Thanks, it was kind of you."

"Maybe you shouldn't read it."

"I think I'll have to."

"Look, if you need us…" he said.

"I know where you are."

The book came with the second post. It was a slender volume, black cover, white lettering. Its title was: *Sorrow*. Nothing more. Inside, on the title page, small lettering added: *Some speculations on the Magpie Murders*.

And under that was printed part of the old rhyme, not quite as Daisy had remembered. *One's sorrow, two's mirth.*

Daisy made toast she did not want and ate portions of it – not the crusts, *My hair won't curl* – and drank more tea. Then she sat down, in her nightshirt, to read *Sorrow*.

It was a strange book. Somehow intensely personal, as if the writer, whose name she kept forgetting, and which did not really matter, had become obsessed with the events at Faithways, and driven his obsession on into the realms of dream, and so the quasi-supernatural. In parts, it touched poetry, and in others the prose was blunt and mundane. It mentioned the victims, not as individuals, like the other book, but as a sort of entity. Only to Margaret Shawn did it devote an individual section.

'For Margaret Shawn, society hostess and celebrated beauty, was in fact also one of the Hunter's victims.'

Testimony was quoted from Margaret's maid, Alice Dimpson, from her diary, and illiterate letters she had penned to friends. How 'Madam' had become fascinated by the murderer, and spoke of him constantly in private, such as when Dimpson was dressing her or doing her hair. 'It was as thow she had a lova,' wrote Dimpson, 'a fance man.' Dimpson indeed found her mistress's interest prurient, without knowing quite how or why. Then, when her mistress began to be absent from the house, saying she had gone to dine alone with Lady Pane-Rosythe, Dimpson realised that Margaret Shawn went to walk the alleys and streets of Faithways, in her black and white dress. 'Masta puts up wiv it,' wrote Dimpson, pragmatically. She believed he thought his wife was seeing another man. Dimpson herself was terrified by now. She reckoned Margaret would be 'sliesed up.' She did not dare to speak.

Faithways, said the author, whose name Daisy kept mislaying, was a corruption of the old Featherways, or Fetherwies. Featherways Lane had run on down to the river, and once there had been both a nunnery and a house of monks situated along its length. These religious buildings had been founded after the visitation of the Black Death.

The summer was erratic, and one night when Margaret Shawn was out walking, a massive storm took place, with torrential rain. Margaret returned about midnight, soaked through.

From this outing, apparently, she contracted a chest cold which swiftly turned to pneumonia.

Alice Dimpson believed Margaret Shawn had gone out courting the Magpie Murderer, instead she met Death in another form. A week later she succumbed.

"Not this way," the author of the book reported Margaret Shawn's dying words to be. "A straw death."

That was what the Vikings had feared, the book said, the 'straw' death – death in bed, as opposed to violent death in battle, which would carry the warrior to Valhalla.

But Margaret Shawn had died through the Magpie Hunter as surely as if he had slashed her in bits; she too was his victim, the ninth. His choicest and most lovely, although he had never met her.

It was three in the afternoon. Daisy went and made coffee instead of tea. She returned to the book with a rabid reluctance.

The dress had not moved. Nothing had. A weird stillness enclosed the flat, into which the noise of traffic came from far away, as if through water.

Faithways, Fetherwies, was a haunted area. Halfway along it, in the fifteenth century, said the book's author, had been a statue of the Virgin. One night a priest from the monastery was found cut to pieces nearby, among the trees at the Lane's edge. He had been used to hear the confessions of the nuns.

'Magpies,' said the author, 'like nuns and monks, in black and white. Magpies, sacred to the Virgin, who had conquered the demon realm of darkness and the moon.'

"No," said Daisy, "that's enough."

She shut the book on the last chapter, which was called 'The Murderer Vanishes'.

She went and had a bath. She felt exhausted. She ate cheese on toast and an apple.

The stillness had persisted. It was twilight now. The day had gone. Why had this book, so much smaller than the other, taken so long to read?

She was confused, too. Images of girls from 1912 in black and white, and mediaeval nuns in black habits...

Finally, she read the concluding chapter, propped up like an invalid in bed. The words blurred, came and went.

'He did not keep his appointment with Margaret Shawn because he had had to escape.'

Apparently, the police had sussed the murderer, and he, getting word of it, fled. He ran from London, out into the rolling orchards and fields of rural Kent.

And so he came to a once-notorious inn, which happened to be named *The Magpie*.

This must be pure invention, Daisy thought.

Yes, certainly, because...

At the inn, he was recognised. And in the night, the village people stormed his room and took him out. They took him to an old gallows across the square, and there they hanged him by the neck until dead.

And this was hushed up, remaining only as a rumour and boast.

The Magpie inn had always, it seemed, vaunted a window which overlooked the gallows. The rich and curious had once paid to take it and watch the hangings of highwaymen. That night the room was empty. They were all down in the square.

They buried his body in an unmarked grave. There was no proof.

But, put down in black and white...

The phone rang.

"Sod it. I woke you again."

"Hello, Tony. I got the book. It's very peculiar."

"Martin says the writer was a known laudanum addict, who wrote under the influence. Most of it's – make-believe."

"What about the inn?" said Daisy.

"Oh, that exists, I checked a Kent guide. A place called Asham."

"Sounds Indian." Daisy closed her eyes. Christ knew what she would dream now.

"Look, I'll call you again in the morning. Agatha's been giving me hell."

"It's all right," said Daisy. "Where's Asham?"

"You can get there from Charing Cross. Off the Dartford Loop somewhere. Should I have told you?"

"Isn't laudanum too late for 1912... whenever?"

"You mean the book? 1913. Apparently not. I'll call you at eleven."

Daisy said, "Got to go to sleep now. Night. Love to Agatha."

She depressed the cradle, and then left the phone off the hook.

Daisy touched the edge of the dress under the banked-up pillows.

"Be gentle. Don't kill me. Or I can't."

She did not recall putting out the light.

5th Feather

In the walled garden, the nun was standing with her arm up-raised.

The walls were high, but clad by roses. Roses like fat pink cabbages with red hearts. There was a small pool, and fish glinted there. Beyond, other higher walls. Grey, yet touched by sunlight.

In the sun, the nun's skin was young, and white as crystal. Despite the black garments and the pallid wimple, she was beautiful. And in her pale lifted fingers was a gob of raw and bloody meat.

Someone came through an arched doorway. Another nun. This one incredibly wrinkled, brown and warty. She hurried to the beauty and tugged at her shoulder.

And the beauty turned her arrogant white perfect face.

Then they spoke.

Daisy could not understand a word. Well, maybe one word in twenty.

It's like Chaucer.

Just vision then, reading of faces, not lips. The young one was proud and disdainful, and the ugly one harassed and bustling; jealous.

Then there was the flap of wings and the beautiful one turned all her attention up into the air, as if at the approach of an angel. And Daisy knew she was saying, *Look! You see?*

The magpie dropped down. It was heavy and solid, black nun-mantle over white, and the wicked beak of a crow, and glowing sideways eyes. It landed on the white arm, where, Daisy now saw, there were already scorings from a hundred such landings.

It took the meat ferociously yet daintily from the girl's grip, and ate, standing there on her slender arm.

The old jealous one had drawn back muttering. She had even made a sort of sign that must be some version of the Cross.

With mouth sewn tight, she waited.

The beautiful one drew something up from under her habit. It was a precious stone, greenish, maybe a beryl. She jinked it under the magpie's beak. She was saying, teasingly, 'Do you want it? Bright, pretty...' And the magpie seized the jewel and, green drop and shreds of bloody flesh dripping from the dagger of its beak, it flapped away. And the girl called after it, some name which meant a faithless lover.

The old one muttered. She told the girl – Daisy understood, as if sub-titles were being printed in her brain – that the young one's brother was coming. And the young one said she did not care to see him. And then she told the old one to go away.

The daughters of the rich had sometimes been allowed to queen it in the nunneries. They must dress as nuns, but otherwise what they did was very much their own province.

And Beauty was of this order. Even to her jewels.

Now her dark eyes rested on the sky, where the magpie had gone. And she smiled.

She was not innocent.

Daisy saw the magpie, like a dot in heaven, wink out.

"No, it's getting muddled." Daisy lay in bed, talking to herself or the dress. "We had 1912. But what's this now?"

The book, *Sorrow*, lay on the floor.

148

What had the laudanum addict said? Margaret Shawn's broken 'appointment' with the killer?

Did Margaret Shawn look like the beautiful, dark-eyed nun?

"All right," said Daisy. "All right."

I'm not being rational.

She washed her hair and dressed, and when Tony phoned her at eleven o'clock, she was already sorting things out for her journey.

"I've got to go to Birmingham. It's a real nuisance. But they insist on seeing me, and they're paying expenses."

Tony sounded relieved. "Well, it will give you a break..."

"Oh, that. I think it's fading out."

When Tony rang off, she phoned British Rail. And then she packed a small bag and put the rolled up Magpie Dress in at the top. And stuffed *Sorrow* down one side.

"Sorry about this," she said to the flat. "Take care."

She felt wild and light, perhaps the way the successful anorexic feels before the pain begins.

The train would take forty-five minutes. The long carriage was empty but for an elderly woman three or four seats further down. The windows were so thick with dirt the landscape outside was distanced, and though notices prohibited smoking, the space reeked of smoke. But perhaps it was only the pollution of the city.

London drew back. Old defamed tower blocks lined the horizon.

Daisy shut her eyes.

I'm not asleep.

Yes, but I was awake in the other dreams too. A fly on the wall.

It was a kind of walkway, with arches, and the beautiful nun was there, standing quite still. She was looking down.

In the stone yard below, a fat woman, also a nun, and with a golden crucifix on her ample bosom, was walking about with a priest.

He was tonsured, and Daisy felt a distaste for this. She sensed that Beauty did too. For the rest of his hair was thick and blond, shining in the summer light.

The important fat nun and the priest were speaking rapidly, and now and then a phrase of strongly-accented Latin drifted up.

This time, Daisy did not take in any of the words, rather she seemed privy to the unspoken phrases of the beautiful nun's body. In her white throat the pulse, beating. And her slender hands grasping the stone of the arch.

Then she called. It was very respectful, addressed to the Mother

Superior, or whatever she was, but both of them looked up, the fat woman and the blond man.

The beautiful nun bobbed a sort of curtsy. She was trembling all over with suppressed laughter, and with something else.

The fat woman was disapproving yet restrained. Obviously, the beautiful nun came of a powerful family, which had granted a large beneficence to this house.

And the priest... He looked only arrogant, proud in the flawlessness of his vocation. If he saw Beauty, he did not show it. He might have been glancing at the stone.

He seemed about thirty-eight years of age, and so probably was in his late twenties, for Daisy imagined that Mediaeval maturity was evidenced early. In the same way, Beauty, who looked twenty-five, was more likely about sixteen.

The priest was painfully handsome. Frighteningly so. And as he turned from the nun on the walk without acknowledgement, Daisy knew the heat of fire, the deep knocking of the excited heart, and the tingling awareness of its own loveliness which suffused the young girl's body.

"Have to get out here," said the station worker, sneering in at Daisy. "Unless you want to go back to Charing Cross."

Daisy got off the train, tumbled off, between two worlds.

She stood on the platform. Everything was grey. She had expected open fields and green hills, flowers and trees, but Asham was not like that.

She wanted him.

Oh yes. Beauty had wanted the priest, all right. Daisy could recall those wonderful awful feelings too well. They stopped you eating and sleeping, and working. But what happened if you were a nun sworn to chastity, and he was at the cold-heat of religious devotion, given to his God, with no room for anything else.

Daisy walked out of the station.

It was a kind of village, but one which had sprawled and overbuilt and become a town. The rolling orchards of *1912* were only now the concrete suburbs of the nineties.

Wake up.

Daisy shook herself, actually and physically.

Above, in the station foyer, she bought herself a diet Coke, the taste of her own time.

On the forecourt were three cars labelled as taxis.

"Do you know the – pub, *The Magpie?*"

"No. Try Jack."

She tried the second car. Jack said he had heard of *The Magpie*, but it was in Sidcup.

"No, it's at Asham. It's famous. They used to hang highwaymen on the square outside."

She expected him to look at her as if she was mad – maybe she was – but instead he shook his head. "That's in *London*."

Daisy took out the book, *Sorrow*, from her bag. She showed Jack the description of the inn.

By now the third one had got out of his car and come over. The first man had no interest and was reading a paper.

"That's the *Old Mag* you want," said the third man. "Blowed if I know where it is, though."

Daisy drew in a deep breath. "Would you be prepared to drive round Asham and help me find it? Whatever it costs, of course."

"Well," said the third driver, "I'll give it a go."

They gave it a go.

They drove through grey, flat Asham, and finally they found the rolling fields after all, but they were cindery, and the trees looked scorched as London trees.

Besides, reaching the outer environs, the driver turned back. "It ain't out here. It's in the centre somewhere."

Back through Asham, up and down.

This pub and that.

The driver got out and asked at the *Red Horse*.

"We'll try up by the railway crossing."

They did so, to no avail.

Daisy felt contrite and determined. Any minute he might get sick of it and ask her to get out. But in fact, the driver now seemed as questing as she. He only asked her if she was still all right to pay.

They found the *Old Mag* about four o'clock. The sky was heavy with summer overcast, and in a narrow street of dress shops and cafés, a timbered front appeared, bulging out, and a sign – of a magpie in flight.

"Oh, thank you," said Daisy, as if he had delivered her baby in the cab, or rescued her cat from a tree, or fed her when she was starving.

"I'm afraid it's twenty-two quid."

She gave him twenty-five and he drove off happy, pleased with victory and money.

The pub was shut. A board told her it would not open until six.

Daisy went into one of the cafés across the street.

She was disconcerted there was no square. As she sat there over her hot ham croissant and Spanish salad, she told herself the square must have been built on.

She drank a lot of tea, and when the cafe filled up at five-thirty, she removed herself for a nervous walk along the street, being careful not to wander too far from the elusive pub.

In this way, she found that *The Magpie* backed onto a concrete apron, packed with tiny shiny Japanese cars. This was what the square had become.

At six sharp she returned to the pub door. She was the first customer.

6th Feather

"You say you're writing a book?"

The woman was blowsy and aggressive.

"That's right."

"About the *Magpie Inn*."

"About the Magpie Murderer."

"Well. I don't know nothing about that. And George don't. We've been here six years, mind."

"It was really the room I was interested in."

"Well, as I say, we don't let rooms."

Daisy, on her second white wine, felt a deep hot desperation. And as the drink took hold, felt too the stupidity of her plight.

For she was in over her head. She did not know what she did. To bring the Magpie Dress to the *Magpie Inn* had seemed logical and sensible, actually consequent. But the dress lay limp, just a crumpled-up bit of black and white silk, fragile enough to tear in two. As indeed had been its owner.

But what had Margaret Shawn, who courted death and died of the wrong brand, to do with the black and white nun and the arrogant priest?

Yes, thought Daisy, *I do know.*

An appointment. A meeting not kept.

"But would you show me the room?"

"I should think not," said the woman nastily, and then softened her voice a touch. "All our old junk up there, and stuff from the pub. Spiders, God knows what."

"What *is* all this?" asked George, coming up.

George was also blowsy, but genial. He liked a tipple and accepted Daisy's offer of a drink, as his wife had not.

After they had talked a while George said, "We could let her see the room, Rita. No harm."

"I don't think..." said Rita.

"Come on," said George to Daisy. He gave her another wine she had not asked for and waited for her to pay. Then he took her out the back, through a brown hall and up some floral stairs that creaked.

The landing was uneven.

"This is it, I reckon."

It was very low, the room, but the beams were long gone. It was also, as promised, full of lumber, boxes and crates, a stag's head, skeins of cobwebs, and a window filthier than on the train, which overlooked the concrete and the cars.

"The square was out there," said George. "I remember old Mick – he had the place before us – he used to say they had hangings there. People used to pay to have the room and watch, in private. Funny things people get up to."

"I'll pay," said Daisy, straight out, "to have the room tonight."

"What?"

"I know you think I'm crazy, but it would help my book."

"But – where'd you sleep?"

"That doesn't matter."

"God help us," said George. "Here, I don't think I can let you do that..."

"Fifty pounds," said Daisy. "In cash."

"Oh, now look..."

"Seventy," said Daisy. "That's it."

Her mouth, despite the wine, was dry. She felt like a bad actor in a bad TV crime play. George was a worse actor. He bumbled away to himself. Then he said, "Rita won't like it. And I'll tell you now, she won't do you breakfast."

"I don't want bloody breakfast," Daisy shouted, astonishing herself, "or a bloody bed. I want to sit in this horrible room for the night and I'm offering you seventy pounds to do it. *Yes?*"

"Just hold on..."

"Yes or no?"

George hung his head. "It's your funeral."

"In fact not."

When he had taken the money and gone out, Daisy leaned on the wall the way Liza Meadows was supposed to have done after her brush with the murderer. Daisy too felt faint and weak. Then she drank off all the third white wine, and went to the bathroom she had glimpsed down the hall. Too bad if they did not want her to use it.

In the bathroom, which was puce, she found like a gift a hanger, and she took it because, for seventy pounds, a pee and some soap and water and a hanger seemed reasonable.

The dark was coming. It was nearly nine.

Down below, noises came from the pub.

Daisy took out the Magpie Dress and smoothed it. She put it on to the hanger, and then hung the hanger on the window-frame. The dress faced out to the concrete apron, and the arrival of evening.

"Here we are," said Daisy. She sat down against one of the crates and began to cry.

After a few minutes, the pain left her.

She thought, *In pieces, but not broken.*

At ten she went down and bought a bottle off George, who stared at her guiltily, and some sandwiches from the bar, which Rita did not want her to have, but what could she do? Daisy was the ultimate paying customer.

Then Daisy went back up to the room with the junk in it and the view of the cars.

She did not know what was the anniversary of the possible, mooted hanging of the Magpie Hunter. But even if she had, would it have been useful? The earth shifted constantly, and time zones subtly altered. Greenwich mean time, daylight saving, leap years – all these would make havoc of exactitude. And if it would happen it would happen.

"Cheers," said Daisy to the Magpie Dress, and drank from the uncorked bottle.

7th Feather and Last

Seven's for Heav'n and eight's for Hell,
And nine's for the Deil, his ain sel.

The noises in the pub went on until midnight, because Rita or George obviously had friends in, drinking after hours. Then Rita and George came to bed, and there were tooth-brushings and lavatory flushings, and a final door slammed. Daisy heard Rita say, "…Might be anyone." But no one came to the closed door of the junk room. No one came to disturb Daisy and the Magpie Dress.

Daisy had drunk most of the bottle, and long ago eaten the sandwiches, which had been, oddly, very nice.

The dress hung in the window, faintly glared on by the suburb lights of Asham, as by the lamps of the capital. It looked thin and flightless.

Daisy thought, *I wish Agatha and Tony were here.*

Then she fell asleep. She was not surprised by what she found there.

Although the chamber of confession was not as Daisy would have guessed it to be. No, it was just a small room, lacking windows, with a crucifix on the wall, and a candle burning.

He stood there, the handsome priest. And he was beautiful. Yes, you would have to be insane not to want to possess him, or else, not a lover of men.

And she was, the girl. She had loved men before.

She was stirred by their bodies. The gorgeous hardness, of muscle, of penis. Their hair and eyes that were like angels'.

And this one, this one...

The young nun spoke as she knelt there. And Daisy, hearing the words, knew them now not like sub-titles, but as if a parallel translation occurred within her inner ear.

"*Mea culpa.* I have sinned."

And he said nothing, only waited.

"I have sinned," said Beauty, her white face bowed, "because all I can think of is you. Not the Christ. You."

And then she stood up, and she looked at him. Her black eyes burned, but his eyes were blue and sere, cold as glaciers. He said nothing.

"Let me," she said, "let me touch you." And she crept to him and put her hand on his chest. "You have a heart," she said, "I feel it beating. Let me – oh, let me..." And she put her other hand on his face and tried to draw him down.

But the handsome face of the blond priest would not allow it. Like a mask, it floated over her. He said, "You will damn yourself. You are giving yourself to the Devil."

"No," she said. "Only to you."

And then she slid her other hand from his heart and put it over his groin.

He moved then, away from her.

He had the face of a king confronted by the most abject and filthy suppliant.

"No," he said. "Hell has got into you. Kneel down."

"I die," she said, "I *burn*..."

"You will burn in Hell. On your knees."

And she lay on her face then, and she wept. She said, "I love you."

Then he lifted her and struck her across the cheek, so that she fell once more. She lay on the ground again, weeping, and she pulled up her habit and her shift, black and white, and showed him the mound of her sex, which was covered with pure blonde hair, as on his own head.

"You are *here*," she said.

"And you are a demon," he said.

She sat up slowly. She was much paler than white. She whimpered. "Others," she said, "led me astray."

Then she confessed to him. How her brother had seduced her. How she had lain with grooms and soldiers. She said the Devil had come to her. She said she wanted to die. And all the while she wept, and her body, although covered up now, glowed like the flame on the shivering candle.

He listened like an icon. And when she was done, he told her he must seek guidance. And then she was afraid, afraid in the midst of lust and love and agony. And she begged him not to betray her, he must not, the seal of the confessional protected her. Only he could save her from the dark.

"No," he said. She was beyond him now.

Daisy went with her down a winding stair and up to a cell, in the shadow. Alone, the beautiful nun wrote a letter to her brother. Her tears fell on it, like blazing acid not yet invented. The letter told how she had been forced to betray their fraternal secret. *Kill him*, the letter said.

And then Daisy saw the old rough track, Fetherwies, by night, no moon, the hard cold points of stars, and the priest walking there in the dark, from which the beautiful nun had asked him to save her.

Near the statue of the Virgin, blanched and dry as a bone, the assassins came to him. There were seven of them but an unseen eighth – her brother – and an unseen ninth – herself.

"Do not forgive me Father, for I have not yet sinned…"

They stabbed and slashed with their blades, and he was cut in pieces, and broken.

His blood made a river under the trees.

When the dawn began to come, an angel did fall from Heaven.

It was the magpie.

It stooped above the carrion of the pale priest, it alighted on his breast. But then it only stared at him, stared and did not plunder. And eventually it lifted up into the gilding sky and flew away.

Karma. They had lived then, died then, and were reborn… She owed him her death, for his, since she had caused his death. And she had loved him. Had he gone looking for her, too, through the alleys and streets of Faithways in 1912? With a knife. Eight times he killed. And then he missed her, though she had gone to meet him. She had caught her death, had died – but wrongly, without his kiss. Margaret Shawn, the frigid nun, and her priest of the knife. *Lovers. Magpies.*

Daisy looked at the window of the junk room. Beyond the dress, there was no light. It was wholly dark, and dim, as if a fog had come and there had also been a power-cut. The room was abysmal.

She got up slowly. And walked to the window.

Outside was – nothing. Nothing at all.

Daisy was giddy. She backed away and sat down on a crate.

She put her hands together, held her own hand.

And then she heard them in the square that was no longer there. The crowd shouting as it pulled him along to the gallows. He had died twice. She heard the lurch and grind of wood. Then silence.

The silence was so thick.

I can't bear it.

But she must.

And then she felt the stirring through the air. Up out of time and night. A touch came on the window like the brush of a wing. And the dress quivered.

A slit shot through the window – and through the dress. Once – twice – again, again. Daisy felt the power of the air and of the dark. She fell sidelong on the floor, still holding her hand.

The knife – invisible – sliced through the dress over and over, over and over again. And in the air, soundless, the high orgasmic scream. Penetration, perfection, payment.

Then it was gone.

It was gone.

Daisy looked.

The glass was cut in shards, none of which had fallen out, like a pattern of strange frost.

And the dress was all in ribbons. Black and white. White and black.

"At last," Daisy said. She put her head into her comforting arms. Peace and quiet. And as the streetlamp light of twentieth-century cities came back into the window, behind the shreds of the slashed and murdered dress, she said again, softly, "At last."

The Persecution Machine

Dedicated to the Matchless Edward Gorey

I: Uncle

My father galloped into the library with a look of terror. "Your uncle is coming!"

"My – uncle? Who do you mean?"

"Constant."

"But I thought…"

"No," said my father, running to the window and glaring out nervously. "He isn't dead. Only mad."

"I see."

"Of course you don't." My father spared a look of distaste for me. As his son, I had had certain duties never properly explained, one of which had been to become a perfect replica of himself in the city of business. Instead I had metamorphosed into a fashionable writer, and it was not in him to forgive me. "Well," he said now, "since you're so clever. I'll leave you to entertain him. Try telling him who you are."

"We've discussed this previously. I'm not clever, only a genius. As for Uncle Constant, if he's calling here, presumably he wishes to see *you*. After all, does he even know of my existence? I'm sure I didn't know of his."

"It was kept from you. I expect *he* will have learned. Twenty years since I saw him. Horrible."

"Is he deformed?" I inquired with pleasant anticipation.

"No. Only his mind. Stall the wretch. Get him to leave if possible."

I shrugged. "Does mother share your aversion?"

"Your mother will faint," said my father, "if he so much as touches the panels of her parlour door."

My mother tended to faint continually when confronted by annoyance. She had already fainted once at my arrival. My father had had the grace only to offer to throw me out. A recent short novel of mine, dealing with forbidden love, very, I may say, tastefully, had caused their latest dislike of me. I, meanwhile, came to visit them from a sense of responsibility, since they were always in want of money.

But what was the motive for mad Constant's arrival?

The doorbell rang below. My father shrieked and rushed from the room.

When Steppings appeared presently in the library door, I accordingly asked him to show the visitor up.

A moment later, my Uncle Constant was revealed to me.

He was a man of about fifty-eight or sixty, corpulent but pale, with a mane of grey hair and disordered clothes. He seemed out of breath, as if he had been running, and he darted a wild look about the room. "Are we alone?" he demanded.

"I believe so."

"Who are you?"

"Your nephew, Charles."

"Who? Oh, never mind it. Only let me sit down. I'm exhausted. They've pursued me all day. Not a second's peace." He fell noisily into a large chair.

Steppings reappeared, mostly from nosiness, but I sent him off to bring some of my father's Madeira. I had no qualms in this, since I had supplied the wine myself.

"Well, uncle. How may I help you?"

"Help? Impossible. No one can help. I ask only a minute's respite." His breathing quietened a little, and he blew his nose into a gigantic handkerchief. "It's no use my explaining. Only I understand what I suffer."

"This may be said of each of us."

"I see you're a philosopher, sir. Did you say we are related? My God, I've run into my brother's house, haven't I?"

"Didn't you know?"

"I will run in anywhere I am able when they are after me."

"Who? Do you mean the police?"

My Uncle Constant was racked with melodramatic laughter.

Steppings came in with the wine and a tray of biscuits.

Constant struck the tray and the biscuits flew in all directions. Steppings did not flinch, merely put on the expression of a surprised chicken, which has seen such good service over the years. I rescued the Madeira and poured two glasses, waving the chicken away as I did so.

"Drink this."

"Is it poison?"

"I don't think so."

"Nothing short of poison is any use to me. I pant to be released from my suffering. But suicide is a sin." After all, Uncle Constant reminded me of my father. He drank the Madeira at a gulp, and I refilled his glass. "They're after me, worse than ever. Their weapons –

If only you knew.

He, as my father had done, bustled to the window. He stared out, I assumed, at the peaceful street.

"Not yet," he muttered. "But soon."

"And you have no matters to consult my father upon?" I asked.

"Who? Who is your father?"

"Your brother."

"I have no brother," said Uncle Constant. "I am cast out into the wilderness." Then his face contorted. It grew red, then blue. "I hear it!" he cried. And flinging the goblet on the ground, or rather the carpet, he sprang away and was gone. I heard his cascade down the stair and the crash of the street door.

I stood by the window and presently saw him emerge and scuttle fatly down the street. He disappeared from view.

2: Uncle's Story

Although I questioned my father and mother about my Uncle Constant, neither told me anything. My father ranted and my mother fainted. Steppings looked like a chicken, and when I tried to enlist his help, only importuned me to persuade my parents to use a new sort of cheese in the mouse-traps. I told him that I disapproved of mouse-traps. Steppings confided that he himself ate the cheese, it was a harmless perversion, during which he sometimes emitted small squeaks.

I was touched by his trust, but it did not help me to discover my uncle.

However, a month later, endless searching led me to a tall gaunt house in the south of the Capital. Here, a gentleman bearing my uncle's name resided. The instant I beheld the house, I knew it must be he.

Large bars were on all the windows, and a sort of portcullis was let down outside the door.

On my ringing the door bell, through the portcullis, no one came.

It was a sunny day, and I sat down across the street on a low wall, to watch and wait.

Presently a maid came out of the house with the low wall.

She attempted some ineffectual dusting of the privet hedge, and then bent to my ear. "He's a madman, that one. You after him for a debt?

"Not at all. I am a long-lost lover of his, come to call on him."

"You're one of them preeverts," said the maid, and ran in.

Half an hour later, two sombrely-clad women, with the figures but not the charm of pigeons, came down the street, mounted my uncle's steps, and banged on the portcullis.

I could tell at a glance they were religious persons, and that a lack of response would not put them off. It did not. Getting no reply, they banged the louder. And the larger lady began to cry: "Open the doors of your hearts, O ye lost children of the Lord! Hear the word of the Master!"

I expected a window to be raised and some missile inserted through the bars and thrown.

Instead, to my surprise and delight, sounds of vast unlockings eventually echoed over the street, the portcullis lifted, and my uncle appeared in the doorway.

He wore a yellow dressing-gown and a look of fear and loathing.

"Be off!" he yelled at the two ladies, "I know your tricks. Where is it? Is it near? I won't be decoyed."

"Repent," said the large lady. "Here is a tract..." But Uncle Constant swept the article from her gloved hand.

"Away!" howled Uncle, and thrust her down the steps.

The lady fell upon the other one and both toppled to the ground. There was the hideous noise of bursting corsets.

Before my uncle could shut the door and the portcullis, I leapt across the street, over the wallowing ladies, and up the steps. I seized Uncle Constant's hand. "Uncle Constant!"

"Aah! Villain! Unhand me."

"I am your nephew, Charles," I intimated, as he tried to run me through with his sword-stick.

"Who?"

"Your nephew. We met a month ago."

"You're not one of their spies?" He peered at me. "No. Your hair's too long and you have no moustache. Come in, then. Quickly. Let me lock the house. I am in deadly peril. If they should once gain a foothold... There! Do you hear it? No. No, you would never hear it."

He slammed the door against the world and we were in a dark hall papered with a design of large red bats, or perhaps prehistoric birds.

"But I did hear..." I began. My uncle took no notice,

Once he had let down the portcullis by means of a switch, locked the door three times and bolted it twice, my uncle led me up a carpeted stair and into a small dim room. The bat wall-paper persisted, but otherwise there were chairs and a sofa and some brandy on a stand. Through the bars of the windows and heavy dusty lace, little was visible, and I imagined that he preferred this to be so.

161

"Sit down," said my uncle, "whoever you are."

"Uncle Constant, I did hear a noise. Perhaps a train?"

My uncle looked at me strangely. He frowned. Then going to the stand, poured out two generous brandies.

He did not, though, give either one to me, or take one himself. He left them where they were as a decoration.

"I will tell you my terrible tale," said my uncle.

"Thank you."

"You must not interrupt."

I nodded mutely.

Assuaged, perhaps, my uncle seated himself in a vast armchair that rather resembled a pig.

"In my youth," he began, "I had no cares. I did very much as I wanted. I had been thought too clever for school, and so a number of tutors had taught me at home. I had no friends and wished for none. My only interest, as I grew older, was collecting young actresses. Then one evening, on my way home from the theatre, I was met by a messenger in the street. My parents had perished in a fire at the house of an ice-cream manufacturer, and I had now inherited the family fortune."

Although I knew that my grandparents were not dead, and that there had never been a family fortune, I did not argue with Uncle Constant at this point. I felt that probably he was instinctively lying in order to give some frame-work to what might follow.

"I fell," he continued, as if gratified by my sensitive abstention, "into a melancholy. I stayed indoors and only wandered from room to room of the house, recalling the unhappy hours I had spent there with my parents, who were both obtuse and ugly. The prettiness of my actress collection came to repel me, and I saw these girls no more. After some months, I ventured out at night, and walked the nastiest thoroughfares of the city, until it was almost dawn. Gradually, as I was returning to the house, I became aware that I was being, and had indeed been for some while, followed, by a number of mysterious shadowy figures. At length, a peculiar noise resounded distantly behind the smoking chimneys and smouldering refuse pits of the alleys."

My uncle looked at me expectantly, but, true to his wish, I did not interrupt. Consoled, he went on.

"I can only describe this noise as that of some curious engine, which also whistled, rather like a factory hooter.

Chug chug, it went, and then *Whoop! Whoop!* Alarmed, I hastened home, but after I was indoors I heard something move down the street and a shadow was cast upon my windows."

My uncle got up, and going to the brandy glasses, he poured their contents into an aspidistra, then refilled them carefully from the decanter. He left them on the stand, and resumed his chair and his tale.

"Soon after this, when I had gone out once more on some necessary business, I was again followed, and after a time I heard repeated the ominous chugging and whooping of the sinister engine. I hurried at once onto a busy thoroughfare, and there the din of the crowd somewhat mitigated the sound of the pursuit. After a few minutes, however, a frightful shooting pain began in my right knee. And then another, worse, in my right arm. I fell against a lamppost, and an old gentleman came up and smote me in the face, accusing me of being drunk. As I partly lay there, I saw, through the ranks of the oblivious and jeering crowd, a fearful thing rolling slowly and mightily down from the end of the street. It was a sort of carriage, yet it had no horses, and from it protruded all manner of pipes and coils, wheels that whirred, and the nozzles of what could only be guns. Suddenly one of these flashed with a cold green fire, and a new pain lanced through my belly. Atop the device was a crew of men clad like explorers in long coats, goggles, and unlikely hats. They had moustaches, and their lips were thin and cruel. From the midst of them a funnel glowed and steamed, and out came the noise. *Chug, chug.* And then *Whoop, whoop.* No one in the street but I could see this evil equipage. I turned and as best I could for my hurts, I ran. The more distance I could put between myself and the engine of torment the more relief I gained, and finally I shut myself into the house and knew an end to my pain. Its four walls, imbued as they were with boring memories of my parents, protected me. But as I crouched behind the door, the machine passed down the street. Its shadow fell again inside the house. From that, day, I have not been free of it."

My uncle rose once more and paced to an empty parrot cage. He stared into it and shook his head.

"So far, they have not gained access to my home. Now and then their spies seek me. The machine never lies in wait for me outside the house... a sporting chance is allowed me – although they are not really fair. If ever the machine can by stealth enter these premises, I am lost."

A vague rumbling sounded in the street. A faint shadow crossed the window and next the ceiling. I got up and went to look out. The street was empty, but for another maid dusting a hedge, and two porters carrying a stuffed bear. The religious ladies had picked themselves up and gone away.

"You may speak now," said my uncle.

"Have you," I asked, "approached no one for help?"

"In the beginning, ceaselessly. I went to the police, and then to private companies. But all laughed me to scorn. An eminent doctor has certified that I am harmlessly mad."

"The engine or machine is invisible to all others but yourself?"

My uncle returned to the brandy stand and drank both glasses of brandy. "I am doomed." He then showed me out of the house.

3. Uncle Pursued

After that second meeting, I took to following my Uncle Constant.

He went out, as can be imagined from his fears, very seldom, and so my vigils were frequently long, dull and unrewarded – except by the emergence of the privet-dusting maid, who seemed to think, despite my 'preeversion' that I fancied her person.

This was rather trying. However.

Finally, my uncle began to slip cautiously out of the house on hobbled rapid errands.

He would first of all open the door a crack, having of course noisily unlocked and unbolted it, and raised the portcullis. He would then gaze fixedly at each side of the street in turn. He never noticed me, even when I had not taken the trouble of obscuring myself behind the hedge. And I noted presently that, even if he looked at me on the street, he never recalled who I was, or that I was anyone but a complete stranger.

Having perused both directions, Uncle Constant would leap forth and bolt one way or the other. Being portly, his quickness soon flagged, but he kept up what pace he could, his arms clutched to his chest, rather in the manner of a squirrel. Now and then he would break into a run. And frequently, he would glare behind him. In doing this, he often saw me, but paid, as I have said, no heed.

I, on the other hand, listened as intently and turned round as often as he.

It seemed to me that I heard a familiar noise in the distance, but I could not be sure how near we might be to some bizarre railway line or extraordinary factory, which might produce such sounds. Then, too, it sometimes seemed to me that shadows appeared at the ends of streets which bisected those pavements along which Uncle Constant rattled. Yet too I was never certain ordinary objects might not somehow have cast these shadows, and besides they were always fleeting.

Meanwhile, other people and things moved all round us in the normal manner. My uncle occasionally barged into them, so oblivious was he of anything but the persecuting pursuit.

He never returned from his expeditions by the same route he had set out on, but always via a roundabout circuit. For presumably he was afraid, if the machine of torment was somewhere behind him, he might otherwise meet it head-on.

Uncle's outings were mundane and sketchy. Sorties upon shops of food and chemists' emporiums, and once a journey to a well-known and reputable bank. On this last foray, he emerged from the august portals amid cries and clangs, and squirreled down the steps, clutching at his left leg and muttering: "They're near." He was obviously in pain, and intercepting his terrified glance, I too looked back along the street.

The vista was thronged with people, and on the road were several carriages. It was apparent that no vehicle could pass unseen, if it were really there. As I gazed, it seemed to me that there was indeed something moving slowly and ponderously under the archway that opened the street. A faint greenish beam was struck from the place that might only be the morning sun upon some harness or other metallic item. My uncle distracted me with a hoarse scream.

I turned and saw he had dropped to his knees. A bank-note fell from his hand, and I ran over, stopping the money before someone should snatch it, and next trying to assist him.

"Uncle - "

"Let me go, wretch!" screeched Uncle Constant, hitting me so violently in the chest that I too was flung on the ground. Before I could right myself, he was up and hobbling and moaning away.

I then decided that, rather than rush after him in the usual fashion, I would wait at the roadside to see if any unusual carriage came past. I was encouraged in this idea by a repetition of the unlikely noise I had heard before – the *chug* and *whoop* of a mad engine, whistle or hooter. Then again, the street was noisy itself and I could not quite be sure.

I waited at the kerb for twenty minutes, by which time all the approaching traffic had gone by and my uncle was completely out of sight.

Irritated, I then stalked back up the road, and found an intersection. Staring down one of the opposing boulevards, I had the impression that something was trundling away there. Before I could go after it, a band of religious choristers enveloped me, and I was forced to give them cash before I could escape. By then, naturally, any hint of what might have been a strange vehicle, or only an optical illusion generated by sympathy and hope for the unnatural, had vanished.

I returned to my uncle's house in a bad mood, and he was already indoors, the portcullis down and all signs of life concealed.

After this jaunt, he did not venture out again, though I waited, for many weeks.

Unfortunately, my own life was becoming complicated. I was supposed to be at work upon a new volume of tasteful obliqueness, and had neglected it sadly. Various creditors were restless, and I was already receiving fewer social invitations. My publisher advised me that unless I took up my employment, the public would forget me, and I feared I would therefore no longer have the money to support my feckless parents, who were just then in the process of buying whole suites of unsuitable furniture, busts of Roman generals and a black parrot.

Regretfully, I left my post at the low wall opposite to my uncle's house. It was a fine evening, the west still flushed with dusk, and a lone light burned in an upper window. And far off, without a doubt at this moment, I heard it in the stillness, *Chug chug chug* and then its *Whoop* on a high weird note. It was circling at a distance, like a beast of prey, the campfire of that solitary lamp.

But I could no longer stay.

I went to my home, and my novel; so much more real than uncle's predicament.

4: The Machine

It was on the afternoon that I delivered the finished manuscript of *The Fateful Kiss of Night* to my publishers that the last act of Uncle Constant's tragedy was played before me, and I was pulled irresistibly into it.

A beautiful afternoon of early summer, it had drawn the idle and the pleasure-seekers into the park. As I walked along beside the river the swans glided past like pillows with white necks, and the nurse-maids wheeled their bonneted toy babies up and down in perambulators. Young men pensively reflected in the glassy water, maidens sat reading under the statues, hoping the young men were secretly watching them, which, usually, they were not.

About two hundred yards off, over the wall of the park and its line of tall trees, an ominous sound came and went, and I had glanced that way in a consternation I did not at first fathom. But although an apparatus was out there, it was only a steam engine, resurfacing the roadway with pitch. With a sense of relief or disappointment, I returned my eyes to the picture-postcard scene of the park.

Across the flower-beds lay a lawn, at the centre of which was a coloured bandstand. Here, the bandsmen were going at full blast, and on the lawn couples bumpily danced a polka.

The warm day lay limpid on the park, with all its safe and proper comings and goings, a postcard view, as I say, into which an unsuitable figure abruptly burst: Uncle Constant.

Of those assembled, I was not the least startled.

How he had come there was beyond ascertaining, he seemed merely to erupt into being. And my premonition of the steam-roller was appropriate. Uncle was as usual in headlong flight. Indeed, he was in the most abject condition I had yet beheld, and through his wheezing, he faintly screamed.

As people hastened from his way, a few turned their heads anxiously to see what it was he fled from, what it was he saw as his head craned at a painful angle over one shoulder. But having turned, they shrugged and one or two made good-mannered gestures relating to insanity, while three pompous gentlemen began to shout for the police.

I also turned, more from habit than from the hope of finding anything.

And so I saw, at last, coming across the wholesome green grass on which little children played and young ladies walked with their parasols, the moving engine of my uncle's terror.

It was unmistakable. It was tall as the second storey of a fashionable house, and it glided smoothly forward on great black runners. Its look was of a monstrous bath-chair, but one which bristled like a porcupine. Pipes and nozzles protruded from it, ornamental and deadly: one glance assured me that each must be a variety of gun. And even as I stared, one indeed gave off a puff of dull viridian smoke followed by a quick white flash. And over the merry noise of the park I heard my uncle howl with pain. I did not look to see if he had fallen. My eyes were fastened to the machine of his persecution.

Aloft, on a sort of balcony above the horseless, rolling carriage-front, were packed about ten persons. Perhaps they were men, they appeared to be, and yet... and yet there was something palpably wrong about them which my study unpleasingly revealed. Their dark overcoats were moulded to their bodies in the same manner that wings mould to the back of a black beetle. Their black moustaches quivered and seemed to move of their own will. And their eyes had been goggled over with curious dark green glasses that were facetted in many tiny winking panes.

Above them, and behind, a funnel rose from the top of the machine. Even as I glared at it, one of the riders touched its side with a gloved hand on which, perhaps, there were two or three extra fingers. The funnel responded with a dim glow and a gout of steam burst from the crown. Over the horrible thundering rattle and chug of the vehicle's progress, shrieked a deafening *Whoop! Whoop!*

Frantically, at last, I gazed about, to observe the bystanders forced to put their hands over their ears.

But, just as they did not appear to see the machine, so they apparently could not hear it.

Even so, even so. As it trundled its inexorable and menacing way forward over the emerald grass, the children gambolled from its path, the girls increased their pace and swept aside. As if at a whim. Yes, as it advanced, the crowd parted before it, but not one of them paid it the slightest overt attention. Not one – save I. And my Uncle Constant.

He had certainly collapsed, but soon struggled up again. And now he limped and tottered on, striving to escape across the park. How desperate he looked. His face was white and blind with fear. He did not think, it was evident, he could on this occasion get to safety.

The machine went by me. It passed within three feet. I too must have taken some instinctive steps aside.

A furnace heat came from the thing, and the terrible chugging was accompanied by showers of cold green sparks from its runners.

Uncle limped over the flower-beds and rambled out onto the dancing sward. Couples bumped into him and waved him aside. He skirted the bandstand and went painfully on towards the wall.

The machine did not, or could not, improve its speed. Yet its unavoidable quality was somehow augmented by its very slowness, as in a dream.

It ploughed in among the dancers, who bounced and swung from its way, not looking at it, not hearing or seeing it. Unlike my uncle, seeming to have to move in a straight line, it came directly at the bandstand, and there, peculiar protuberances, like the rubbery legs of some enormous fly, poured out and raised the runners, and so walked the whole contraption up into the midst of the band, the top of the machine only narrowly missing knocking off the roof.

The musicians were forced to scramble to the perimeters, juggling their instruments.

And yet – even in this extremity – not one man regarded the invader, and not *one* lost the beat of their foolish dance.

And then the horror had marched on, and over, and was down on the lawn again, and all the band resettled, banging and tooting the jolly tune without a break.

A fierce ray flashed.

I saw my uncle sprawl headfirst.

Instantly he had pushed himself up, but now he could not rise from his knees. He began to crawl towards the wall of the park.

For a moment, I stood at a loss. And then some primal spirit took hold of me.

I raced.

I sprinted over the lawn, scattering and possibly felling the polkists left and right. I tore past the machine itself, and felt again its awful heat, and smelled its metals and its odour of a chemical swamp, and of some location inexplicable.

Even past my Uncle Constant I sprang, and reaching the wall, I bolted through the gate.

Outside, the steamroller majestically moved, and its motion was very like that other one, that wallow of the machine. I flung myself upon the steam engine and wasted no time in hauling myself up its side. The driver was startled as I barged in beside him. I thrust some coins into his palm and cast him out, and he plummeted angrily on to the pitchy road, shouting.

I turned the steam engine with difficulty but with determination, and drove it back through the gates.

My uncle was crawling steadfastly on, but thank God he had the sense to pull himself from my road. I cranked my colossus onward, until I beheld the persecution machine exactly in my path.

It did not veer, perhaps it could not. No expression crossed the faces – if such they were – of its malefic crew. Only the moustaches wrinkled and the goggles glittered, and from the stack of the funnel went up another gout of white and another fiendish whistle.

I sent the steamroller headlong. With a grinding of gears and a furious hissing, it pounded forward into battle.

Until I could see every beaded decoration on the nozzles of the ray guns, I held to my post. Then I jumped away. I landed in a rhododendron bush. And at that moment the two leviathans came together.

There was an explosion like the Trump of Doom. And then a tumult only like that of some apocalyptic train crash.

A light like an incendiary burst, and out of it huge pieces of things were hurled into the air and dashed all about, boiling and gushing, and black metal rods, wheels, plates, cogs, screws, all types of mechanical and peculiar debris smashed down over the park.

Not a single cry or scream attended this.

But looking up from my bush, I saw the monstrous crew of the machine also hurtling through space, and they were broken in a way human creatures do not break. Black blood or slime rained all around. It smelled medicinal and acid.

Presently the hurricane ceased, and a great stillness should have settled, but did not, for the park had gone on at its music and its chat uninterrupted.

I stared. Swans swam peacefully among black irregular objects in the river. Young ladies, blood-splattered, danced brightly with their bloodied gentlemen, between rivets and black smoking shafts stuck down in the earth like flaming bones. Craters had appeared. And these the dancers carelessly circled. While the band played on, despite the green-goggled heads, which had fallen on the bandstand roof, the instruments streaked with blood and coiled with what were, conceivably, alien entrails.

Of the machine, nothing but a sort of heaving slag remained. There was little either of the noble steamroller.

I went to my uncle and helped him up.

"It is over," I said.

"Who are you?" he demanded.

Outside the wall, the driver of the steam engine had left off his complaints. He sat smoking at the roadside, as if that was his only purpose, and touched his cap to me.

I assisted my uncle to his house.

Flower Water

Lady Emeraldine Morrow vanished, or died, yesterday, and the circumstances were reported in many of the papers. It was the bizarre nature of events and their number of witnesses, which led to the publicity.

In the midst of a private festival, as the sun began to set, Lady Emeraldine was rowed across her small private lake, to her small private island. Just visible from shore, she there commenced to regale her three hundred guests with vivid torrents of music on her harp.

Her many accomplishments coupled to her great beauty, have been well-known and much publicised for years. Also, her enormous good humour, her happy, light-hearted disposition. And, in some circles, her apparent callousness.

The music rang out, chords, glissandi, and the sun sank into the woods, and the sky turned from crimson to the coolest mauve.

It was at this moment, in the last of the twilight, that Lady Emeraldine ceased playing, in the very middle of a spirited improvisation. As startled applause broke forth, a loud cry soared upwards from the island. Then came a burst of flame, a sort of explosion. Something quite small, dark and hard, shot into the air, then fell down into the lake, and with a sizzle, disappeared.

Guests swam or rowed in swarms to the island. They found a charred place beside the harp, which was itself unscathed. Of Lady Emeraldine there was no evidence at all.

There has of course been talk of spontaneous combustion, or of abduction by fiery creatures from some other world. Myself, I am strongly inclined to think that Lady Emeraldine was one of us.

Until I met him, under the coloured lamps of the Public Gardens, I had had an unpleasant life. My story is all too common. Father a drunkard; Mother a washerwoman. Put out at fifteen on the streets. Here I unoriginally plied my trade in the oldest profession on earth, and with limited success, being neither very attractive, nor very enthusiastic, and by no means a talented actress.

As the years passed, I had been also beaten and abused. I had thieved and been thieved from. I developed the expected passion for gin, and lost the last of my slight looks. Some of my teeth dropped out, my eyes were dim, my balance unpredictable. In this state, at twenty-four, here I was in the Gardens, not looking for custom, certainly, but tottering up and down, blearily eying the paper lanterns in mawkish solitude, before a police constable should behold and move me along.

When he spoke to me, indeed I took him for the police.

"Can't a poor old girl come in and joy herself for five minutes for no cost, without she gets herded away?" I whined, in traditional, useless obstinacy.

"I don't suggest you go," he said, with a voice too educated for any of the police I had come across, which had been many. "No, stay with me."

"What, you want a walk with me, do you?" I croaked.

I said, I was no actress, and though I had been trying to act the pathetic, sodden old harlot I had become, for at least five years, was really no good at it.

"I'd like to hear your story," said he.

"Soon told. For the price of a gin."

"Champagne," said he.

At that I felt I should straighten up. "For the likes of me? What are you after? What's your game?"

He was young, rich and handsome. He shone with health and wealth and grooming. He must therefore have some perverted whim. Fill me with expensive liquor and then slice me in scollops.

"We can remain at all times in the general gaze," he said. "I was only moved by your plight." But when he said that, he suddenly burst out laughing. I could see, in fact, he had the most carefree face I had ever looked at. I have seen one more such, since then. But I will come to that.

"Lead on then, Charlie," I said, thinking he was truly mad.

"My name is Raphael Pemberton. And yours?"

"Lizzie Lines."

We shook hands, and all about, very likely, the fashionable persons in the park glanced askance at us.

He took me to the open ballroom in the centre of the Gardens, and straight off ordered two bottles of a famous champagne, on ice, also plates of oysters, bits of geese in aspic, jellies, cakes, and heaven knows what.

As I sat there, I thought, *He must be going to poison me, slip something in my glass. Blame my demise on my weak condition.* I wracked my brains to remember strange deaths of blowsy, nasty whores in public thoroughfares, with a handsome gentleman nearby. Probably I had only missed hearing of them.

In any event, my life was not so grand I yearned that much to keep it, or so it seemed after a couple of draughts of the champagne.

Raphael Pemberton meanwhile, began to question me. He wanted to learn about this vile existence I had had. He could see, he told me, I had suffered.

As I regaled him with my history, thickly laying on all the horrors, and inventing several new ones – my dying mother's bedside with the non-existent little ones snivelling in my skirts, my noble father renouncing the drink, and dying of want of it – actually he had been squashed by a run-away beer barrel – Raphael stared at me, his face working as if with grief until, every few moments, he burst out laughing again.

With the champagne, I too began to see the funny side of me, and soon we were rolling in the aisles, a sideshow for the adjoining tables.

Additionally, I forgot to act my part. I became myself.

At last he said, between our gulps and hiccups, "You seem improved, Lizzie."

"Well," I said, "both my parents trod the boards – the stage, that is – before their luck changed. I had no talent, but I learned how to speak. Is that," I added, "why you're so amused?"

His pretty face fell. "No. Oh no, Lizzie." Then he bloomed, I have to say, like the rose in his buttonhole. "What a beautiful night."

"Not bad," said I.

"Tell me, Lizzie," said Raphael Pemberton, as we began upon the third bottle, "would you like to be young and lovely again?"

"I'm not so old as I look. It's the gin wot's done for me, guv'nor. I was *never* lovely."

"For the first, then, Lizzie. How about it?"

"If you're buying."

"Selling, in a way. How old would you say *I* was?"

I squinted. Strong drink, by removing all pretence at focus, had oddly improved my vision. "Twenty-one," I said.

"Wrong, Lizzie. Seventy-one would be nearer the mark."

I smiled. Humour the fool. We were, as he had said, in the general gaze. And it seemed he had not poisoned me. Yet.

"You don't believe me, Lizzie Lines. Of course not. I look young. I'm handsome. And, evidently, well-off. The latter springs from the former. It can for you. I feel so happy, Lizzie. How do you feel?"

"I feel splendid. When the drink wears off, I'll be back where I was."

"Just imagine," said Raphael Pemberton, "there was a drink that never wore off at all."

"Oh yes?"

"A drink that, after one swallow, made you feel so well, so glad, as if – as if your heart was full of stars. Always just a little tipsy. Never a bad day. Never a sad night. No pain. No sorrow. Think of it, Lizzie."

"I am."

"Does it appeal?"

"What do you think? Besides, obviously, it makes you young. Twenty-one, seventy-one. And good-looking. And it makes you rich, too?"

"Wealth comes from the rest. If you're utterly healthy, completely attractive, and your mind sharp, and your attitude merry at all times – you can't avoid riches, Lizzie, getting to be rich. Just think what you could have done, with all that."

"Well, Raphie, I didn't have the chance, did I?"

"You have it now."

He gazed at me soberly for all of three seconds. Then he grinned. Well-being flashed and flamed from him. You could never think a blazing torch looked sick.

"This is a drink," I said.

"Yes, Lizzie. And I offer it to you."

"Why?"

"I have just one dose, and I must give it to someone."

"And why is that?"

"Because, outside the human frame, it's indestructible. I can't pour it away. Not down a drain. Not into the sea.

I don't even want to lock it up, because, in a thousand years, someone might find it. But you. I think you deserve it, Lizzie."

"Oh, yes. And why is *that*? For my terrible life?"

"Because you're such a bitch."

He told me then, as the dancers cavorted on the ballroom floor and the lamps burned lower in the trees, and the fourth bottle came, and I knew that, jolly as a jack-rabbit, in the morning I was going to wish I was dead – he told me about Aquaflora,

Someone had found a hidden spring, it transpired, beneath a temple in Italy dedicated, in pagan times, to the goddess of nature, Flora.

This someone, whose name Raphael Pemberton claimed not to know, had drawn from the spring – reputed, according to a Latin inscription above the fount, to restore, heal and bless – one flask. An ancient legend declared that barren women had sought the fount and drunk there in order to bear children, also that cripples had washed in it and grown whole, elderly men got back their youth, and many other such tales. What had become of all these recipients of miracles had never been said, but in the end, the spring was shut away by the priestess for reasons of spite.

The modern explorer who found the spring did not think for a moment it possessed any unusual qualities. He took the water as a curiosity. A day later, returning to the spot on other exploratory business, he found the spring had mysteriously quite dried up again. With the other excitements of his trip, he soon forgot the matter.

It was over a year later, once more at home, that the traveller again took notice of the flask from Flora's spring. By this time, he desired to impress a young lady, and so he bore the flask to her house, told her that here was the wine of the goddess of flowers, and she, out of bravura, poured a few drops into her tea cup, and drank them.

Within a quarter of an hour, a change became apparent. Her undeniable prettiness had escalated to a potent glamour. A strain in her left foot that had been annoying her for days, vanished. Her hair, which was not very thick, took such a turn towards the luxuriant that all the pins fell out in a downpour. Within the day, she could see farther than the most far-sighted man in her father's regiment, could hear a bat squeak, and had mastered the pianoforte, which so far had eluded her, to the point of rendering the Minute Waltz in forty seconds. Her skin was like cream, her grace that of a swan, and two missing teeth had grown back.

Her unnamed swain, the traveller, lost no time himself in sampling the juice from the holy spring.

Presently two of the most attractive people in the country walked to the altar.

"And lived happily ever after," said I. "I suppose, in *fact*, for ever?"

"No," said Raphael Pemberton.

It seemed that the fortunate couple had somehow slipped from the annals of history, and after them only the flask had remained, its contents next portioned out in several equal measures.

"How many?" I asked.

"That I can't say. The last will and testament which brought me mine, informed me of nothing but the basic tale, and that the fluid, which might be called the Elixir or Life, but which was only named as Aquaflora, would give me health, youth, physical glory, luck, and perpetual happiness." At which Raphael Pemberton lifted his marvellous face to the sky. "And it has! Oh God, it has!"

"But there are others?"

"Many. How many I have no idea. Sometimes – I believe I have unearthed one. People of great beauty and talent. People who are never for a moment sad. I read once of a fellow screaming with mirth at a funeral. I sought him out. I'd been wrong, he was only subject to a rare laughing disease."

We drank a little more champagne. The sixth bottle now, I thought.

"You said," said I, "that you reckoned me a bitch."

"Well you are, aren't you," said my host, smiling lovingly at me. "All around me I can see the poor and ill and needy and broken. But you're a clown, Lizzie. You mock us all and you mean no one any good, not even yourself."

"Fine words for a fine gentleman," squawked I.

But, "Look," said Raphael. And from his coat he drew out a tiny little phial full of a muddy brown mess. "With my own mouthful of the water came this other one. It may be these were the two last measures from the flask. One for me. One for someone of my choosing."

"So you want to waste it on me. On a bitch. What about your mother? Your wife? Your mistress? Your fancy boy?"

"All of those," said Raphael, careless, light of heart, "are long dead. You see, when I took my dram, I was aging and almost alone. I didn't hesitate. And when I looked into my mirror, what a roar I sent up. I've been roaring ever since. Oh Lizzie. The worst news can't shake me. When I learned my only son had died, I had to hide my habitual, genuine, smiles with a copy of The Times. If the world were to end, there I'd be in space, charming as a comet, spinning with pleasure. *Nothing*, Lizzie, can bring me down. Think of it, Lizzie."

"But you want it for me as a *punishment?*"

"Not quite. It will suit you, Lizzie. You laugh at us all. It's in you already."

"There must be some catch."

"Can you think of one?" he asked.

I looked at him. After all the booze, I did believe the story, and the filthy-looking muck in the glass vial might well be a magic potion. My days had been devoid of any nice thing. Was I not due for some colossal change in fortune?

"It's poison," I said.

"It's water of flowers."

I had a strange notion then. I remembered some flowers in a vase in a public house where I had been sitting on a sailor's lap, and the flowers were past their best. In the obligatory fight which followed, the vase was knocked down and the flowers spilled and the water ran out on the edge of my dress. What a stink it had, that flower water.

But the lights were growing dull, and I bethought me of the Last Chance, the Final Risk, which, in fairy stories, and the silly dramas my parents had acted on the stage, must be taken, or lost for ever.

So I uncorked the phial, sniffed it – it had actually no odour – and sipped. I waited a little after that, to see if there were any burning or discomfort. Nothing happened. So I tipped the contents, the Aquaflora, down my throat.

"Cheers."

"Cheers, Lizzie," said Raphael.

And then he got up, and we went on to the floor, and danced a polka.

I knew I was drunk enough to try, but soon enough I understood that now I had a mastery of this polka that is not given to many. And by the time they had cleared the floor to watch us, and by the time the orchestra itself surrendered and stood applauding, and I felt my back was straight, and my corset loose at my waist, and my hair tumbling down the colour of polished coal, and my hand white on his sleeve, and I could see every tree to the termination of the mile-long avenue, and hear every individual hand clapping, I knew he had not lied.

The champagne was gone. I would never need a drink again. The world – was my oyster.

"I feel quite wonderful," I cried to Raphael.

"So do we all," he said, and his voice, for a moment, was black as iron in a pit, before he burst out laughing, and I with him, in ecstatic joy.

When I went home with Raphael Pemberton to his fine house in the square, I believed I was going there for the eternal reason, and for the first time in my life, I was looking forward to it. And perhaps, even more than that, to the bathroom he promised with the enormous mirror, where I could see to the full what so far I could only feel.

The servants were in bed – or perhaps dismissed, I now sometimes conclude – and he led me up the stairs by low light, and opened the door of the bathing apartment, which led off his chamber.

I left that door ajar, and outside I heard him in his vast bachelor bedroom, talking to me as I stripped under the gas-lamps, and showed myself the new Lizzie Lines.

I am accustomed to her now, this paragon of raven hair and hand-span waist and skin like lilies. But then I could not see enough, turning this way, that way. And licking round all my new growing teeth, and admiring my cornless feet, and washing myself the while in delicious pomades that now I could have for myself simply by smiling at a man – and to smile, when one is feeling so incredibly well and strong, and brave – and victorious – and safe, and confident – is easy.

Meantime, Raphael went on with a sort of monologue.

To start, I scarcely listened. But now, I piece it together somewhat, for in the end, I heard the end.

He spoke of all his shining days of happiness, not one with any flaw. And of his nights of blissful sleep unmarred even by any unappealing dream.

He spoke of his rise to wealth. Of all those idyllic spots he had visited and all those impossible conquests he had made. Of business ventures of pure success. Of the realisation that, whatever he wished for, would soon enough be his.

And laughing, sometimes breaking into snatches of happy music and song, unable to restrain the sweeping delight in all and everything, which I too now had within me, Raphael related how he had observed the miseries of the world, had looked upon its torments and its tears, even on its blood, and futile sacrifice, and never once had their shadows touched him.

"I've seen a woman hoarsely weeping at her husband's grave. I've seen the dead brought up in hundreds from a mine, I've seen a hopping child wasted by plague, and a city under a flood, and I've sung this very song, Lizzie.

"Lizzie, do you hear any strain in my voice? Do you, Lizzie? Regret, guilt, pain? No? I'm enwrapped in sweetness. For ever and a day."

I went out then, naked, in my exquisite flesh, and there he stood, Raphael Pemberton.

"Have you heard of the Last Straw, Lizzie? The one that breaks the back of the camel much overloaded? You, Lizzie, are it."

I laughed. I always laugh, now. Show me your wounds, I will lave them with laughter. If heaven falls, I shall fly above heaven. I cannot do otherwise.

"Perhaps you won't believe me, Lizzie Lines. I've offered this single phial of the elixir of life, this Aquaflora, seven hundred and eighty times, before I came to you. To the drunk I've offered it, and to the sober. To the rich and the destitute. To the sick, the dying, the agonised, and the mad. They all refused. This gave me some hope, Lizzie. But then, tonight, you crossed my path. I knew you at once. She'll take it, thought I. And so you did, Lizzie, you bitch."

And then Raphael Pemberton convulsed in a paean of hilarity, content and pleasure, and as he did so, there broke from him one howl of anger louder than any thunder. Then he was on fire. He went up like a firework. Vanished in a few seconds. Lightnings, sparks and gushes – I jumped back – laughing, of course laughing.

It took about a minute for all of him to be consumed in that golden detonation. And out of it there showered down only a veil of slightest ash, to touch the carpet scorched merely where he had stood. But one tiny, wizened black thing there was, that shot up and fell back, and lay there, which might have been his heart. All that is, that a lifetime of fulfilment, happiness, and perfect peace, had left of his heart.

There is no other phial of Aquaflora in existence, at least, I have none. Enviously I deduce, you would read of the delirious winders of my life, if I paused to repeat them. I have had all I want. More. A cornucopia. And, with good reason, I have never been sad. But, more to the point, even in the presence of the darkest and most awful, rent and desolate horror of this earth, never have I felt the faintest hint of hurt or sorrow. As for despair, I cannot even recall that angel with its sallow, leaden wings.

I look at you, without pity, for pity grows from fear. Your sufferings. Your endings.

With my heart brim-full of melody, I say, I, the smiling, beautiful and blessed, you cannot be more envious than I.

Your lovely pain, your tortures and your anguish that I cannot even in a dream recapture. Your loss, your rage, expressed in the poetry of words and souls, tragedy, romance – cheated, I.

Melody and laughter have shrivelled, by now, my heart, little as a raisin, like the heart of Raphael Pemberton, who gave me this.

Far, far off, like a mist glimpsed fading on a hill, I think I see – nights when I sobbed or stormed, the glories of agony. The power of riven love. And my destitution, and my bad sight, and how my teeth left my mouth. My triumph over these paltry terrible things. My dignity. My inheritance, my rights, the sword's edge, honing me, telling me of my life. But perhaps it did not, and I was only what he said, and deserved only what I got from him.

One day I too will flare up and be gone. Like Emeraldine Morrow, whose withered heart dropped in a lake.

For now, all is lovely. All is well. It cannot be otherwise. Aquaflora. Stinking water from those stagnant flowers.

I have only had ten years of it. One was enough.

What will bring to me the explosion of release, and let Lizzie from her prison of interminable heavenly joy?

For me, as for all of them, perhaps, though quite unfelt, it is that last being freed from a Pandora's box of human truth. *Exasperation.*

Stars Above, Stars Below

When the dust-storm had ended, Taira walked out into the desert. A court woman, she could not travel quite unattended. But she left her guard at the Temple of the Gate, pretending she was going in to pray. And her little slave, Aspa, she left in the last oasis by the road. By now, used to her whims, Aspa did not scold her; he was ten years old, at eight he had been impossible.

Taira walked along the road, then off the road into the rust-coloured desert, which was, in the sunfall, the soft shade of a fading, browning rose.

One final palm tree stood up from the dunes. A huge red palm, with beneath it a small altar to the desert God. Votary offerings left there had been covered with fine pink sand from the storm-breath of the God, who was savage, thankless and unkind.

Taira's feet were bare, for court women went barefoot in the palace and the city, whose floors and upper streets were kept smooth as glass. Warmth remained in the sand like a caress. She found this comforting, yet the comfort was useless. Everything had been tinged by utter loss. It was so enormous that she scarcely felt it as anything separate. The loss had become like breathing, or even awareness. Loss was now the condition of life.

Since the age of fourteen, Taira had served the priestess-queen Het-Ambaret. And this month, Het-Ambaret had died. Already the death ritual had been spoken. There was one line of it, which said: *The lamp of my heart has been put out. Though it may again be lighted, never again will it burn with this same flame of love.*

Tonight, when the Lion Moon rose, the death barge would set sail upon the river. Taira would stand in the barge, behind the sarcophagus of Het-Ambaret. It was a journey of three nights and two days, to reach the Tomb.

Taira, the chief maiden of a priestess-queen, was proud. She did not wish anyone to see her weep. So she walked into the desert of Kmur Ar to do it. And here she was, a mile from the marble city, a mile from the cool river.

Dimly on the sky, the city lights glimmered, and Taira caught the strands of some music, teased out by the last wind-breath of the desert God. Above, the stars had unveiled themselves, and the little moon,

180

the Kid, was coming up, tiny and almost opaque; but later the smallest of all, the Blue Moon would rise, glowing, the Virgin.

Peace lay in the cup of the desert, as well as terror and violence. For this Taira had come here. But as she stood alone, and composed herself for grief, no tears rushed from her eyes. She felt their pain, their scald, but no release.

She thought that she, a being of red amber like the planet, must now be growing dry like the planet, barren of water. But the planet was old, and she was young.

Taira thought deeply of Het-Ambaret. Her grace and beauty, her playfulness, her serenity, her gentleness. She had never struck Taira, or any of her women. And once, when Taira had been sad, over some love-affair, Het-Ambaret had singled her out, and come to console her, staying with her a whole afternoon. A skilled huntress, Het-Ambaret had even once brought Taira a portion of the kill, a sign of high favour, at which the surrounding court clapped, laughing, praising Taira and wishing her good fortune.

And now Het-Amaret lay in her gilded coffin-box, which showed on its painted lid the image of the priestess-queen as she had been in life.

Thinking still, Taira could not weep.

So she thought of Het-Ambaret divining in the temple of her Goddess, moving among the sacred things, pausing, selecting, while the priests wrote her findings on their slates. She had seldom been wrong, even in great age. As, in age, she had never lost her beauty, becoming only thinner, and more inclined to meditate and to sleep. At last, she slept and did not wake. It was Taira who found her, in her gilded chair on the terrace. The moons were high in the sky, all three, the blue Virgin the smallest and lowest and brightest of them, giving her lucency to the night like water.

Long ago, Het-Ambaret would have gone up to the highest roof, and sat there, all her ladies about her, if they had the energy to climb so far the palace steps; sometimes Taira followed alone. And then quite often Het-Ambaret would vanish away. The cool of night would grow chilly, even in summer. The women often walked down again without their queen, knowing she had sought solitude, and was communing with the heavens.

Thinking, thinking, still, still Taira could not weep. She gazed up into the sky. The little pale grey moon had moved some way, and already she should turn back.

She had not shed her tears. They lay inside her like drops of hot iron.

Dry like the planet, dry with sorrow, Taira returned across the desert.

At the oasis, Aspa came out without a word, and pattered after her, carrying her folded wooden parasol. At the Temple of the Gate, the guardsman, not knowing where Taira had gone, complacently fell in behind the boy.

Along the glass-smooth marble streets they went, towards the palace of columns, the stair, the quay where the barge waited on the river.

Gongs sounded from the temples, and all the high places of the city, to mark the rising of the Lion Moon, which was white, like the lions of the desert.

The death barge of Het-Ambaret slid from the quay, itself a phantom.

The women sang: *she will go up…*

Ten rowers dipped and stirred with their oars, making hardly any sound start from the thick shining waters of the river. Above, against the darkness, lit by all its red and rosy lights, the polished sandstone columns railed the facades of slender buildings, the great open windows, hung each one with a fretted golden or silver lamp. To the river's edge descended terraced gardens, planted with palms and traceried tinsel trees, where night birds called in wild moon-voices. But all these things swam by, and were soon gone. The lesser, more sombre fringes of the city appeared, and wharfs lit by fire-baskets, where soldiers stood, raising their spears to salute the barge. Then the wharfs gave way to vineyards and to fields, pierced by canals, until everything melted into the desert. Presently, on the farthest inland horizon, three tall volcanic mountains were visible, and farthest of all the volcano called the Torch, on which a blush of flame faintly flickered always.

The river grew wider then, opening out, and the desert, and its intermittent garland of palms, moved to a distance.

Now there was predominantly only night and water.

It became cold. The river flowed here from the Mountains of Ice. All rivers flowed from these mountains, crossing by and through the cities built mathematically on their banks, and so down to the abstract Sea of Smokes.

But the place of Tombs was not so far away as that.

The Kid was low in the sky now, and the blue Virgin smouldered between the volcanoes. Around the white Lion, stars burned in clusters. The river, shone, but nothing reflected in its movement save in fragments, not even stars or moons.

In an arbour at the boat's centre, the painted case lay, with the queen in it. How small the coffin looked.

Two ladies sat on either side, and two at the front. But Taira must stand behind the coffin, a sentinel. It was her duty, and the honour shown her.

Over her head hung the veil of mourning.

The women sang, sobbing sometimes, the death hymn. Taira listened. But the hymn seemed remote, not even sorrowful. The barge was ghostly, and the passing of the city, the threads of land now unravelling on either side, here and there set with an oasis, or some monument or statue, interested her vaguely, so her mind wandered.

She will go up among the stars.
Like a star she will live among the stars.
She will be winged as the stars
Are winged, with light.

The soft drum beat in the stern, making the stroke for the rowers.

If one looked carefully, on a clear night, a lion's face might be made out on the surface of the Lion Moon. But Taira could not see it. And after an hour or so, another dust-storm, rising elsewhere on the land, obscured the lion's face with a tawny veil like Taira's own.

The colouring of Taira's people was inside one spectrum. The hair, if undyed, mahogany red, the eyes reddish bronze, jasper, amber, the skin all the tones of reddish tan, from shades like powder to the depth of a copper mirror. But Het-Ambaret had been of another kind. She was generally black, and her eyes gold, freckled with shadow.

This the painting on the cask-lid showed exactly.

As the barge continued downriver, sometimes people came by day to the banks, and threw flowers into the water. Or, at certain points, where temples of the Goddess had been built, a privileged few might row out, and be permitted, while the barge was at anchor, to step on board.

Children stared at the painting of Het-Ambaret in wonder.

There were others of the queen's kind, but in this region only seven, now that she was gone.

"Was she truly so black?" the children asked Taira.

"As black as night," said Taira.

"But her eyes were golden stars," said a little boy, prophetically. Taira thought of Aspa, who was not prophetic at all.

The other women were moved. They cried openly. But Taira's tears stayed locked inside, hurting against her.

"She was the loveliest and best," said Taira, in a calm voice.

This was on the first day, and in the purple sky the sun blazed.

At noon, the barge again put down anchor. Under an awning, the women slept, as the rowers slept at their oars. Taira did not sleep. This was part of the ritual, and a herbal wine had been prepared, to help her stay wakeful. But Taira felt no need to sleep, had forgotten sleep.

The women had begun to tell her, from a few days after the queen's death, that they saw Het-Ambaret in their dreams. The priestess-queen was alive then, and spoke to them in her own magical language, which they had partly come over the years to understand. Her voice, as they recalled, was like a pale golden chime.

In the dreams, she was as she had been in her youth, plumper, and silken haired, but also she now, of course, had wings.

From Taira alone, pain apparently excluded such a visitation. Not once had she dreamed of the priestess-queen, though during Het-Ambaret's life, Taira had often dreamed of her. And as the post-mortem dreams failed Taira, so she had gradually given up sleep. In a way, it was similar with her tears, she would not, then could not, shed them.

Today, as the rest slept, she sat by the coffin-cask, and leaned her cheek against the planed wood. She spoke to Het-Ambaret in her mind. There were no reproaches – Why did you leave me? – mortal things had little choice.

Instead Taira thought, *Do you remember all those years ago, when we were so young, and we played the ball game in the court?* Or: *Remember how happy we were when you predicted an end to the drought, and rain came, the first in two years...* But then: *Oh, where are you?*

In the ancient time of myth, there had been a Flood, which covered all things. But before that time, the stories said, the people had been winged even in life, and had flown out to the moons, even to a place on the tiny Blue Moon, and built cities there. This country of the Blue Moon was like Kmur Ar, the Red Land, also a desert, with one vast river.

Myth told too how the Land of Life beyond life had its entrance in the skies between the planet and the Blue Moon. Here, the planet's river flowed up mysteriously into the purple sky. At first there was sunset, and then night, black night sown thick with stars. But one would know it was not the night of the land of mortal life. Because all at once the river, though still it flowed onwards, turned also to utter black, and was set with stars. So you drifted in your boat of death, between the star-gilded banks, where silver palm trees grew, and stars shone bright above, and just as bright and fixed they shone below in the river, and there was the sound of mystical sweet pure singing, beyond all physical voices ever heard.

At last, a sunrise would commence at the end of the river of stars, and here the Afterlife began.

The Afterlife held no censure, no punishment for any, and even for the worst transgression there was merely teaching, grief, empathic penitence and expiation. Which would at last fade away into the delight and freedom of eternity. But no one had described, even in myth, the nature of the Afterlife, beyond its indescribable bliss. They told only of the river of stars above and stars below which led serenely into it.

Het-Ambaret was supposedly there.

I must recollect that she is, thought Taira. *I must hope that she is…*

And she was, if so, glad for Het-Ambaret. So glad. But she thought too that never again in ordinary life would she, Taira, be able to see or hear Het-Ambaret, or softly smooth and comb her hair, or feel the warmth of her touch, or smell the fragrance of her – not once. This was as if it had been said to Taira, *Summer will never return* – or worse – *Summer never was real.*

They passed three more cities. At the third, a great ceremony was held, and hundreds of voices soared in the hymn to the dead. Gold and silver and jewels flashed, and flocks of birds clouded from the trees, while the sacred Ibu dippered their beaks in the river. The scaled river serpents which had legs, paddled up to the bank. They were thrown bread soaked in wine and red honey. They snapped the loaves up, jaws clashing, and the Ibu drew back, offended.

Taira, many nights and days now without sleep, her blood full of unshed tears, felt pain like a spike driven through her. So much *life* – and this little death that filled the world. She seemed to herself so light her feet did not meet the deck of the boat.

She drank some of the herbal wine. Not to keep from slumber – for surely she would never sleep again – but to stop her thirst – her dryness, her drought.

They poured honey before Met-Ambaret's cask, and put down dishes of baked meat and river fish, and beer and milk, for her Goddess received all these things, and she had liked some of them.

A handsome man from a high family, leant over the coffin and laid on it a pink lily, the kind that grew tall among the reeds. Het-Ambaret's women fluttered, even in their sadness. On his long dark hair, the sun found streams of brilliant copper red, his eyes and skin were very dark.

That evening, just before the barge departed on the last stretch of the journey, this man came aboard again, and bowed to Taira. "Lady, may I hope to see you again, in happier times?"

"You are kind," she said, "to wish me happier times."

"At the great city below the Torch, in a month, might I visit you? Meanwhile, may your sorrow leave you and joy return."

She saw in his dark eyes a promise of sexual desire, and perhaps more, perhaps the ember of love. Only these had made him precipitate. He was not unsympathetic. At any other hour, she would have quickened. But not now.

She smiled sadly at him. She was too courteous to say, *Do not trouble*.

The rowers rowed them away.

The swift sunset poured out like the red honey into moments of a lilac twilight. The night rose, with all the stars above.

Taira thought of Het-Ambaret, her body held firm and pristine by the embalming of the priests.

Taira thought of kissing for the last time the soft brow of the priestess-queen, which had grown cold, and hollow and doll-like with death. And of her shut eyes, the suns of which would never be revealed again.

Taira's tears moved behind her whole face, a wall of water, a Flood, the inundation. But all her doors were locked against them. She had lost the key.

On the third night, they came to the City of the Dead, which lay far downriver, but still many miles from the Sea of Smokes, where all the planet's waters finally perished in boiling steam – so travellers declared.

The drum had stopped beating. The rowers raised their oars. The barge rocked mildly, and the current alone moved it.

They drifted in among rows of towering tombs, which ran for miles beside the river and out into the dunes, and even went down into the water itself, like marble and sandstone animals, which had come there to drink.

Reeds grew here taller than a palace guard, whose head must always at least touch the lintel of each city's Soldiers' House. The pink lilies had gathered in nets, and the purple irises, which matched the sky. But now the lilies were simply pale, and the iris black.

There was a colonnade of pillars that led away from the river. The river ran off in a canal there, between them. The barge went into the canal without any guidance.

A current existed in the canal, perhaps natural, quite swift.

The rowers sat silent at their oars, and the women sat silent. But Taira raised her head and saw the stars above the columns, and under her hands she felt the wood of the painted box. She thought, *Now they will take even this from me.*

The death temple of Het-Ambaret's Goddess came from the night at the end of the canal. Before it, had been made a great statue of the Goddess. Though a giant, she was formed like any woman of Taira's people, but from the way her face had been carved, her nose and eyes and ears and mouth, one saw she was really of Het-Ambaret's kind.

She had a collar of skeins of coloured precious stones, and earrings of gold. In her carven skirt was a door. Which, as the barge approached, moved slowly open without a sound.

The barge slipped in through the door, and dropped anchor.

Steps ascended from the water, to a terrace, where priests and priestesses were gathering now. They carried tapers, which burned like a thousand golden eyes of the dead.

The painted casket of the queen was taken up, and carried among the priesthood, and Taira walked after, her head held high. They were singing in the voices of life, the praises of Het-Ambaret. And Taira sang with them.

Suddenly, without shame or fear, without thought, the tears flooded easily from Taira's eyes, and dropped like heavy rain, striking her feet in hot, wet, unhurtful blows. It was so easy to weep, after all. It was so easy, so simple. The light of the tapers glittered on her tears.

The hymn said now:

Her body is here, her body held in memory,
The memorial of our respect and honour,
The avowal of her beauty and virtue.
But she is in the land of life,
Where for ever she is living,
As in the heart, for ever she is loved.

All Het-Ambaret's women wept, loudly now, sobbing, and holding each other's hands. Taira with them.

The voices of the priesthood sang high up, sweet and pure, the prologue of supernatural songs to come.

For the beauty of the world was only an echo of a higher world.

All things must die, every man and woman, every beast, every tree and reed. Even the planet, Kmur Ar, the Red Land, one day would be a husk that lay empty upon the shore of a dusty sky. But the river of the stars would remain.

Taira thought, *I could not weep, it was impossible, and now I weep. It is so simple to weep. I could not love any other, but now I can, it is so simple to love. And I have thought it is impossible to live beyond death. But I shall live beyond death, and I shall see her again, and hold her in my arms, my queen, who lives beyond death now. And this too will be simple and easy. As easy as weeping.*

For a moment, neither a vision nor a dream, only a thought, Taira saw Het-Ambaret flying, winged, with a star on her forehead. And Taira's tears in the taper light made the stone roof above sparkle, as if with stars, and where her tears had fallen on the stone of the floor, they sparkled too like the stars below.

Author's Note:

To speculate an ancient race might once have lived on the planet we call Mars, is fanciful, but not entirely ridiculous. More fanciful is, perhaps, the notion that at one time 'Martians' reached the planet called by us Earth, and validated our own species. That a younger Mars generated water-courses seems to be a fact. But if so, fancy again conjures a recognisable resemblance between a waning desert Mars, her civilization clinging to the banks of yet-fertile rivers, and the Black Land of Egypt, a desert quenched only by the nurturing Nile.

In Egypt, certainly, the cat – whose kind may well have originated there – was loved and reverenced. Used in the temples as diviners, and worshipped directly in the person of the cat goddess Bastet, (Bast, Pasht) cats had servants and slaves allocated to them, and lived royally.

If anyone killed a cat, the sentence was death – if the crowd had not already stoned the murderers or torn them in pieces. After their lives, sacred cats, like high-caste humans, were mummified, and buried, sometimes with regal and priestly rites, as the cat necropolis at Bubastis on the Nile bears witness.

As for the mysteries of true love and true loss, they have many forms, and are surely universal among any race, human or otherwise, which possesses imagination, compassion, and emotion.

Unlocking the Golden Cage

To be poor, not young, unlovely – and alone – is a composite fate inflicted on many by the Angel of Misery. And so it was upon Agnes Drale, who, thirty-three years of age, and in a faded gown and unfashionable bonnet, walked up the two miles of the drive, to her late Uncle's manor, carrying her bag, one evening in the early autumn of 18—.

Another might have had high hopes, but not Agnes. Although it seemed, by the terms of the curious will, she was now supposedly to want for nothing, she understood quite well that the house and grounds, the title, and the coffers of the fortune had passed to her eighteen-year-old cousin, Genevieve, who was already wealthy and notoriously fair. Agnes was to be this woman's supplicant. And although, as the will stated, Agnes was to live in the great house, and have everything she required, it was to come to her by means of asking.

Throughout her life, Agnes had learned, utterly, that asking was ruinous, and mostly unwise. In church, at the age of ten, and on her knees by her narrow bed for three years more, she had asked God daily, nightly, to improve her looks. But God preferred to keep her as she was, thin and sallow; indeed He liked this so well, He added artistically to her appearance by bending her back and blearing her eyes, in the service of ungrateful and sometimes vicious children, so that now she had a sort of hump, and wore spectacles.

Other than God, the human race provided evidence of the inadvisability of asking: those who did not wish to employ her or, having done so, pay her; those who did not care to take a cup of tea with her in her room, preferring other friends more galvanic; those, like her father who, when she was twelve, refused her desperate plea not to die and leave her.

Agnes had never met her Uncle, but he seemed to her, rather than a benefactor, a cruel and perverse man, wishing to play some game even from the grave – for things were said of him, of his journeys in the East, and his private pleasures, which included alcohol and perhaps other stimulants more foreign.

Genevieve, of course, he had once visited, when she was a glimmering, ormolu child of fourteen. Agnes, he had never bothered with. The tone of his testament, conveyed to her by the lawyer, was of impatient remorse. As she did most others, Agnes had apparently annoyed him with her lack of means, and must be tidied up, like spilt milk, before he could depart the world.

Having just been ousted from her work as governess in a drab, unclean, and misogynist household, Agnes had already packed her bag. She next came across the length of England, through the first flame of September, in a cheap, close, and bouncing public carriage. And so now walked up this drive, through this glorious park which, presently, was faintly tinged itself with the shades of butter, copper kettles, honey, rust, amber, and ruby wine.

When she reached the house portico, arranged with the Greek columns that showed one of the flighty turns of the building, Agnes activated the bell and stood in its clanging, to wait. Governess, servant, dependent, drooping under her hump at the great front door, she expected insults, and having to explain herself. But despite her droop, she was ready. For suffering and ill-treatment had done to Agnes Drale that which they usually do — soured and twisted her, made her bitter as the aloe, and hard, under the layers of her physical weakness, as a cold and ancient stone.

The cousins, Genevieve and Agnes, did not meet until the evening, the hour of dining, in the Old Hall of the manor.

The Old Hall was not, in actuality, very ancient, but had been arranged in the Gothic way, with a vast fireplace, black beams, and shields and swords to mingle with the portraits on the walls. An angled passage led from the Hall directly to the chapel, done in the same mode, that had, so the lawyer had informed Agnes, a royal crimson ceiling, with hammered silver stars. No one had worshipped in this chapel since its erection. The lawyer opined that Agnes might care to, holding, it seemed, to the common belief that the higher-class female destitute soon learned a rigid habit of prayer.

Now, amid the candlelight before the fire, Agnes observed, in her cousin, a pure example of the redundancy of praying.

Genevieve was a being of gold. She might have stepped from the heart of the sun. From her head poured loops and coils of golden hair, shining like the flames of the hearth. Her eyes, the colour of chestnuts, had each a golden sequin, that could have been caused by the candles, or by some inner, ever-present combustion. Her flawless skin was softly flushed, as if gilded. She glowed, she gleamed. While her dress of gold-leaf satin had been fashioned to match all.

Agnes, sitting in her one shabby, dark, 'dinner gown,' her hair pulled tight, could only smile her twisted, little, invisible smile.

"This must be amusing for you, Agnes," said Genevieve. "Do you like Italian wine? I expect the French vintage was too dry for you. Or do you like dry things?"

Agnes, used to the quips and cuts of numerous employers, answered only when needful. Genevieve was patently furious that her cousin had dared to come. Genevieve had already made quite clear the fact that Agnes was normally to dine in her own sitting-room upstairs. Genevieve had explained that, while hairdressers and dressmakers and other slaves might arrive regularly at the house, and Agnes must feel at liberty to engage them as and when she wished, Genevieve did not predict Agnes to wish for very much. Agnes would have simple tastes. Agnes, unused to opulence, would intend, circumspectly, to avoid it. And so, to the frequent dinner parties, to the evenings of dancing, she must naturally consider herself, under the post-mortem avuncular law, invited – but Genevieve would not be offended by her absence.

"I made quite sure, Agnes," said Genevieve, as she ate the chocolate fruits, "a Bible was put beside your bed." Raising her dessert wine, golden as she, Genevieve declared, "I've no doubt you have several favourite passages in the Godly Book. Do tell me one. I'm sure it would admonish me to be virtuous, and I'm sure I need reminding."

"I seldom read the Bible," said Agnes.

"Oh, your weak eyes. How thoughtless of me. But then, doubtless you have large portions of the holy work by heart."

Agnes sipped the wine. It was sweet as the pain of toothache she had so often experienced. She said quietly, "Curse God, and die."

Genevieve started. She seemed shocked, or perhaps only behaved as if she were so. "Whatever is that?"

"The Bible. You will find it in Job."

Genevieve smiled. "What a serpent you are, in your dark dress. You must have something brighter. We must see your true colours."

Upstairs, in the large bedchamber, which was now hers, Agnes looked from her window and beheld night upon the park, the huge, blazing autumnal oaks and beeches put out, and crowned solely with midnight. Stars shone, dull as hammered silver. Below, to her left, she made out the chapel, stretching away from the side of the house. It had seven long windows, each caught in a spider web of iron, and through these nothing was visible. The chapel seemed to Agnes more like an orangery than anything else, the skittish styles of the house here mixed to an extreme of unlikeliness.

On impulse, before blowing out her candle, Agnes opened the

Bible at random. Running her finger down the page, she read this: All wickedness is but little to the wickedness of a woman.

A week passed. Agnes Drale became re-acquainted with familiar, anticipated things. Firstly, her despisement by the servants, and their carelessness with her, manifested in their short replies, the cold and muddled food brought to her rooms, the way in which her furniture, of all the building, was left undusted. Secondly, her exclusion from the life of the mistress of the house, Lady Genevieve.

There were, however, new, and quite unknown, comforts – the softness of the bed, even undusted and not well-made, the tastiness and variety of breakfasts, luncheons, teas, and dinners, even tardily and untidily presented. To have her own private place at last, and somewhere to put her books, allied to the chance that she might purchase more. Soon enough, she barred the sneering or glowering maids from her sanctum, and herself, not reluctantly, made up her own bed, her fire, and dusted the fine old chests and chairs. The park, too, with its massing of fiery dying colours, afforded her long and fascinating opportunities for exercise. Agnes did not know any more, it is true, how to be happy, but she had never had before a life such as this.

She met, during that week, only once with Genevieve. This was in a lower hall, near dusk. Genevieve was returning aflame, in a riding habit of Prussian Burgundy, with two or three gallant young men.

"Oh, Agnes, if you wish to join us for dinner... but I don't suppose you do. She is most retiring," Genevieve added to her court, and they laughed, a laugh that such women as Agnes have had from such women and men as these, since humankind was evicted from Eden.

Needless to relate, Agnes did not attend the dinner. Nor did she have plans to intrude upon the other, more lavish, dinner Genevieve proposed to give, to dignify her eighteenth birthday. This celebration had been carried from its correct date in August, due to the business of her having come just then into the inheritance of the manor. She was a child, unsurprisingly, of Leo. Agnes, whose Virgoean birthdate fell curiously on the very day of Genevieve's extravaganza, imagined only that the onset of her thirty-fourth year would pass without notice among Genevieve's birthday flambeaux and fireworks.

This was not, however, exactly the case. Five days before the event, one of the maids rapped harshly on Agnes' door.

"Lady Genevieve says you are to go down. Lawyer's come."

Agnes felt a clutch at her heart. From her past history, she knew at once a trepidation that some successful act had been made to exile her, after all, from her anchorage, despite all self-effacement.

Grey and rigid, she entered the drawing-room, and there posed Genevieve, herself like a ray of the sunshine which burst in at the casements, the lawyer fawning and sunning himself in her contemptuous light.

"It seems there's some box Uncle left for us, to mark our birthdays. Apparently, he believed they lay closer together than they do." She expressed a glitter of distaste at such a notion. "This gentleman," the word spoke volumes of disdain, "has said that we must be present when the box is unlocked."

The lawyer uttered, trying – in vain – to impress by privy knowledge, "As I have said, my lady, the receptacle has never been opened, not since it was brought to his estate by your Uncle. But the documents assert that it contains a most valuable, indeed unique piece of jewellery, as I believe, of Eastern origin."

All this was rather lost upon Agnes, who, flooded by relief, had blushed a sudden, unbecoming red.

Nevertheless, she went, as instructed by the lawyer, and stood nearby, while the container was produced and a key set in its lock.

The box was of some black wood, and intensely carved with coiled and embracing designs. The lock was horrible, although well-oiled, and gave out such a screech that Agnes' hair rose on her neck. Inside the box, alone on a nest of papers, shone out the roar of gold.

Agnes did not, immediately, determine what this golden article might be. But strangely it came to her, how different this was, this deep, hot, heavy, and mysterious alchemical metal, how unlike the golden gildedness of Genevieve, which even she, Agnes Drale, had confused with it.

"A bracelet," said Genevieve. She seemed amused, idle, neither impressed nor curious.

But as the lawyer lifted it out, and held it for her, ready, the rich lushness of its gold drained the sunlight, drained even, for a moment, Genevieve.

Genevieve said, maliciously sweetly, "Come and see, Agnes. Which of us can he have meant it for?"

"Evidently, for you," said Agnes, in a leaden voice.

It was only her now-ingrained servitude that spoke, her resignation. And yet, her voice sounded ominous, and cold as a bell.

Genevieve took the jewellery, an intricately-worked band, having in the midst of its circle a sunburst. With no scruple or hesitation, Genevieve undid the clasp and fitted and secured it to her wrist, the right one, brushing aside the lawyer's offers of assistance.

Slinking back, he said, "The papers relating to the ornament are here."

"Yes, no doubt. Reading of any sort bores me terribly. It harms the eyes, you know, and makes them dull, and blind."

She drifted to the window once more, holding her trophy – who could think of it as other than hers? – before her, outstretched the length of her creamy, rounded, lower arm.

The lawyer took from the box a paper, and put it on the table. Agnes leaned, almost involuntarily, to see. The writing was highly decorative, and did not look like the rather slovenly script of her late Uncle.

This wrist-ring, or bracelet, is known as the Fraanghi or Frengeh. Although very beautiful, in the land from which it was taken, it was thought to convey a curse.

The lawyer sucked his lower lip. "Dear me."

At the window, seethed in light, Genevieve, the lion's daughter, did not seem to hear.

Agnes read on, with her dull and blinded and bespectacled eyes.

A wise king, having this jewel, lived a full, long, and sanguine life. But, once the adornment passed to his son, this son, boastful and proud, made many enemies. It happened that he was found, then, the arrogant one, with the gem upon his wrist, but he was torn asunder. Then arose another king, a braggart, a cruel man, and he, wearing the jewel, was also found, stripped to his bones in the forest. Beware then, for not randomly does the object keep its name.

Agnes turned to the lawyer. "What language is it, what does it mean? Frengeh – Fraanghi…?"

The lawyer glanced at her. He said, "Your Uncle was a great traveller in India, Persia, and the East."

Agnes said, "There is another paper."

This time, he took it out and handed it to her.

She read aloud, "The gemstone is purported to be that Fata Morgana, a yellow ruby, of which there are few or no examples. Those who have conversely suspected the jewel to be a topaz, of the red variety, amend that such stones are not often found in that region."

There was nothing else in the box, but for a deep shadow. Agnes said, "There is no jewel. The gold is plain."

"It seems so," replied the lawyer.

Genevieve spoke in the incandescence of her window. "A jewel? Is there a jewel in it?"

"No, my lady. It must be that it has lost the jewel…" Agnes looked, and the flash from the bracelet blinded her for sure. The light had sprung from its central part, the sunburst. Before the darkness cleared from her eyes, she heard herself speak distinctly. "Perhaps the boss opens."

"Let me see."

For an instant, Agnes beheld her glorious cousin clawing at her own wrist, the way a cat will at something it does not like, or likes too well.

There was a loud click. It was a noise a clock might make, in the moment before it stops.

"Oh! Agnes, come and see…"

No malice was apparent now. Genevieve cried out, as had the precocious, lovely, repellent, and greedy child she had been at fourteen years of age, the day her Uncle had visited her and brought her such wonderful presents, and she had danced for him the 'Dance of the Pretty Fairy,' and recited some sentimental ode, and everyone had sighed, and clapped, but he had only gazed, with his thin, brown face and narrow, evil eyes – that she, the fool, had been too young and too self- enamoured to interpret.

Agnes moved to Genevieve across the room. She entered the flaming crystal of the light. And in the light, Genevieve became the palest ghost, but on her wrist, freed now from its cover, there scorched, amid the curve of gold, a gem, the red topaz or yellow ruby, just as the paper had specified.

Agnes, once more, heard from her throat the voice arise, as if another uttered within her. "It might have been made with you in mind, Genevieve."

On the evening of Genevieve's deferred birthday party, which was really her own, Agnes Drale descended the main stairway in good time.

Most of the upper house had been decked with gilt ribbons and swags of velvet roses. Tall, ivory candles burned at every turn, as if gas had never been invented.

A few heads were rotated as Agnes came into the reception room. Not at her beauty, nor in mockery, in mere perplexity. In the past slender number of days, she had called upon the harassed dressmakers and coiffeurs, and had so changed her appearance that Genevieve, in the midst of admirers, did not for some time recognise her. Agnes had not aimed for the impossibility of charm or the veneer of sweetness. She wore an expensive gown of jet black silk, whose tailored shawling collar quite concealed the upper curve of her spine. On this was pinned a watch of finest silver, with seed pearls, tiny and of impeccable design. Her hair had been re-invented, in a style more classic and less severely placatory, and had given her face, now mildly powdered, the stern and implacable look of the Roman dignitaries found on antique coins. Agnes, who had been, seemingly, bowed and apologetic, now looked more what she secretly was, formidable and unforgiving. As her eyes passed over the assembly, assisted by her improved and gold-rimmed spectacles, no one was moved to laugh at her. *Best be wary*, was the instinctive if hidden thought. They took her not for a governess, or poor relation, but some steely aunt, ready to despoil their pleasure if they were not careful, to cast them down. If one cannot ever be loved, it may be better, in the interests of self-preservation, to be feared.

In some way, Agnes perfectly understood this. Her glance, fortified also by a glass of malt-coloured sherry, was unwavering. Although she could not have said exactly how she had come by her abrupt assurance.

It was only Genevieve who, recognising her cousin suddenly, burst into a peal of mirth. Genevieve, herself in a dress of saffron, her hair raised like golden fruits in a basket of combs, half spilling on her enamel shoulders, was even then extending her fair arm, for everyone wished to study her bracelet – the single ornament she had put on. Agnes, despite seeing the jewel on its emergence, was also drawn to do so once again.

"Why, Agnes, how magnificent you are!" But Genevieve's sparkling voice passed over Agnes' bending head.

There in its socket of gold, the huge, polished gem, substance of the wristlet called the Frengeh. Yellow ruby or not, one could not mistake what it was like. The clear reddish upper water that melted through the tinge of nasturtiums, to a base the shade, perhaps, of a Harvest Moon. And over its face, a flaw, which must, being so remarkable, have made it even more valuable and curious, more esoteric, bizarre, and even sinister. This flaw showed itself as three soft bars of shadow, that were, unmistakably, like three stripes upon the pelt of a tiger.

"A tigerish stone," said the plump young lord who stood at Genevieve's elbow. "A tiger for a lioness, since her birthday, you know, falls more properly in Leo."

"The tiger abhors the lion," said someone.

"Does it not suit me, then?" asked Genevieve, playfully.

Her gallants laughed loudly. They laughed with countenances angled aside – they did not wish to dispute with the grim and elegant aunt, who had spoken such ill-omened words.

As Genevieve glided away, they passed with her, like a cloud clinging to a sunrise. And Agnes remained alone, wondering what she had said. It was strange, was it not, that the golden bracelet, which had closely fitted the strong arms of kings, would be small enough to cling to the slim wrist of Genevieve. But men in the East were often small of bone.

Agnes turned her head, and saw, as if her reverie had conjured it, an apparition. Against one wall, was positioned a small and slender man, clad in garments that, to Agnes, suggested the East, his head bound in a scarlet cloth. His skin was smoky, his eyes as black as her dress. Seeing that she looked at him, he bowed, his hands beneath his chin.

But then the crowd of Genevieve's guests washed between them, he was gone, and all that was left, for a moment, was the impression of a woman's amber-coloured gown, moving away, as it almost appeared, with no one inside it.

The dinner was held in the Old Hall. As decreed, torches burned. Gilded candles pointed from garlands of autumn leaves and forced red flowers. An artifice, a palm tree with gilt fronds, dominated the table's centre.

Through the many courses, the soups and meats and side dishes, the desserts and savouries, the selections of wines, Genevieve was Queen. Her radiance beamed the table's length. As Agnes sat, eating her sparing, precise mouthfuls, she felt swell within her her own murderous hate, that which never before had she been able truly to acknowledge. As the gaiety and high spirits emblazoned the hot, fragrant, and over-powering air, Agnes mused inwardly on all the mean cruelties inflicted upon, and the careless wrongs done to her. A host of horrors marched across her mind, and in their wake swept Genevieve, a sun in splendour, putting all other light, all other slight, to shame.

After the feast, out they went, on to the terraces above the descending lawns, and watched as, garnet and diamond, fireworks were let off against the backdrop of black trees and night.

Agnes Drale noted the little slender man in his turban, hurrying about the pitch, ordering the incendiary shows. While, as the fireworks soared, bursting with sharp bangs like artillery into their kaleidoscopes of flame, Agnes beheld how they reflected in the lines of the windows of her Uncle's unused chapel, unsanctified by prayer, throwing up crimson flares on its ceiling, where the still stars hung, as if it too were burning.

It was later yet, after midnight, when the cold champagne was served in the Old Hall, back into which they had mobbed to get warm, that the Eastern man approached Genevieve, and bowing low, hands joined, produced from thin air a yellow rose, unlike all the other madder roses, and put it at her feet.

"Oh, bravo!" exclaimed her lovers, who had arranged presumably for his participation. "Shall he read your future, Jenny?"

"Do say 'yes'," cried the ladies, who wanted to have read their own.

Then Genevieve sat in a chair, the pivot of all things, a golden lamp; and Agnes waited in the distance, like a shadow. The Eastern man crouched by Genevieve's knee. He stared into her palm. He said, in a rhythm fluctuating like an autumn wind, "You are walking your true path, lady. Before you is your Fate."

A woman shrilled, tipsy and excited, "What is it to be?"

"It is shining," said the man, "like the morning. It turns towards you its golden eyes. Your Destiny is beautiful, lady, and you will not fail to meet with it. It purrs, like a cat."

Genevieve clapped her hands. The Frengeh flashed, another firework, its gold, the astonishing stone that ran from ruby to topaz, and was striped like a tiger.

"What about that, eh?" asked the lordling, "Cursed, ain't it?" He grinned.

The man from the East smiled, his eyes lowered to the floor where, applauded but untended, the yellow rose had been trampled.

"The jewel will have caused the death of mighty kings," he said. "But what need this lady fear? She is in England."

At that they howled with proud laughter. And Agnes Drale stood watching, smiling a little, just as he did. Yet through the smirch and haze of sinking lights, she saw now, deep inside the crowd, a woman in an amber dress. Her hair was dark, springing and trailing all around her face and throat. Her skin was tawny, and the lights ran on it like water. Her eyes seemed to come and go, now pale and flame-like, and now dark as the sky beyond the house, as if fireworks went on in them still. And as she turned a little, her gown might be seen to be striped, barred, an unusual pattern, just before she was gone.

Agnes shivered in the scalding room. And raising her sour and flat champagne, she drank it down. She was in the grip of that most primal and appalling and triumphant fright, which the ancients knew to call Terror. She was aware that all things were altered now, and that the drab world held more than she had thought, and that God, in some form, some fierce and unimaginable and awful form, existed.

There is a wretch of a gypsy in my park," said Genevieve, peevishly, shedding her riding gloves. "She wore a dress of dull orange, and her dark hair all loose. I shall have men scour the grounds. She must be evicted."

Agnes did not argue with this statement. She ate her breakfast, there in the dining-room with its marble and velvet, where now she took her early meals. But as she bit into her kedgeree, Agnes recollected how, even prior to Genevieve's ride, she, Agnes Drale, had walked in the manor woods, and sensed that something was slinking behind her, hot in the frosty morning, something that smouldered on and off between the trees. And on the lake, the ducks kept to their island, while now and then, above, the song of the over-wintering finches fell mysteriously quiet.

Two grooms and three footmen were sent out from the house; they left jesting, and returned silent. Seeking for the gypsy they had found nothing at all, save the burnt leaves down from the trees, the berries like blood, and feathers of some bird a fox had taken.

The servants were different now, in their attentions to Agnes Drale. In a matter of a month, they had come to respect her. As the last leaves scattered from the trees, so were discarded the prejudices and the glee of certain ill-used things for another ill-used creature supposed more vulnerable. Agnes was not as she had seemed.

When she brought back the surly young women to clean and tidy her suite of rooms, they took one fresh look at her, this Agnes seeming taller in her faultless black, straight and hard as the winter trees were coming to be, strong and impervious. And when their first efforts were not good enough, then she brought them back again by a couple of clipped words, to re-make her bed, to replace her higgledy-piggled ornaments in a reasonable order. They said, presently, she was obdurate, but just. After all, she knew what was right.

They did not say they had formerly sought to jibe at and prey on her weakness. They said they had mistaken her, been misled by a temporary loss of character on her part, and so not initially discerned that she was a lady and so she expected – and deserved – their best.

It was Genevieve now they took to task, Genevieve who had always been capable of viciousness, throwing at them her hairbrushes, retracting their wages, her unsuitable whims and extravagances, her manner that had, they now affirmed, no dignity. She had hardly worn mourning black for her Uncle, and that was a disgrace, he had been dead only half a year. She slept most of the day, until eleven o'clock, like a pig, and then was out gadding in the town, or rode about the park until the poor horse was lathered, and carried marks on its side of her wicked little whip, so the head groom frowned and cursed under his breath. She said something had frightened her in the park, under the oak trees, something, some vagrant, a cry or call or sound – but she was profligate and drank too much for a lady, a bottle of wine now at her luncheon, and two or more at night. With these sudden unaristocratic humours and alarms, a look had come into the exquisite face of Genevieve, that puffed it out and dredged away its lovely colour. She appeared more human now, standing in her hallway, under the chandelier, which tinkled and faintly glinted in the cold October afternoon dimness, twisting her whip in her hands, her eyes roving, screeching like a fish-wife for lights, like that guilty king in that clever play Miss Agnes had mentioned.

And now Genevieve, their Lady, had lashed them all with her tongue. She swore they had a criminal here – she had seen the woman, she, Genevieve, had *seen* the gypsy bitch – such a word! No lady would use it, Miss Agnes would not – seen her in an upper corridor. Not only some no doubt impecunious and thievish relation of the servants taken in secretly under her ladyship's roof, but permitted to steal about the rooms of their betters, pilfering. In vain they protested, scandalised themselves, for they laid claim, the servants, only to relatives of the purest sort, and with here and there merely the by-blow of some exalted person, who had loved their grandmothers or their great aunts unwisely but extremely well.

As the girl nightly brushed Agnes' hair, found to be long and strong and wiry, with its strands of steel, and the sparks flew off it, she told Agnes of Genevieve's strange, new, and troublous ways.

"I think, Miss Agnes, if you'll excuse me…"

"And what is that, Beryl?"

"I think she may've taken her Uncle's own road."

"Which road would that be, Beryl?"

"It was – Hump, Miss Agnes."

"Hump… ? Oh, hemp. I see. Opium."

"He was haddicked, Miss. Terribly so. The drug makes you mad."

"So I've heard."

"She ups and screams at me, Miss, yesterday, as I was going through the lower hall – 'Look! Look there!' She gives me a proper turn. I dropped all the napkins. And then she struck me. 'Can't you even smell it, you stupid…' Well, then she called me a nasty name. I said I couldn't smell nothing but for the fire burning in the little sitting- room, which was smoking. She says, 'Beryl, you… that name again – and she hit me across the face. 'It's a dog,' *she cries.* 'One of the dogs is in – that filthy orange one – fetch someone to put it out!'"

Beryl brushed, and Agnes Drale's hair crackled. The sparks flew past the lamp, and the little clock chimed eleven.

"But there was a smell. I did catch it. A whiff; like the zoological gardens in the city. It seemed – beg your pardon – to come from her ladyship. Perhaps something picked up on her skirt…"

Agnes thanked Beryl, and Beryl put down the brush, and drew open the neat and perfect bed. Inside the hour, lying on the laundered sheets, Agnes slept her now-usual sound and dreamless sleep, which as a rule continued until seven in the morning.

However, about four, something woke her. She did not know what it was, but yet she was impelled to rise at once, and seek the window.

How icy the panes of glass were behind the thickness of the curtains, and beyond this flimsy barrier, lay the great park, stripped bare now to its black bones, and holding up a canopy of stars. Her eyes, her neck, her head – turned, and Agnes looked towards the star-hung chapel that ran out from the house.

She was bemused by sleep, and yet awake. She saw calmly, clearly, the long black window-spaces in their iron webs, and next, faint and glowing, how some occult light passed up and down inside. It was the shade of a dying lamp, reddish or ochre. It reminded her of how she had seen the reflected fireworks display upon the crimson ceiling. Yet, conversely, it moved low down.

"What can this be? Who's there? Oh, what?" Agnes murmured. She trembled and her heart beat wildly, and yet she was removed from her own self; from the expressive emotion of her familiar body. She sat high up within the walled chamber of her skull, and watched the moving glow, now yellowish, now red, until it ceased to move and faded away like a dying, or a sleeping, fire.

Then, returning to the bed, she too regained her sleep and in the morning, perhaps, had quite forgotten.

That evening, Agnes Drale was summoned by her cousin Genevieve, to dine in the Old Hall. Here, every night, Genevieve had partaken of her dinner, alone or in noisy, festive company. While Agnes had kept to her modest if luxurious rooms, now her own meal was always served hot, and decorously arranged.

No one but Genevieve waited in the Hall. Of all things, a cold repast, on this frigid night that conceivably promised snow, was laid beneath the illumination of a mere ten candles. The gas was out. The fire burned sluggishly about a handful of logs.

"The heat – the smell of recently cooked food," said Genevieve, turning rapidly to Agnes, "excites – something." She added, feverishly, "Animals in the park – come to the windows."

"As the wolves do, in Russia," supplied Agnes, coolly.

"Just so. Indeed. What an isolate place this is. I may remove to town. Lord E——, you recall him, I expect, has offered me the use of his Small House, only fifty rooms, but I must manage. You, of course, won't mind remaining here."

"No, I should think it very cosy," said Agnes, amenably.

They went to the table, its waste of white cloth, and helped themselves from the dishes.

"The servants..." said Genevieve. "It's because I must speak to you very privately, Agnes. No prying ears or eyes. They gossip about me..." Genevieve was pallid, her face, on another, might have been described as engorged, swollen. Her grasp was unsteady upon the silver utensils, and three times they dropped from her fingers.

Agnes ate at a slow and even pace, and sipped from her crystal glass the apricot-coloured wine. Genevieve ate nothing, but drank eagerly. On her wrist was a dull mark; perhaps the bracelet, the Frengeh, had bruised her. Occasionally Genevieve would encircle this bruise with her other hand. At last she said, "Do you remember the jewel, Uncle's silly foreign bangle – it's so heavy... those times when I put it on. But the gemstone is spoiled. Three dark scorings across it – surely there's no such thing as a yellow ruby."

Agnes ate a tartlet. It was cold in the vast room, the fire soaking ever lower, casting a dark cinnabar glare, the candles flickering. The voluminous curtains were drawn fast at the long windows, to close out any wild beasts that might be gathering in the park.

"Agnes," said Genevieve, "I don't suppose you were ever – fanciful?"

"In what way?"

"In – the way – oh, of ghosts, nightmares. Such things."

"Perhaps," said Agnes quietly.

"It is stupid of me," said Genevieve. "Never in my life – something is following me about, Agnes."

"Something is following..."

"*Some* thing"

"How exactly do you mean?"

Genevieve drained her glass, rose abruptly, and flung it from her. It smashed in stars at the edge of the hearth.

"It is preposterous and absurd. But – I know that it happens. I hear it. I – smell it. I see it pass, sometimes near and sometimes at a distance."

"But what do you see – or hear or smell?"

"I can never be sure what it is – the smell is hot and pungent. Spicy. Or – a dirty smell. Or there is a noise – soft, like – a cat, walking over the floors, but a big cat, Agnes, very big. And sometimes..." Genevieve stared at Agnes' face, not seeing her, "I hear it – breathing."

"You're overwrought," said Agnes.

Genevieve gave a squeal of laughter. "I am terrified!"

"How could there be such a thing?"

"The bracelet," said Genevieve. She wilted suddenly; she drooped. Such a stance, over thirty-three years, had brought about Agnes' stoop. To Genevieve it was a posture novel as darkness to one who had never beheld the night.

"The bracelet Uncle left for you," clarified Agnes, diligently.

"Yes, yes that horrible, gaudy gew-gaw. Oh God! I shut it up in its box again. I hid it in my dressing-room. And still – still – Oh, Agnes, I can't eat or sleep. I think I'll wake to find it crouching on my breast. I dream of it. It – purrs. Such a dreadful purr, rasping – like nails tearing velvet. I shall go mad!"

Agnes drank another mouthful of wine. She said, "You're unnerved, my dear cousin. Naturally, no such thing exists. But if you're in this state of mind, there is, after all, a certain recourse."

"Tell me! Quickly! Agnes – I beg you..."

"You must," said Agnes, raising her eyes, her spectacles gleaming bright, "turn to God. No other, my dear, can help you. Pray, Genevieve."

"Pray? Pray? Do you think..."

"I know it, Genevieve. God is attentive to every sincere plea. And only recollect, our Uncle built here a chapel, consecrated and ready for the most urgent use."

"The chapel," said Genevieve. And she spun about in the direction of that narrow door, which led from the Old Hall, out into the angled passage, and so to the folly of the chapel with its orangery windows and ceiling of stars.

At this moment, the most curious sound stirred against the huge room. It might have come from outside the walls, or down the chimney, or out of the very air itself. It was indescribable, but as Genevieve heard it, she uttered a shriek, and Agnes rose to her feet, the skin crawling on her bones.

"Take a candle, Genevieve," said Agnes.

"Oh, Agnes – I'm too afraid – in the darkness..."

"Then I'll go before you. I'll go and see, and ignite the gas lamps that I've been told are fitted there, as here."

"But the light..." cried Genevieve, "...may attract..."

"It is," said Agnes, in an iron voice, "the place of God."

"*Yes.* Yes, then. I will. If you – will go there first."

"Stay here, and I'll return for you," said Agnes.

And taking up one of the faltering candle-branches, she walked across the Hall, her spine erect, as if fletched with the quills of lizards, her hands colder than the promised snow.

At the narrow door, she paused. The sweat started icily on Agnes' brow. She said, "Take courage, Genevieve. All will be well." And passed into the corridor beyond.

Perhaps, because it had no windows, the corridor, that ran between other rooms unseen, was close and warm. It had a scent of fruits dried for cake – raisins, prunes, such items. At the turn, Agnes halted. The candles dipped and lifted up again their nervous flames. She went on.

The right-angle of the passage was only some four or five yards in length. At the end was a large door, secured only by a simple latch.

As Agnes approached it, she seemed to hear a strange, muted noise, like tiny tinsel bells. She shivered again, touched the latch, and opened the door wide.

The chapel stretched before her, long and dim, its elongated windows dark, lit sidelong in a peculiar manner, by the vague, curtained lamps of the house. It was a slender oblong in shape, this chamber, and at its extremity a carved lectern stood, and before that, to either side, three carven pews with their backs to her. On the floor lay a red runner, velvet perhaps, and above soared the red arch of the ceiling, where the silver stars winked back the candlelight.

Possibly it was the apprehension of Agnes Drale that made the atmosphere seem to tremble and ring. She had had so often to be brave in the face of many humiliations, attacks, and reversals, that courage was habitual with her.

Nevertheless, she moved stiffly, and put up her hand like a stick to the gas fitment she had perceived on the wall. The gas fluttered and popped, and slowly the flame bloomed up, spreading down the aisle of the chapel and polishing the carvings on the backs of the pews. The second fitment was set adjacent to the lectern, and Agnes gathered herself to go there and attend to it. For she was not yet quite ready.

Beyond the long windows, only the night finally showed, the glim of the manor put out. Around the lectern shadows clung, ascending into the crimson roof. It is now and then to be seen, this phenomenon, how a light, placed in an unexpected or unaccustomed position, may seem to throw a shadow that bears no relation to anything revealed by its rays.

Agnes stared, and then, intuitively, her glance descended and rested on the last of the right-hand pews, that which stood the nearest to the lectern. Its back was high, and nothing was to be seen, but the air was now so very hot, so intensely smothering, as if before some tropical storm. And in this choking, shimmering air, the quivering bells rang on, making dizzy Agnes Drale, so that she swayed, and her candles sank and died in her hand.

Something was rising after all, over the back of the last pew. Something was sitting up, a curve, a hump of darkness that rose into the light. Its colour slowly changed to amber, rich and royal, and over the amber scored the dark streaks and bars, and a stream of gold that ran from the lamps, on silk, or fur. It was the back – of an enormous beast, of a tiger, and yet, and yet, it was turning now, the golden sheen shifting, turning its head, to look at her.

Agnes Drale opened her mouth, but no sound came from her. She slumped against the wall, and was pinned there, unable to drop down.

It is a woman's face, but a woman's face that is the face of a beast, a face of amber, with human eyes that are the eyes of a demon, yellow as topaz, red as ruby, eyes that are not windows, for no soul is behind them, yet something is behind them, and looks out. And the jaws are wide, and the long teeth, brown and stronger than steel, protrude from it. The dark hair falls that might be mistaken for a woman's hair, but not now. And a hand that is a paw rests on the edge of the holy seat, and the claws unsheathe, and they draw one thin line along the wood, delicate, soft, and never, never will be forgotten the noise they make, as this is done, nor the rasping ripple of a speechless voice, coaxing and impatient. And the thud, the lash of the tail.

It is hot now as the centre of a furnace, or a dying sun.

Come, Agnes Drale, leave your candles where they lie, go backwards slowly and with caution, feel for the door, slip out, and close it carefully once more, behind you.

Agnes re-entered the Hall, firm, not breathless, and Genevieve sprang up at once.

"Everything is ready," said Agnes.

"The gaslight…"

"There is light," said Agnes. "And God is there, awaiting you."

Genevieve draws herself up, haughtily. "Then I shall go alone." If it is between her and God, no other is needed.

Ten minutes after, Agnes is in her bedroom, while Beryl brushes her hair. Across the park, once, twice, three or four or five times, they have heard an odd note, a shrill, distorted, soulless scream.

"It must be an owl," says Beryl. "There it is again. It does go on so. I hope it won't disturb you, Miss."

"Not at all," says Agnes.

In the sombre month of November, when the white snow was down about the manor, the lawyer finished his work for Agnes Drale, the legal proceedings necessary now that the house, and its estate, were hers. As she sat like a queen in her black tussore, he offered her a last paper.

"You were curious, I remember, Lady Agnes," he said, making intent use, as he had throughout, of her inherited title, "about that bracelet your Uncle had brought from the East. I confess I was a little, too, myself."

"An unlucky gem, as prophesied," said Agnes. "It's locked away, and no longer in my keeping."

"I hope, my lady," said the lawyer, "that you also affixed the golden sun-shaped cap once more over the stone?" He chuckled frivolously. "You will see why, when you regard this document I have procured from the city museum."

"Oh, yes. I did do that. My servants were very uneasy. They had learned the jewel was cursed. Poor Genevieve."

The lawyer touched his heart in an affectation of feeling. "And the criminal is still at large…! A madman. Such a terrible, such an unthinkable end – eviscerated, rent, ripped, the blood splattered – the face torn off…" He displayed the purest ghoulishness of his time, or most times.

"There is a general belief," said Agnes, "that gypsies and their ferocious dogs…"

"Several had been seen, I gather," agreed the lawyer. "But to enter the chapel…"

"No one can explain," said Agnes. She nodded. The subject was closed; one did not argue with her.

She unfolded her palms and took the paper, and read it. As she did so, the lawyer, a true slave, and generously remunerated, stood respectfully smiling, to show how he was aware what nonsense he had just handed her.

This piece of jewellery is mentioned in several ancient texts, and seems to date from the fourteenth century. The jewel is itself not mooted as a mineral but as a living energy, or *animal*. When let loose in particular conditions, it may evoke, it is thought, violent and horrible death, the ingredients for this seeming to involve the emotions of hatred and jealousy, in opposition to callous greed. In the case of one ruler said to have died through it, the matter is proposed as the actual opposition of the two elements of the stone itself – vividity and hardness.

The bracelet, which is formed of gold, also entails an enclosement over the stone, which, if the wrong or provoking elements are present, should in no circumstance be removed.

Thus, it is the bracelet, the setting of the jewel, which is named Frengeh, or Fraanghi, deriving of course from the Musselman word, meaning, A Cage.

Scarlet and Gold

There were two brothers. But, as the day is not much like the night, so they were, or were not, to each other. The fact was, they had had the same father, the lord of the great Village of Seven-Willow, but their mothers were different. Chegahr had been got by the lord on a girl little better than a slave, one midwinter's night, in a barn, while the wolves were composing their songs to the moon. Chegahr was strong and square-built, swarthy and dark-eyed, and with the white-blond hair of the North. But Velonin, whom his father had got on his priest-law lady wife, respectably under a sheet in the High House, was slim and tall, with hair like a mountain panther's pelt and blue eyes like the best china plate.

My story does not begin there, however, (or perhaps it does, since without their being born, they would not be in it), but in the hour before sunrise some eighteen, nineteen or twenty years later.

At this hour, be certain, Velonin was yet lying fast asleep, with his head on swansdown pillows. Chegahr, though, was out on the plain beyond Seven-Willow, dragging along his sled, for which he could afford neither pony nor dog, and loading it where he could with fallen branches, which the snow had brought down. Trees grew thick on the plain, and southwards became a forest, but being the son of a slave, he was not permitted to cut any tree, even a dead one. So his share of firewood depended on sloughings.

It was winter again, and the scene was worth a look, if Chegahr had had the space and the spirit to look at it. And he did. When you have not much, there is not much to interrupt you. So he stood and saw, in the narrow, silver light that comes before the dawn, the sweep of the white world, which was like a vellum page in some rich man's book, but a book not yet written on. Unless the woods and forest might be the words of some tale, the birch and the pine, all coated white, but here and there with a little of themselves still visible. For miles the plain ran, and at its end, which Chegahr had been told – he had never gone so far – was ten days' journey off, stood the wall of the Iron Heart Mountains. And they too were shouldered and crowned with white, against the ghostly sky.

Chegahr looked, and he saw it all, and he fed his hungry eyes. Even on the three white hares he saw playing not much distance off. And if he wondered, should he bring one down quickly with a stone for his dinner, he then thought better of it. He had bread and cheese and a jug of potato beer, which he had earned by his work for others. Let the hares keep their lives, until he would lose his without them.

Meanwhile, the night got on with its departure. It rinsed the bright stars off the sky, carelessly muddying and fading them as it always did, before stuffing them in its pockets, and slipping away over the western horizon behind Seven-Willow Village. And the sun began to stain the east over the mountains, spilling pails of itself up the stairs of the sky as usual, in its rush to get back and spy on what was going on.

Chegahr watched, and he enjoyed the rich red flush of the coming sun and the torn gold stitches of the clouds, just as he would have enjoyed his breakfast, if he had had any.

And then, ah, then. The sun did a new and very strange thing. Instead of rising blindingly up as always through the gap in the mountains, it shot right through the gap, fast as an arrow, and began to race towards Chegahr.

Chegahr stared, and then he prudently moved himself and his sled some yards to one side. At the same moment the three white hares went leaping away, and Chegahr pondered if he too should take to his heels. But instead he only planted his feet more firmly. For if the sun was running straight towards him, it was yet much smaller than he would have expected, and although it flashed and sparkled, it seemed to burn nothing, not even, properly, his eyes.

After some minutes the actual sun rose in the normal way, up from the Iron Heart Mountains. And then the bit of the sun, which seemed to have been fired out of it, began to cast a long blue shadow. And next Chegahr began to see what it really was.

"Well," said Chegahr, "is this less or more wonderful than the sun rolling towards me?"

Just then, the less-or-more-wonderful thing turned sharply sidelong, and Chegahr beheld properly what it was. And what it was, was this: It was a great gambolling sled, and it seemed to be made of hardened gold. Its sides were gold, and its runners, and its high seat, and all its curlicues and elegances, and it had a prow that was in the shape of a wild face, human, but with the beak of a bird. And this was all gold, as I say, ripe red-gold, that shone and glowed. The sled was drawn not by a horse or dogs, but by a team of snow-white wolves. And Chegahr had no doubt about that at all. They were hitched very oddly, in two lines of six, with one enormous one, big as a lion, he thought, at the very front, who bounded forward, dragging the rest behind. These wolves were harnessed in deep red, and hung with golden bells, and by now Chegahr could hear the hiss and rush of the sled, and the pound of the four-times-thirteen pads that sprang up and pounced down on the snow. Was this not enough? Of course not, for the sled must have a traveller in it, and so it did.

Chegahr stared, blinked and stared the harder. In the sled was a young woman, and he was sure she was young, for she was only a hundred feet away – what was that? – and if the sun was beyond her, even so, she seemed lit up like a lamp, and he could tell she had skin like cream, without one blemish or wrinkle in it, and eyes like hot chestnuts and lips like red currants. But she wore a blood-red gown and, oh, but was it not embroidered in a border three hands high (and Chegahr's large hands at that) in golden patterns? And at her wrists were golden armlets and round her slender white neck a necklace of hammered gold, and on her head a cap of scarlet velvet, trimmed with golden discs. And was not *this* enough? Yes, and too much, indeed. But there was more, for as with most such sights, marvels vulgarly outdo themselves. So, from her pure pale temples sprang out a mane of golden hair, not vivid gold, as the sled and bells and discs and other paraphernalia, but *icy* gold, like the sun gleaming through a milk-glass window. And this hair, believe me or not, (and I hold nothing against you if you refuse, for even Chegahr, who saw it, afterwards partly thought he had not), this hair poured over and down like a wind of light, blown out through the top of her head, and swirled on and on behind her, over her gown, out of the sled, over the white snow, over the plain, back as far, it looked, as the mountains. And all the while, the red cap bobbing on it, like a stopper coming loose in a bottle of bubbling wine.

But then the wolves pulled the sled away among the trees, down the aisles of the wood, where the snow-coated pines soon hid it. And after some ten or twenty minutes more, which Chegahr counted out as carefully as he was able, (imagining in his head, the tick of the clock in church), the last of the *hair* was drawn in too, and vanished after the maiden and her sled, into the wood.

Then Chegahr took up again the ropes of his own sled, and turning, he walked back to the Village, whistling.

Let me assure you, Chegahr had no intention of speaking a word of what he had seen. It is possible that, on Witch Eve or Christmas Eve next, when he might have gone to the church, and next the tavern, if some had begun telling fairy tales and legends of the Village, he might have added this anecdote:

"One morning I saw..." But in no other form would he have risked it. He was the son of a slave who had been rash enough, before she died, to boast her baby was the child of the lord in the High House, and that was tale enough to hang about him, as thrown stones, spittle and other kindnesses had swiftly shown.

However.

As Chegahr was walking across Church Square, to reach the alley behind the cemetery, where he had his hut, five men were standing by the church door to smoke their pipes. And they were important men of Seven-Willow, the chair-maker and the horse-doctor, the rat-catcher and the roof-patcher, and the elder of the two priests whose skin was thin as silk from spirits in a bottle.

As Chegahr came near, generally speaking, they would have paid him no heed. Except one might have muttered something, or one might jeeringly have laughed. Even if any of the nine hundred persons in the Village had work for Chegahr, they tended to send their servants or slaves to tell him so. And even the slaves were impertinent and sullen, for they were owned and had some value. By the by, too, Chegahr's mother's master had died in the year Chegahr was born. And this master had been the Village muck-carrier, who tended the midden and cleaned the privies. Even as a slave, Chegahr would have had no status. But if you are wanting to tell me that Chegahr would have done better to have left the Village of Seven-Willow the day after his mother's death, when he was just twelve years old, I may say he had often thought so himself. But then, the mountains were ten days away, and crossing them was another matter, more like scaling the vertical air to reach the moon. While south and north were other obstacles, the haunted forest, a vast raging river, and anyway there were everywhere only other villages very like Seven-Willow, which to strangers were reported unfriendly, or treacherous. And though everyone spoke of a city to the north, and another to the west, whoever came from there and could prove it, or going there – returned?

Besides, which is more to the point, now and then Chegahr looked up and saw the rise above the Village where stood the High House, inside its walls. But I shall come to that, as will Chegahr, presently.

Now, though, the five important men stared at Chegahr.

And the rat-catcher gave an oath, and the old priest marked himself with the cross. It was the chair-maker who roared, straight at Chegahr, "Hey, you dog, what do you mean by it?"

Chegahr stopped. He put on his mildest glance. Trouble had no interest for him, for its own sake. It wasted his time, which might be spent in more fruitful ways, such as gazing, thinking and dreaming. He did suspect this bother might be about some Village girl, for sometimes it was. Although the Village men did not much like him, now and then a young woman might cast him half a look of a different sort. He was too wise to give the look back, but occasionally even modest indifference was not enough. (As with the scholar's wife, who had once stridden up to Chegahr, one summer as he was minding the Village goats on the plain, and slapped his face hard.

"I dreamed last night you laid me on my back and straddled me!" had cried this amiable woman. "There's for that!" And then she had fetched him another slap. "And that's for making me like it." Her name was Majlena, but it was not the time for him to find out.)

"How did you get it?" now bellowed the roof-patcher angrily.

"What?" asked Chegahr.

"Behold him stand there and deny it," growled the horse-doctor. "See this, wretch? It's a pill to cleanse thoroughly a horse's bowels. Do *you* want to try it?"

"My thanks, I decline."

"Then tell your news."

"I have none."

"The scut!" cried the rat-catcher, "I'll stuff a rat up him, I will."

"Peace, peace," said the old priest, "we are before God's house. Chegahr, you must tell us the truth."

"It has snowed," said Chegahr. "The sun has risen. This is called the Village of Seven-Willow and I am Chegahr. What other truth is there? Enlighten me. I'll speak it."

Then the horse-doctor and the rat-catcher and the roof-patcher and *almost* the chair-maker – who began then decided against it – rushed at Chegahr and grabbed him hard and fast. And Chegahr, who might fairly easily have thrust them off and mashed their noses for them, did not. Because other than they, there were the rest of the eight hundred and ninety-five persons of Seven-Willow, not to mention the immediate chair-maker and priest, and even women, who made love with him in dreams, slapped him twice in daylight.

"What now? Fetch my tongs!" inventively shouted the horse-doctor. And, "I'll nail him on a roof," improvised the roof-patcher, but the priest said, "He must go up to the High House. His lordship must see and decide."

Chegahr was quite in the dark about all this. And stayed in the dark all the way up the path to the top of the rise, during which trek, various other people came to join the procession, including the boot-maker and the tavern-owner, and the scholar, (he of the wife), many children, and sixteen young girls from Seven-Willow's five wells. And it was not until Chegahr got face to face with a glass mirror in his father's house, which was now the house of Velonin, his half-brother, that he knew. But I will explain at once. Chegahr had returned from the snowy winter plain with a most beautiful golden summer tan. It covered, uninterrupted, his face and throat, and had even bleached his blond hair at the front to white.

The High House had high walls, and within was an orchard of cherry and peach trees, now hidden in the snow. But before the house, which was partly of stone and partly timbered, lay an open snowy space, on which balanced one mournful statue. It was of a naked boy and two bare-looking dogs, from which the ice had mostly melted off. This statue, a wonder of Seven-Willow, had been brought to the house as a curious bit of the dowry of Velonin's deceased mother. Chegahr, who had heard of it but never seen – this being the first time he had entered his father's gates – thought only that the marble boy looked very cold, and was shut out of the house. But perhaps he had some cause for thinking in that way.

Then the great door was knocked upon and a house servant came, dressed better, of course, than any Villager, save perhaps for the horse-doctor and the boot-maker.

To begin with, everyone waited in a big cold hall, with tiles underfoot and a long window of coloured glass, showing a scene that looked religious, but not religious enough. In one corner lurked a clock, twice the size of that in the church, and variously about were set a barometer, a musical box, (silent) and a ship in a bottle.

Then, from up the oak staircase, (imported), came a loud bang and a slither, which was Velonin, throwing a large book at the announcing servant in vexation, and the servant falling over.

Then Velonin appeared in person on the carved gallery above the stair. All but hatless Chegahr doffed their caps and bowed.

"What in the devil's name do you want?" shouted his lordship.

The Villagers grovelled. Many began to blame Chegahr, while the priest made a sort of bleating noise, the rat-catcher swore, and the girls from the wells gazed blushing at their lord.

"Devil take you," said Velonin, "cluttering up the place." And he strode down the stair, into the hall, his breakfast napkin still in his hand. There he stood, glaring from his best-blue eyes, and in his coat of pale blue satin.

There were three gold rings on his fingers – and next down the stair, as if wishing only to stay with him, there wafted the scent of hot white bread and butter, roast chops, and a rare coffee, brought years ago, with cases of wine and champagne, it was said, from one of the mythic cities far away.

"You," said Velonin, pointing at the horse-doctor, whom he slightly knew, having met him now and then in the house stables, "what's up?"

But the horse-doctor gave Chegahr a push. "Look, your lordship can see, it's written all over his face."

And it was then that Velonin, who was the half-brother of Chegahr, stared right into Chegahr's face, and into his eyes. And Chegahr did the same with Velonin.

"Then who the devil are *you*?" demanded Velonin, sensing insolence more than noticing the tan.

So Chegahr told him, "Your father's son."

"Stuff and nonsense. You look nothing like him," declared Velonin, going straight to the point.

"Neither do you," announced Chegahr. "You're pale and dark and delicate like your mother. Just as I'm burly and blond like mine. But what's wrong with my face, then?"

And at that Velonin reached into his satin pocket and took out a silvered round of mirror held in a gilded frame.

Chegahr peered. He saw. He gave Velonin once more look for look. "Then I'll tell you," said he, "seeing as you're kin."

And on the gale of gasps at his effrontery, there before them all, and the barometer and the music box and the bottled ship, Chegahr told what he had seen. That was, the sled drawn by thirteen white wolves, the maiden in scarlet and gold, and her golden hair that poured behind her and passed into the wood after her, ten or twenty minutes after *she* was gone from sight.

Throughout Chegahr's recital there was not another sound. Even the clock seemed to give over its ticking to hear. While the young lord, Velonin, sat down on the stair, careless of his coat.

But as Chegahr finished it was the scholar (he of the wife) who cried out, "It is a Soracsh!"

And then the priest said, "Hush, good sir. Such goblins do not exist."

But, "What is a Soracsh?" inquired Velonin.

At which Chegahr, not the scholar, thoughtfully answered, "My mother once told me of those. They are common enough in the North, it seems. A Soracsh is a sorceress. She has power over wild beasts, and her hair has abilities all its own."

But the scholar pushed through the other Villagers and stood frowning there, as if he had a quarrel with Chegahr, yet did not know quite what the quarrel was. "More than a sorceress," said the scholar, "for a Soracsh is related to the wolves. She has their blood in her veins.

But, my lord, do not believe this oaf, Chegahr. He is only trying to make dupes of us. He has rubbed grease on his skin and burnt it at the fire to make it brown."

At which Velonin stood up again. "Well," he said, and slapped his napkin on his smooth, clean palm for emphasis, "get off with you. But you and you, come upstairs."

At which the scholar and Chegahr exchanged an uneasy glance, and followed the lord up his stair, while two servants ushered the rest out, being only careful to tip the priest and the horse-doctor with enough to buy brandy.

In the dining room above, an elbow of a huge stove, enamelled black, white and blue, gave heat and cheer. Chegahr and the scholar were seated on two gilded chairs, quite near the servant who had earlier been felled by the book, and still lay prone. Velonin sat back to the table, and picked up his bread, dipped it in the coffee, and ate it.

"Now," said Velonin presently, "what I need is a plan. Put on your thinking-caps."

Chegahr said nothing, but the scholar asked, "A plan, sir? For what? If you valiantly mean to try to be rid of the Soracsh, that would be most unwise because…"

"Be rid of her? What do you take me for? I'm eager to meet the lady. The trouble with this village," added Velonin, turning to Chegahr, "is its lack of cultural excitement. Take a city now. There would be cafés and loose women and the opera. But here what have you? In summer, there is drought, and in winter there is snow. What else? A zero. Don't you think so?" Velonin added in a peculiarly familiar way to Chegahr. "What do you say?"

"To what?"

"To what I have said, of course."

"I say you'd be happier in a city."

"Oh come," said Velonin, taking a pinch of snuff elegantly, as if sniffing a wayside flower. "In any city, I'd be thought a turnip. No, I must make do, lording it over you foul and hapless peasants. But a witch in the forest, now. That fires me up."

"For God's sake," said the scholar, "don't go near her, whatever you do. She's not a witch, but a Soracsh, part wolf and part woman and part spirit, and all of her terrible."

"Oh stuff," said Velonin, "get out, you klutz."

So the scholar got up and got out, and outside, to reassure himself he was not a peasant, he took a pinch of his own inferior snuff, and horribly sneezed three times as he went down the stair.

"Well then," said Velonin to Chegahr, "what do you think?"

"I think you are one year older than I," said Chegahr, "but act like a child of six. I think you faultlessly arrogant and perfectly rude, and probably heartless and witless to boot. And I think that God, if God exists, is anxious to call you back to Him that He may beat you soundly, and put you to bed in a grave with no supper, which is anyway more than you deserve. I think therefore also, that if you desire to court a Soracsh, which being I now recall my ma told me is quite likely to devour a man alive and raw, then go do it, with my blessing. It won't be the opera, but nor do you deserve the opera. You deserve the Soracsh. And *now* I think I shall go home."

At which Chegahr rose. But Velonin burst out laughing. He laughed so hard he knocked over his porcelain coffee-cup and it broke. So hard, the stunned servant, (who anyway had been shamming), came to and crawled hastily away across the room and left them entirely alone.

"You *are* my father's son," cried Velonin. "Where else did you get such a voice and a wardrobe of such words?"

"From my mother," replied Chegahr staunchly, "who on her death-bed, called out to the angels, 'Leave preening your wings, you vain creatures, and heft me to the stars'."

At that Velonin stopped laughing. He said, quietly, "Mine only whimpered. She was afraid God would be like Father. You seem to think so, too, with your beatings and supperless graves."

"You care a deal what I think."

"Maybe I do. Come, have some coffee, or there's Aqua Vita, there. What the old priest drinks, but better."

Chegahr only looked at him.

Velonin said, "How's this. You mind my house here. Keep it up to scratch. Kick the servants, sleep in the best bed, and so on. I'll take *your* fate and go after the Soracsh."

"*My* fate?"

"What else? Who saw the creature? You. And she tanned your hide for you. She left her book-mark in your pages."

Chegahr shrugged, but his heart was banging now like a drum.

Velonin jumped up. He took off his fine coat and dropped it on the floor. "And if I catch the Soracsh, I'll make her my wife. That'll set things right."

"Oh, how?" asked Chegahr.

"I don't like unkindness to women," said Velonin. "I've seen plenty. Our dad. (Your mother was spared, not living with the brute.) That scholar who was here starves his wife 'for her own good', and speaks to her only at mealtimes, while she goes hungry and he eats.

Even that servant who was lying by your chair gave his wife a black eye last night, which is why I took the opportunity to give him one this morning. Yes, viciousness to the sweeter sex seems natural in a man. Why suppose I'm different? So, if I live, I'll have a Soracsh-wife, who I won't dare anger."

That said, he strode from the room, and Chegahr was left standing in it, between the still-laden breakfast table, with its white cloth and plate of roast chops, and the warm grumbling stove-pipe.

Now Chegahr was left inwardly debating the actions and speeches of his half-brother, as you or I might briefly do, (or not), wondering if Lord Velonin were superficial, thoughtful, careless, caring, rotten or simply deranged. But we, (you and I), must now leave Chegahr to his debate, and to his bizarre possession of that lavish house, and follow Velonin, done up in his fur coat and hat, and his boots, and with, despite all his words, a sharp knife to hand and a gun with an ivory stock, into the woods beyond Seven-Willow.

Naturally Velonin had known the plain and these woods since childhood. He had ridden about them on a horse, or even, sometimes, tramped about them with his father, various servants and hangers-on, or now and then with some party of other rural aristocrats from neighbouring villages. He thought of the woods, and the plain, as belonging rightfully to himself. But not being mad, or not mad in this way, he had the sense to know the southern forest, which the woods soon became, was no more his than the Iron Heart Mountains in the east.

The change from the woods to the forest was very strange, for it was not sudden, and yet it was suddenly felt. One moment the trees were scattered, and sunlight seemed to litter about from a cloudy or clear sky. And then the light was gone, to be replaced by a sort of dim luminescence. But in fact the trees had closed their ranks only gradually. With the loss of light, there came a monumental sense, as of terrific architecture. It was like being shut in some ancient church, among great crowds of tall, thick columns, whose crowns met vastly high up, in a beamed and coffered roof without a single window or lamp. This overpowering awareness was the same, both summer and winter, save in summer it was a black-green church, and in winter a white-blue one. That was all the difference. Also, the forest was very silent. Among the woods, even in winter, red grouse flickered, birds and hares, sables, ermines, and other animals were to be glimpsed and heard. In deepest winter, wolves and ghostly deer foraged even among the thinnest trees. Once into the church of the forest, however, nothing stirred or made any sound. Whatever lived there kept itself hidden – or was invisible. So, with the crushing sense of enclosure and dimness came the idea of deafness and isolation.

Velonin had entered the forest before, surely, but never alone. And if he had noticed all these sensations, never before had he acknowledged them. Now he did so. And this made him stop quite still, staring about him, and up into the windowless roof of frozen boughs and shadow.

Just then some snow did fall somewhere among the trees. It was like a giant's dull gun being fired, and Velonin jumped in his skin.

Then he only smiled. "What better place for a sorceress who is half wolf?" asked Velonin of the trees.

All this time, he had been guided by the spoor of his quarry, for all over the softer snow the runners of the sled and the paws of the thirteen wolves had left their impress, while from this point he noticed, twined like exquisite gilded thread among the roots and snowy scrub, occasional slender, long, long skeins of shed pale golden hair.

Velonin now bent and picked up some of this hair. It was fine as silk, yet very strong. Only with difficulty did he snap a single hair, and that across the edge of his knife. It had a faint perfume too, like burning incense, and like peach-blossom, and like fresh cold milk. In fact, it had so many scents, these three and others, he began to think the magical hair had enchanted him and really had no smell at all.

Velonin had come out for adventure. He had come because he was impossibly bored. And because the Soracsh was now his fate, not Chegahr's.

So, quite quickly, he coiled up the strands of hair in his pocket, and went on.

The forest grew more and more grandiose and ponderous, until he felt himself almost bent double under its weight.

The trees were very old, hundreds of years, perhaps centuries, and here oily indigo hemlocks loomed among the snow-wrapped pines and spruce, and black firs, which also had let the snow slip from them. At last Velonin leaned on a trunk and took out his pocket-watch. He saw from this he had been walking most of the day, and also that the watch had stopped, and then he seemed to realise night was coming or had arrived.

Just at that moment, craning his neck, he beheld what seemed an extraordinary sight. In the roof of the forest was motionlessly gliding a huge, pitted white lantern, which touched everything to silver fire. It was the moon, risen high up in a patch of coal-blue clouds, and below, before Velonin, there opened a wide clearing.

Even as he grasped this, and wondered if the clearing had been there a moment before, Velonin noticed another arresting thing. The further end of the clearing was not closed by trees but by a sort of stone-piled cliff. And even as Velonin gazed at it, in the cliff wall, one by one, a row of lovely tapering amber lights bloomed up. Then he saw that they were windows, and that the cliff was the side of some great house, which made the High House at Seven-Willow into a cowshed.

On the moon-whitened snow beneath, the amber windows dropped reflections. And then in one flame-lit window, and in its reflection too, came a slender shape, like the slim dark wick dividing a candle-flame.

Out into the night rippled a wordless calling cry, that made Velonin's hair stand on end. And yet, it heated his blood at the very same instant.

"There, sure enough, is the Soracsh," said Velonin, "and she is calling to see if anyone is here at last." So he stepped forward boldly into the clearing, swept off his hat and bowed low to all the windows.

She was only a silhouette, so he could not tell if she was as Chegahr had described her, but then there came a flash of light like three hundred tinders struck all at once, and over the window-sill poured a waterfall of shimmering gold.

Only when it slid quivering and gleaming along the snow at his feet, did Velonin see she had thrown down into the forest the ends of some of her sorcerous hair. And then he heard her laugh.

There was no door in the wall. No trees grew near. Velonin looked at the fall of hair, which even a knife had trouble in breaking. Then he asked her, "Do you mean me to be so ungentlemanly as to climb up by your tresses?"

And the Soracsh called down at once in her wild voice, "Do you dare?"

"If it won't hurt you, lady."

"Oh, nor it will," said the Soracsh.

So Velonin put his boot to the wall and gripped the stream of her hair in both hands, and swung himself upward.

And but for being so silken-slippery, the hair proved a serviceable rope, so Velonin climbed on and on, up the rough flints of the wall, up and up to her high lit window, and there she leaned, with her hands on the sill, laughing at him, her lips like red currants and her coffee-coloured eyes that had reminded Chegahr only of chestnuts, and her skin like alabaster.

Velonin hung in her hair with his booted feet braced on the wall, and he thought she had only to cut loose this streamer of her crowning glory, she would hardly miss it, and he would tumble and break his neck. But he said cheerfully, "Good evening, fair lady. I hope my weight doesn't pull at your scalp?"

"Not at all," said the Soracsh, "but put your foot now on the sill, and I'll help you in."

So Velonin swung himself up on to the sill, and she gave him her white hand, and he sprang down into the chamber.

I do not know what places you have seen, or what buildings you have ever gone into, but I myself never entered a room like that in the Soracsh's house.

First of all, the walls were encased in a glowing gold and bronzy green that seemed at first to be caused by the adherence of thousands of polished gems. But then you saw it was the static carapaces of thousands of beetles, but whether alive or dead, or ensorcelled, or only sleeping, one could not say. The ceiling of the chamber, however, the Soracsh herself presently explained. It was covered – or formed of – hundreds of flying birds, large and small, among which were even bluebirds and canaries, peacocks and swans. They all hung there, static as the beetles, their wings spread wide, and all the shades of emerald and beryl, agate, turquoise and nacre and, seeing Velonin admiring them, (with his mouth open), the Soracsh idly said, "When birds sleep, they dream of flying. These dreams I catch in a net, and there they are." So perhaps the beetles on the walls were likewise meant to be the *dreams* of beetles. Meanwhile, lamps floated in the air to illumine all this, and they were distressingly like great burning eyes… so Velonin did not look at them for long.

The floor of the chamber, though, was more simple. It was solid glass, but in the glass, just below the surface, great fish swam about, tawny pike, and huge carp of brass and coral. Seeing him look, even more idly, the Soracsh then remarked, "Oh, it is a lake."

"Indeed," said Velonin, but he sensed her slight displeasure, and realised that, as with many other women he had met, and several men too, she preferred her guest's attention upon herself.

So Velonin gazed at her, raised her hand and kissed it, (and when he kissed her hand, it was in some particular way, like drinking the best chocolate, or taking a mouthful of roses and cream.)

She wore a scarlet gown, but not the gown she had worn for the sled. This one left bare her milk-white shoulders. But her throat and waist were clasped by gold and on her head she wore a tall golden tiara, set with scorching diamonds. (It must have been about this time that Velonin for ever mislaid his knife and gun.)

The Soracsh then clapped her hands, and a door, (which seemed to be made of two bears with smouldering eyes), flew open. In walked a pair of beings that Velonin took to be her servants. They were men clothed in black velvet, but for their heads and faces, which were those of wolves.

"Here is my good friend, Velonin," said the Soracsh to the wolf-men. (And how she knew his name is a mystery. But then, she was a Soracsh.) "Is dinner prepared?"

The wolf-men bowed, and stood aside, and the Soracsh took Velonin's arm, and they strolled through the bears into another chamber. And this chamber only had walls made of static waterfalls, but against them stood gigantic flowers on stalks like birch trees, and in their bells burned unseen lights. There was a table of glass, (perhaps), laid with silver and gold cutlery and dishes, and goblets of crystal. For the dinner, it was meats and pastries and puddings and delicacies. And there were hot-house fruits, the like of which Velonin had only ever heard described, or seen in books.

The Soracsh sat at one end of the table and Velonin was seated at the other. And he noted that one of the wolf-men stood behind his chair. But then, the other stood behind the chair of the Soracsh, and their prime wolfish purpose seemed to be to help their mistress and her guest to food and drink.

Of course, Velonin was not quite ignorant of uncanny matters. He had had a nurse as a child, and knew from her that to eat or drink anything in the house of a mere sorceress, let alone a Soracsh, would render him her slave. So he toyed with the choice cuts and slices, and did not put them in his mouth, and he pretended to sip the choice wines, and did not swallow any. But every so often, one of the lit flowers would bend towards him, and he would see another of those shining eyes peering at him through the petals, obviously watching.

"Well, madam," said Velonin, once they had been at table a while, "you must wonder what my purpose is, in calling on you."

"Not at all," said the Soracsh.

"Then you have read my mind, perhaps?"

"No need."

"I am beneath your interest? That grieves me." The Soracsh smiled, and Velonin became aware that she also did not eat or drink anything from the table, only played with it as he did. And he wondered if she had another dish in mind, which was raw dead man's flesh. And this notion made him smile as well, and he said, "My reason for visiting you, lady, was to ask if I might court you for my wife."

"I am," said the Soracsh, "a great deal older than you."

"Oh come. We are too sophisticated to be upset by such trifles. What are a few hundred years between friends?"

"Also," said the Soracsh, "I am unbelievably wealthy, and you only somewhat rich."

"That's true. But then, if you wed me, by law your wealth comes also to me, and I shall be as well set up as you."

"Besides," said the Soracsh, "we have nothing in common."

"Quite wrong. We have in common one most influencing thing."

"And what is that?"

"We both of us," said Velonin, "adore you."

The Soracsh only nodded. "That's not enough. In any case, you came to me because any who see me must so come. That is my power, or one of my powers."

Velonin said, "I think you may be wrong. But we'll let that go."

"No, no," said the Soracsh, frowning, "are you saying that one has seen me and not come to me?"

"I heard some such tale. Doubtless a lie."

But he realised how close the flowers were leaning now and their eyes popping out at him, while behind his chair the wolf-headed man leaned so close, Velonin could smell his meaty breath.

"Why," said the Soracsh, "will you not eat and drink?"

"Madam, I'm in love. My appetite therefore is gone. Since your beauty is all the feast I desire."

But the Soracsh got to her feet, and when she did this, she seemed very tall, and suddenly the dining room was much darker, and Velonin began to think that he felt most uncomfortable, like a child put in an adult chair too big for it. And it was then he noticed the ceiling, and it was full of faces, but all these faces moved and made mouths at him, screwing up their eyes and wrinkling their noses and poking out their tongues. It was very disagreeable and unaesthetic.

"Velonin," said the Soracsh, "you fear that to eat with me will give me extra power over you."

"Not at all. I already adore you. What power can you gain greater than that?" But when Velonin spoke, his educated and pleasant voice sounded quite odd to him. And then he found himself slipping off the chair on to the floor. And the floor was made of snow. It was cold and silent, and he saw how his feet and hands left prints in it, but the prints were of the wrong shape. "Ah now," said Velonin, "I've been a great fool," but he did not hear his voice at all now, only another noise, which he had never made before.

And she, the Soracsh, had become tall as a pillar, tall as a tree, and she stood there and, oh, how stupid he thought he had been not to ask himself where all her miles of hair had gone, (for it should have been piled up on the floor), but now he saw that hair, and he and she and the two wolf servants were all tangled up in it, and out of it now there dissolved the illusions or maybe the realities she had conjured, the birds and beetles, the flowers and fish and burning eyes. They had all been made, thought Velonin, out of her hair, even the *dinner* had been made of hair. And now only her hair remained. And it was like the web of a ruby and golden spider, and he hung in that web, and heard her say, "Do you think I need such nonsense to entrap you? No. When once you kissed my hand, you were mine. And now you're mine for ever."

"I have earned no better," agreed Velonin. But the only thing that came out was a yowl. Then all the colour and eye-lamplight winked away, and there was simply a horrible, ruinous white garden under the walls of a cold dark house. And the unkind moon stared pitilessly down, for she had seen everything long ago; nothing was new to her or worth a second look.

For nearly a month, Chegahr lived in the High House at Seven-Willow. One may say he lived like a lord, but also the role did not fit him, just as Velonin's fine coats, breeches and shirts did not – although, perhaps oddly, in boots and shoes they were of a size. A tailor had soon crept from the Village, and brought Chegahr some quite tasteful apparel, ready-made, and Chegahr had chosen a few items. But he would not pay for them from Velonin's money-chest, and had no money of his own beyond a few coins in a broken pot, left at home in his hut by the cemetery. So he was in debt to the tailor. But the tailor only beamed and fawned, sure now Chegahr had gone up in the world. Likewise, the others who came to call – the younger priest, with his silver cross a-bump on his chest, the horse-doctor – now leering with would-be friendship – the vintner, the apothecary, and so on. Chegahr sent them all away. He had needed nothing but a few new clothes, so as not to dirty or untidy his brother's house.

And that was how Chegahr thought of it, the house. As his brother's.

Which was itself strange, because all his life until then, if he had been honest, which generally he was, Chegahr would have said, "That house is partly mine, by rights." But of course, he had never thought he would live in it. And now he did, he felt he rattled in it like a die in a box. He was not comfortable, in fact. The rooms were too big and he could not find things in them. Their beauty he did not find beautiful – he preferred mountains, woods and sunsets. He got lost in the corridors and could not discover the indoor privy, which anyway he thought unhygienic. The bed was too soft. The servants seemed to spy on him – they were always underfoot. The luxurious food was over-spiced, too sweet, too complicated. The fine coffee, which is a stimulant to most people, made him bad-tempered and sleepy.

All that disappointed him, as well. Here was the life he had, vaguely, envied. But he had no use for it. The only hours that still pleased him were those when he could escape the servants and pace about, or sit near a window, doing what he always did when he could, dreaming, gazing, thinking.

So in the end, he dreamed of Velonin, and in the dream Velonin was at the bottom of a long steep place, and howling. And when Chegahr had sat up and lit the candle, the light fell on a book, which had been Velonin's, and it was poetry, but Chegahr could not read it, so he somehow imagined the black print said: "Help! Help! Oh, half-brother, help me or I'm done for!" And then when Chegahr thought about it, he recalled that Velonin had been gone a long while, far longer than he had needed to go into the forest and find the Soracsh, drop on one knee, offer a ring, give her a kiss and bring her back for a priest-law wedding, and the better truer wedding in the wide soft bed.

"But what is he to me or I to him that I should bother myself? When I was in the hut, with only the recollection of a dry crust to eat, did nice Velonin ever trouble himself? If I hadn't seen the Soracsh pass, he and I would never have met, even though we lived only half a hill's distance from each other."

But then the servants came bursting in, as they always did, and Velonin saw it was morning, the candle had burnt out, and wax had splashed the book. He saw it, as the servants threw wide the silk curtains, and the light thundered in. The wax on the book had formed the shape of an animal with four legs and a tail, and its mouth was open howling, as if it cried, "Help! Help! Help!"

"Devil take the pest," shouted Chegahr, who to his dismay had, in the house, begun to speak sometimes rather as Velonin did, as if Velonin's speech had stayed like a haunt. "Devil take him," he added. "Or the devil _has_ taken him. I should never have let him go. It was _my_ fate. He knew it, and so did I. If I had the wit to resist my fate, the wit even not to know there was anything _to_ resist – I had the wit to stop Velonin as well."

Then Chegahr had his breakfast, put on some of the plain new clothes, and going out, walked down through the Village of Seven-Willow, where everyone stared at him, and even dogs trotted at his heels, wagging their tails.

When he reached the scholar's house, in a secluded lane, Chegahr halted. He knocked loudly on the door. The maid opened it, and she cried at once, apparently satisfied, "Master's away!"

Chegahr scowled. "When is he back?"

"Not for seven days. He is off to the funeral of another scholar, in the village of Tall-Wheat."

Just then the scholar's wife appeared. She looked thin and pinched, but when she saw Chegahr, her face flamed and her eyes grew very bright. And suddenly Chegahr saw that she was young enough to be the scholar's daughter, and also Chegahr remembered that Velonin had said the scholar starved her 'for her own good'.

"Let me in," said Chegahr.

"Never!" cried the scholar's wife in a shrill excited voice.

Then Chegahr stared at the maid, and as Velonin might have, "Be off, you goose," he said. And the maid ran away. Chegahr then said to the scholar's wife, "Madam, you slapped me twice. You owe me two words in exchange."

At this she stood dumbfounded.

Chegahr said, "The two words are, Forgive me."

Her mouth dropped open. He saw it was a pretty mouth. Her eyes were deep as pools and sad as the hearts of dark flowers.

Chegahr said, "What I did in your dream was very wrong. What can I say? None of us can control what we do in our dreams."

Then she blushed, and lowering her long black lashes, the scholar's wife said to Chegahr, "It was my fault. In the dream, I made you go and pick poppies with me in a field. And then I flirted. I said, 'My husband is away from home'. And then – I kissed you on the lips. Naturally you felt able to take liberties afterwards."

"I'm sorry I don't remember it as you do," said Chegahr, thinking that perhaps he was, too. "But in that case I must give you the two slaps back."

"Why not?" said she. "The scholar is always slapping me."

So then Chegahr stepped inside the house, shut the door, and kissed the scholar's wife gently, first on one cheek, then on the other. Then on her eyelids, and next on her lips.

"Oh, Chegahr," sighed the scholar's wife, "I have loved you wildly for three years." She no longer seemed thin and pinched, but only slender, and aflame. "Come up the stairs, and let me show you the bedroom."

So they went upstairs, and Chegahr saw the bedroom, which had a good hard solid bed. And here the scholar's wife flung off her garments, and she was pretty all over, her body like a slim white dress set with two pink pearl buttons, and honey trimmings.

Near afternoon, by which time Chegahr had finally learned her name was Majlena, he put to her the questions he had meant to put to her husband. And as he had begun to suspect, Majlena knew all the scholar knew, and quite a lot more, (as she had recently proved in the bed.)

Chegahr left the house after supper, as dusk was coming down, and went up the street whistling. But when he came to the foot of the rise where stood the High House, Chegahr did not turn that way, but went on walking.

And those that saw him pass said, "There goes the lord's son, Chegahr," and the dogs dribbled and wagged their tails, but Chegahr spared them not a glance, for he had things on his mind.

It had taken all one day for Velonin to get deep into the forest. But then he had not been following his fate, but another's. Chegahr walked for a brace of hours, and then he only sensed that he was in deep enough.

All around the ancient church of trees stood still and silent, but here and there the cold heartless moon pierced through. And to Chegahr she was not heartless at all, only secretive.

He knew now all he had to do, for Majlena had told him, taking care he should memorise everything. This had not been so very hard either; it was as if some part of him had already been lessoned in it.

First Chegahr made a fire. Then he drew all round the fire with a stick a black circle in the snow, and sprinkled it with salt. Then he took off every stitch, (just as he had earlier in the day.)

Then Chegahr recited the rhyme Majlena had taught him.

He recited its four lines facing all four directions, starting with the west and ending with the south.

When he had done this, a great wind bowled through the forest, and the vast branches and boughs rustled overhead, and snow fell from them. But after the wind was gone, another snow began to fall, straight down from the sky. Chegahr nevertheless felt warm as a cooking potato, and when he glanced at the fire, it was a strange clear yellow. Chegahr felt his eyes drink this colour up, and they turned yellow too. And then he put back his head, and please believe me, he gave such a howl that every wolf in the land may have heard it. After which, he crouched down on all fours, and he turned this way and that way, and then he heard it coming, heard it far better than that first time, the hissing of the runners of the Soracsh's sled.

Sure enough, she soon appeared, and she passed, as the wind had done, and through the white lace of the dropping snow he saw her, in her scarlet and gold, and the thirteen white wolves running six by six, with the huge one in front, and the gold bells ringing, and the gold sled rushing over the ground, with a white spray going up on either side, like two white wings. The Soracsh looked only straight ahead of her.

No sooner was she past, and off between the trees, than Chegahr leapt out of the circle, taking care not to touch it with his feet. And then he ran to where the flowing train of hair was still streaming on in her wake. There he waited, counting, and when he had reached nine or nineteen minutes, he jumped forward and caught hold of some of the hair in both his fists. The speed at which it was going pulled him over, but he landed soft on the hair, and after that he let it pull him on.

Presently, the sled ran into a vast clearing, and directly ahead, in the moonlight, was a high wall of piled stones. The sled raced on, and Chegahr, borne so far behind, expected some magic door to open in the wall. But this was not what happened. Instead, the lead-wolf ran straight up the wall, and after it the other twelve, six by six, and next the sled ran up, with the Soracsh upright in it, and standing out now horizontally from the wall like a red and gold nail.

Chegahr may have uttered an oath, I am not sure at this point, but whatever else, he clung on tight to the ropes of hair, and next minute he too was hauled right up the wall, after the sled, and only the silken thickness of the strands saved him from a grazing and, seeing how he was dressed, from rather worse. Over the wall's top had gone the wolves and the sled, and over the wall's top was dashed Chegahr. And there, on the far side, was a lighted ballroom, such as he had heard of now and then, in those cities far away. But not quite.

Rather than being dragged down into it, Chegahr now found himself all at once lying on a golden staircase, and so he got up and leisurely descended, looking about him all the way.

Chandeliers with flaming roses in them floated in mid-air. Below were walls like marble, and a floor like polished silver, and everywhere grew slender blossoming trees, frothy with pink and purple and blue, and golden snakes were coiled in them, with eyes like topazes, and from the boughs hung golden apples and silver pears. Where the snow fell into the ballroom, it became sweets, the fashionable kind called *bonbons*.

In the middle of all this stood the golden sled, but it had altered to a golden chair, and in it sat the Soracsh, (and Chegahr wondered where it was that all her hair had gone, for now it only reached her scarlet slippers.) As for the thirteen wolves, they had changed, or were changing, into men in black velvet, and it looked very odd as they did this, as if they pulled their bodies up over their heads like a nightshirt.

But even though they became men, and had men's faces, this time, they had the eyes of wolves still, intelligent, and far more human than human eyes. And as they laughed and called out to each other, they only barked and yipped and made similar wolf sounds, apparently disdaining speech. Even the lead-wolf, who was brawny, swaggering and tall, did no differently.

Chegahr reached the foot of the stair, and then he noticed that now he wore satin breeches and a shirt of silk and a coat of golden tissue.

"Well, Chegahr," said the Soracsh, "here you are."

Chegahr thought it no surprise she knew his name. "I am here," said Chegahr, "to ask you about my half-brother, Velonin."

"No. You are here because you are in my power, and I made you be here."

Chegahr felt the fine clothes itch him, and when he looked at the marble walls, he thought he saw mountains and seas and skies inside them. And in the floor under his feet glittered stars, and all at once, there under his gold-buckled shoes, the priestess moon appeared, veiled in light clouds, at whom now, he might look *down* in wonder.

Just then, a great golden table sailed through the air and squatted before the Soracsh, and after that a second golden chair. On the table was a landscape of food, the like of which Chegahr had never seen, even in the house of Velonin – no, not even in his hungriest dreams.

Chegahr regarded it, and two of the wolf-men ran up to him, but they ran up on their hands and knees, and panted, with great red tongues hanging out.

Chegahr stepped around them, went up to the table, and stared along it at the Soracsh.

"Eat and drink," said the Soracsh.

"Pardon me," said Chegahr, "I ate supper before I left home."

"Some wine, then, Chegahr. See how good it is."

"Your pardon again. Wine makes me bad company," said Chegahr. "I shouldn't like to offend you."

"Well, but already you do," said the Soracsh, getting up now and coming around the table. "Oh, Chegahr, wouldn't you like to give me a kiss?"

"I have had kisses too, before I left home. Enough to last a little while."

Then the Soracsh stood very near to Chegahr, and she smiled at him. "Your eyes are yellow, Chegahr, and I had thought your eyes would be black. Why is that?"

"I have the wolf-blood, lady," said Chegahr, "just as you do. When I was made, the wolves sang loudly. But how this coat itches. I think it's tailored from your hair. Like the table there, and the roasts and cakes, and like the magical walls and floor, and all the lamps. What do you say?"

"I say I will have you, Chegahr," said the Soracsh, and she suddenly bared her teeth. They were white as the snow, but they were the teeth of a wolf, and her tongue was blue.

"Oh, that," said Chegahr. "Didn't you hear me say, I'm part wolf too? I can't live in a fine house. I can't wear fine clothes. I like to dream and play. I like the woods. Just tell me where you've put my brother, Velonin. He's only a man, and is unhappy here."

The Soracsh snarled. Her chestnut eyes turned red as live coals. She clapped her hands and everything flew up in the air, the table, the blossom-trees, the entire ballroom, (even the moon in the floor), and Chegahr and the wolf-men were floundering and staggering in the midst of it, and it was all a writhing mass of golden hair.

"Now," said the Soracsh, "I'll show you your Velonin."

And she gave Chegahr a shove in his (again) naked chest that sent him hurtling: he landed on a cold cushion of snow, in an old garden that lay at the foot of a high, dank, dark towering wall. The Soracsh stood on the wall top, snarling down at him, gnashing her fangs. She looked small as a doll.

And in the snow beside him was another tiny toy. It was a little wolf, made perhaps of dark wood. But as Chegahr stared at it, it spoke to him in a little wolf squeak, as if a mouse were trying to howl. Through this noise, Chegahr plainly heard the words, "Help me, brother!" Here was Velonin.

Generally, in Velonin's life, it had been thought gracious and cultivated to talk. In his childhood, too, he had been given lessons in oratory and debating. So now he began to tell Chegahr, in dramatic detail, all that had occurred to him. But he could only squeak in his little wolf squeak. And all the time, the Soracsh stood on the wall top, gnashing her fangs.

So then Chegahr said, "Be quiet, Velonin. You need only know this. *She* is dangerous as life and death together, but blood is thicker than scarlet, and I find I have a heart of gold. Besides, I am mysteriously unhurt after being flung off the wall, which is encouraging. This is what I'll do. I'll put you into my mouth, and you must wrap your front paws round one of my lower canine teeth. And then, with the help of the cunning spells of the scholar's wife, which have already saved me a broken neck, I shall run very fast away."

Velonin may have wished to argue, but he had no chance. Into the wide-open mouth of Chegahr he was popped – and Chegahr's mouth seemed, even to little Velonin, very much larger than it had been. And the strong teeth stood very tall in it, especially the canines. Velonin therefore had no difficulty in gripping a left one with his wolf paws.

No sooner was this done, than Chegahr gave a huge spring, and up the wall he ran, straight up over the flints and stones, on his bare feet, which were hard and tough as pads on a beast. Only once or twice did he need the use of his hands in this frantic endeavour. And he moved as quickly as a lizard.

The Soracsh to be sure darted back, but at the top he went right by her, and she spat at him, and her spit was fiery stuff, but it missed him, and instead burned a hole out of the wall. Meanwhile, he was leaping from the wall's other side. Down he sailed, and hit the ground of the clearing, as if he had springs in his heels, (from all of which we might conclude, you and I, the scholar's wife truly knew a thing or two.) And then Chegahr ran in good earnest.

Never in all his days had Chegahr sprinted so fast, nor would he ever have had to sprint so far. But he knew he was no longer quite himself, or perhaps he was *more* himself, for his yellow eyes showed him all the forest clear as day, and his limbs had muscles of steel.

"Do you hold tight, brother?" he grunted, as the white towers of trees roared by.

And Velonin squeaked that he did, but he cowered in fear, clinging to that tooth, now blasted by the icy cold air rushing in, and now by the scalding hot breath, (tinted by a hot supper and Majlena's kisses), gushing out, nearly champed as Chegahr spoke, afraid of being swallowed whole, soaked by saliva and bounced up and down.

But Chegahr pounded on, and as he did, he did not know if he were any longer a man, with a wolf in his mouth, or a wolf that bore along a man. Nor did he know if he ran upright on two legs, or parallel to the earth on four. And then he heard the thick *plush-slush-ssrrrh* of the sled behind him, and the bounding footfalls of the thirteen wolves.

So Chegahr, who had only been running: well, you see, now he *ran.*

At this new speed, the trees disappeared. They became a pouring wave of white-black, that here and there dazzled with the light of the stars which still fell, or maybe it was the softly falling snow. And now and then, he leaped high over some narrow streamlet or slight chasm, or some arched root wide as a crocodile shown in one of Velonin's books – but saw none of them.

But he heard *her* behind him, the push and hiss, and the thudding of the four-times-thirteen feet. And he heard her crack a whip, too, and sensed its golden flare across the flying dark, like the striking tongue of a serpent.

Then, what should happen, but Chegahr heard also the lead-wolf calling to him, and now it either spoke in the human language, or he had come to understand its growls.

"Halt, stay, give in! There's nothing to fear. My mistress is charming. Have I not served her all this while?"

Chegahr knew better than to shout over his shoulder what he thought of that. Besides he did not want to deafen Velonin in his mouth.

But then the lead-wolf began to call in a sort of singing way that matched the rhythm of their running, both the white wolves' and Chegahr's.

"Won't you run with us? Wouldn't you like to? You could even take my place and lead, a fine one like you. Oh, I lived as a man, once. I took a man's pride and pleasures. I smacked my wife soundly and laid her on the bed. I drank my beer and ate my meat, and once a year I bathed and read a book. Oh, it was a comfortable life, that. But would I now exchange what I have? Ah, what it is to feel the kiss of the golden whip. What it is to fawn on her scarlet slippers. She is the fate of all men, Chegahr. But it takes wisdom to know it. Yes, she may belittle you, or throw you down. But in the end, you are necessary to pull her through the world."

Chegahr thought, and the thought was like the single wink of a spangle in the whirl of his running, "If you want that, that you may have."

But he knew by then where it was he ran to, although perhaps he had already known.

I cannot say how long Chegahr cannoned through the forest and the night, with the Soracsh after him, her whip cracking, her tongue blue, and her spit all fire. Possibly it was scores of hours, the night constantly renewing itself, as one might over and over sew up a tear in a sock. Or perhaps he ran for many nights together, all the nights it needed to prove to the Soracsh she had not caught him, or to him that he had not been caught. Then again, he ran so fast, and so speedily did she follow, maybe they reached the brink of the forest in half an hour.

For reach its brink they did.

And then Chegahr sped through the thin woods, and over the plain, while the snow tinkled down like white china broken and dropped in heaven.

And at last Chegahr saw, (although Velonin did not, for if a wolf can faint, he had done so, though still with his paws locked fast about that great wolf's tooth), Chegahr saw the dull sparse lights of Seven-Willow, some of which always sophisticatedly burned on through the dark.

Even so, in the east, though Chegahr did not notice it yet, a hollowness had come to indicate night's end.

Accordingly, as he burst across the last distances of the plain, a cock crowed in the Village. It was early, to be sure, but not by much.

At the cock's alarm, Chegahr sprang again, he sprang among the streets and lanes, under the shadow of the houses. And so stopped running. To any other who had made such speed, and curtailed it so suddenly, it might have seemed the sky fell on his back – but not so, and God bless the scholar's wife.

When Chegahr looked round, his sides merely heaving, and streaming sweat in the white cold of ending night, he beheld the sled too had come to a standstill, there, at the Village's edge, and all the thirteen wolves stamped up and down, while their tongues lolled, and in the air, coiling and boiling, was the golden whip, and also billows of the Soracsh's hair, embroidering the dark, weaving between the falling snow, her hair which was running yet to catch up with her. But strangest of all to him in that moment was the beaked prow on the sled, which all at once seemed to have the face of Chegahr's father, the lord of Seven-Willow – but doubtless he imagined it.

And then he forgot, for he heard the Soracsh cry out.

She *screamed*, no less, and in no language he had ever heard, though he had translated the words of her wolf-pack.

But some heard her. Some knew. Oh, indeed.

All through the night-ending Village, there was a banging and shouting, a bumping and scurrying. And then an unlocking and opening, a slamming and damning and hurry.

Out they came, as Chegahr later said, like rats from a drain.

Some had their lighted candles and some a lit lamp. Some were in their night-attire and some in no attire at all, and some had put on their Sunday best.

There was the horse-doctor, a quarter in his coat, and three-quarters not, and there the blacksmith in only his apron. And there came the shepherd too, all unshaven-woolly like a sheep. And there was – but I hope you will pardon my not listing everyone. For there were many others, with however among them, two servants from the High House, in two of Velonin's own nightshirts, and, and here I lay an emphasis, there was the scholar, who very luckily had returned extremely and suspiciously early, by means of a horse and cart.

Chegahr stood aside, and as he did he prized his little wolf-brother out of his teeth, and held him wrapped up for warmth in one hand.

"See, Velonin. Not your fate, nor mine. The fate of Seven-Willow. She gets what she deserves, and so do they. But she was too stupid to know it; it's we that have shown her. She'll hardly miss us now."

Just then the sled spun round, and all the thirteen white wolves spun round with it, *it* pulling *them*. And with a blood-curdling merry shriek, the Soracsh was flying off again, while her golden hair flapped and flew behind her. And so the crowds of men in the streets, and in all there were one hundred and fifty-six of them, pelted after her as fast as they could. As they went, they yelled, they dropped their lights, and hats and shoes put on now fell off, and now and then they pushed each other out of the way, or, at other moments, yanked each other forward. Until finally, every one of them, (again, very luckily including the scholar), had tumbled down among the rolling, retreating wave of the Soracsh's hair. And wound round in it, clutching and clawing at it, like kittens in yarn, they were carried away across the snow. And it seemed to Chegahr that now the direction of the fatal sled was not that of the forest, but straight on, back into the east, towards the paling sky and the stone and flint wall of the Iron Heart Mountains.

So he wished them much joy of each other and of it, one and all.

As Majlena threw open the door, which the scholar, bumbling out, had yet possessively closed, she cried, "But Chegahr, how big and yellow your eyes are, how large and sharp your teeth – and I never recall you were so hairy!"

But Chegahr seemed to gaze right through her to her sweet bones, and he said, "What you see is only another side of me."

So then she kissed him. And after that she led him, and his brother Velonin, a curled-up wolf that could have sat in a little box, to the bath she had prepared. In the bath were thyme and olibanum, myrrh and saffron, pepper and aniseed and califrass. Best of all, it was warm.

As she sponged them, Majlena, who was a real scholar, even in her dreams, sang over them old words. And as she sang, she washed off the hair and the yellow stares, she washed off the wolf teeth and the wolf form, and in the very end she washed off Velonin's reduction, so he would no longer fit in a box – unless it was man-size. And so at last in the firelight and the copper bath, there sat crowded the two brothers, two young men white with fatigue, which one could barely see, since the proximity of the Soracsh had tanned them both golden all over.

Then Velonin wept. Chegahr thought, *Now he will start thanking me in flowery phrases, on and on.*

But Velonin only said, "Oh, but I loved her, that Soracsh."

Chegahr answered, "She had a blue tongue."

"It would," said Velonin, "have matched my eyes."

For some while after, in the way of a hero in a play, or an opera, Velonin wrote poems to his lost love, the Soracsh. He wandered forlornly the snowy woods, declaiming, until one day, near evening, he noticed that every tree was strung like a harp with notes of green. And then he went back to the High House and ate a large supper. After which he threw out the skeins of gold hair he had kept – they had faded anyway, and smelled of frogs. Then he wrote to another village lord, at Tall-Wheat, as it happened. This lord had a daughter, and inside the year, she and Velonin were wed. She was a lovely girl, with flawless skin, and sensibilities. He was very kind to her, and became immensely witty. And her word was Law. Yet also she loved him.

But Chegahr and Majlena, they bought a wagon and two strong horses, and wandered away across the world. At night, by their wayside fires, they would tell each other stories, and teach each other all they knew. In the end, they were, each one, as clever as the other, equal as two stars that give the same blue light, but they had only one heart between them.

As for the Soracsh, I cannot say I have ever seen her, but I have met those who reckon to have glimpsed her sled. They relate how it is made of hard gold, and her hair of filmy, milky gold, and that her red dresses are dyed in the blood of men she has devoured raw.

Once, I did see where the sled had gone by. I was shown, in the mud of spring, the tracks of the runners. And of course, the prints of huge wolf paws, which in number were then thirteen-times-thirteen. She had harnessed them in sixteen rows of ten, and two rows of four, with one huge beast at the front, all alone. Those that have seen it in person, say it runs like a scholar.

An Iron Bride

Mirabeau said: 'War is the national industry of Prussia.' In the eighteenth and nineteenth centuries, Prussia asked her rich citizens to give up their gold and jewels to support a war, and rendered in their place, replicas of the ornaments in iron. These replicas were apparently so exquisite, that other countries tried to copy the method - inadequately. None was as good, it seems, as war-mongering Prussia.

This stern stony city in the snow, who would think that it could ever be summer here? But once it was. The lime trees had opened their parasols of aching green, birds flew about the red roofs, and in the gardens there were coloured lamps at dusk, and soft music, and laughter. Along the boulevards the carriages rattled. The sky was flowered with stars.

It was at the end of this lovely summer that they were to be married, Marten and Klovia. They had had to wait a year, as was customary. But they had not minded so very much. Though young, both were possessed of a curious maturity. Meeting each other, they knew, each of them, that they would be together for the rest of their days, and perhaps, beyond life. It was a love match, strange for their social position and era. They had been very lucky. Good luck always says, *Now I am with you, to the ending of the world.* And is believed.

Both were remarkable, he handsome and fair, she beautiful and very dark of hair and eyes. In this way, then, descending to some ballroom, he golden in his black clothes, and she crowned by night in her white dress and skin. They were the talk of the city, these two. No one wished them any ill. Sometimes perfection awakens in human things an innate nobility and spiritual height. Marten and Klovia were like a talisman, like clear weather or a winter festival. Like a promise to everyone, of what might be. And then there blew through the lavish corridor of summer the coarse trumpet note of war. Some had looked for it, and others, caught up in their own lives, not. The lovers raised their heads and saw, on the horizon, the march of men, banners and cannon, and the black smoke that follows like a raven. He held her in his arms. He said, "I'll soon be home. It will have to be an autumn wedding after all."

She said, "Kiss me."

In the dark he went away, late in the night, but when the sun rose next day, it did not rise for her. The light was gone.

235

Klovia's aunt came to the house of her mother. In the salon they drank tea, and beyond the doors, the charming garden stretched. Klovia did not eat the little cakes, and no one pressed her.

"It's been asked," said the aunt, who had once been beautiful, and now was only cruel.

"But surely…" said the mother.

"No. How can it be wrong to make a sacrifice for one's country?"

Klovia looked at her aunt stilly. In the green shade of a tree, through which the sun, meaningless, was shining, the aunt glowed with purpose.

Klovia said, "I'll do it."

"Of course," said the aunt. "There you are. The young are sometimes able to teach us."

Klovia's mother put her hand dubiously to the golden pendant that hung about her own neck. "Why do they need such things?"

"To pay for this war," said the aunt. "Do you think we should bow to our enemies?"

"But – a necklace…"

"It will be melted down. And look, do you see what's given in return? The badge of patriotism."

The aunt displayed the black cruel claws of her brooch. It was of iron. In return for an ornament of gold and pearls, they had given her an exact iron replica. It was very delicate, like a briar of thorns. Klovia undid her golden bracelet and took the two filigree golden drops from her ears.

"What else do you have?" asked the aunt.

Klovia's mother said, "Wait…"

"Many things," said Klovia.

"Fetch them," said the aunt, imperiously.

As they walked along the boulevard in their slim pale dresses, the aunt told Klovia of the virtue of what she did. It was the pride of women now to wear iron jewellery, showing they had given their riches for their country.

At a tall white building, they went in, and were treated most respectfully. Klovia placed her casket in the hands of a man who gasped in turn at this and her beauty. She was awarded a receipt written very carefully and stamped with the seal of the city.

Her aunt left her after this, and at home her mother wept over the loss of the jewels, as if she had lost her son or husband.

Klovia looked at the bare column of her slender neck, her empty wrists, the white lobes of her ears. She did not know why she had done what she did. That she would be praised for it, faintly, distantly, annoyed her. This was irrelevant.

After a week, the iron jewellery came. It was brought ceremoniously, and the banner of her land nodded in the street as the things were presented. Every item had been faithfully copied.

Klovia set them out, the rings and earrings, bracelets and necklaces and combs. Like the sun, they had grown dark and hard.

A ball was held. Klovia entered. She wore midnight blue that was nearly black. At her throat and in her ears, delicate black metal, like traceries of ink. And the other women – all the same. The men were like ghosts, only those the war had spared. Elderly men, invalids, the very young, the blind and halt and lame. Klovia danced, and did not see who she danced with. All around the bright dresses and the black iron jewellery. On the terrace of the ballroom she looked up, and there was the black iron sky set with diamonds.

An old man said to her, "I fear you find me thirty years too late."

Klovia smiled at him. She realised that one day she too must be old and all things left behind, like shells on a beach. But she had thought she would be old with Marten.

She left early. She said to her mother, "Don't ask me to go to such places anymore."

"But, my dear, you'll be talked about. It's our duty to maintain the spirit of the country."

Klovia went to her room and took out of a drawer a pair of gloves that belonged to Marten. She held them, but they were only gloves.

There had been one letter. It was full of repressed misery. She knew he would not write to her often, because there was only horror to tell her of. Even when he wrote of his love for her, it had become part of the horror, as if, by loving her, he had made himself the reasonable prey of war. It seemed to her she did not exactly miss him or grieve. It was only as if half herself had been cut away.

She took off the iron jewellery and went to bed and slept, for she was healthy and youthful still. Outside, a nightingale sang in a garden tree. She dreamed she stood in the garden with Marten, as she had often done, and the nightingale sang on. When she touched her lover's hand, it was cold.

"What does the nightingale say?" she asked.

"That I love you."

But she knew it was no longer so. He had surely ceased to love her, for love had become a piece with the desperate darkness of war. And when the sun rose in the dream, it was black, with rays like thorns.

After three months, Klovia knew she would never see Marten again. When acquaintances spoke of him, boldly and gladly, to cheer or please her, she smiled politely, as she had to the old man at the ball. Marten in turn had become unreal. Perhaps he had never existed, and she and her mother, and all these other people, had simply imagined him. Before her stretched her life, which now had no meaning or interest. She had been trained from childhood, as rich women of her country had always been, to show nothing publicly of her deeper emotions, possibly not really to think of them.

Her gracious fortitude and bravery became a by-word of the city. They understood, if she must not, what she had been deprived of.

The summer passed into a russet golden autumn. There was a tall white church, and here Klovia and her mother and hundreds of others regularly went, to praise God for His grossly imperfect world and His faulty erratic genius, and to thank Him for any occasional fortune or happiness they might have scavenged.

From this temple Klovia was coming out, when the news was brought her, in front of five hundred people, on the steps, that Marten had been killed. Klovia stood quite still in her dark red gown, holding the letter in her gloved hands that had a bracelet of black iron. The captain saluted her and spoke in ringing tones of Marten's courage, and how he had sacrificed his life for the honour of his land.

The crowd stood hushed. The crisp blue air was electric. Klovia nodded, and bowed her head.

"He is a hero," cried the captain. "His name will be remembered for ever."

A strange thing happened to Klovia. For a moment, only that, she could not remember Marten's name at all.

Klovia sat waiting through the autumn. She did not know for what she waited. Perhaps for them to bring her, again, the bad news. Her mother wept copiously and even the maids in the fine house shed tears over the loss of Marten. Klovia did not cry. It was as if she did not have the proper mechanism. She wondered if she ever had cried – in childhood certainly. She recalled as a child how her doll was broken – she had cried then. And when a favourite cat had died, then too. But now her eyes were as empty as her life. No one now expected her to do anything in the way of social things. It was accepted she would be reclusive. Only to the church she was still supposed to go, as she was supposed to pray to God, who had presumably permitted the death of Marten in horrible circumstances of blood and maiming, for the care of Marten's soul. She did go to the church, but did not pray at all. She closed her eyes and thought of trivial things, that a new button must be sewn on her cuff, that she was thirsty. However, every day, although no other social obligations were entailed, Klovia must rise and dress, breakfast and lunch and dine, attend her weeping mother, and listen to her mother's curious entreaties that she too, Klovia, should burst into loud sobbing.

"What's wrong with you?" cried Klovia's mother. "Are you unfeeling?"

But Klovia's aunt said, "Don't be foolish. Klovia's grief is assuaged by her pride in him. He died for his country."

Sometimes the war was mentioned. It was going very well.

One morning, an important official arrived at the house. He showed Klovia and her mother a complex document with the seal of the city. Klovia waited politely, looking at his face, and sometimes modestly lowering her eyes. But she did not hear much of what he said. She was thinking that the leaves would soon be gone from all the garden trees, turning them from gold to black.

"And today, this very evening, it will be brought here."

"It is a great honour," said Klovia's mother. "We are touched. My daughter's very sensible of this kindness."

Klovia raised her eyes. "It is more than I deserve," she said.

The official was gratified. He assured her that her stamina in loss had been an inspiration to the whole city. He went out.

Klovia's mother was flushed and excited. She exclaimed that she must send a message at once to the aunt.

Klovia said, "It... will come this evening."

"Yes. And a perfect likeness. No one else has been recognised in this way."

Klovia was puzzled. She lowered her eyes now to the complicated paper, and slowly read it. So she learned at last that she was to be given a life-size statue of her lover, Marten, modelled precisely to resemble him, and the face also, for a mould had been taken of this after death. Her city regretted that no valuable material was available because of the war. The statue was made of black iron.

As evening fell, the statue arrived with great circumstance, and was carried into the house and so out into the garden to a suitable site. After a lot had been said, and Klovia had made her thanks, she was left alone to stand beside the iron Marten, staring up into the face that had been constructed from a death-mask, and then its eyelids opened. Indeed, it did look just like him, handsome and graceful, the high intelligent forehead and strong jaw, the classical mouth and nose, wide eyes, and fall of hair. There was a secretive smiling look to the face, however, that he had never worn in life. He knew things now that living persons did not.

Night sank down to the grass, and Klovia was summoned into the lamplit house to dress and dine with her mother and aunt, and two or three officials. After this, in her black necklace and bracelets, Klovia slipped out again, and stood under the trees, looking up into the black eyes of Marten. No one tried to dissuade her.

Nevertheless, far into the night, she was called in again, to go through the decorum of undressing and lying down in bed.

About two in the morning, she descended through the house and let herself out once more. Once more she stood beside the statue.

The night was cold and crystalline with frost, and no nightingale sang, but Klovia did not think of this. Although when she touched the statue, the cold of it burned her.

It was the same height that Marten had been. In the darkness it truly might have been he, except it had no light or warmth. It did not speak or move. It did not think.

Klovia had remained puzzled. She gazed on and on into the black face and eyes, trying to undo the riddle. In place of her golden lover, they had given her an iron bridegroom. What did this mean? At last she gave it up, stopped considering it at all. She stepped between the statue's arms and stood against it, her hands loose at her sides, looking up even now, as if to receive, the pressure of his kiss.

At the hour of arising, no one could find Klovia. They searched through the house and finally went out into the garden. Initially they did not discover her. However, at length, her mother noticed that the iron statue under the trees, the statue, of Marten, had altered. Presently Klovia's mother fell on the lawn in a faint. No one went to her aid for some while. They were arrested in contemplation of the statue – which had overnight become that of two persons, a handsome young man, and a lovely young girl, gazing up into his face as though awaiting some caress. Both figures were of black iron, and the frost had webbed them over with delicate filigree which, catching the sunlight appeared to be made of gold.

Girls in Green Dresses

This is for John Kaiine, who, on my mentioning the story-less title, told me who they were, and promptly recounted most of the tale of Elrahn.

In the dim diluted light an hour before the dawn, the girl's father took her hand. And soon after they set out on the long walk to the lake among the reeds.

The river flows into the lake from the hills, then flows away again, down to the sea. It is a green river, and the lake, tidal but also capable of deep stillness, is green too. The tallest reeds grow there, taller far than a child-girl of thirteen years, as was Elaidh that morning. Men and women, and children too, go there now and then to cut the reeds for the thatch, and for their healing value. But not so often any more. Since the lake is thought an unsafe and mysterious place, not gentle with humankind.

Yet it looked well, that morning, the water a milky green among the circle of the round hills, and the mist just stealing away as the sun came up unseen, only the sky lighting to show its path. A heron rose from the reeds, steel-pale in the twilight, but every stem shivered, and the ripples fled over the lake as a woman gathers her stitches when she sews a cloth. But then the reeds were once more still as if made of iron, and the lake was like a plate of misty glass. And silence spoke with its own voice.

"Are you cold?" asked the father, Elrahn.

"No, Dadda."

"Are you afraid?"

"No, Dadda."

"We'll sit, then. We must wait. We'll eat our breakfast on the shore."

So in the lea of a willow they ate their bread, dipped in sweet black tea. They waited. He did not tell her the story then, for he had already told her, over and over, all the years of her life that she could listen. Only the silence spoke, then sang

He had been a baby, Elrahn, when he took the snow-sickness Not many take it, nor live that take it. Those that do are ever after marked.

And that was how he grew up then a fine young man, but with hair

241

and skin so white, and his face and body, all his fleshly surface, pitted by the silvery pocks the fever had made on him, that are like a mountain leopard's paw-marks in the snow.

"He will have second sight," said the old women. But he did not.

"He'll go off for a soldier," said the men. He never did.

"Religion is always a refuge and consolement," said the priest, standing lonely under the church's dome. But Elrahn did not come to be taught about God.

"He will never wed," said the girls, "though we should like him, if it were not for his snow-leopard skin."

And Elrahn did not court or marry. He did not even glance at the girls, and if he thought of them when he was not with them, it was impossible for them to say.

His mother was a widow – his father was long dead of the spirit that he had brewed at his own still. But when Elrahn was seventeen or so, the mother too died. And besides she had never liked Elrahn much nor been very kind to him, preferring her other sons. These presently kicked him out, and it was winter too. "Go cuddle the snow or find a leopard to live with, or a wolf, Elrahn. It's sick of the sight of your white scales we are."

Elrahn did not answer. He seldom said a lot. He picked himself up and walked off along the village street through the snow, not looking back once. Only the priest followed him a little way, shouting, "Return, dear Elrahn. God loves you." But Elrahn did not return.

Elrahn walked all through the dark, white day, and when he was hungry and thirsty, he took up some of the snow, or plucked an icicle and sucked it. Later he found a barn to sleep in and there was a cow there with a calf, and he had a little of the warm milk

The next day Elrahn met a kind of travelling show. There were three painted wagons strung with bells, and drawn by shaggy ponies, and in the wagons were those who danced or jumped through fire, or performed magic tricks for money. And also there was a woman pretty enough to make you blink, but she was only the height of the back of a young dog. And also there was a dog, that had wings. Though it could not fly until hoisted up in a harness from invisible wires by night, to deceive the ignorant in various villages.

The show-master was a man in a fine coat with brass buttons. He gave Elrahn a piece of cheese with bread and a cup of liquor. "Well, my handsome fellow, are you marked like that all over? What do you say to going with us? You can be our serpent prince, the child of a man and a female snake. Your food, and one hundredth of whatever we'll take in coins."

Elrahn was staring at a blue ape that could walk across the tops of narrow sticks and was doing so. The cheese was tasty, and besides the pretty dwarf had given him a sort of look he had never been given – or noticed he was given – before.

"I will," said Elrahn.

Some while Elrahn was with the show-wagons. In the villages and little rambling stone towns, he stood naked but for a kilt and some ornament painted to look like gold. The people gaped, for in those parts they had never even heard of the snow-sickness. And when he stuck out his tongue, stained black for purpose, they gasped.

Life among the wagons was not bad. It was better than it had been in the village and with the mother and her other sons.

The blue ape was full of jokes and the winged dog liked running, and would warm your feet by the fire. The troupe were daring. And besides, there was the lovely dwarf.

But then one day, in a town above a high forest, a rich man saw the dwarf and he made her an offer of love and marriage.

"Elrahn," said she, "we have been good friends, but I would be a fool to refuse this chance. He is a kind man, if not good-looking or young. And I am coming to the end of my bloom. You'll tire of me, in any case."

Another man in Elrahn's place might have said, Never! But Elrahn said nothing like that. Nor did he say, You are breaking my heart, or, You are a bitch. Only his eyes filled with tears, but he looked away, and she did not see, or if she did she did not say. Instead he answered, "I wish you well and happy."

After the dwarf woman was gone, Elrahn had less interest in the wagons. He told the master so.

"Ah, then, just come down to the reedlands with me," said the man, "for they say there you can find a mermaid, and I should like, I would, to have a mermaid among my show."

Elrahn agreed to this. He thought he might as well go on with them until he found some other thing to do.

The spring was begun, and the reedlands were green. The greenest place on earth they seemed, as they always do then, and in the summer. Even the sky looks green, in its way, between the stems, and from willow islands in the rivers, the emerald ducks fly out in swarms like bees.

There was a big old inn, and here the three wagons stopped for several days.

As he drank beer under the low beams, the show-master asked to hear the local tales.

So then they were telling him everything, of giants in the hills who had left the ruins of their castles there, of ghosts that dance on the thirteenth night of every month and of the demon-fox that steals babies left in the fields and changes them to foxes.

The show-master and his troupe listened to all this, but Elrahn could see the master was impatient. Elrahn wondered why the master did not ask straight out for the tale he wanted, the story of the mermaids. But as Elrahn never said a lot, he never said a single word now.

And then an old man came over and held out his mug for some beer.

"Welcome, Grandda," said the master. "What tale do you have, then?"

"No tale at all," said the old man. "Only this warning. Do not go down to the lake in these days of the spring."

"And why is that, Grandda?"

"If you do, you may see there the girls in green dresses. And then no man alive, nor God in His sky, can save you."

A great thick hush had fallen. Even the fire dropped down on the hearth, and the winged dog folded his wings close, and went under the table.

"Why is that, then, Grandda? Are they so terrible, these girls in green dresses?"

"So they are."

"And *why* are they?"

The old man said, "Ask the dead, for they know."

Then the show-master nodded, and refilled the old man's beer-mug, and said the ape would dance on the rafters upside down, which it did. And the other matter was let go.

Except that, near midnight, as they were all in bed, the master woke Elrahn up. "Tomorrow, at first light, we walk to the lake, you and I."

"Do you want?"

"Are you a dunce, or what? Do you not know what the old man said?"

Elrahn said he did not.

"Listen then. They call them that here, girls in green dresses. There are *mermaids* in spring in this lake. And we shall catch one or I'll be hanged by my tassel."

They say the mermaids would come in from the sea, up the river to the lake, in spring. As salmon come in, to spawn. But a mermaid is a fish only up to her middle, and from there she is a naked woman. So, if she should stand upright on her tail out of the water among the green reeds, she may look like a girl clad in green...

All this the master explained to Elrahn as down to the lake they went, brushing through the spangle-dew before sunrise.

The sun was just opening its eye when they reached the shore. A sight of beauty it was, the coin of water lying there so still among the misty hills, and the rim of the flame-green reeds, and the sun just touching the world with one crystal finger. And then the dawn wind stirred and blew on the reeds, and they rattled like harp-strings struck by an unseen hand.

But when the wind was gone, all was still again. And Elrahn was taken with the idea that human things and animals breathe, and so are always in a sort of motion, while they live. But the land and the heaven and the water, which do not breathe at all, may lie as still as if turned to glass.

Then the master spoke in a fierce quick whisper. "See! Do you see, *there?*"

Elrahn looked. A duck was swimming along the lake. No, it was a great fish. And he thought they might have brought a rod or net, to catch some fish for breakfast. And then he thought, curiously, of the Bible, which the priest had kept telling him of, and of the thing spoken to a fisher-man, saying he should be a fisher of men.

Just then the fish broke the surface of the lake, and oh, it was not any fish at all, but a young girl with skin as white as winter snow and hair as green as water. And then down she dived again and there was the flip of her tail, and the unbreathing lake was turned once more to glass.

Elrahn was amazed, but the show-master was already going out between the reeds, standing himself on the shore. And in his hands he held a shining string that looked like gold, but Elrahn knew it would only be painted.

He thinks that will catch her, thought Elrahn. But he himself knew nothing about mermaids, and perhaps it would.

Presently there came again a rippling and whirling in the water, and suddenly the water broke in a hundred pieces, and up out of it burst two creatures, and they were, without any doubt, mermaids, the pair of them.

"See my sweet girls—" boldly cried the master, "look—a golden chain! I have heard how you like to gather treasures. Should you like this golden chain?"

And then they looked and they laughed, the two mermaids.

Elrahn thought he had never heard a sound so charming or so cruel.

It was true they were naked to the waist, and a little below. They had long slim arms and throats, and round white breasts with centres pink as coral. Their lips were pink like that, and the long nails on their hands, and as they laughed he saw their teeth, which were white and very sharp. And Elrahn remembered he had heard once a sailor speak of big fish in the sea with teeth, called sharks.

Their hair was long and green and wrapped them over as they moved and then uncovered them. Their tails were a silvery green, and utterly the tails of fish, with silver fins like fans. Their eyes were pale so he could not be sure of their colour, but it was somewhere between the other colours of them, green and white and silver – and also pink.

"Come, sweetlets, come to me and take the chain…" cried the show-master, gambolling along the shore and jinking the painted string, and the mermaids laughed, and dived and whirled and came up again, always nearer the shore, and then they clove through a reed-bank and stood up among the reeds, tall on their tails, and they were two girls in green dresses.

"Come away," called Elrahn to the show-master.

But the master did not hear. He thought he fished for mermaids and held out the bait, and would soon catch both – and once on land they would be helpless as any fish thrashing and rolling and at the mercy of anything on legs. Yet Elrahn saw their playful strength and suppleness and their sharp teeth and the pink under the green of their eyes. Elrahn heard the old Grandda at the inn saying, "Then no man alive, nor God in His sky, can save you."

"Master – come away!" called Elrahn, now loudly.

And when he did this the mermaids both turned their heads as one, and stared right at him.

And under the silver-green and pink of their eyes, was black, a black as deep as the unsounded depths of the outermost seas, from which they had come.

What a journey it must be for them, with all the trial and danger the in-running salmon finds. The terrible currents and waiting enemies, the rocks and tides, the change from salt to soft water. Yes, they were strong, these girls, and cunning too, for they had survived. Yet why, he wondered, why did they come in at all? For the salmon came to mate, but surely these ones – *their* kind lived in the sea?

Right then, one of the mermaids dived down under the reeds. She vanished, but the other lingered there flirting still and smiling at the master, and at Elrahn too, and waving her hands now, in a sort of amorous half-embracing way.

Elrahn strode out towards the master. This man had, after all, taken him in even if for profit, fed him, and been polite, and even bought him drink the night the dwarf lady was wed.

When she saw Elrahn also was striding towards the lake, the mermaid in the reeds shook her shimmering hair for pleasure. Then Elrahn broke into a run.

But he had not yet reached the master when out of the purling water at the master's very feet, the first mermaid broke like a shining spear up from the lake.

The master shouted and held the golden string high to entice her on. But in the next moment, she seemed to sink down over on him like a wave. Elrahn saw her arms about the master's neck, and her hair falling all across him, and then the gleaming fish's tail swung up and round, and the master, held in the coil of it as if in the coils of a snake, was falling over. Over into the lake he fell, all twined in tail and hair and arms. There was a sparkling slither and a splash. Elrahn beheld the fan-like tail-fins flash from the water once, then go under.

Both had gone under, the mermaid-girl and the show-master – gone without a trace. And the water closed shut upon them.

Elrahn stood there with his heart drumming, and he thought he must run back now to the inn and get what help he could. And as he thought this, he knew there was no use at all in it. But he had forgotten the other one, the other mermaid, and in that very instant in her turn she was there.

What he had only seen with his eyes a moment ago, now happened to him.

Her arms were cool and silken and her clasp unbreakable, and her hair like the green reeds and smelling of spring flowers and mud. Her mouth, which was a woman's, laughed in his face and her breath smelled of the open sea. Then the horror of her tail, muscular as the body of a leopard, seized him. And he was pulled over at once before he could do anything, into the white slap of the water and down into the dark of the dark below.

If he had thought a single last thing, which he had not, Elrahn would have said a prayer, knowing it must be death he went to. And, it is no lie, in any other case it would have been death.

The mermaids came up the river to the lake in spring to fish for men. And when they caught them, they ate them – but this Elrahn only learned later, when he had learned too something of the mer-language. They told him then, or *she* told him, the one who caught him, that just as men relished fish, so certain fish relished the flesh of men. Indeed, she said, a mermaid would not eat a fish, for mermaids were themselves partly of fish-kind. "But you are also of mankind!" exclaimed Elrahn. She said this was not so. Mermaids in their other half were of *woman*kind. And so they would not eat a woman either. Not a fish or a woman or a human child. Only a man. And they preferred, as some humans prefer fresh-water fish – fresh-water men.

The name of this mermaid, who had caught and thereafter owned him, was Trisaphee. Hers was the only name among them he ever learned, for the sounds of their tongue still bewildered him even after he came to understand it somewhat. Their voices too, under the lake, were also like water. He never heard them speak or sing or call in the sea, for when the time came for them to return there, his days with them were over and done.

That *first* day, Elrahn woke up lying not, in darkness, but in dimness. What he could see was water, and there could be no doubt of what it was. The movement of it was like that of thin cloths drawn over and against each other, but bubbles littered through, all bright. And even the sun shone in with one smoky shaft, though far off.

And he saw too that *they* were going to and fro, swimming over and about each other in an endless dance.

There were many hundreds of them. A clan of them. A host. All were female, with breasts and long, long hair, and all were fish from a little below the waist.

They were very lovely, to be sure. The loveliest thing he ever looked on, apart from the full moon. But at this hour he thought of their beauty less than his own terror and the place he was in.

After a while, he next realised that he, a breathing thing of the world, still breathed.

Then he got up, and he went about to see how it was that he could. And *then* he found he had been shut up in a cage, but it was a cage of air, a great round bubble that somehow had been formed, and when he put his fists against it, its walls did not rupture, only trembled.

All this while the mermaids swam about him, some paying him no attention, but some staring in. And their eyes, like this, under the lake, were sombre green and beautiful and quite human in their shape and form – yet too, they were luminous as the eyes of cats or *demons*.

Soon, *she* was there. That is, Trisaphee, only then he did not know her name. She came and she shook her hair at him, which underwater was like a sequinned veil.

"Let me go, you witch," said Elrahn.

But the instant he said it he thought he had been a fool. For though she seemed to grasp what he said – and many of them, he after found, knew the language of men – she was the more powerful, and his foe.

However, even through the vast bubble of air, she said something to him. He knew not a word of it, even if he could make out the liquid sounds. But then she spoke in his own tongue, and she said, "Stay still, you Man. You belong to me, and we will not harm you."

This done, she swam away.

Then all of them swam off, and not long after the shaft of sun faded, and everything was darkness.

Perhaps he slept, or simply lost his wits again from fear. Waking once more, he saw the moonlight pierced the water as the sun had done. And in the rays of the moon, more dreadful than any sight he ever saw before or after, Elrahn made out the skull and bones, and something of the body, what had been left of it, of the show-master, lying there on his own fine coat with the brass buttons, with the gold-painted string of bait tangled between.

How long exactly Elrahn lived in the bubble he was afterwards unsure. But he said that he kept some count, by the gilded shaft of sun and the bluish one of the moon, and maybe it was a fortnight.

The very second day, the master's bones were cleared. But he knew that was not for any Godly burial, for he saw one of the mermaids gnawing at a thigh bone – and some while after this one returned, and lo and behold, she had refashioned the bone as a pipe and she played on it a low, mournful, underwater song, which Elrahn took a mortal hatred for.

But then too, Elrahn thought, the master would have caught a mermaid if he could and put her in his show. Perhaps she would have had less kindness than he gave the dog or the ape—she would have been a slave, and crippled on the land by her tail.

It was Trisaphee who took care of Elrahn.

She brought him fresh fish, newly killed and cleaned, and though he must eat them raw in the bubble, they were not so bad. Also she brought him ducks' eggs, and once or twice human bread, and once a bottle of tea with some berry jam stirred in—but these last things he would not bring himself to swallow, for they had certainly come from others who had been killed and devoured.

Why had she not slain and eaten Elrahn? He never had to ask her, for in the end, he fathomed it for himself. It was his skin. His skin which, though that of a man, stayed – save at the head and groin—hairless and clear white as any mermaid's. Also was he not, from the snow-sickness, pocked and scaled like a snake or a fish?

He came to see, between the clocks of the sun and the moon, that he was kept by Trisaphee as her pet. She fed him, and even she pushed in—like the food through the sides of the bubble, by some uncanny aperture of which he was never certain – lake water in a crock that, he might drink and wash himself.

As a prisoner will, where they are able, he tried to keep himself in health, and keep his brain in sanity and his soul in hope.

But one morning, by the sun-shaft clock, Trisaphee came and she lashed the side of the bubble with her tail, and the lake gushed through. The water covered all and in a minute or less, Elrahn was drowned.

And then he thought, *But I am not.* Nor was he. And so he found that, by a magical means in the bubble, which was itself, maybe, part air and part water, he had mastered the art of breathing liquid. Then out he swam, and in the marvel of this wonder, he turned and saw Trisaphee was smiling at him in a loving, tender way. And she stroked his hair and kissed him with her icy mouth, between the eyes, before she put on to him the harness and the lead.

He was her dog, then. Where she went, he might go with her, if so she wished. But when she did not wish it, she tied him to some post or rock or curious aqueous stalagmite under the lake.

To the surface they never ascended. But now and then into the depths they did go, where it was so black he could not see, and then she shortened the leash, and guided him, with her other hand resting on his neck.

What did he think of this? He was angry, but also he liked her touch. Yes, even though she was what she was and had done what she had done. And not long after, as he learned from her pieces of her language and she spoke somewhat in his own, she announced to him she herself had not eaten any of the body of his friend, the show-master. And when Elrahn, hearing that, swore an oath, she too swore she was blameless of it, and this in his own tongue. And she swore on the name of God.

This gave Elrahn pause. For the priest in his birthplace had once assured him no soulless or evil thing could speak God's name.

Then again, Trisaphee gave Elrahn presents. He did not, of course, want the leash, though it was plainly of real gold, a very proper metal, and set with pearls. But also she gave him a silver ring fixed with a jewel like a fox's eye, and then she regaled him with stories of treasure hoards in the seas to which her kind had access. And when his clothes wore out in the water, she brought him leggings of some strange stuff. She said they had been made from the skin of a shark her kind had killed in war.

"Do you fight, then, Trisaphee?"

She assured him they must, to live.

"How were you born?" he asked her once, one time when they rested under a cliff far down in the lake to watch the clouds of fish, which blew about there.

"In the usual way," said she.

"But," he said, "seeing you are a woman but also – a fish, like these, and also because you say your kind are *only* female..."

But she would not answer him directly, and only said she had lived many hundreds of years and would live many hundreds more, and could not recall her start.

At this time, it must be admitted, he felt he understood the tongue of her kind better than perhaps he did, and so may have mistaken her words. But also she had spoken partly in his own tongue, and he could have had the right of it.

Always he had been an outcast. And even when he had journeyed with the wagons, Elrahn had not existed as most men do, nor lived by the normal laws. In this way, for him, this being under the lake among the green fish-girls was only another eccentric phase of his odd life. While he himself had been well taught he was a monster of some type.

He flowed along with his fate therefore, resisting only a little, and that only in the matter of the harness and lead, and those moral issues to do with eating human flesh. He flowed with the currents, and in the company of Trisaphee. And now and then he saw not only that she was beautiful but that she was a living thing, and even under the lake she breathed, as he did, and was not made of glass or water.

One morning – the sun shaft was there – Trisaphee took him away up the lake to a spot they had never before swum to. Wide watery caves ran into the under-side of the hills above. They were black as night, yet things clung in them, lichens and weeds and stones that glowed.

Trisaphee sat herself on a rock, and only her hair kept up its furling spun-silk motion. A mermaid's hair is never so beautiful above the water as it is below.

Presently she spoke in Elrahn's language, which – as only years later he came to see – she had grown more accomplished at as her time with him progressed.

"You have been with me now a while, my Man. If I were to ask what you would like most in the world that I could give you, what should it be?"

Elrahn looked at her. He said not a word.

"Well," said she, "it's tired out by the lake you must be. And so it is with us. Soon we shall be turning down the rivers to the sea. And there I will not take you, for there I could never keep you safe. What shall I be doing with you, then?"

When it seemed she would wait on and on for his answer, he looked her in the eye and he said, "So *now* you will murder me."

"No," said Trisaphee. "You shall live. But what would you like?"

"To live, then," he said, "and to go free."

"It's tired of me too, so you are," she said.

"How not, seeing you keep me on a chain like your dog?"

"Have I not fed and cared for you, am I not kind and loving to you?"

"As to your dog."

Then she stretched out her hand and tapped the harness where it circled him, and it flew off and went bounding away through the water.

"Be free," said Trisaphee, "and not my dog."

He thanked her.

"But what will you have?" she inquired.

"You have given it. And if you'll let me go up now to the light and air – that is all I ask."

"Ask for something more," said she.

Elrahn showed her the ring on his finger. "I have this of you, which is worth money in the world. That is enough, if I can keep it."

"Oh, keep it, keep it, sell it and forget me," said Trisaphee.

"How can I *forget* you?" he angrily asked. "Do you think I am *mad?* You are a mermaid of the deeps."

Then she smiled. "Then what would you have?" she asked again.

Elrahn had not been much with women, but he had been with one, the dwarf lady, and so at last, a tinkling bell rang somewhere in his brain. He widened his eyes at Trisaphee, wondering if he could be mistaken. And if he were not, whether he wished he were.

"I do not presume," said Elrahn prudently.

Then Trisaphee left the rock and she came and wrapped him round with her arms and body and hair and tail. It was as it had been that first time when she caught him and pulled him over into the lake. Yet, much more gentle, and to say he did not care for it would be to speak falsely. Then she kissed his mouth, and it was the kiss a woman gives her lover, though her lips tasted of brine and her tongue of silver water.

And could there be any man in such an embrace who would not

wonder what he must do next, seeing she was formed as she was. But before he could attempt a single thing with her, she suddenly let him go, and floated from him with a look so sad and ancient now, he believed at last she was old as the oceans and full of sorrow, and the salt in her was not only sea but unshed tears.

"I will tell you now, my Man. You may swim up to the land. And not one of us will harm you. But when you come ashore you will feel a hurt in your chest. Have no fear of it. It is only the air coming back into your body. Spit the moisture from your mouth and void it from your nose and all will be well with you. But never again will you be able to breathe in the water."

"Very well." said Elrahn "but…"

"I am not done," said she. "Listen well to me. Tonight you will dream of me, and everything you might like to have of me you will have, but only in sleep. When you wake, you will discover there is yet something left with you that is ours, yours and mine. And heed me now, care for it, that thing, or I will curse you. Thirteen years from this day's night, you must come back to this water's edge, and prove to me you have done as I say. And on that night before that morning, distant by thirteen years, which to me are like thirteen quarters of an hour, you will see me again in a dream. But in the daybreak you will see and meet me among the reeds. And you will have with you that thing I have left with you now. Or else woe betide you."

All the while she spoke to him in this way, Elrahn felt his skin crawl with a strange thin fear. And even as he felt the fear he felt a sort of love for her and a sadness for her, and besides, he lusted for her.

"Say yes, now," she said. "Let me hear you say yes, so that I know I have made you understand."

"I understand nothing, but I will say yes, to make you happy."

"Ah," said Trisaphee, "what is happiness? I am familiar with a joy your kind can never know, except in heaven."

And then she turned in the water, brilliant as a star, and swift as a dart she shot away.

Elrahn hesitated only a moment or so. Then he too raced from the cave, and raising his arms, he rushed for the surface.

All the while he was diving up, with the little fishes storming off before him, he was certain others of her tribe might come and attack him. But he saw none of them, and in a space of minutes, the water turned from sable to fair and then to jade and so to gold. And then he broke the skin of the lake and swam wildly for the nearest shore. And a pain began in his chest and lungs as if he breathed in molten bronze.

When at last he fell out among the reeds, he coughed and choked and hawked and spat away the spell and the water. And then he lay a time under the sun, until he was able to get up and go on his way.

Elrahn did not walk towards the inn, nor did he really recognise the place where he had beached, to find that inn. He walked away from the reedlands, and up into the hills, and everything he saw was a great marvel to him, from the tall trees to the little sparrows, and the grey hares that sprang along in the fields. As for the sky, he could hardly bear to look at it, it was so mighty and so lighted up, so *blue*. When night came on, the stars made him weep. It seemed, even by starshine, he had never seen such colours.

How long had he been in the lake? A week or two, a month or two. But he might have been gone a lifetime.

And he resolved he would tell no one the story of what had befallen him, for who would believe it but for the people of the inn, or the people from the wagons who would blame him for the death of their master?

Last of all he thought he might not sleep, but keep himself awake, and he was hungry enough he fancied that would not be so difficult. Truth to tell, he was frightened now by what she had said to him, the mermaid, about the dream and that something would be left between them, and he must care for it and show her, in thirteen years, he had, or be cursed. He was afraid at last, if *all* the truth be told, of everything that had happened.

But in the end, sitting up staring under the burning stars, he slept.

And he dreamed what many a man would, things being as they were. He dreamed of Trisaphee, and that he lay in the reeds above the lake with her, and she had wrapped him in her reedy hair and her fish's tail, caressing him while he caressed her, and without possessing her, yet he *possessed* her. And so vast was the pleasure that he cried out loud. And in a while he looked her in her fiery eyes, and he said, "Yes, there is one other joy, under heaven, that I know."

But waking a second later, he was aware that he had *not* possessed her in any way, but only given his seed to the grass. And with a bitter sigh, he moved his sleeping place. And after that he slumbered dreamless till the morning.

The sun was over the trees by the time he roused again. The birds were singing, and he lay in rapture to hear them, after all those shadow days of the mournful, heartless songs of the mermaid kind.

When he got up, he saw how in parts the dew still sparkled on the grass. And then he saw that one bead of dew was larger than all the rest. And when he went to see, he found a big gleaming pearl that lay in the lap of the earth. But even as he stood there watching it, the pearl swelled larger and greater and soon it was the size of a thumbnail, and then the head of a spoon and then of a cup and then of a plate, and then it cracked open, and out fell a tiny child, white and translucent as an asphodel.

This child, a girl, lay in the grass with her dreamy eyes gazing at him. Next she seemed to harden over, her flesh losing its fairy look of flowers. Soon she was opaque, and big nearly as a baby two months old. She breathed, and she hiccupped, and then she cried.

"What on God's earth shall I do with this?" said Elrahn. But anyway he picked her up, and took her where they could both find food and shelter. And here he told the people a tale not the facts. Such fact he told to her alone, to the child from the pearl, that in a while he called Elaidh, his daughter, through a kind of birth, by the mermaid Trisaphee.

Now, as they sat on the shore of the morning lake, to which they had come back in her thirteenth spring, Elaidh looked up when again her father spoke.

"These have been good years together, child."

"Yes, Dadda."

"I have loved you, Elaidh. But you were never more than half mine, and this I have told you often, from as soon as you might hear."

"I am a mermaid's daughter," said Elaidh.

She was solemn as the quietness of the lake, and her long hair was the pale brown of a duck's wing, but her eyes were green.

"Now and then," said Elrahn, as if idly, but not looking at her at all, "I thought I would see you grow to be a woman, and I should dance at your wedding when the fiddler played his best tunes."

Elaidh said "I would like that, Dadda. But now I love you first."

"Do not be loving me," said Elrahn, "and I must not love you, for it's your mother loves you best. She made you with me, which is how all her clan make their children, by a sort of magic, and they are always daughters. Last night I saw her again in a dream, only the second dream I ever had of her. I never saw her all these years till then. But it was as she promised or she warned me. She told me this, Elaidh. And she told me she will swim up in a while today, out of the lake. And when you see her, she is that lovely, Elaidh, and young still as when I met her last. She will never grow old, and not for an age will she die. Her kind live for centuries, perhaps they do for ever. And this too she said I must say to you: How they roam all the waters, the fresh and the salt, the endless oceans that lead one into another, and the rivers and the lakes that pierce and cross the land. How they own vast treasures, huge rubies and diamonds and hoards of golden coins that have gone down with ships, and pearls that grow in the shells of creatures in the sea. How they play on sands miles under water, lit at night by a moon so vigorous its light is as the summer at midday. And how they sing and make music. And how they are free as the tides. And their beauty, Elaidh, and I should know it, is like a secret of the heart."

"Yes, Dadda?" asked the child, all attention.

"You and I," said he, "have had our life together. A chancy travelling existence. Doing this and that, mending, fetching, or pulling trick birds from a scarf to tickle crowds. I have taught you the little I know, little enough it could fit inside an acorn. That was all I could do, but it was given to me to do it. And at first it seemed too much for me, the task. And then it was only simple as to breathe. And now, it's done. For when she comes from the lake, your mother Trisaphee, she will offer another life to you. She will offer to take you among her own kind, half of which kind you are. By her spell, your hair will turn to the colour of the reeds, and you will have a tail like a fish, strong as a leopard. And water and air will be alike to your lungs. You will live for centuries never growing old. You will journey through the oceans, free as the tides, playing with rubies and pearls. You will be a mermaid, if so you wish it."

The child stared. She said, "But if not?"

Elrahn said. "Then you'll stay with me and be my daughter. You will wed a man and bear his children, not as she and I bore you, but in pain and labour. You will likely be poor, and certainly hard-worked, and you will wither with the years, a piece of time which to a mermaid is like an afternoon. Then you will die and be dust. Unless, as the priest said, you have a soul. We have been good friends – but oh, a mermaid – you would be a fool to refuse this chance."

Then all at once Elaidh had turned from him and Elrahn knew why. He heard the murmur of the water, the flutter of it as if a great fish swam just under the surface. Then came a dash of light and water-drops.

Turning himself, he saw Trisaphee standing there, as in the second dream he had, lifted on her tail in the reeds, a girl dressed all in green.

And she held out her smiling arms, not to him, but to Elaidh, and Elaidh jumped to her feet and ran towards her mother and the lake, the centuries and the shadows, to sing and laugh, and to bite the bones of men.

Elaidh had her foot even on the water's hem. She had let her hand almost into the hand of the tall green girl, her mother, who seemed only five or seven years her older. Already Elaidh felt the coolness of the lake, the freedom of a fish, she smelled the ocean and the opening of infinity.

But then, she glanced back.

There *he* stood, her father, straight and scaled and calm, no longer young. And he raised his hand in farewell. "Elaidh, my love, I wish you well and happy."

But she saw his eyes, they were full of salty water, full of tears.

Elaidh took her foot out of the lake's edge, and put down her hands. She stood on the lakeshore and looked at her wonderful mother, the mermaid.

"Mother," said Elaidh, "thank you so kindly for your queenly offer. But I will stay here with mankind. I'll stay with my da."

And Trisaphee made a sound, that might have been the human word *Why?*

"Oh," said Elaidh, "because they kept me when you let me go, and he lets me go when I *would* go and you would take me. Because they can cry salt water. Tears – that is ocean enough for me. I will stay with my da."

And turning, Elaidh walked back along the shore, into the land.

Behind her came a splash they say, as if every mirror in the world had been smashed in fragments. No more but that, and the reeds again were empty, green, and silent as the moon.

The Sea Was In Her Eyes

This sequel to "Girls in Green Dresses" is also for John Kaiine – who told me something too, of Elaidh

Day by day the great ship swung across the ocean. She was rigged so full she seemed to carry the clouds above her decks. At first, the passengers had looked up, wondering, at these. Then they looked down and about, and most of them saw the young woman, for she was the only human female thing aboard.

"She's a fine-looking girl, she is so," they said. Her hair was brown and piled up heavily on her head.

She was slender and green-eyed. Her clothes were good, but more than those, they noted three ruby rings on her fingers and the long rope of pearls, nearly long as she was tall, that she wore at night to dinner in the saloon.

"She's alone. Such a girl should have some company," said they.

They generously tried to give her company then, the older men and the younger men, the sailors and the passengers both. She was quiet and graceful with them all, but they slid from her surface as fishes slip through water.

"It's a pity she is a tease," they said.

"She's plain as dough," they said, "despite her rubies and pearls."

"She has emeralds for eyes and a cold green heart."

The sea was wide as the sky, but now and then a bit of land appeared, the thin strip of a coast. Here passengers got off and new passengers walked on. At one land-strip, which had an edging of mountains, a young man stepped aboard, with six brass-bound boxes and a chest, and two servants, two white horses and two black dogs, and an owl that would sit on his arm. His hair was dark and his skin fair. He was handsome, too, and like everything else, his looks came aboard with him.

Half the day he would sit reading, and the other half playing the piano in the saloon. He was rich. A prince, they said.

"Prince Cuzarion," they said, bowing to him. And they tried to win his money off him at cards, or by means of bets and wagers, inviting him to race his dogs against other dogs on board, or to set the owl on some passing gull. But they never won a penny, and the dogs did not

258

race, and the owl never chased the gull.

Sometimes the passengers would tell stories in the saloon after the dinner.

One night the prince, if so he was, told a marvellous and clever story, about a prince who, on a voyage, was carried down into the deep by a mermaid where he lived with her some while—she having, by then, taught him how to breathe under the sea.

"Is that what you'd like, then?" they asked.

"I am already betrothed," said Prince Cuzarion. "Although perhaps I might not mind it, for a month or so."

All this while, the girl had sat in her usual corner, drinking her glass of wine, the rubies burning on her white hands and the pearls weeping down her dress.

Maybe some of them had noticed she would often glance at the prince. Maybe some of them had even seen her gaze at him very long.

So now, one of the other men said to her, "Well, my lady, what do you think of mermaids?"

Although she was so young, she was never discomposed. And now she spoke calmly and clearly, with neither arrogance or shyness.

"I think that they exist," she said, "but they are not as you imagine, being a cruel race, who like to eat men raw and sometimes alive, spitting out the bones to make flutes."

This shocked everyone. The idea itself, and that this young girl should speak of it. So they said no more to her. But Prince Cuzarion, he flipped her one look. It was probably only the second he had ever given her, for she had not taken his fancy, though perhaps he had taken hers.

That night a storm came up out of the sea, boiling and black. It put out the stars and smashed the plate of the moon. That done, it scanned about for something to harm, but though the land was not far off, it did not want the land. Then, it saw a ship dancing along, rigged with clouds, and with lights shining from the port-holes and in the lanterns, and under the howl of the wind fluttered the notes of a piano.

"I'll have you," said the storm, and flung itself forward, kicking the waves from its path.

When the storm hit the vessel buffeting blows, the ship's world went to pieces. Lights and wine glasses and coffee-pots flew one way, and with them the chairs and boxes, and the piano even. And all the passengers. Then everything went another way

There was a great yelling and praying. From the depths of the ship the pair of horses neighed, and above, dogs barked. But in the ship's seams the rats looked philosophically about, for they always knew things might end in tears, and tonight it would be the tears of the sea.

None saw, or if they did they paid no heed, to the slight young girl with her hair blown from its pins, standing on the upper deck, and staring over at the churning waves.

Then the ship split from one end of herself to the other, and everything spilled out into the sea.

That moment, the girl jumped over the side. And if any had spied her, they would have seen she was naked as a knife, but for her ruby rings and the rope of pearls, and her long brown hair.

Cuzarion—and he was a prince – had a great many accomplishments. He had matchlessly waltzed in glittering ballrooms, and faultlessly fought on foot and on horseback; he could play the piano better than most. But swim he could not.

So now, as the cold black water closed over him, he thought with wrathful despair of all he would miss, and gave himself up to darkness.

But in the dark, just as the last light in his brain was going out, he felt a cool warmth pressed all the length of his body, and through the shadow saw a naked woman held him, while her hair swirled round them through the currents like a huge flag. She pressed her lips to his, but all he could taste was salt. Then she blew into his mouth.

"Why have I not died?" Cuzarion presently asked the deeps of the icy sea. But then he thought that probably he had, and just did not know it yet.

Up above, on the surface of the water, which was as tumultuous as the lower reaches were almost still, a curious thing happened.

Among the floating spars and smashed rails, which were all that was left of the ship, amid the turmoil of night and waves, the storm, having successfully broken something, was ebbing away to sleep, but the elements remained all disturbed and out of kilter. Now a lantern bobbed by, still burning in the murk, and you might see two pale horses swimming, led by long brown reins, and it was a girl leading them on, and hair that made the reins. And then several dogs went by, balanced companionable on a piece of stiff sail, and towed along. And an owl perched on a shattered mast, to which twenty men were also clinging, lifting its wings above the brine.

Later, when they had come to shore – and not one of them was lost, although, to be exact, they thought that one of them of them had been – they told this strangest tale. Of a woman in the sea who drew them up from the ocean and hung them out like her washing on the bars and stays and wreckage of the ship. Who bound them there with wet wippy weed from the under-shores of the sea, and pressed, with small slender hands as strong as steel, the water from their lungs, then dragged them in, by a net of weed – and some said of brown hair – to the shores of the land.

There then, in the last of the awful night, men stood by the driftwood fires they had made, wringing out their washing-wet clothes and fear-sodden souls, while the horses stamped and the dogs ran about and the owl dried its feathers. Then rescuers came, with torches and brandy, from the nearby town.

"It is a miracle – is every man here?"

"Every man and every beast. Look, even the bloody rats are saved and brought ashore!"

"No, no," cried one of the servants, "we have lost our prince."

"They have lost their prince."

"And her, we've lost the young lady…" cried another. But when he said this, the rest shushed him.

"She was no girl or maid or lady."

"What then? What?"

"The sea she was."

He woke on a far coast like none he had ever seen, though, being well-read, he had read of such a place, now and then.

Palms like green spiders on stilts swept the sand with their legs. The water was a blue turquoise. Above rose wooded hills, from which blew the scent of orange groves, and the dim ringing of the bells of a monastery on a high rock.

Nearby sat a girl in a satin dress and a rope of pearls, toasting fish over a small fire.

"We're ship-wrecked, then," said the prince. "Only you and I. The other poor devils have all gone down. But I grieve too for my horses and dogs, and the owl. Although perhaps the owl at least may reach land."

"Grieve for none," said the girl, "all have reached the shore, though another shore than this."

"Indeed," said Cuzarion. But a memory was coming back to him, like a remembered dream. "I think you saved me," said he.

"So I did. I saved each and all."

"That is most praise-worthy and talented of you," said Cuzarion, raising his brows. "How, pray, did you do it?"

Then the girl brought him some fish, and he ate this hungrily, and then drank from the bottle of wine she had also set by, which was very nicely aged.

"Did people bring these provisions out of pity for us? And these clothes – this fine shirt and breeches I have on, which are never mine – and your dress, since – I hope you'll forgive me – you seemed without one earlier."

The girl smiled, not looking at him. She put back her mass of hair with one hand.

"I brought the fish and the wine, and the clothes too from chests, out of the deeps of the sea."

"Did you now," said Cuzarion.

"Up from the deeps, out of which I brought you all. It is work I set myself to do."

Cuzarion made no comment. But then he said. "It's a noble thing to be so busy, and at your young age too."

"How old do you make me out to be?" said she, tossing her head a little.

"Oh, a great age – eighteen or so."

"One hundred and eight is nearer the mark."

"Ah."

Then she laughed. "You think I lie, of course. But I tell you true. My name is Elaidh. My mother was a mermaid, and she got me by a human man, and left me in his care, the way the mermaids do, for all that race are female. Then when I was thirteen years old, my mother wanted me, to transform me to her kind, with a long silver tail and hair green as grass. But I loved my da, and so I stayed with him. I thought I should only be a woman, but it seems I have great powers from my mother, though she was cruel, as mermaids are. I am long-lived, and the ocean is familiar to me. I can breathe in water easy as air, and I can give my gift to humankind for a little while, when I blow in their mouths. Also, I can tell the ships that may go down. I walk about the quays, and suss them out. Then I go sailing on them, and when they sink, save everyone I can. With your ship, I had great luck, and saved every living thing."

"I must thank you, then," said Cuzarion, attempting to laugh, but seeming uneasy. He added, "Do your pearls and rubies come from the sea, too?"

"Oh yes. There are great hoards of jewels and other riches that lie there, mermaid-trove, that I steal from them. My da and I were rich, while he yet lived."

"Yet a pity," said Cuzarion, looking under his lids at her, "that you only blew the breath of life into my mouth. All this while I'd been thinking it was a kiss."

Then she sat back and looked quietly at him.

"Oh, do you see me now?" she asked.

Cuzarion, though a prince, had the grace to blush. But then, he was young as a child beside her.

Some while they were on that coast.

Elaidh taught Cuzarion to swim, and sometimes she would whisper the magic air into his mouth so he might swim under the sea, but not very far down. Even so, he saw wonderful sights there. Peculiar creatures that moved about below the rocks, and mysterious plants and corals, and fish of rainbow colours.

By day, he and she would swim then, or walk about the country. Going inland, they went by mustard fields and fields of lavender, and on the hills the bees rose in clouds, just as the fish rose in the sea at their passing. Now and then they met with people, who spoke a language Cuzarion, for all his education, did not know. But Elaidh knew it. She told him frankly she knew by now most of the languages of the earth, for she had journeyed nearly everywhere. "There's no land," said she, "the water cannot take me."

In a village under the monastery rock, they went into a cool blue church whose walls were figured with saints. And Cuzarion was amazed Elaidh could do this, and more amazed when she bowed to the cross, for he had heard mermaids, and their kin, could not have one single thing to do with God.

As time went on, Cuzarion began to think less and less of who he was, who he had been, his other life. He thought more and more of Elaidh. And as he thought more of her, he saw her more and more clearly. At first, she seemed plain, but very graceful. Then she seemed lovely, and then beautiful. At last she seemed the only living thing, so that if a bird exquisitely sang, somehow it was Elaidh, and when it flew, it was Elaidh. And the dawn was Elaidh, and the evening star, and the moon.

"I should like to stay with you," said Cuzarion, "for ever."

"That is hardly possible," said Elaidh.

"Because you will never die, and I shall?"

"One day I shall die."

She led him into the wood at dusk. The grass was thick with clovers and warm still from the sun. They became lovers with finesse, and ease, for each had been a lover before.

And at first Cuzarion was most happy. But then, he was less happy. He became content, then static, then restless. And Elaidh became again only beautiful.

"Elaidh, I must get home. How long have I been away?"

"One month," said she.

"So long – it seems only a day or so…"

But she knew he lied.

"You'll understand my difficulty," said Prince Cuzarion. "My father is old and gives over much of the running of things to me. Besides – I was to marry."

"She'll be that impatient." said Elaidh. From her face, you could tell little, only perhaps that she had spoken in this way before, once, twice.

"Yes, she's a royal girl, and she will be very angry."

"What is her name?"

"Oh – some royal name Sapphyra, that's her name."

"Will you not give her up," said Elaidh, "for me?" But she spoke in a light and mocking manner, and Cuzarion smiled.

"Would that I could," he said. "Kingdoms depend on it."

"Go up to the monastery," said Elaidh. "Say the sea cast you here, but now you'd be going home. The priests are wealthy and wise and will find you a ship."

"Come with me, Elaidh."

"I? Come with you where, and to what?"

"In my own country – maybe we can make an arrangement, you and I. It's not unknown. I must marry the princess, but even so, there will be times when I can get free of her."

"No, then. I will not be going with you for that."

Cuzarion was sorry. He felt badly about himself. And so he walked off through the fields of mustard and lavender and mint, and among the olive groves where, as the soft wind blew, every leaf flashed, like the silver tails of a thousand fish.

When he came back near evening, Elaidh was not there. He searched a long while, even standing at the edge of the dark blue sea, calling her. But she was gone. She was gone for good. After a day or so, he walked up to the monastery where the priests were gracious to him, for he was a prince, charming, and well-read.

The ocean is not made of tears, though one might think it. No, it is the other way about, for the water of the sea is in us, in our blood, and when we cry, we cry the sea's own salt water.

The princess whose name was Sapphyra, had herself done some crying, but that was now over. She had a fair face of sharp features, and raven-black hair.

"How good it is, to see her cheerful again," said her maids. "A year ago, when she thought him dead, she grieved so." They did not add that while she grieved, she had pinched and slapped them every day.

Now the princess, and her three highest attendants, were gathering flowers, in the palace's wild gardens that ran to the shore. In one more day, Sapphyra would be married to the Prince Cuzarion, and the garlands – which others would weave from the flowers – were for her wedding: A quaint custom.

"Who is that?" said the First Attendant, straightening up with her armful of lilies.

"Some great lady," said the Second Attendant, "standing by to watch."

"She's only a girl, she is," said the Third Attendant.

Then Sapphyra turned and looked.

There the woman stood, under a tamarisk tree. In the sunlight, she shone like a church window. Her gown was silver, there were diamonds in her hair, and on her fingers three red ruby rings of incalculable price.

"Good day, madam," said Sapphyra, feeling quite undressed in her embroidered morning-wear.

The woman nodded. "You are the Princess Sapphyra?"

"I have that joy."

"Long then, may you be joyful," said the woman.

"But let me ask," said the princess, frowning somewhat, "your own name, and your purpose."

"My name is Elaidh, and my mother was a mermaid. I am here to offer you my wedding-gift."

A great silence had fallen in the wild gardens. Even the daylight nightingale had left off her song.

"A gift? Why should I deserve one from you?"

"Ah," said Elaidh, sadly, "you must take my word for that."

The three Attendants were in a fuss.

They bustled about, and everywhere flowers fell from their hands and out of their gilded baskets. But Sapphyra said, "If I should accept your gift, how am I to receive it?"

"You must come down to the shore," said Elaidh.

The Attendants did not wish to. But Sapphyra took hold of them and shook them.

"Do you know nothing? The mermaid-kind are wealthy beyond all thought. And see – the gems all over her – why, even her two shoes are studded with pearls."

"And why should she need shoes," said the Third Attendant pertly, "if her mother was a fish?"

But Elaidh was walking slowly away by now, and Sapphyra soon followed. The Attendants unhappily went after.

The sea came gently to the gardens, it was there an ocean of low tides.

But Elaidh stood, with her pearl shoes in the water. "Now, princess Sapphyra, you must be brave, and trust me. For I'm set to show you an astonishment of this world, which is a treasure-hoard of the mermaids. But to see it, you must come down with me, under the waves."

At this, all three Attendants began to scream, but such silly little screams, like operatic mice.

Besides, Sapphyra turned and slapped them. One! Two! Three! After which there was only snivelling.

"They must come down too," said Sapphyra, spitefully.

"Very well," said Elaidh.

So she stepped up to each of the women, and kissed her on the lips, and as she did so, into each of their mouths she blew her pure salt breath.

This dazed them a touch. So, when she walked out into the sea, they went after her, lifting their skirts foolishly, to keep them dry, until the water closed over their heads.

Down and down sank the princess and her maids, after the swift form of Elaidh – who seemed to fly through the water.

The light left the sea. It grew dark and then black. But everywhere in the black it was lit up by gleaming objects, some of which were stones, or plants, and some of which were glowing fish with eyes like candle-flames.

Huge rock-faces rose about them, and from the ledges of these, bloated shapes sometimes launched themselves, and flapped off like crows. Then they came into an orchard of corals, which were all in razor blossom.

Now and then Elaidh spoke to Sapphyra and her ladies, and through the sorcery of her breath, or her mind, they heard her, although they themselves could not utter at all.

"There is a giant octopus," said Elaidh. "Never fear him, he knows not to be discourteous to me." Or, "Look there, the wreck of an antique galleon." The octopus was a cause of discomfort to the princess and her ladies, though he did no more than blink his eye at them. The galleon filled them with terror, for the bones of men lay over its decks, and even the figurehead had become a skeleton.

But then Elaidh led them through a forest of tall seaweeds, every one of which was like a long, six-fingered hand. And then they passed through a tunnel of the rock, and coming out, they were in a vast cavern, elsewhere open only at its top. But somehow, through this opening, miles up, the sunlight entered, and came down and illuminated the space, and the floor of fine, moon-white sand.

Sapphyra and her ladies stopped, balanced in the sea, and staring.

"Here," said Elaidh, "as I promised you, is a treasure of the mermaid-kind."

On every side went up heaps and actual towers of riches, such as would surpass the trophy chambers of an emperor. There were caskets and chests of golden coins and silver, and cascades of pearls, emeralds and diamonds. There were statues of solid gold with eyes of opal, and unusual artefacts of gold, one of which was a model of a golden palace, very intricate, and large enough a child could have played in it. It had windows of carnelian, amethyst and chrysoprase, and roofs of polished ivory.

The ladies seemed to forget their terror. They floated to and fro, handling things and exclaiming silently, so crystal bubbles blew out of their mouths like words.

"You may take anything you can carry," said Elaidh.

At this, Sapphyra strove to pick up the gold palace, but Elaidh came to her and pressed her arm. "For you, princess, there is another treasure."

Then Elaidh drew Sapphyra aside into a second cave. And here Sapphyra lost all her composure. For from the floor to the ceiling, the cave was piled with jewels of a shining, heavenly blueness, some set in gold and some strung in ropes, some burnished, and some cut so they had become like stars of the northern pole. And some were larger than a man's hand. They were sapphires.

"For your name," said Elaidh. "Take whatever you want."

Then Sapphyra made an apron of her skirt, and she darted about the cave, until she had gathered everything she could, and rather more. And still she was digging out rings and necklaces and putting them on, and tying others into her corset ribbons and her black hair.

After a time, however, a louring weariness seemed to overtake her. She sat down on the sand, holding the treasure to her. Then she spoke to Elaidh, and though no words were to be heard, Elaidh heard them.

"Madam," said Elaidh, "it is a great disservice I have done you, although I did it without malice, or intent, without thinking. Listen now. Keep these jewels from your husband, the prince. Then, when a time comes that what you wish for most you find you do not have, put on some of these gems, and go to him. Then he will give you back what I have taken from you. And if it is really mine, it is also his, and shall be yours."

Riddles! said the crystal bubbles from the lips of the princess.

But next moment Elaidh raised her up, and gave her a push that sent her spinning, and Sapphyra found, to her indignation, she was rushing out of the cave, and up and up through the light-changing water, with the three Attendants whirling around her. Until all four broke the skin of the sea, and fell out on the sands of the earth. And there lay the tame wild gardens of the palace, and all around the gold and jewels that had tumbled from their skirts.

Years passed. To the prince and princess, they seemed only a few in number. So that, should they add them up, they were startled always. To others, the number of the years was more than twenty-five.

They were not often together, the prince, the princess.

She would be at cards, or at her dressmakers, or she would be lying on her sofa, eating something that had to do with chocolate. Or in the theatre, in a dream.

He would be riding, and then he would be aching from the ride. He would be up all night to drink or gamble. Or, now and then, with one of the scatter of his mistresses. Or he would play the piano in the echoing marble music-room of the palace, surprising himself by how often his fingers stumbled on the keys.

There was a solitary odd story told of the royal couple.

At the start, for a decade, almost, they had been childless. Then one day the princess had given birth – astounding the physicians who had, it seemed, burst in too late to do more than ponder the flawless child – and shake their heads over its largeness and the adjacent slenderness of the princess, which had persisted throughout her term, right up to the morning of the child's unheralded appearance.

Once, at a dinner some months later, the princess had drunk a great deal of champagne. Pointing at a sapphire necklace she had on, she exclaimed, "Do you see this? This is the reason for my child." Which was thought, by the assembly, very daring, perhaps rather too bold, and also most curious.

More curious still was the truth. But there came a night the prince told it to his heir, the son the Princess Sapphyra had shown to him that morning, eighteen years before.

The boy entered the music-room, and found his father, the prince, seated there at the piano.

Cuzarion was no longer young. His hair had turned grey, and though his court, and the mistresses, still lauded him as handsome, it was a sort of handsomeness which might have looked better on a statue than a man.

But the boy – oh, the boy. He was like the morning sun, so young and straight and fair, his hair the light brown of acorns, his eyes the green of apples. In honesty, he resembled neither his father nor his mother, the princess, at all.

In the tradition of the royal household, the prince's son had the same name as his father, just as the prince had had his own father's name. Cuzarion, they were all named that.

"Cuzarion," therefore said Cuzarion, to his son, "I've called you to me to tell you a tale that you will think a lie. Or else you'll think I have gone mad."

But Prince Cuzarion's son, Prince Cuzarion, smiled kindly at his father.

"No, sir. I would never think that."

"Well, then, we'll sit here. Let me tell it through, and then decide, for you have reached a proper age, both to hear it, and to judge."

Then the elder prince spoke of the voyage he had made those few years, more than twenty-five, in his past. Of the storm and the sinking ship, of how Elaidh had saved him and every other living thing aboard. But then he told of how he had loved Elaidh, and lain with Elaidh, and presently left Elaidh to come home and resume his life. To do him credit, the elder Prince Cuzarion did not paint his love for Elaidh as anything more than it had been, the passion of a month, nor himself as any more than he was, a man capable only of a month's fidelity.

And the younger prince listened gravely. Even when his father explained how Elaidh was a magical being, the daughter of a human man and a mermaid of the deeps of the ocean.

Then the elder prince mentioned his marriage to the Princess Sapphyra. That it was pleasant enough. That it went by. And that one day he found her sobbing, and she said, "We have no children, you and I."

"And we had done everything that humans may do," said the elder prince, "to ensure a child between us. Yet none arrived."

"But then I did arrive," said the young prince. "It is most sorry I am, to have kept you and mother waiting."

"My son," said the elder prince, "you were born of a spell. You are my child, it is a fact, but not the child of the princess. The mermaids have their children by another means. It is the father brings them forth, having carried them a while, without knowing it. It seems Elaidh visited the princess before her wedding. Elaidh gave her sapphires, for her name, from the depths of the sea. And one night Sapphyra came to me in a necklace of these jewels. Later, as I slept, I dreamed of

Elaidh, and in my sleep I possessed Elaidh as a man possesses a woman. And when I woke, the sheet was damp from my lust." He glanced here at his son, a little afraid to have embarrassed him. But the younger prince was not ashamed. Still he sat gravely, listening, as if in his heart he somehow knew it all.

"Sapphyra too," said the elder prince, "lay in the bed that night. In the dawn, a ray of sun fell on the coverlet. Then she and I woke, for something stirred on the mattress between us. And when she threw off the covers, a baby lay there, white as the sea-foam, and clean as the morning.

"And this was I?"

"And this, my son, my mermaid's son, was you."

"Then," said the young man, "Elaidh is my mother."

"So she must be."

"Shall I ever meet her?"

The eider prince sighed. "Perhaps. I hope you may. But I think it will never be in my lifetime. For I think I shall never meet that lovely girl again, she that was the evening star to me, and the flight of a bird. She that I forgot then, as I forget now how to play my piano, and everything – but her."

But the boy was in a sort of trance, and could only look glad, thinking of his new history. He said, "How shall I know her, if she should come here?"

"Ah," said the elder Cuzarion. "Easily enough. She will look, I think, just as she did. Eighteen she will look, your own age now. For her kind live long but never grow old. And she is in her colouring also like you. Her hair is brown that has a spirit of green in it. Her skin is clear as waters."

"And since she is half mermaid, how will I notice that?"

"As I did, my son, if I'd looked as I should. For though she shed no single tear, the sea was in her eyes."

La Vampiresse

Up in the elevator, he felt a wave of depression so intense at what he was about to do, that he almost rushed out at another floor. But then what would he see? The eerie elongate building was frosted with a dry desert cold. On the ground floor he had already encountered strange sliding, creeping or slipping shades. He had glimpsed creatures – things – he didn't want to be at large among. And anyway, there was the man with him in the lift, 'helping' him to reach the proper place.

"How is she today?" he had asked, when they first got in.

"As always."

"Ah."

And that was all.

Ornamental, the elevator had fretted screens of delicately-wrought white metal. Its internal light was soft, but not warm, and when the cage finally rattled to a halt, and the screens parted, a cold blast hit him from an open window.

"Is that safe?"

"What?" asked the man.

"That window – surely…"

"That's fine. See the grille?"

He looked and saw the grille. And in any case, now they were in the heart of a desert night. The sunset had been sucked under, sucked up like red blood, in the minute or so of the elevator's ascent. Stars glittered out in the black sky, undimmed even by the lights of this immense, automated mansion. Soon a moon would rise.

"Thanks," he said humbly, to the attendant. Should he tip him? Perhaps not. The man was already undoing a door and it seemed *he* should go through – go through alone. And now, after the depression, for a moment, he was afraid.

"Am I okay in there?" He tried to sound flippant.

The attendant smiled suddenly, contemptuous as a wolf. "Sure. It's alright, you know. She's sated."

"She is?"

"Yes. Quite."

"Sated."

"Yes."

"How?" he heard himself ask. The ghoulish word hung there in the slightly-warmed cold air.

The attendant said, "Best not to ask, mister."

"No..."

"Best not to ask," the man repeated, as fools or the nervous or the indomitable often did.

But this time, he resisted, himself, doing so.

And then he was through the door, which - as it seemed with its own laughter - shut fast and closed him in.

The first thing he saw in the great wide room was the Christmas tree. It was that blue-green variety, about two metres tall and growing in a stone pot. He knew of the tree, had indeed seen pictures of it. Probably not the same tree, but the *same* type of tree, and decorated approximately in the same way, for it was hung with long pearl necklaces.

The room was luxurious. Thickly-carpeted, with deep chairs upholstered in what looked like velvet, or leather. The drapes were looped back from two windows, in one of which the moon was now coming up from the desert.

In fact, this whole room was very like the other room, the room he had seen photographs of. Not absolutely, he supposed, but enough.

He looked around carefully. On a gallery up a stair were book-stacks lined with volumes of calf and silk, gilded. A globe stood up there on a table, and down here, one long decanter filled with dark fluid, and two crystal goblets.

"It isn't blood."

He snapped around so fast a muscle twanged at the top of his neck.

Christ. She had risen up silent as the moon rose, out of that chair in the corner, in the half-light beyond the lamps, a shadow.

"No, truly, not blood. Alcohol. I keep it for my guests."

He knew what to do. And if he hadn't known, he had had it droned into him by everyone he had had to deal with, lawyers, his own office, and inevitably, the people here. So he bowed to her, the short military bow of a culture and a world long over. But not, of course, for her.

"Madame Chaikassia."

"Ah," she said. "At last. One who knows how to say my name."

Naturally he knew. He had known from the day he saw her in an interview on TV. Rather as he had seen the actress Bette Davis in an interview years before, and she had been asked how her first name was pronounced. So that he therefore knew it was *not* pronounced, as most persons now did, in the French way, Bett, but – for he had heard the actress herself reply – as Betty. And in the same way he knew the female being before him now did not pronounce her name as so many did, Che Kasee-ah, but Ch'high-kazya.

She did not ask who *he* was. They would have told her, when they said he would be coming. After all, without her permission, he would never have been allowed into this room. And all the way here, if the truth were known, he had been sweating, thinking she would, after his journey of two thousand miles and more, suddenly change her mind.

"Help yourself," she said idly, "to a drink."

So he thanked her, and went and poured himself one. To his surprise, when he sipped it, it was a decent malt whisky. Despite her words, he had expected anything but alcohol. Yet obviously, they knew *she* would never drink *this*.

When she beckoned to him, he sat down facing her, where she had once more sat down. The side lamps cast the mildest glow, but behind her the harsh white neon of moon was coming up with incredible rapidity. It would shine into his face, not hers.

In the soft, flattering light, he studied her.

Even under these lamps, she looked old. He had been prepared for that. No-one knew her exact age, or those who did kept quiet. But twenty, twenty-five years ago, when he had seen her in that interview, or more recently in little remaining clips of film, she had looked only a glamorous thirty, forty. Now he would have said she was well into her sixties. She looked like that, except, of course, she was still glamorous, and still she had her wonderful mask of bones, on which the flesh stayed pinned, not by surgery, but by that random good luck that chance sometimes handed out, just now and then, to the chosen few.

In fact, she was still beautiful, and he had a feeling that even when she looked seventy, eighty, one hundred, she would even then keep those two things, the glamour and the beauty.

Although again, probably she wouldn't live that long, not now. Now she was in captivity, and ruined.

She lost a little more each day, they had told him that. A little more. But you'd never know.

Her hair was long, as in the old pictures, and just as lustrous and thick, though fine silver wires of the best kind of grey silked through it. She wore a minimum of make-up, eye-shadow and false lashes. No powder he could detect. And though her lips were a startling scarlet, it was a softer scarlet, to suit the aging of her face.

Her body, like her throat, was long and slender. She wore one of those long black gowns, just close enough in fit he had seen; in her rising and sitting, her figure looked, at least when clothed, like that of a woman half her apparent age.

And she had on high heels – black velvet pumps on slender tapering pins. She had surrendered very little, that way.

As for her hands, always the big giveaway, she wore mittens of thin black lace, and her nails were long and painted dull gold.

"Well," she said. "What do you wish to know?"

"Whatever you're kind enough to tell me."

"There is so much."

"Yes."

"Time," she said. She shrugged.

"We have some time."

"I mean, my time. Such a great amount. Like the snows and the forests. Like the mountains I saw from the beginning of my life. And always in moonlight or the light of the stars. So many nights. Centuries, and all in the dark."

She had hypnotised him. He felt it. He didn't struggle.

But she said, "Don't be nervous," as if he had stuttered or flinched or drawn back. "You know, don't you, you are perfectly safe with me tonight?"

"Yes, Madame Chaikassia."

"That's good. Not everyone is able to relax."

"I know," he said, "that you've given your word. And you never break your word."

She smiled then. She had beautiful teeth, but they were all caps. Thank God, he thought, with a rare compassion, she had not needed new teeth until such excellent dentistry had become available.

He could remember the little headline in a scurrilous magazine: *False Fangs for a Vampire.*

"Do you know my story?" she asked, not coyly, but with dignity.

Surely it would be impossible not to respond to this pride and self-control? At least, for him.

"Something of it. But only from the movies, and the book."

"Oh, my book." She was dismissive. Any authorial arrogance had left her, or else she had never had any. "I did not write everything I should have done. Or they would not let me. Always there are these restraints."

"Yes," he said.

She said, "It must surprise you to find me here."

He waited, careful.

She sighed. She said, "As the world shrinks, I have been taken like an exotic animal and put into this zoo – this menagerie. And I have allowed it, for there was nothing else I could do. I am the last of my kind. A unique exhibit. And of course, they feed me."

At the vulgar flick of her last words, he found, to his slight dismay, the hair crawled on his scalp. Then curiosity, his stock-in-trade, made him say, "Can I ask you, Madame, in the realm of food, on what do they...?"

"On what do you *think?*"

She leaned forward. Her black eyes, that had no aging mark on them beyond a faint reddening at their corners, burned into his. And he felt, and was glad to feel, an electric weakening in his spine.

If only I could give you what you need.

He heard the line in his head, as he had heard and read it on several occasions. But he kept the sense not to say it.

She had given her word, *La Vampiresse*, that she would not harm him. But there was one story, if real or false he hadn't been able to find out. One journalistic interviewer had teasingly gone too far with her, and left this place in an ambulance.

So he only waited, letting the recorder tick unheard in his pocket – they had said she didn't object to such machines, provided she didn't have to see or hear them.

And she leaned back after a moment and said, "They bring me what I must have. It is taken quite legally. And only from the willing, and the healthy."

He risked it. "Blood, Madame."

"*Blood,* monsieur. But I will tell you something. They must, by law, disguise what it is."

"How is that possible?"

"They add a little juice, some little meat extract or other. This is required by the government. Astonishing, their hypocrisy, would you not say?"

"I'd say so, yes."

"For everyone knows what I am, and what I must have, to live. But in order to protect the sensibility of a few, they perpetrate a travesty. However," she folded her hands, her rings dark as her eyes, "I can taste what it really is, under its camouflage. And it does what it must. As you see. I am still alive."

He had been an adolescent when he saw her first, and that was on film. He was not the only one whose earliest sexual fantasies had been lit up all through by *La Vampiresse*.

But also, romantically, he had fallen in love with her world, recreated so earnestly on the screen. A country and landscape of forests, mountains, spired cities on frozen rivers, of winter palaces and sleighs and wolves, and of darkness, always that, where the full moon was the only sun. Russia, or some component of Russia, but a Russia vanished far away, where the aristocrats spoke French and the slavery of serfdom persisted.

As he grew up, he found fleshly women that, for all their faults, were actually embraceable, actually penetrable, he lost the dreams of blood and moonlight. And with them, perhaps strangely, or not, lost too the romance of *place*. So that when, all these years after, he had been looking again at the film, or at those bits of it that had been – aptly – dug up, he was amused. At himself, for ever liking these scenarios at all. At the scenarios themselves, their naivety and censored charms. Oh yes, the imagination, in those days, sexual and otherwise, had had to work overtime. And from doing it, the imagination had grown muscular and strong. So that in memory after, you saw what you had *not* been shown, the fondling behind the smoky drape, that closed boudoir door, or even the rending among that hustle of far-off feeding wolves ...

Altogether, he was sorry the romance had died for him with his youth. What was more, though they had only been, to begin with, such images, a recreation, coming here he grew rather afraid she too, *La Vampiresse* herself, would also disappoint. Worse, that she would horrify him, with scorn or pity or disgust.

But now, as he sat facing her, he had to admit he was nearly aroused. Oh, not in any erotic way. Better than that – *imaginatively*. Those strong imagination-muscles hadn't after all wasted completely away. For here and now he was filling in once more the hidden or obscured vision. So that under her age, still, he could make out what she had been and was, in her own manner.

And when she spoke of her food, the blood, he didn't want to smile behind his hand or gag at the thing she had told him. He felt a kind of wild rejoicing. Despite the fact she was here in this building in the desert, despite her growing old and – nearly – tame, she had remained *Chaikassia*. Everything else had gone, or was in retreat. Not that.

Because of this, he was finding it easy to talk to her, and would find it easy to perform the interview. And he wondered if others had found this too. He even wondered if that had been the problem for the one who left under the care of paramedics – it had been, for him, *too* easy.

At the nineteenth hour, when the moon was at the top of the first window and crossing to the top of the second, someone came in to check on them.

They had been talking about two and a half hours.

Verbally, they had crossed vast tracts of land, lingered in crypts and on high towers, seen armies gleam and sink, and sunrise slit the edge of air like a knife. And she had been, through memory, a child, a girl, a woman.

She had spoken of much of her life, even of her childhood, of which, until now, he had known little. A vampire's childhood, unrevealed in her book, or in any other medium. He had even been able to glimpse her own adolescence, where she stood for him, frosted like the finest glass with candleshine and ghostly falling snow.

As the door was knocked on, this contemporary and unforgivable door, in such an old-fashioned and fake way, Chaikassia threw back her head and laughed. "They must come in. To see if I have attacked you."

He knew quite well that there were three concealed cameras in the room, perhaps for her protection as much as his. He suspected she knew about these cameras too.

But he said, "They see, surely, you would never do that."

She glanced playfully at him. "But I might after all be tempted."

He said, "You're flattering me."

"Yes," she said. "But also I am telling you a fact. But again, I have given my word, and you are safe."

Then a uniformed man and woman were in the room. Both gave a little brief bow to *La Vampiresse*. Then the man came over and handed her a beaker like a little silver thimble on a silver tray.

"Oh," she said, "is it time for this, now?"

"Yes, Madame."

She glanced at him again. "Did you know, they make me also swallow such drugs?"

"I knew something about it."

"Here is the proof. For my health, they say. Do you not?" she added to the man. *He* smiled and stood waiting. Chaikassia tipped the contents of the silver thimble into her mouth. Her throat moved smoothly, used to this. "But really, it is to subdue me," she murmured softly. And then, more softly, almost lovingly, "As if it ever could."

The uniformed woman had come over and stood by his chair. She said to him politely, "Do you wish for coffee, sir, hot tea, or a soft drink?"

"No, thank you."

"I must remind you, sir, that your three hours are nearly through."

"Yes, I'm keeping count."

When they had gone out again, Chaikassia stood up. "Three hours," she murmured. "Have we talked so long?"

"We have twenty-four minutes left."

"Twenty-four. So exact. Ah, monsieur, what a captain you would have made."

He too had got up, courteous, in the old style. He saw now, taken aback for a moment, that even in her high heels she was shorter than he. He had gained the impression, entering, approaching, she was about a tenth of a metre taller, for he wasn't tall.

She had always seemed tall to him, as well. Perhaps she had shrunk a little. Despite their best efforts – the diet she now lived on ... like the loss of her own teeth.

"What else shall I tell you?" she asked.

"Anything, Madame. Everything you wish to."

So she began again one of her vivid rambling anecdotes. Only now and then did he require to lead her with a question, or comment. Of all the things she had already told him, many he recognised from the other material. Yet others had proved changeable, or quite fresh, like the childhood scenes, different and new. He was aware they alone might make a book. The tape chugged on over his heart, a full four hours of it, to be on the safe side, its clever receptor catching every nuance, even when, for a moment, she might turn her head. And he marvelled at her coherence. So much and all so perfectly rendered. If she repeated herself, he barely noticed. It didn't matter. This was a reality more real than anything else, surely? More impactful and apposite than any tragedy that was human.

"Look at the moon," she suddenly said. "How arid and cold and old she is tonight." Her voice altered. "Have they told you? I'm always better, when the moon's up. When it's full. I wonder why the hell that is? Crazy, isn't it?"

And something in him stumbled, as it seemed something had done in her. For not only the pattern of her speech had altered, the faint accent wiped away, but as she looked back at him her face was fallen and stricken. And from her eyes ran out two thin shining tears. Lost tears, all alone.

Made dumb, he stood there, seeing her oldness and her shrunkenness. Then he heard his voice come from him, and for a second was afraid of what would say.

"Madame Chaikassia, how you must miss your freedom. It must be so intense, the lonely sorrow of all these hundreds of years you have lived – and you are the last of your kind. You must feel the moon is your only friend – at last, the only thing that can comprehend you."

And then her face was smoothing over, the strength of imagination working its power upon her. The trite banality of his words, like some splash of bad dialogue from the worst of the scripts, but able to change her, give her back her courage and her centre. So that again she rose, towering over him, her eyes wiser than a thousand nights, older than a million moons.

"You are a poet, monsieur. And you are perceptive. Come to the window. Do you see? The bars are of finest steel, otherwise, they think, my captors, I will escape them. But they have forgotten – oh, shall I tell you my secret?"

They leaned together by the cold glass, observing the slender bars.

She said, "Unlike most of my kind, I am able to make myself visible, monsieur, in mirrors – have they ever told you? Oh, yes, an old trick. How else was I able for so long to deceive your race and live among you? But there is, through this, a reverse ability. I can pass through glass. Through *this* glass, through these *bars*. I do go out, therefore, into the vastness of the night. But I am then invisible. I see you believe me."

"Yes, Madame Chaikassia. Many of us have long thought this was what you must be doing."

She leaned back from him, triumphant, and laughed sharply again. He caught the faint antiseptic tang of the drug on her breath, the drug they gave her to 'subdue' her.

"I fly by night. And though I return then to this prison-cage – one night, one night when I am ready – believe me, *I shall be gone forever.*"

Her eyes glittered back the stars.

He knew what to do. He took her hand, and brushed the air above it with his lips.

"I'm so glad, so very glad, Madame, you are no longer shut in. I salute your intrepid spirit, and your freedom."

"You will tell no-one." Not a plea, an order. (Yes, she had now forgotten the cameras.)

"I *swear* I will tell no-one."

"Nor when you print your story-piece about me."

"Nor even then. Of *course* not then."

Flirtatiously she said, "You are afraid I will kill you otherwise?"

"Madame," he said, "you could kill me, I'm well aware, at any instant. But you've given your word and will not. Now I have given *my* word, and your secret is secure with me, to my grave."

He found his eyes had filled, as hers had, with tears. This would embarrass him later, but at the time it had been, maybe, necessary.

She saw his emotion. Still smiling, she turned from him and walked away across the room, and up the steps to her gallery of books. She did this with the sublime indifference of her superior state, dismissing him, now and utterly, for all her unfathomable length of time, in which he had been only one tiny dot.

So he went to the door and pressed the button, but it opened at once, because the cameras had shown the interview was over.

A copy of the piece he wrote – less story or interview than article – would be sent to her, apparently. She had stipulated this as part of the deal.

And so had he. He had made sure, too, the copy she received, which would be only one of three, one for her, one for himself, and one for the archive, was exactly and precisely right. Which meant that it stayed faithful to the flawless lie she was now living.

He didn't want her, or intend her, ever to see the real article, the commissioned one. Nobody wanted her to see that. But that one was the one the public would see. Christ, he would cut his throat if she ever saw *that* one – well, perhaps not go so far as cutting his throat... But he had made absolutely certain. The truth was the truth, but he'd never grasped why truth always had to be used to hurt someone. To her, life had done enough. And death would do the rest.

So in his version of the article that Chaikassia would later receive and glance over in her great room, in the tall building in the cold, moon-bled desert, an article complete with a most beautiful photograph of her, taken some twenty years before, she would see, if she looked, only what she might expect from one devoted, loyal and bound by her magical spell. But that was not what the rest of them would read, marvelling and sneering, or simply turned to stone by fear at the tricks destiny or God could play.

But the real article would anyway make little stir. It wasn't even going to be very lucrative for him, since the travel expenses had been so high. And it was of interest only to certain cliques and cults and elderly admirers, and to himself, of course, which was why he had agreed to write it, provided he could interview her, by which he had meant meet her, look at her, be with her those three hours.

The photograph used in the real article was chosen by his editor. It was *very* cruel. It showed her as she had become – not even, he thought, as she had appeared to *him*. But perhaps some of them, with imaginative muscles, would still see something in it of who she was, had been. Was, *was*. This phantom of his adolescence, who would now be the haunting of his dying middle-age.

Who Remembers Pella Blai?

She was once said to be one of the most beautiful women in the world, or at least on TV. She had the eponymous role in that fantasy series of the previous century, *La Vampiresse*.

The storylines of the series were gorgeous if slender. It was all about a (seemingly – somewhat) Russian vampire, located (somewhere) between the Caucasus and Siberia, though God knows where. A winter country around 18-something, of moonlit gardens and gravestones, and wolf-scrambled forest. And here she flew by night under the moon, gliding at first light down into her coffin, as any vampire must.

Though never at the top of the tree, (not even her famous pearl-hung Christmas Tree at Bel Delores), Pella enjoyed much success, and most of us forty years and up know the name. But then the whole ethos of this kind of romantic celluloid vampirism slunk from prominence.

What she did with her between-years remains something of a mystery. And even the lady herself never now talks of them. But there is one very good reason for that.

Diagnosed in her fifties with Alzheimer's disease, Pella lives out her final years in a luxurious private clinic, somewhere south of the northern USA. It is a clinic for the rich and damned, a salutary lesson for any visitor of what fate may bring. But in the case of Pella Blai, there is one extraordinary factor.

For the strangest thing has happened. Another blow of fate – but whether savage or benign, who dare say? For Pella Blai's disintegrating brain has by now wholly convinced her that she is not herself at all, but the heroine she played all those years back on TV, on screen, and about whom she wrote her own novel: the one true vampire left alive on Earth.

Her only memories then, and perhaps continually reinvented, concern the role she acted and has now come to live, Chaikassia, the eternal vampire. (And please note that is pronounced Ch'high-kazya.)

Bizarrely, inside this framework, she is pretty damn near perfectly coherent. It is only, they tell you, when she comes out of it, and just now and then she does, that she grows confused, distressed, forgetful and enraged. When she is

Chaikassia, and that takes up around ninety percent of her time – she's word-perfect. No-one seems to know why that is. But having spoken some while to her, I can confirm the fact.

Chaikassia's wants and wishes too, are all those of a vampire – let me add, a graceful and well-bred vampire. And to this end, the amenable if expensive clinic permits her to sleep in some sort of box through the day. While at mealtimes she is served 'blood' - which is actually a concoction of fruit juice, bouillon and vitamins – the only nourishment she will knowingly take. They can even leave a decanter of malt whisky in her room. She never touches it – what decent vampire would? 'For guests,' she tells you, with her Russian aristocrat's grace, learnt in her earliest youth in a winter palace of the mind – *her* mind. Which is all so very unlike the real Pella Blai, the hard-drinking daughter of an immigrant family, dragged up somewhere in lower London, England.

Frankly, having met her only last month, I venture to say there is nothing left of that real Pella at all. Instead I talked with a being who can make herself *appear* in mirrors to deceive us all, and who passes at will out through the bars of her nocturnal windows. A being too who never takes your blood if she has promised not to, but who once, with one of the fake books from her gallery, broke the nose of a reporter who offended her.

And this being lives in a high white tower in the middle of a moon-leached desert, as far away from the rest of us as it is possible to get. And, until the last of her mind sets in oblivion and night, and finally lets her free forever, I swear to you she is, without any doubt – *La Vampiresse.*

Where All Things Perish

From a Tailored Concept by John Kaiine

1

It was glimpsing Polleto again, between trains, at that hotel in Vymart, which made me remember. Which in its way, is quite curious, for however could I have forgotten such a thing? So impossible and *terrible* a thing. And yet, the human mind is a strange mechanism, and the human heart far stranger. Sometimes, the most trivial events haunt our waking hours, even our dreams, for years after they have happened. While episodes of incredible moment, perhaps only because they have been marked indelibly upon us, stand back in the shadows, mute and motionless, until some chance ray of mental light discovers them. And then they are there, burning bright, towering and undismissible once more. At such times, one knows they are more than memories, more than the mere furniture of the brain. Rather, they have become part of it, a part of oneself.

"What is it, Frederick, that you are staring at?"

"That little man at the table over there."

"What, that little clerkish chap in the dusty overcoat? He hardly looks worthy of your curiosity. Of anyone's, come to that."

"No, he probably isn't. A very ordinary fellow, the sort you wouldn't recall, I suppose, in the normal way of things."

"I should think not. But you do?"

"Well, as it happens, he was resident in a place where something very odd once happened to me. And not to myself alone."

"He was involved in this odd thing? He looks blameless to the point of criminality."

"I imagine that he is. No, he was simply living there at the time, had been there two or three years, if I remember correctly. I met him once, in the street, and my aunt introduced him as a Mr Polleto. We exchanged civilities, that was all. He had the faintest trace of a foreign accent, but otherwise seemed a nonentity. My aunt confessed they had all been very disappointed in him because, learning his name before his arrival, they'd hoped for some sort of flamboyant Italian theatrical gentleman, or something of the sort. "

"He looks more like a grocer."

"My aunt's words exactly. Those were the probable facts, too, I believe. He'd been a shop-keeper, but come into some funds through a legacy. He bought a house in Steepleford, which was where I was visiting my aunt."

"This is a remarkably dull story, Frederick."

"Yes." I hesitated then. I added, "The other story isn't, I can assure you."

"The story which you recollect only since you caught sight of your Mr Polleto? Well, are you going to blab? We have four long hours before the Wassenhaur train. Let's refresh our glasses, and then you can tell me your tale."

"Perhaps not."

"Oh, come, this is too flirtatious. What have you been doing all this while, but trying to engage my attention in it?"

"I protest."

But the brandy bottle intervened. And presently, sitting on that sunny terrace of the hotel Alpius, I recounted to my friend and travelling companion the story which I will now relate. That was the first time I ever told it to anyone. And this, now, I trust, will be the last.

2

The modest town of Steepleford had some slight notoriety in the eighteenth century, when it was one of the centres of a cult known as the Lilyites. These people believed so absolutely in the teachings of Christ, and acted upon them so unswervingly, that they soon turned the entire Christian church against them. There were a few hangings and some riots, as is often the way in these cases, until at last the cult lost both dedication and adherents, and ebbed away. Even so, through the succeeding years, (from about 1750 to 1783), now and then some murmur might be heard of the Lilyites. Being however still generally feared and loathed for their extreme habits, they were soon rooted out and disposed of, one way or another. The last hint of the cult seemed to surface, nevertheless, in sleepy Steepleford. During the July of 1783, one, Josebaar Hawkins, was harangued in Market Square, for holding a secret meeting of seventeen persons, at which they had, allegedly, sworn to slough their worldly goods and to love all men as themselves, in the celebrated Lilyite manner.

At his impromptu trial, Hawkins either denied all this, or ably recanted. He was said to have laughed heartily at the notion of giving up his fine house, which was the product of successful dealings in the textile industry, and stood to the side of Salter's Lane, in its own grounds. He asked, it seems, if the worthies now questioning him thought he would also abandon his new and beautiful young wife, who went by the unusual name of Amber Maria, or drag her with him in the Lilyite fashion, shoeless and penniless, about the countryside.

Hawkins was presently acquitted of belonging to the sect. No others were even interviewed upon the matter. Thereafter no more is heard, in the annals of Steepleford, of the Lilyites, but there is one more mention of Hawkins and his wife. This record states that in 1788, Amber Maria, being then twenty years of age, (which must have made her fifteen or less at her wedding), was taken ill and died within a month. Hawkins, not wishing to part from her even dead, obtained sanction for her burial in the grounds of his house.

All this, though possibly of local interest in Steepleford, where as a rule a horse casting its shoe in the street might cause great excitement, is of small apparent value on the slate of the world. Yet I must myself now add that even in my own short and irregular visits to the town, I had been, perhaps inattentively, aware of a strangeness that somehow attached itself to the Hawkins house, which still stood to the side of Salter's Lane.

The Lane ran up from Market Gate Street. It was a long and winding track, with fields at first on both sides, leading in turn to thick woodland, that in places was ancient, great green oaks and mighty chestnuts and beeches, some over two hundred years of age. I can confirm from walks I have taken, that there exist, or existed, areas in these woods which seemed old nearly as civilisation, and when an elderly country fellow once pointed out to me a group of trees which had, he said, stood as saplings in the reign of King John, I more than half believed him. But this, of course, may be attributable merely to an imaginative man's fancy.

Some two miles up its length, Salter's Lane takes a sharp turn towards the London Road. At this juncture stands the house of Josebaar Hawkins.

It was built in the flat-faced style of those times, with tall, comfit-box-framed windows and a couple of impressive chimneys like towers, behind a high brick wall. Although lavish enough for a cloth merchant and his wife, the 'grounds' were not vast, more gardens, and by the time I first happened on the place, these had become overgrown to a wilderness. Even so, one might make out sections of brickwork, and the chimney tops, above the trees.

I asked my aunt about the house, having found it, idly enough I am sure. She replied, also idly, that it was some architectural monstrosity a century out of date, standing always shut up and empty, since no one would either buy it or pull it down. Perhaps I asked her even then why no one lived there. I know I did ask at some adjacent point, for I retain her answer. She replied, "Oh, there's some story, dear boy, that a man bricked up his wife alive in a room there. She belonged to some wild sect or other, with which he lost patience. But she had, I think, an interesting name... now what can that have been?" My aunt then seemed to mislay the topic. However, a few hours, or it may have been days, later, she presented me, after dinner one night, with a musty thick volume from her library. "I have marked the place."

"The place of what, pray?" I inquired.

"The section which concerns the house of Josebaar Hawkins."

I was baffled enough, not then knowing the name, to sit down at once in the smoking-room, and read the passage indicated. So it was I learned of the Lilyites, of whom neither had I ever heard anything until then, and of Hawkins and his house off Salter's Lane. Included in the piece was the account from which I have excerpted my own note above on Hawkins' impromptu 'trial'. It also contained a portion quoted from Steepleford's parish register, with record of both the marriage and the death of Amber Maria Hawkins. This was followed by the notice of her burial in the grounds of the house, which had been overseen both by the priest, and certain officers of the town. Then my aunt's book, having set history fair and straight, proceeded, in the way of such tomes, to undermine it.

According to this treatise, Hawkins, first an enraptured husband, had come suddenly and utterly to think his wife an evil witch, and growing afraid of her, he tricked her to an attic room of the house, and here succeeded in locking her in. Thereafter, he had both the door and the window bricked up, by men who, being sworn in on the scheme with him, turned blind and deaf eyes and ears to her screams and cries for pity. My aunt's book was in small doubt that both the priest, and the officers who later pretended to Amber Maria's death and burial, were accomplices in this hideous and extraordinary act. (I have to say that, perusing this, some memory did vaguely stir in me, but it was of so incoherent, slight and indeed uncheerful a nature, having to do, I thought, with a children's rhyme of the locale, that I did not search after it at all diligently.)

As I have already remarked, I seldom then visited Steepleford. On that visit, I may have offered some comment on my reading, or my aunt may have done. I fail to recollect. Certainly, the rest of my visit was soon over, nor, having gone away, did I return there for more than a year, and during my next dutiful brief holiday, I remember nothing seen or said of the house in Salter's Lane.

But now I come to my next relevant visit, which occurred almost three years after those I have just described.

I had been in Greece for ten months, and come back full of the spirit of that place, thinking to find England dull and drab. But it was May, and a nice May, too, and by the time the train stopped at the Halt, I had decided to walk the rest of the way to the town through the woods and fields. So, inevitably, I found myself, just past midday, on the winding path of Salter's Lane. It was the most perfect of afternoons. The sky was that clear milky blue, which certain poets compare, (quite wrongly, to my mind), with the eyes of children. Among the oaks, which clasped the track, green piled on green, wild flowers had set fire to the hedges and the grass, and sunlight festooned everything with shining jewels. Birds sang in a storm, and my heart lifted high. *What is Greece to this?* thought I, staring off between breaks in the trees at luminous glades, steeped in the most elder shadows. Why, this might *be* Greece, in her morning.

And then, between one step and another, there fell the strangest thing, which I could and can only describe as a sudden quietness; less silence than absence. I stopped, and looked about, still smiling, thinking the world of nature had fallen prone, as is its wont, to some threat or fascination too small or obscure for human eye or mind to note. I waited patiently too, for the lovely rain of birdsong to scatter down on me once more. It did not come.

Then, and how curious it sounded to me, as if I had never before heard such a thing, I picked up the song of a blackbird – but it seemed miles off up the Lane, the way I had come. And precisely at that moment, turning again, I saw something of a dull, dry red, that thrust between the leaves. At once I knew it for a chimney of the Hawkins house.

I was taken aback. Imaginative, as I freely admit I am, I would not say I was especially superstitious. But something now disturbed me, and that very much, and not being able to divine what it was, beyond the presence of that wry old house, discomposed me further.

Accordingly, I stared at the house, right at it, and crossing over, gazed up the outer wall, over which the vines and ivies hung so thickly. What an ugly house it was, I thought, and no mistake. Even its windows of filthy glass, largely overgrown by creeper, were ugly. While that window there, above, was the ugliest of all, an absolute eyesore, stuck on at quite the wrong architectural moment.

While I was thinking this, and standing there, staring so feverishly and insolently, with no warning the childish rhyme came back into my head, from out of some store-cupboard of the brain. And with it a host of tiny bits and pieces that, over the years of my visits here, and all unconsidered, I had apparently garnered. I heard my aunt say again how a woman had been bricked up in 'that house', and a friend of my aunt's, a titled lady I barely knew, I heard saying once again, as she must have done years before: "Oh, the peasantry won't go by the place after dark. No, it's a fact. They go all out of their way by Joiner's Crossing. And this, mark you because of a tale more than a hundred years old."

And the rhyme? I had doubtless heard children singing it in play, in the streets and yards of Steepleford, and maybe they still do so, although, I wonder if they do. I will set it down, for having remembered it, I have never since forgotten.

She looks through water,
She looks through air,
She leaps at the moon
And she looks in.

Give her silver,
Give her gold,
And bind her eyes
With a brick and a pin.

"Aunt Alice," I said to her that evening, when we were pursuing some sherry before the meal, "I want to tell you about something I saw on my walk today, coming here to the town."

Pleased to see me, she turned to me a willing, expectant face, but no sooner did I mention the house in Salter Lane, than she laughed. "Dear boy, I shall have to think you obsessed by the place. Are you intending to buy it? I should certainly be delighted to have you live in the town, but not in such a miserable property."

I replied, rather irritably, that nothing was further from my desires, and looking rather crushed, she amended, "I'm sorry, Frederick. I am sure that London is more suited to your temperament than such a dreary backwater as Steepleford." After which much of the evening was spent in my praising Steepleford and herself, for I felt ashamed of my bad temper. When I was a boy, this aunt had been very kind to me, and deserved far better of me than three-yearly visits laced with petty ill-humour.

By ten o'clock we were friends again and playing cards, and so I reintroduced my topic. Although, I admit I stuck strictly to facts as I saw them, omitting all the other sensations I have outlined.

"The oddest thing, Aunt, is that I could swear the window which I saw had not been there previously. It was very high up, almost into the roof, rather small, yet somehow extremely noticeable. Although I have only once – to my recollection – looked at the house before, yet I thought I remembered it quite well, and I truly believe there never was a window in that position – however fantastic this may sound."

As women will, my aunt then said something damningly practical. "So many of the house windows there are closed up with ivy and creeper. Could some of this overgrowth simply have fallen away, and so revealed the casement you speak of?"

Such a banal solution had not occurred to me. I agreed that she was probably correct. To myself I said that I must put up with the necessary boredom of my visit, and not try preposterously to dress it up with invented supernatural flights.

The following morning, I penitently accompanied my aunt on her round of social calls. By midday, my face had set like cement in a polite smile, and thus, as we crossed Market Gate Street, I found myself beaming at a small, nondescript man in unostentatious dress, who had touched his hat to us.

"Ah, Mr Polleto," said my aunt, magnanimous to a fault. "What fine weather we are having."

Mr Polleto conceded that we were. He had a flat, dusty voice, old even beyond his bent and well-aged appearance. In it, my ears caught just the trace of some foreignness. Then I found myself introduced, and not standing on ceremony, as my aunt had not, I shook hands with him. What a hand he had. It was neither cold nor hot, not damp, but rather dry – it did not have much strength in it, certainly, yet nor was it a weak hand. But an uncomfortable hand it was. It did not seem to *fit* in mine, and I sensed it would not fit in anyone's.

"Mr Polleto has resided in the town for quite three years now, I believe," said my aunt, when we had parted from him. She then told me of the general disappointment that he had not lived up to his name. "He has the cottage by the old tiltyard."

But I was not interested in Mr Polleto and his indescribable handshake; his face I had already mislaid, for he was one of those men who are eternally unmemorable, or seem so – for if ever seen again, somehow they are known at once, as I have already demonstrated, and later must demonstrate further.

However, now I wanted my lunch, and was dismayed to find my aunt was leading me to yet another doorstep. I rallied rather feebly. "And which lady is this, Aunt Alice?"

"No lady, Frederick. This is the house of our local scholar. I have some purchases to make and will leave you here, with Mr Farbody, who has written and published pamphlets."

"Indeed," said I, but just then the maid let me in, and presently I was taking a glass of very drinkable Madeira, in a sunlit library, with Mr Farbody, who had at once addressed me with: "My good sir, I understand you are interested in the history of the Hawkins house."

"Well, it is a curious tale," Farbody continued, requiring little prompting from me. "Did you know that the farm-hands hereabouts, and workers and their families in the town, have kept up a tradition that the spot is cursed?"

"I remember someone saying that people refuse to go along Salter's Lane by night."

"Well that, of course, isn't always to be avoided, but they make a to-do about it. The thing is, it seems, not to *look* at the building. I've heard of girls, if due to be married, still binding their eyes with a scarf and having to be led, if they should need to pass the house even in daylight."

"And all this because Amber Maria Hawkins was thought a witch?"

"Ah, she *was* a witch, if the tales may be believed." And here he winked at me. "She could see treasure in the ground, for one thing. No one knows her origins. Josebaar said he came across her one day in the woods. She was probably a gypsy girl, but all alone, bright-haired and straying with her arms full of wild flowers. He took a fancy for her, and perhaps she for him, it seems so – or else she liked the idea of his status in the town. He had already made some money, and his family was an old one. And if she was a gypsy or itinerant, homeless and without kin, all that may have appealed to her – do you see? So there and then she is supposed to have said to him, 'You may sport with me, and I will let you. Or you may marry me and I will make you rich.' And he said, 'How might that be, seeing you are in rags?' To which Amber Maria replied simply, 'You I will bring silver and gold'."

At this, the rhyme came into my head again and I interrupted. "I thought it was she was to have the gold and silver?"

Farbody smiled, and lit his pipe. "It does seem she might have been rich on her own account, for sure, if she'd cared to be, for the next thing she did was point at the ground under a tree and say to Hawkins, 'Dig there, and you will find a large store of coins'. Even money likes money, so he dug in the ground, and *hey presto*! found a box of gold pieces, deep down and undisturbed for a century. When he asked her how she knew where to dig, she shrugged and said, 'I saw them.' Nor did Amber do this only once, but several times, apparently. And in the same way, she could find items that had been lost. And once she is supposed to have seen a sheep that had fallen down a deep well, which animal was then got out alive. She could see, you understand, *through* things. Through the earth, through stone, and through certain other natural materials, though not, I think, through metal, which may account for the metals in the rhyme."

"What does the rhyme mean?" I asked him.

"It's essentially to do with binding her, shutting her up where she couldn't do harm. You see, Hawkins was besotted with her some while, but then he began to be afraid of her. He's said to have told the priest, 'She will sit quiet all day and only look at me', and when the priest said that many a man would be thankful for such a placid, adoring wife, Hawkins replied she did not look *on* him, but *into* him. And he said that once he had told her hotly to leave off, for he was a sinner, like all men, and if she would keep on staring in such a way, she would see his foul and mortal corruption. To which she gave this strange response: 'Men say always they are wretched and tainted by flesh and sin, but in all men there is such goodness and beauty, as in the earth and all living things, that it is to me like my food and drink, and I can never be tired of having it'."

When Farbody told me this, there in that warm and pleasant room, the sunlight on the books and the domestic pipe-smoke mild in the air, the hair rose on my neck.

"In heaven's name," I said.

The scholar smiled again, pleased with himself, and with the peculiar tale he had memorised so well. "Yes, something in that gives you a turn, doesn't it? She seems to be speaking so charmingly, innocently, and it makes the skin creep. I can tell you, sir, I read this story first when I was a boy of eleven, and I was awake nights after, until my mother scolded some reason into me and hid the volume I'd been reading. Which may explain," he amiably added, "my life-long quest for such hidden trifles of knowledge."

Farbody then went on with the narrative.

Josebaar turned quickly from love to shrinking horror at his young wife. At first, he tried to arrange a separation between them, but she would have none of this. Then he had thoughts of escaping her by going overseas. But she guessed his course, and is said to have assured him she loved him too well to let him go. If he must leave, she would find and follow him, and he did not doubt that she had the powers to do so.

In the end, Hawkins, pale and harried, went to his friends, among whom was the priest, and confessed he was in such fear he should not 'soon remain alive, since the woman eats me up from the inside out'. By what grim stages the others came round to Hawkins' state of mind, Farbody said one might only conjecture, and similarly if any money was involved in it. "But those were ignorant and superstitious times," he reflected. "Alas, they are still." Whatever went on, or the span of its duration, a plan was presently constructed to rid Josebaar Hawkins of the woman.

"He pretended to her that he had only been testing her with his talk of going off, to see how much she loved him. And finding her so faithful, he meant to reward her. He told her he had put by an especial gift for her, an heirloom of his family, kept in a wooden chest in the attics of the house. But it would amuse him if she would go up and look first *through the wood* of the lid, and so say what she saw, before he unlocked the chest and gave her the trophy. Well, it seems she could easily see through wood but not through her husband, and up she went. No sooner was she in the room with the empty chest, than he slammed closed the door and secured it. And then at once came a gang of men and bricked the door up, and others came along the roof to seal and brick up the window."

The bizarre quality of Farbody's recitation was added to, for me, by a sense of historical fact which seemed to underlie the whole. I found I asked abruptly, "Could she not have opened the window – or broken the pane, before the roof-gang reached her?"

"No, dear sir. Remember, the glass in those days was of much thicker and sturdier stuff than the flimsy crystal of our day. Besides, he had previously *pinned* the window shut. I mean, he had driven iron' pins through the frame to the brickwork, and hammered in long pins lengthwise all across."

"Hence the horrible rhyme, a brick and a pin."

"Just so. Besides too, she was very high up, and the men anyway would have thrust her back; she was physically no match for them. They must have been a harsh crew. All the while they were doing it, blocking her in to die the slow death of starvation and thirst, Amber Maria was shrieking and imploring them. And after they had finished, she screamed and howled in her prison uncountable days and nights, before she fell silent for ever. There are many reports of this."

I shuddered. "In God's name, you speak as if it happened."

He looked at me. "My dear sir, it did. I can make no claims for her sorcery, but the facts of her death are undoubtedly true. Some years after, Josebaar Hawkins was hanged for her murder. For he confessed to it, having had not a quiet hour since."

"And then. Did they unlock the room?"

"That they did not. The story concludes with that asseveration. No one would go near the house, let alone pull bricks away from any part of it. That they left, and leave, to the mercy of God."

I sat some while in silence. Perhaps, very likely, I looked grim or rattled, for the scholar came and refilled my glass and moved the biscuit plate nearer my elbow.

"The children's rhyme," said Farbody, "as you're aware, has its own oddities. The brick and the pin relate to the window and door, the sealing of the room. I've come across one text which states that Amber Maria could see only through natural substances, and that therefore a brick, which is man-mixed, would defeat her gaze, just as would refined metal; obviously the very reason why she could detect coins in the ground, rather than see through these also. But do you recall that other line, *She leaps at the moon?*"

I said that I did.

"Salter's Lane," said the scholar, "has nothing to do with the salting trade. Indeed, one wouldn't expect it, so far as we are here from the sea. No, the word *salter* relates to the Latin, *Saltare, to leap*. In Mediaeval times, that area of the woods was known to be a place where witches held their revels, and danced the Wild Dance for their lord, Satan, 'leaping high as the moon'. Which moon, of course, is a calendar feature of the sabbat, whether full or horned for the Devil."

Just then, the door-bell jangled. My aunt had returned for me. I was astonished to see, glancing at Farbody's clock, that only half an hour had elapsed. But then I suppose, I was struggling back to my own time, across the centuries.

I thanked him, and going out with my aunt into the summer street, I resolved to shake myself free of the unnaturally strong emotion that had dropped upon me. And so we went to our luncheon.

Three or four days later I, reluctantly, but evincing cheerfulness, accompanied my aunt to a church tea-party, in honour of the new bell, which had recently been installed, and for which everyone had, the year before, been engaged in fund-raising. Here the social classes mingled with uneasy and ill-founded camaraderie, and I was revealed to a succession of people of all types, to whom it seemed my aunt wished to show off her nephew. Touched by her pride in me, I did my best to be jolly.

"And look," said Aunt Alice, "there is Daffodil Sempson. Or rather, Mrs King, as she is married to a hotelkeeper at St Leonards now, and has come for the first time to visit her sister. They are somewhat an estranged family. None of them is in service now, but in her youth, Daffodil was lady's maid to the Misses Condimer, and travelled all over Europe with them, before she was even seventeen. A great advantage for any girl."

Struck I admit by the name Daffodil, I turned, and saw a very pleasing young woman, dressed most stylishly, a trick no doubt learnt during her travels with the minor aristocracy.

"By all means introduce me to her," I told my aunt, with a more genuine enthusiasm.

But neither of us was able to catch the lady's eye.

She seemed to be fixedly interested in something that went on at the far end of the room, where several people were walking about, and the tables groaned beneath their cakes and lemonade.

"I wonder what has engaged her attention so," speculated my aunt.

Mrs King, *née* Sempson, was staring now almost unnaturally. Then I saw her turn her pretty head, seem to check, and then once more compulsively gaze back towards the tables.

Suddenly, she quite changed colour. I have been witness to several instances of abrupt illness, slight or extreme. Mrs King seemed in the grip of the latter. Her face took on not a white, but a thickly-shining, greenish pallor. Without thinking I moved towards her. But in that moment, she dropped to the ground.

At once she was surrounded by women, one of whom must have been her sister. Presently she was carried away.

On all sides were sympathetic murmurs concerning the heat.

To my sorrow, Mrs King did not return to enjoy the over-bountiful Tea. My aunt made enquiries of her sister, who said that Daffodil was been obliged to be sent home in the pony-cart. "It is a great nuisance, as she intended returning to St Leonards tomorrow, and now she won't be well enough."

"Is her indisposition more serious than we had hoped?" asked my aunt.

"Oh," said the sister, blinking at me with eyes not half so fine as her sibling's, "she makes a fuss about it. She has these delicate ways from her younger years. I may say, she'd never have dared go on so *then*. They would have dismissed her."

"I thought," said I sternly, "that she seemed most unwell."

"No, it isn't that she's ill," declared the vulgar sister, whose hat might have been a lesson to us all in the virtues of regret. "She says it's something that she saw in Austria, once." My aunt and I evidenced incomprehension. The sister said, "I can say nothing of it. She refuses to explain. She says it's too dreadful, and it's taken her these six years to put it from her, and now she's been reminded and will need to stay in bed, with me expected to be flapping round her all day long, and neglecting my duties and Pa."

We extricated ourselves from the uninspiring Miss Sempson and soon after left the Tea-Party. As we were going out, I remember that Aunt Alice said to me, "There is disappointing Mr Polleto. I understand he contributed generously to the bell-fund, which I find curious, since he's far from affluent, and never attends the church. Nor is he sociable. Did you happen to notice him this afternoon?"

I said he might easily go unnoticed, but that I had not, I thought, seen him. Nor had I.

The day before my departure from Steepleford, I had planned a walk through the woods. Whether or not I would approach the stretch of Lane that ran by Josebaar Hawkins' house I was myself unsure. In any event a sudden thunderstorm erupted. Its violence and tenacity were such that I gave over any idea of walking, and spent all that last day with my aunt. The following morning we parted most affectionately, and I returned to London. A month later I went abroad, and spent the rest of the year in Rome, in which ancient, imperial and legend-haunted city it may be supposed Steepleford, and all its tales, sank in my memory to a depth of fathoms.

Just after the New Year, I employed a day or so again at Steepleford. This time, there was snow down, but a flawless snow, thick and solid to tread upon, the weather chill and fine. Had I truly forgotten the house in Salter's Lane? I think that I had in everything but my heart. I took my way across the white fields, admiring the shapes of everything, each changed by its cover of pale fleece, then strayed off into the ancient woods, which were like a cathedral of purest ice.

And then somehow, in the way these things turn out, I took at random another of the silent avenues, and found myself ten minutes later at one of the several openings of the Lane. I had been walking by then more than two hours, and it seemed foolish not to follow this path back to the town.

Soon I reckoned I had been wise to do so. The low afternoon sun was clouding over and a mauve cast had the sky. So, I strode briskly, and thinking of a warm fire ahead, and other cheer, I came level with the high wall of Josebaar Hawkins' ill-starred house.

At first I think I did not recognise it, for like everything else it was plastered with white. But then I got a great shock, and stopped dead in my tracks.

"What has happened here?" I asked, perhaps aloud. Until that time, the trees of the old estate had made a second wall behind the first, and the pile of the building been visible only in portions, as I have previously described. Now, beyond the range of one huge holly tree, I gained abruptly a view of the entire front aspect, all of it, its timber, stone and brickwork, the roof and chimneys, and every cold window, glaring as if it were eye to eye with me, like some person who has suddenly whipped from their face a mask.

Astonished, I attempted to reason how this should be. It was not that the trees were bare. No, it was that every tree, saving the holly, which in any case stood this side of the wall, had been brought down.

I confess that meeting the house like this, head-on, unnerved me. I made to myself no secret of that. But in a moment or so, I had a rational thought. Some vandal had been at work in the 'grounds'. They had chopped down the trees and carted them away, no doubt to provide firewood for needy winter hearths.

On the wing of this rationale, an unusual, perhaps a boy's desire took me, having seen so much, to scale the wall and peer over into the precincts of the house, now open to be studied. I have to say too that my peculiar eagerness to do this was prompted, I now think, more by an *aversion* to doing it, rather than a longing after secrets. It was like a dare one must not evade, for fear of being thought – and worst of all by oneself – a coward.

I am quite strong and fit. The wall had inconsistences and irregular stones in plenty. Despite the snow, I got up it in less than three minutes, and, perched there on the top, stared down into the gardens.

They were the most desolate sight. The snow lay all about, but it had turned dark, and in places black, partly melting away, as on some of the higher trees it did. There was a good reason for this. Any sun which fell here must fall directly over all, since nothing now stood between, only the house and its ground. While every tree and shrub which had grown, rampantly and untended, within the walls, had been levelled and presumably taken away. And I wondered who could have made so bold after all these hundred and more years.

Then, something else caught my eye. There was, towards the side of the house, a sort of ornamental little building, perhaps a folly. It was ruinous and falling down, and its demise seemed hastened by a young oak tree, which had toppled aslant upon its roof, and leaned there yet.

And why then, I wondered, had the wood-stealing vandal not carted off also this ready-felled tree? There it lay, as useful as any other timber, bare and lean, its dislocated branches creaking in some unfelt wind, clear as complaining voices in the stillness.

There were no birds, of course. There was, as before, no sound. But this effect had been common through much of the woods, as the day advanced and the winter sun prepared to leave the earth. This time, I had not noted it particularly only here.

Now I did. For here the absence of all sound, save that sinister creaking whine of broken branches, seemed heavy with presage. The air smelled sour, and faintly dirty, like what one might expect in the centre of an industrial town, where smoke and cinders fall and make each breath lifeless, and potent with disease.

And then, even as I sat there gazing at it, the unlikeliest thing occurred. The leaning dead oak tree swayed, and out of it there burst a shower of dry pieces, splinters of wood ejected, and then one whole limb snapped off and dropped, disintegrating even as it went, so that by the instant it touched the ground, there was no more of it than dust. What had occasioned such a thing? The action of some animal? – no animal was in the vicinity, so much was plain. The simple process of a slow decay then, electing to finish its work coincidentally with my scrutiny. I had the strangest notion that, by *staring* at the tree, I had hastened the breaking off and dissolution.

And then, and then, I knew it was not I. *I* had not caused it. Across my scalp my hair crawled as if filled by icy tricklings. Against my will, it seemed to me, yet no more resistible than as if at the pull of a chain of steel, my head turned and tilted back, and I looked up at the unmasked face of that house, towards its highest casements.

There was not a creeper left upon any of them. Even the snow had been leached away. But oh, something white there was, which stood at the window, looking out, and out.

I can put down here only what I saw. I saw a woman's shape. Her gown I cannot detail, nor how her hair was dressed, though it seemed to me that both were disordered. Her features I could not see, and that had nothing to do with distance, and I believe nothing to do with light or shade.

She *had* no features, none. That is, she had only one feature. She had two eyes. But her eyes were set in that featureless whiteness of a shape like two burned holes. They were not eyes at all – but, they were eyes, more eyes than are possible to any thing which lives.

I remember little of my descent of the wall. Perhaps I fell from it. Certainly, I think some of it crumbled and broke away too, as I slipped down. And then I fled along the Lane, and this I do recall. I fled and I whimpered like a man pursued by the dogs of hell, that are really fiends, and they will tear him, even his soul, if they catch him. But they did not catch me, and I reached the town. And then came maybe the most sinister and curious thing of all.

For running out into Market Gate Street, in the wintry dusk, a carriage passed me, and in the carriage a friend of my aunt's, who greeted me as she went by, most graciously. And I raised my hat, and nodded, and then walked on to my aunt's door, like some man who has not just met the devil on the road.

"Aunt," I said to her that evening, "why not come up to London for a spell?"

"Oh, no, dear boy," she said. "I'm too comfortable here. Why should I wish to be in London?"

"Well, I am there. And half a dozen theatres and shops and museums that are the envy of the country."

But she would not be moved, saying it would put me against her, if she encroached upon my 'London World'.

And so, after another day I went again away from Steepleford. And naturally, I had spoken to no one of what I had seen, and no one had asked me what I had seen. Nor did I hear a single mention about the town of Hawkins' house, or its current state, let alone of anything else.

However, as I sat in the train, I took myself sternly to one side, and told myself that perhaps ghosts did exist, for there are nowadays even photographs of some of them, but of all things, the dead could not harm the living, their power was done.

3

Less than a month later, I was at a supper given by my then acquaintance, Lord D----. The food was of the best and the wines Olympian, which made up, somewhat, for the conversation. At midnight, I well remember we had some music, amongst the rest an attractive rendition, given by a female singer of superb voice, of the words of Alexander Pope's *Pastorals*, the melody being, I think, Handel's. As it finished, one of the servants came discretely in, and presently handed me a telegram.

To my dismay, I read that my aunt had fallen seriously ill, and begged my attendance on her. My own man had taken alarm and brought the message directly on to me.

I hurried to my rooms and flung some things together, and was next on the train for Steepleford Halt.

I have said, I had great affection for my aunt, and with good reason. My agitation was increased because she had never, until then, that I knew, been afflicted with any ailment more than trifling and swiftly over. Other thoughts I believe I dismissed from my mind.

The morning was young when we arrived at the Halt, where her carriage had been sent in readiness. It was a dismal day in February, sleety and cold, with leaden skies. Everything looked horrible to me in the deadly light of it, and the light of my anxiety, and all the station buildings, the gaunt trees, covered by an air of desuetude and darkness. This impression only increased as we bumped among the wintry woods, and I cannot describe my abrupt unease, as I thought we must turn into Salter's Lane. Then the carriage veered away, and went instead by the other route, to the Crossing. On asking the coachman, he told me that some trees had come down in the Lane, which made it impassable, and I dare say I was ridiculously relieved.

I barely noted the town. No sooner had we reached my aunt's than I sprang from the carriage and hastened indoors.

In the hall, I met her doctor, a solid man, who reassured me somewhat. "It is a kind of low fever we've been seeing in the town recently. Unfortunately, given your aunt's age, it has stayed with her longer than one might have hoped." Then he frowned, and I asked him why he did so. He said, "Ah, well, there have been rather a lot of such cases in the past month. But there. The old and the very young are always vulnerable. Your aunt, of course, is not yet sixty."

I said, "Have there been fatalities?"

"No, no, nothing like that."

None of this prepared me for the sight of my aunt, who, lying propped on her pillows, looked white, and, to me, near death. I took her hand, and she murmured at once, "I called you here, my dear, because I was afraid I might not be able to remain much longer. But today I feel rather better."

I told her she was a fraud, and that I was happy to find her so.

Despite my nervousness, my aunt rallied. She improved. But she did not entirely get well. Two weeks later, when pressing concerns of my own urged me to go back to London, she too implored me to leave. "I was being very foolish," she said. "What nonsense. I shall see the New Century, I am determined on it." And I realised I made her more uncertain by remaining so faithfully, as if hourly fearful of her collapse.

The doctor too grew confident. "She is completely out of danger, or I'd never concur with your departure. And she has the best of care.

I'd like to see more progress, but then her age has been against her a little. When the spring weather comes, then we should see a change for the better. Although," he added, rather insensitively and ominously, "I find that all those who have succumbed to this pernicious malady take a great while over mending. There's a young woman I have heard of, of only three-and-twenty, of the working families, you understand, but well-nourished and fit, and the mother of healthy children, who has been sick with this same fever off and on for eight weeks. She was one of the first to contract it, and again and again she seems to throw it off, only to sink down once more."

Receiving this news, I was now in two minds whether or not to go. However, in the end, a telegram arriving the other way, from the metropolis, forced my hand, and I caught the train.

Truth to tell, it was a relief to escape the atmosphere of a convalescent house, not to mention all Steepleford, which had seemed unbearably dreary and run down in the rain and mud of a new-born and unfriendly March. Indeed, I had never seen the place look so forlorn; it had depressed me. And when, having been returned to the city only a few days, a firmly-written letter came from my aunt, assuring me she had now taken the upward path, and even given a tea-party for some friends, I resolved to stay where I was. Soon after this, and in the light of a further optimistic bright epistle from Steepleford, I allowed myself to be lured to France with Nash and his brother, and then was persuaded on to Italy again.

In retrospect, I gain a terrible impression of my short time there in the awakening summer, and of that previous more leisurely summer I had spent in Rome, happily gravitating among the bronzes and the marbles, both inanimate and human, while concurrently there ran on and on, behind the veils of distance and inattention, that dreadful horror of which I could know nothing, and yet which I do believe I sensed, for had it not shown itself to me behind its own shadow, brushed me with its noiseless wing?

I shall not try to excuse myself. Perhaps I was afraid. I might have seen there was good reason to be.

Certainly, I did not ponder that chance vision I had had of a 'ghost' in the window of Josebaar Hawkins house. I did not even offer the experience as a suitable gothic tale, one hot Tuscan night among the soft blue hills, when others were telling ghost stories. Did I even call it to mind? Perhaps, I cannot remember. But of course, too, what I had seen was not a ghost. Not that at all.

Needless to say, when I got back to England late in July, I was at once assailed by feelings of unquiet and guilt, and instantly wrote to Aunt Alice – there had been no letters from her waiting for me, but as a general rule she did not constantly put pen to paper. I asked how she did, and if I might come down and see her.

After a little delay, I received her reply, which was brief and penned in a careful, rigid style. She said she was in her usual health, and would be glad if I would 'take time to call on her'. I thought the whole tone of her letter sulky, and was peeved she had not mentioned some presents I had sent her on my travels, for which may I be forgiven.

For some reason, as I saw to the packing of my bag, I had upon my brain that fragment of Pope's *Pastorals*, which I had heard the very evening the telegram reached me of my aunt's illness. The gracious verse was in every way unlike the rhyme which had accrued about Amber Hawkins and her murdering spouse, yet now it too lodged fast in my head, and repeated itself over and over. Never came warning in a stranger guise. The words are well-known, of course, but I shall put them down even so, such is their unconscionable significance to me now:

Where'er you walk, cool gales shall fan the glade,
Trees where you sit shall crowd into a shade;
Where'er you tread, the blushing flowers shall rise,
And all things flourish where you turn your eyes.

The train reached Steepleford Halt soon after three o'clock of a peerless summer afternoon. London had been somewhat stuffy and overheated, but as we entered the countryside beyond, a wonderful honeyed peace descended, balmy, lazy, and a-flicker with butterflies. Flowers blazed from every hedge and bank, the trees were laden with heavy green, the sky as blue as the mysotis.

Descending from my carriage, I was struck initially only by the sense of the huge sun, which was hammering the earth, but looking about me, I perceived at once a quality in the light, both dry and harsh. Where it fell, not only did the sight seem wounded, but the place beneath. Everything looked to me, in this glare, drained of colour, faded like a woman's lovely gown worn too often.

The veteran who oversaw the station was standing to one side, consulting his watch as the train pulled out again. It was my habit to exchange a few pleasantries with him when I met him, and I prepared to do so now, but he forestalled me. Looking up, his face was not as it had been, less older than used up. He nodded with no smile. "Good day. I regret the train was late."

"No matter. It was a delightful journey today."

"But a poor arrival, I dare to think," he said. He sounded surly, which surprised me very much; he was not of this sort. Then he pointed straight by me. "D'you see that tree?"

I turned, to humour him, and gazed towards an old copper beech, which had guarded the ground above the railway for as long as I had been coming there, and no doubt some regiments of years before that. "The tree? Indeed I do."

"See how it leans?"

"Why yes — what can have happened?"

"The good Lord knows," said he. "The roots are out to one side. Dying it is."

"What a great pity. Can nothing be done?"

He made a noise. He was angry, not merely at my paltry concern, but at all things, which had somehow conspired to ruin the beauty of the tree. "It's got to be felled," he said, "tomorrow. A danger to the trains if it falls, d'you see?"

I said again I was very sorry, as I was, and gave him something for his trouble, at which he looked as if it were the Thirty Pieces of Silver themselves.

I was glad to get out of the station after this.

My intention had not been to walk, it was too sultry, and here for sure there was a dull storminess to the air that already made my head ache. The station further up the line lay five miles beyond the town, but in an outpost where a cab might be accosted. Here, however, I had been promised my aunt's carriage, which now, going out on to the path, I did not find. This I could have understood more readily if the train had been early, or on time.

I half turned back to ask the station-master if a carriage might be procured from the local inn, but then thought better of it. The walk to the town would not take so long, providing I struck off at once for Salters Lane, and followed that to Steepleford.

There I idled then, on the gravel, under the impoverished shade of some spindly, desiccated sycamores, as if a decision must still be made. I was reluctant to go on. But go on I must, and would.

Until this moment, I had, I think, almost entirely suppressed or driven away my utter unease at the prospect of the Lane, where witches once had leaped in their revels, and where lay the house of a murderer, and his wife who, as I had seen and still credited, haunted its window. Now my fears rushed in, like the sea tearing through one small crack in a dam, and carrying all before it.

I broke out into a sweat, which even the leaden heat had not occasioned, for it was cold, and my heart thudded in my breast.

Come, I thought, *in heaven's name, you are not a baby. What is there to be afraid of? If the wretched nook affects you so, do what the others do, and look away from it.*

What finally galvanised me was a dawning grasp of what the absence of the carriage might mean. In the past, when it was promised, it had been reliable. If my aunt had forgotten to order it forth, or her coachman not brought it, then something must have occurred to interrupt the mission. And all at once I was vastly unsettled as to what.

Then I did set off, striding the path between the fields, towards the woodland which lay, like a smoky cloud, upon the nearest horizon.

I must have noticed as I went, the state of those fields. They were bleached and barren-looking, the grain in parts fallen, and where upright, then not usual in its colour, and in areas seeming burnt. At the time, I suspected a fire had taken place, or infestation of some sort. My mind was not truly on the fields, or did not want to be.

But then I reached the edges of the woods. And with the best will in the world, I could no longer delude myself very much.

Only after the most serious of gales would so many great trees have fallen. Looking in, at what had been the greenest of green shades, I now beheld bald, wide avenues, all railwayed with these broken pillars, which had tumbled in every direction, taking in every case more than one or two fellows with them. Besides these fallen giants, the standing wood was sickly. There could be no mistaking it.

A yellowish tinge was on each leaf, or worse, a blackened scorching, as if some acid had been thrown over and among them all. The canopy besides showed great holes.

I advanced like some soldier into enemy territory, where any lethal hazard or trap may be encountered. No sooner was I in, however, than again I paused. Upon the raddled ground, bare of anything but for the most hardy weeds and brackens, (and these burnt and brown), I had begun to see strange heaps and drifts of a dark dust. I knew at once what these were, but going over to one of the fallen trees, I tapped it, nor very hard, with a strong-looking stick I had found on the outer path, and picked up thoughtlessly, as one sometimes does on a walk. No sooner did the stick make contact, than the bole of the prone trunk, for about five feet either side the light blow, gave way in a shower of what appeared to be the finest black sugar. The sturdy-looking stick also snapped in half, brittle as charcoal. And the sugar-like substance sprayed out also from this. I dropped the stick then. As it hit the ground, it shattered into some twenty further fragments. The dust – the dust was all that persisted of trees which, last summer, had seemed to touch the sky.

But I must go on through this wreckage of a poisoned wood. I followed the carriage-ride doggedly, which normally at this time of year would have been rather overgrown. Surely I had seen it so myself – with sprinklings of woodland flowers everywhere the sun could penetrate, thick moss and large lacy ferns where it did not. There was no hint of that now. Not even the toadstools and other funguses, that colonise any woodland, good or bad, had ventured in. Nor was anything else to be come on. No beasts or birds ran or fluttered or fluted through the trees, or played about the tracks. Silence ruled the woods. Absence ruled them. And here was I, forging on perforce, like the last man quick upon a dying earth. And my feelings of horror and dejection increased with every step I took.

By the time I got out into Salter's Lane, I may say I was prepared for anything. Had I not been, the quantity of felled trees which marked the exit point, would have alerted me, and the expanses of the deadly dust, which resembled here nothing so much as the encroachment of a desert.

Even prepared, yet I halted where I stood. I looked down the Lane, and knew it for an avenue accursed. It was – and I do not exaggerate – like some landscape of the damned.

Nothing stood in it, its length was paved by horizontal trees, and between, the dust had formed mounds which had partly solidified, in a friable, hopeless manner, perhaps from the direct action of weather. Where hedges had been, there were sometimes left some bare black twigs and poles. I did not want to enter the Lane, I did not want to travel it over.

I had no choice, unless I turned back and retrod my path, then going on to Joiner's Crossing, which would now add almost an hour to my hurrying journey.

So, I went on. I walked into the Lane and advanced, having, every yard or so, to get over the fallen trees, most of which gave way under my feet, meaning I must scramble and jump to save myself also from a fall. The mounds of dust were much the same; I sank in them as in the dunes of some hellish beach, or else the humps of powdery 'soil' they had formed crumbled, and I unsafely slithered.

This was very exhausting, and addedly foul from the dust, which was constantly clouding up, as if purposely to stifle me.

Above, the sky was no longer blue. It had a tarnished sheen to it, like unpolished metal. True clouds were hung out on it, grimy-looking and peculiar in shape, like torn banners, each a mile across.

Of course, I knew I must come to the house. I knew I must pass it.

I had vowed I would not give it one glance. The perils and obstacles of the Lane would assist me, surely, in that, since I needed all my attention for the road.

However, I reached the house of Josebaar Hawkins, and did not keep to my vow.

The holly tree was gone. There was no trace of it; it had become one with the dusts. The wall too had come down. It lay scattered all over the Lane, the bricks and bits of stonework disintegrating, like everything else. Behind the wall stretched a vast piece of ground that was like a bare, swept floor. It had nothing at all growing upon it, and even the dust had blown or died away. It was a nothingness, in colour greyish. And upon this table of death there rose – the house. With by it the little ornamental building I had spied on my last excursion here. This I now saw, with an unnerving pang, had been a small mausoleum, no doubt the supposed resting-place of Hawkins' wife. Now it comprised a part of a roof upon a couple of columns, and within, too, was nothing. Of the toppled oak, which had leant there, naturally, there was no sign.

Of everything which had been there, of nature or contrivance, that house alone remained, but not intact. Its roof had come away in broad segments, one saw the gaping joists and beams, which were in turn disbanding. Both chimneys were down, crashed inwards. On the lower floors was not a window that held its antique glass, or its boxed decorations. The creepers had slipped from it, and after them the bricks had tried, and still tried, to come out. Yet the building, what there was of it, jutted upright. And in that spot, this made it a thing of unbelievable terror. Ruined and dislodged, and every moment giving more, nevertheless *it* had so far *stayed*, where nothing else had been enabled.

All this while I had not raised my eyes beyond the lower floors, or where I had raised them, I had selected their progress with much care. But in the end, I knew I would have to do it, would have to look full on at the upper window under the roof.

I had been in Rome, I had been in Siena and Venice. Among the hills and waters, among the bronzes, had I not somehow understood that *she* stood here, on and on, stood here looking out, eating with her eyes first the bricks and mortar, then the pins, that sealed her up, patient as only a hopeless thing can be, taking a century over it; next eating out the glass, and next, what lay beyond the glass, the trees, the air, the Lane, the countryside.

They must have known, the people of Steepleford town, in 1788, when they passed by on the Lane, hearing her weeping and shrieking in agony and fear, all those endless days and nights. They must have known what he had done to her. What then did *they* do, but cross themselves perhaps, or use some older, less acceptable mark. But they knew, they knew.

She had loved too well, that was her sole crime. She had seen too much in mankind that was beautiful and good, and for sure too much in him, in Josebaar Hawkins, and for this they had condemned her and killed her. How she must then have hated them. How she must have *looked*, fixing despairingly her mad eyes upon the impenetrable dark. And if she had not survived her death, *something* that came of her, and of her hatred, and of those eyes – and which learned too new skills whereby to use those eyes – that did survive, and lived still, and saw and looked – and fed. And it was there, there in that window, drawing up the whole world in its slow and bottomless net.

"Oh, God, Amber Maria, poor lost pitiable hideous residue…"

My eyes were on her window, her death's window. My eyes were stuck there and now could not pull away. I felt my heart turn to water inside me, and the occluded atmosphere blackened over.

I did not quite lose my senses. Instead I found I leaned on my hands, kneeling in the desert of dust among the slaughter of the trees.

To myself I said, *But what did I see this time?*

For I had not seen a single thing. The window – *her* window – was empty of everything. Of creeper, and of bricks, pins and glass. Of light and shadow, and of any shape. As with the rest, nothing was there. And yet… the nothing which was in that window was not empty. No. She was there in it, there in the core of it, as things hide in darkness. Or, her eyes were there, those pits of seeing, her *looking* was there, her *looking* looked out. It had looked even into me, and through me, and away, to have all else.

Presently I got up, and as before I ran.

The town – I wondered after why the station-master had not warned me. I wondered too why the newspapers and journals in London had not carried some mention of it, why no sensational word seemed to have escaped from it. Perhaps there had been some news which was disbelieved – or believed too well and suppressed. Besides, events had raced to their final act as swiftly as a wave.

I have read of times of siege and plague in Mediaeval Germany, Italy, France, and in certain of those occult little towns, crouched at the foot of deep valleys, hung like baskets from the sides of cliffs, the dim and winding alleys make such images still but too conjurable. But Steepleford was a slow, flat, gentle settlement, prosperous and mild, where the horse, casting its shoe, caused a stir, and they had longed for a foreign theatrical gentleman to liven them up.

Getting near the outskirts, I saw a cloud hung over the fields and town. It was a wreath of smoke. The dead gardens along the approach I had scarcely noticed, nor the untended houses, which seemed to have been afflicted too by a kind of partial hurricane, ripping the tiles from roofs, and setting askew anything that had been in the slightest vulnerable. There was a dearth of people brisk at their trade or gossip. Instead, there hung there a *presence* of incredible raw heat and turgid staleness. I have never smelled such air, even in the sinks of greater Europe.

I came into Market Gate Street before I properly knew it, and there, as in some canvas by Hieronymus Bosch, I saw what I took at once for plague fires burning in arches and at the corners of houses, reeking of sulphur and other purgatives.

The fumes by now were thick nearly as a London fog, and in them, as I moved on, persons came and went unknown, their heads down and swathed in scarves, none looking at another. They were creatures from the self-same painting, at large between torments.

Then came the River Styx, for the street was awash with a black, stinking body of fluid. I had splashed into it before I could prevent myself, but in any case, there was no other way across.

Up towards my aunt's part of the town, a pony and trap leapt rattling by, the unhappy animal tossing its head, and red-eyed as the horses of Pluto from the smoke. A man hailed me and pulled the horse in. Amazed to be recognised in the Inferno, I stopped. There was my aunt's doctor, peering down.

"Thank God you've arrived, young man. We sent off a wire this very morning."

My heart clutched at me. "It must have missed me by an inch. Is she so bad, then?"

"I fear she is, now. It's the same all over the town. The deuce knows what the illness is. We have three specialists down from London, and one from the Low Countries, and they have drawn a blank on it. My own sister, who has never taken sick in her life – well. But besides all this business of burst pipes and subsiding walls across the entire town… But I won't trouble you with that, either." The pony shook its head violently. The doctor raised his voice to curse. "Be damned to these confounded fires. What do the fools think they're doing? Have they heard nothing of modern hygiene, our only reliable ally against disease – to fill up the air with such muck? Superstition, ignorance… Make haste to get on!" And with this baleful cry, either to me or the pony, I was unsure, the doctor whipped the beast on, and like King Death himself flung off into the smother.

But I ran again, and so reached my aunt's house. And ten minutes later I was in her bedroom, by the side of her bed, but she, although living yet, did not see or hear me.

When I was a small boy, and my youthful mother died suddenly and without warning, this aunt of mine, then an elegant and pretty fashion-plate of an Alice, herself not much above thirty-five, sheathed in softest clothes and scented by vanilla, took me in her arms and let me sob out my soul. And now again I leaned by her, and I wept. But she never knew it, now. And oh, any pity I had felt for that other, for that thing once known as Amber Maria Hawkins, you can be sure I had given it up.

So now I must come to the strangest part of my abnormal tale. To a conclusion, indeed, which any writer of fiction would be ashamed to set before his audience, having brought them thus far, and by such a fearful road. Therefore, prior to the last scenes of the drama, I will say this: one piece evidently missing from my narrative has since been supplied, and only the discovery of that unique absentee has brought me, at this time, and so many years after these occurrences took place, to write them down at all.

My aunt, where she lay on the bed, did not stir. Only the faintest movement demonstrated that she breathed at all. I looked ardently for this proof, and once or twice it seemed to me it faltered, and then I too held my breath. But always the slight rise and fall of her breast resumed. At least she was not in pain or distress. That was all, at this time, I might be thankful for.

Near midnight the doctor called again. He was worn out, as I could see, by his conscientious tours up and down the stricken town, through the acrid fumes of the fires, the stenchful spilled waters, and the furnace heat, which even nightfall had not abated. When he was done with his examination, a frighteningly swift one, I had them bring him some brandy, and he thanked me, then solemnly announced that he 'did not think it would be long.'

"Is there nothing can be done?" I asked, like a child.

He shook his head. He was doubtless exhausted too by this question, which must have been asked of him everywhere that night, by tearful wives and white-faced husbands, by daughters, by fathers, by one third of the folk of Steepleford, who in that hour had been made the people of Egypt, when the Angel of Death did not pass over them, but took from them, across all the boundaries of age and condition, their first-born.

After the doctor had gone, I sat down again, and drank some of the wine, which had been brought me on an untouched dinner tray. Then I think I must have slipped into a doze.

I was woken, as were some countless others, by the most fearsome noise I have ever heard.

Starting up, I gave a cry, and as I did so, heard below and above me in the house, and everywhere about, many other throats exercised in similar startled exclamation.

The sound I can only describe as being like an exact representation of that phrase: The Crack of Doom. It was as if a thunderbolt had been hurled from heaven and struck the town, cracking it open with one awful brazen clang.

Finding myself unharmed, and the house still entire about me, I turned in fear to the bed. But a glance at my aunt showed her still insensible. Going to the window then, I stared out, but the street was thick in smoke and darkness, its few lamps half blind. Worse for being unseen, vague noises of fright and panic had risen all around, and I made out windows lighting up here and there like red eyes. Then a man came running by. I opened the casement and called down to him. "What was that sound? Do you know?"

But he only raised to me a face peeled by terror, and flew on.

I truly believed some apocalyptic conclusion was about to rush upon us all. The most primal urge came on me, and going to her, I meant to lift up my poor aunt in my arms, so we might at least perish together. But as I reached the bedside, I stopped dead once more. For I saw her eyes were open and looking at me lucidly. And where the lamp shone on her face, her colour had come back, not feverish but soft, even attractive.

"How nice to see you, Frederick," said my aunt. "I have had the most refreshing sleep and feel so much better now." Her voice was not weak, nor did she seem to be lying to console me. She added, nearly winsomely, "I hate to trouble cook, I know the hour is late, but perhaps Sally might boil me an egg? An egg with a little toast. And oh, a cup of tea. I'm so thirsty."

And then, before my astounded gaze, she was sitting herself up in the bed, and as I sprang to forestall and help her, she laughed. "You're gallant, dear boy."

When accordingly I went out into the passage, I found the maid, Sally, standing there and looking at me with great eyes. Before I could speak of the wonder concerning my aunt, Sally announced, "They say the new church bell has fallen right down the spire and landed in the chancel. The roof there is all damaged and come down, too. Did you hear the horrible noise, sir? We thought the End had come."

Distractedly I asked, "Was anyone hurt?"

"They say not." (I learned later 'they' was the carter's boy, who had bustled in with the news.) "But the whole town has been woke up."

This was, it turned out, true in more than one way, if the process of waking may be associated with revival. For my aunt was not alone in her abrupt and miraculous feat of recovery. It transpired, as over succeeding days I learned in more detail, that of all the six hundred odd persons lying sick that night, or even at the point, it was thought, of death, not one but did not rouse up an instant or so after the app-alling clangour of the bell. And not one thereafter but did not take quickly a swift and easy path to full recovery. (Even, or so I was assured, a cat, which that been failing, grew suddenly well, and a canary, that had sunk to the floor or its cage, flew up on its perch and began to sing.)

Shamelessly it was spoken of as a miracle, this reversal of extreme illness to good health. And there were those who spoke religiously of the falling bell, some claiming that it had cast itself down in some curious form of sacrifice, which it achieved, having cracked and buckled itself beyond use. Others averred that it had been itself unlucky, or impure in some sensational but mysterious way, and therefore fell like an evil angel, at God's will, after which the town was freed from its curse.

These notions, of course, were ludicrous, but everywhere for a while one heard them, and small surprise. For the saving of so many of the town's lives, both young and old, affluent and poor, and in so abrupt and unheralded a form, did smack of divine intervention. While I did not for a moment credit this, yet I thanked God with every other there. And as the days went on, and Steepleford hoisted itself, slowly but surely from its own ashes, the streets cleared of water and debris, the baleful fires vanished, and the summer sun took pity and shone with greater brightness and less heat. The smell of furnaces and dungeons melted away.

Ten days later, accompanying my aunt on her first walk up and down the thoroughfares, I saw fresh roses flaming in twenty gardens, and now and then, where a tree had come down or been axed, new growth rioting, shining green, from the stumps.

They had found by then that the bell-rope had been eaten away. By rats, some said, as Steepleford moved, a rescued ship, back upon its even keel.

"Such a nuisance," added my aunt, flighty as a girl. "Now the rector will want another one."

I said that this would mean more fund-raising bacchanals, and Aunt Alice remarked that the strange Mr Polleto at least would spare them all his disappointing presence. "Lady Constance, when she called, told me he had left the town only last Monday. Generally, such a thing would never have caught her attention, but it seems, the cottage is now for sale, and she wishes to buy it for a young painter she has found."

But I had then no interest at all in Mr Polleto.

My aunt, meanwhile, had more than become herself again. She seemed to me younger and more active than she had been for years. The doctor too assured me he now thought her good for 'three decades'. And when she said to me one evening, "Do you know, dear boy, I think being ill has done me good," I could only agree. And so it must be confessed, at liberty to do so, I began to hanker after my own life.

Of course, I was bemused too. I wanted time to myself to think over events. One instant, I felt I had been the involuntary party to a delusion. At another, the unreal seemed actual. But we seldom trust ourselves upon such matters, I mean upon matters that may contain the supernatural. There is always some other explanation that surely must be the proper one.

I am not unduly superstitious, but now, in the glow of returning normality, I began to prefer to think myself to have been in the grasp of a wild obsession, where I had imagined some things and brooded upon others, until I could make them fit my vivid scenario.

When finally I commenced my preparations to leave Steepleford, I was told, in passing, by a neighbour, that no carriage could be got now along Salter's Lane.

"Are the fallen trees still uncleared?"

"No, no. It's the new growth shooting out there. It's become one great coppice, with trees bursting, they say, from the stumps. Those that have seen say they've never had a sight like it. But there's a deal going on with trees and other plants, after that drought we had." Here he gave me a long list of things, which I will not reproduce, then, as I was tiring, said this: "Perhaps you may have noticed the old beech at the station? A fine old tree, but it was twisting and due for the axe, but now spared, and they say the roots have dug down again, if such a thing is to be believed, and the trunk is straight again too. And the leaves coming out on it, as if it were May not August. A strange business and no mistake. Did you ever get a peep at that house in the Lane? The Witch House some call it."

Sombrely I replied that I had.

"Well, that's all come down, like a house of cards. Not a wall of it standing, nor one stone on another. A great heap of rubble."

I had a dream, not while I remained in the town, but a month later, when Nash had persuaded me back to France, in the south, in a little village among the chestnut woods. I dreamed I was on the roofs of Steepleford church, and pale, glassy arrows flew by through the air, that were the looks of a woman who stood at a window in Salter's Lane. These arrows severed the rope of the bell in the church spire.

And when it fell, there was no sound, only a great nothingness. But in the nothingness, I knew that woman was no more.

"What's up?" said Nash, finding me out in the village street, smoking, at four in the morning, the dawn just lifting its silver lids beyond the trees.

"Do you suppose," I said, "that something thought fully virtuous, if attacked, might rebound on the attacker, might destroy them?"

"History and experience relate otherwise," said Nash.

And so they do.

4

That then, was my story of Steepleford, all I had of it at the time, but which I gave to my companion, Jeffers, on the terrace of the Hotel Alpius, as we waited for the Wassenhaur train.

I was nevertheless moved to regret to him the unsatisfactory lack of explanation concerning the final outcome of events.

"I haven't been back now to the place for years," I finished, "and so can add nothing. My aunt, you see, grew sprightly – she still is – and moved to London, where she has a fine town house."

"Hmm," said my companion. He drew upon his cigar, and looked covertly again at the instigator of my tale, that same quaint little shop-keeper Polleto, who still sat at his adjacent table.

Precisely then the untoward took place. Or perhaps I should say the apt, as it had happened before, and neither of us could now miss its significance.

A party of three gentlemen and two ladies had just now been coming across the terrace, and taken their seats to my right. So it was I heard, from behind my right ear, a stifled little cry, and next the splintering crash of a water glass dropped on the paving.

Jeffers and I both turned sharply, and in time to see that the second young lady of the party, ashen in colour, was being supported by her friends. As they fussed and produced a smelling-bottle, and called loudly for spirits, Polleto darted to his feet and went gliding quickly from the terrace.

"Now I fancy," said Jeffers, "you've witnessed something of this sort before. And I too, in a way, since you told me of it."

"You mean Daffodil King, who fainted at the church Tea. "

"Just so."

"You imagine that she, and the lady over there, gave way for a similar cause – that they had seen Mr Polleto?"

"Don't you imagine it?" asked Jeffers laconically.

I thought, and answered honestly, "Yes. But why?"

"I wonder," said Jeffers, infuriatingly. Then he added, "No, I'm not being fair to you. You see, I've read of the case, and viewed a rather poor photograph once, in a police museum, in circumstances I shan't bore you with. When you first pointed him out, I had a half suspicion. But in the light of both ladies swooning at the sight of the man... Recollect, Austria is only over the border here. I believe you told me the charming Daffodil had been in Austria once, and said she had seen something there so awful, it had taken her six years to recover from it?"

"Yes, or so her sister informed me."

"What she saw then was that same man, Polleto, in the street probably, on the day that the people of a well-known Austrian spa almost lynched him. I have no doubts the other lady to our right, saw him in a similar style. Unless she had the singular misfortune to have met him."

"Then he's notorious?"

"No. Of course, his real name *isn't* Polleto. I was never told what his real name was. The documents referred to him only as The Criminal. And the crime too was hushed up in the end, and rich acquaintances got him away to avoid a most resounding scandal, which would, I believe, have brought down the Austrian government of the hour."

"In God's name – what had he done?"

Jeffers shrugged. "That's the thing, Frederick, what *had* he done? No one would say. Not even the file on him, which I was shown, would say anything as to the *nature* of his crime. Not even the policemen I spoke with. It was something so vile, so disgusting, so inhuman, that no scrap of it has ever been revealed by anyone who knows. They won't – can't – speak of it. They try to push it from their minds. And if they see him, like that lady across the terrace, some part of them withers. There now, she's looking a little better. All the better, no doubt, since what made her ill has left the vicinity."

I sat staring at him.

Presently I said, "Are you then saying to me what I suppose you must be?"

Jeffers stretched himself in his chair, and smiled at me. "Even you," said he, "asked yourself whether or not something of great perceived virtue, like a church bell, could have halted Amber Maria, should she set her sights on it. But it wasn't virtue she avoided, was it? She loved the earth and all the people in it. I, too, Frederick, have heard of the Lilyite sect, and of course she must have been a member of that sect. No doubt Josebaar Hawkins let her have her meetings in his house, and protected her after by lying. But maybe in the later years he feared that in her too, that she was one of the Lilyites and put the teachings of Jesus before all other things. What did she do but love others and want to help them with her precious gift of seeing, from which she herself had never tried to profit? She saw good and beauty in all men and all things, and loved them like – loved them *better* – than herself. And where have you heard such philosophy before, save from the lips of Christ?"

I was shocked a little, to have missed this clue. Humbly I waited for him to go on. He did so.

"Amber Maria looked with her eating eyes through her window, and after the blocked-up bricks and pins, she had the glass, and then, as you said, the trees, the air and the Lane. And next Steepleford she ate up with her eyes. And it would have gone on like this, like rings spreading from a pebble thrown into a pool, and God knows where it could have ended. But ended it must have done, at last. For in this world, along with all those who, despite their colossal failings, carry in them the seeds of goodness and beauty, there are a few, only a few, I trust, who have nothing like that inside them. Who are composed only of the grossest and most foul of atoms, who are, though human, like things of the Pit. In them there is not, I daresay, one hint of light. Perhaps there is no soul. And meeting one of these persons, Amber Maria, who fed on goodness and beauty and drained it to dust, fed instead upon the worst poison, that which would scald away the psychic core of any such vampire. It was Polleto, you see, Polleto, that little ghastly human demon, whose crime is so unspeakable that never is it spoken, Polleto who had come to live in the town, placating it by helping it buy a bell, Polleto that at last her devouring eyes reached. Like everything else then, she tried to eat him up. And then she must have tried to spew him out. But it was too late. She had touched and tasted in a manner only vampires know. She who had once loved God and once loved others as herself, until they let her die in that atrocious manner. And after that, she who hated, and would have eaten the world, save in due course she came to Polleto and ate at Polleto. *Polleto!* And it killed her, Frederick, in all and every way. It killed her to a death more deep than any grave, more cold than any stone."

Flicker of a Winter Star

As so often, from an idea by John Kaiine

Ernestine was seventy-six when she went to live at Gracious Pines, and it felt like her first day at school.

"This is the library. There is the conservatory. And now we have the dining-room, Ernestine."

It was all first names, both residents and staff. Here there were no such formalities – or were they courtesies? – as Mr or Mrs or Miss. And when they called you *ma'am*, it was a kind of joke. As if, by growing old, (as by being very young), you had forfeited any right to – to what? Perhaps simply... a little distance.

But this was: We are all a team. And above all, though you were paying through the nose for it, be grateful. Be *cheerful*. "Why such a long face, May-Ellen? That's better, Donald, you're in a good mood today."

Loathing herself, Ernestine smiled too, nodded and looked pleased, appreciative and willing.

Inside, she thought, *When is this awful young woman going to let me go?*

They reached Ernestine's private room, and the Awful Young Woman, who was tall, pink and pushy, with a scrubbed face and hardly any eyes, (creased away by constant smiles?), herded her through the door.

"Here's the bed, the blinds, the bathroom."

Some strange shadows, Ernestine thought, almost like – but she was always over-imaginative, even Jim had used to say that. Besides, no time to daydream – the AYW was firmly announcing: "And here's the bell, if you have an accident or when you don't feel so good."

"Am I very likely not to?" Ernestine inquired archly, and could have kicked herself.

The AYW peered at her, beaming. "We have to take care, don't we, Ernestine?"

When she was gone, Ernestine saw the odd shadows had vanished. Instead, she wondered if she should search the two rooms for hidden devices of surveillance. There were some outside, here and there, in the corridors and the main rooms.

Other elderly occupants of Gracious Pines had seemed to find them amusing, staring at themselves on camera as they went by, some chuckling, even pulling faces or preening. They had looked, despite the accident-and-not-feeling-good comments, a well-dressed and healthy lot. Gracious Pines did not accept anyone, of course, with a history of any serious mental or physical illness. And, (like school again), after a certain age, in this case eighty years, no one need apply.

It was Lois who started it, last year, or even the year before that. Which meant it was probably Greg.

"Oh, Mom, you can't go on living in this house on your own."

"Why not?" Ernestine had asked her daughter, slightly surprised.

"Mom – you're seventy-seven..."

"Seventy-five, dear."

"OK, seventy-five. And you don't need all this running up and down stairs..."

"I have never run up and down the stairs. Any stairs. Ever."

"Look, Mom, don't be clever..." (That too, like a mother with a child, which they were, except it was the wrong way around for this kind of dialogue). "I worry about you. Out here, miles from anyplace."

"I am absolutely fine."

"I have to be frank, Mom."

"Do you?"

"You're fine now. But what about in three more years, or ten more years?"

"What about it?"

"Greg has heard of this really great place. It's like a luxury hotel."

The trouble was, Greg, Lois's husband, had money and influence, and Ernestine had very little of either. The old house was wearing out, as she apparently was. One night, there was a storm. It came up like blown breaths from the swamplands and the deep watery forests, and heaved off a quarter of the roof, and a falling shingle cut Ernestine's leg, so she fetched up in the hospital. She was only there two days, but after that her daughter and Greg the Gruesome, as Ernestine had always thought of him, had their way. Oh, it was easier to give in. She had had a fright.

It was as if familiar things had turned on her like a rabid dog. What had been loving and secure and loyal was now dangerous and must be dispatched. Only it was she who was dispatched, and the house sold to developers. From its proceeds, and forcefully guided by Gruesome Greg, Ernestine soon found herself here.

Breakfast was served at 8 and dinner at 6.30. When told of this, Ernestine had shrugged. One was too late and one too early – she had generally breakfasted at 7 am, even 6 in summer, and eaten dinner at 8.30 or 9. But she was back at school now. She could only accept the regime

The food was quite good, if resolutely on the health and fitness side. Ernestine rather liked large salads and fresh vegetables, but she objected to the rationing of eggs (cholesterol) and booze. An occasional drinker, when she drank, she had never seen why she should not finish the bottle of wine – which at Gracious Pines was rapidly whisked away from her before she was quite half through, to be corked up and 'kept cold' for her 'tomorrow'. "But I haven't finished."

"Now, now, Ernestine. We'll have to keep an eye on *you*."

"Actually, then," she said, giving in, "would you mind *not* putting the bottle in the refrigerator? It's a red Burgundy, and I'd prefer it room temperature."

"Sure thing," said the whisker-away.

And next evening Ernestine was presented with the stale half-bottle, almost frozen and standing in a cooler. There was a bar, too, where they let you purchase a couple of drinks before dinner, (alcohol was not covered by the overall fees, like the library and the cinema-room). The bar had no idea of how to make a proper old-fashioned.

Still, Ernestine supposed they were lucky to be allowed to drink at all, in sixth grade.

The grounds, (they were definitely grounds), were beautiful, as the great, stuccoed, mock-Italianate house was. There were terraces and flower-beds, long shallow pools with lilies and alpacas. And surrounding everything, the massive pines, which gave the place its name. Were they gracious, these trees? No, Ernestine thought not. They were too tall and strong, too powerful for that. Age had *not* withered *them*. Two hundred years old, some of them, so the brochure had said. They had been kept inside the walls, as if to encourage the residents, most of whom, going on statistics, would reach a hundred and ten or so before graduation.

The shadows returned to her room on the third night.

Coming in and switching on the side-lamps, she looked at them and said aloud, (one of the supposedly bad habits of living so long alone), "Now, I guess you're here again tonight because I'm getting bored."

It was strange, though. The shadows were not as they had been the first morning, between the lifted blinds and the bed, trailing over a little on the satin comforter. Now the shadows were between the armoire, (you could *not* call it a clothes closet), and the bathroom door. And even so, they were the *same* shadows.

"I wonder," said Ernestine aloud, "what makes you."

It was probably the stale wine making her tipsy, where fresh would not have done. Anyway, Ernestine went over and tried to see around the lamp, around the armoire, the doors of which she opened and closed several times. She discovered nothing except an overlooked spider, which she left in peace. The shadows had gone again.

"Oh well, I suppose it's none of my business. I don't mind you. Do as you want."

That night, as Ernestine lay in the dark in bed, her curtains parted and one blind raised just a crack to show her starlight over the gardens, she heard a wolf howl across the lawns of Gracious Pines. No, it was not a dog. She knew what a dog sounded like. Wolves too, from long ago, camping with Jim high in those mountains, all those miles from here, and from now. Lovely fearful lonely sound, redolent of night, open spaces, and the moon. Then it stopped, and silence came again.

Ernestine slipped out of the bed, like a young girl wakened by some magical intuition. Standing at the window, she raised the blind higher. Below, the vast backyard lay with its stone urns. In the starlight – despite the howls, no moon was visible – the manicured grass, the balustrades, looked cool and blue. There was a smoky sheen to bushes and to trees, and the lilies poised sleeping on the nearest pool, like white pods containing exciting dangers, aliens, or unborn swans...

Ernestine chided herself. She heard Jim's voice in her head, "You should write a story, honey. You sure got all the ideas for one." But she had never needed to write. These dreams were not for others, not even to be revealed to pen and paper. Just for herself, and sometimes Jim.

The wolf howled again. Ernestine jumped, and stared across the lawns, into the luminous dark depths of the pines. Her distance vision was pretty good...

What was that? There, running, low and curious, animal, yet not entirely – but so swift and – *boneless*...

Gone now. Quite gone. Things... did go.

Descending to the dining-room next morning, Ernestine met Coral, the gossipy woman who wore a silk tent to breakfast, pearls to lunch, and diamonds at dinner.

Perhaps, Ernestine thought, she could ask Coral, who spoke constantly about everyone and thing, as they bore relation to herself, if wolves were ever come across in this neck of the woods, and if Coral had heard the one last night. Coral forestalled her.

"There's been a *demise*."

"Oh, dear."

"Not what you think. Not just some old-timer cashing in his chips." Coral was a mere infant, sixty, or so she said. "A *violent* death."

"Really?" Ernestine sounded, she herself felt, heartlessly fascinated. One could only blame boredom for so much. "Who was it?"

"Well, I heard it was Donald."

"What happened?"

"Why, someone killed him. Out in the grounds last night."

This is too obvious, Ernestine thought. She frowned, and Coral took that as a judgement.

"You can look as disapproving as you like. They say it was an animal, but animals don't get in *here*. The walls are too high and the gate is closed up nights. And we have our private patrol-men. *They* were the ones found Donald, I heard."

"How was he – I mean…"

"You want the grisly details, huh? His throat was cut. Yes! And I'd take a bet it was Louisa. He's been stringing her along for three whole years. A girl can only take so much."

The dining-room was horribly perked-up, Ernestine saw at once.

"Come sit at my table," said Coral bestowingly, sweeping through in her silk and scent of *Avoir Chaud*. "I'll take the orange and grapefruit juice, and whole-wheat toast with the raspberry preserve. Black tea. Oh, Louisa, come sit with us."

Normally death was a repetitious and dreary event, ominous to the inmates and irksome to the staff. But this death by violence was more like the times of youth, when others fell by the wayside and could be pitied and picked over, often without personal alarm.

"Now tell me," said Coral to the woman who was serving their food, "Nancy, come on, what happened to Donald?"

"You'll know soon enough. The way I figure, wild dog musta got him. A real mess."

"Did you sleep well, Louisa?" Coral asked pointedly, but Louisa only stared at her oatmeal and did not eat any.

"I'm sorry, Louisa," said Ernestine.

But Louisa did not answer.

Across from them, Lionel barked, "Pack of lies. I saw that body. Fell down the goddam steps in the dark and bruk his neck, the old fool."

"Should he have been outside?" Ernestine asked innocently.

"Always up to something," said Lionel, who had once been connected, in a minor way, to the Senate, it was reported, doubtless falsely. "Goddam maniac. They need to fix those goddam steps."

Coral flounced. Whether at the expletives or the ordinariness of neck-breakage, Ernestine was not sure.

The police came an hour after. They had driven all the way up from Lake Tarho, in two indiscreet cars, with some paramedics in another vehicle.

The residents gaped from windows at LTPD antics on the lawns and among the urns. Everyone was high as kites, sparkling with animation and speculation, and Coral blatantly ordered a glass of champagne with her lunch: It's the only thing'll quiet my nerves."

Of course, no one told them anything now, and when they asked they were headed off. George, who had ambled out and tried to get a closer look, was sent back in, in disgrace.

"Didn't see a blame thing. Just some cop's butt stuck up in the air. Cute police gal, though."

Presently the ambulance drove away, and the police cars with it. Some of the higher caste of the staff then came into the lounge, where most of the residents still lingered, to address them.

It appeared than Donald had had an accident, falling down the stair from the terrace, where he had been most ill-advised to be so late at night – after *ten*, it seemed. The accident had caused his 'passing'.

Findlay spoke up from the front rank. "Yep, I guess it did. Neck bruk and all. Or was it *torn out*?"

The information committee was not flustered by this. They laughed a little sadly and shook their heads, commending Findlay on his imaginative powers – but of course, he had been a writer, had he not?

"Still am," said Findlay, visibly nettled. "Just don't sell no more. That don't stop me being what I am."

Of course it did not. But it did mean he had over-coloured somewhat the distressing facts of Donald's mishap. It was the shock of the fall which had brought on the fatal coronary. No, Donald had not been attacked by any savage animal.

Later, Nancy serving more coffee in the lounge, was surrounded by ladies, mostly Coral. "A wild dog?"

"Don't you say I said so," said Nancy. "But heck, there was some *gnawing*."

"Rats," said Lionel. "Goddam place is infested. Jesus Christ, nine hundred dollars to pick your nose, and rats every place."

Ernestine, standing near the fringes of all this, sipped her coffee and thought how wild things would always come to an unattended body. There need be nothing sinister about it. She could remember when Jim and she went camping those times... And here there were the pine woods, naturally, where all kinds of small things lived, hungry and feral in their habits, and not respectful of old people called only by their first names...

The shadows gathered early that evening.

Actually, one shadow. This time it lay across the floor, along the rug.

Ernestine looked up and saw, in the window, something which was not there even in the second she glimpsed it.

So she went slowly over to the window, and looked out.

Dusk lay on Gracious Pines, and tonight there would be moonlight. A new moon, delicate and glassy, had been hung on the navy sky.

Below there were the usual things. Whatever had reached the window must have sprung away again, vanished into the bushes or around the side of the house.

What was it?

All she was certain of, she thought, was its colour, a whitish grey, yet silvery too, nearly phosphorescent. The shadow though, on the rug, had been much more clear, as really it always had been when it showed itself before, sometimes in segments, strewn about the bed and walls.

The shadow was of a kind of man shape, but the hands were not hands, and the head was not the head of a man.

There had been eyes too, Ernestine decided, not in the shadow, but over there on the ledge by the window. These were also silvery, but darker, a kind of pewter shade. Jim had had an old watch like that, in pewter, and it was the colour of the eyes which had looked in through the window, from the head which was not a man's but a wolf's.

"What are you reading?" said Findlay.

The library was Findlay's domain, and this a challenge more than a courtesy. Most of the other residents drifted in and out, but Findlay would park himself there most days. Now here was Ernestine, reading in one of the easy chairs, a pile of books beside her.

"An old story."

"What's it about?"

"A werewolf," said Ernestine.

Findlay leered wolfishly. "You like that stuff, huh? How about these ones here?"

"The same," said Ernestine.

Findlay clawed up and squinted at a couple of the volumes. He did not yet need glasses, which was a source of glee to him. Ernestine had been warned, sometimes he would steal the glasses belonging to others, in order to cause consternation, which, obviously, it always did.

"Saki," said Findlay. "Yep, he's a weird 'un." He moved away, then called back in a whispery voice across the room, "That what you think it is?"

"Yes," said Ernestine.

"You're pretty crazy for an old woman."

Ernestine shrugged.

The furore over Donald had died down by now. His funeral had, for obscure family reasons, been held in Sacramento, so no one from Gracious Pines had gone.

Ernestine finished the story, closed the book, turned to another one. Some she had already read, like the Saki tale, *Gabriel Ernest*. Saki's werewolf was physically all wolf, or all boy when *not* wolf. Both the creature and the boy had a fearful glamorous pagan quality, sharpened by Saki's cruel wit. Some of the other works were less well-written, but even so they provided lessons in werewolfery. In fact, Ernestine was not surprised to discover how much she already knew. The other versions of the beast included something which, once shape-changed from the human, still stayed partly manlike, the transformation most apparent in its coating of hair, wolfish feet and hands, and the large wolf-like head, often ruffed, set with burning eyes and rapacious fangs.

"Grrrr," growled Findlay behind her in the darkening afternoon. "Going to catch it, then, with a grass rope?"

"That is a unicorn," said Ernestine with asperity.

"I guess it is. Hypnotise it with a diamond, then."

"I don't have any diamonds."

"Coral, the human seal, has some."

"They belong to Coral."

"Aw, come on. You're not gonna let a little thing like that..."

Ernestine stood up and left the library to Findlay, who had written and sold fantasy and detective fiction, enough to make him quite rich. Or at least, rich enough for Gracious Pines.

She did not want to discuss any of this with him, even though she had sensed she would be unwise to lie to him. And she had kept a firm attention on her glasses. (She suspected it would have been, forty years ago, the hooks of her brassiere.)

Really, she just did believe her own eyes, and ears. Perhaps Donald had not been murdered and savaged – surely there would have been more fuss if he had; a combing of the woods, a police presence that asked questions of the inmates. But even so. Probably he had gone out for a stroll, residents did, although it was discouraged, naturally, at night. And then – had something *frightened* him? Frightened him so badly that he suffered a heart attack and was dead before he fell all down the steps?

Ernestine met Nancy in a corridor.

"Oh, Nancy, do you know, how is Louisa now?"

"She's doing great. That spell with her son is just what she needs. I heard there's talk of her going to live over there. Seems they gotta spare house, something like that. These wealthy folks... when I gotta take the step, I guess it'll be a state place for me. My son's wife, she hates the sight of me. Take no notice now. I'm just rattled."

"I'm sorry. This sort of thing *is* upsetting." Deliberately switching track as if misunderstanding, she added, "Even if it was a heart attack."

"That. For my money, something scared the shit outa Donald. None of you saw the guy's face. Oh sure, he was sick, but it was more than that. And this kinda stuff happened here before. When was it – about twelve, thirteen years back."

Through Ernestine's mind, irresistible, the flashing of a kingfisher's turquoise wing: not thirteen, but fifty years ago, *When I was young, and Jim and I...* It was not death you minded, it was loss. Each loss worse, heavier to bear, when added to the others.

"What happened, Nancy, thirteen years back?" Ernestine heard herself asking in a little voice, that Nancy would no doubt attribute to interested and ghoulish fright, but which came from her sudden grief.

"Well, seems this house was owned private then, and the woods come right up to the lawns. Wolves, they reckoned. A man died. I forget how it was. And later someone else..." Becoming vague, Nancy shook her head, losing her authority as story-teller. "The way I heard it anyhow, they shot this thing, whatever it was. Shot it stone dead. Silver bullet, that was it. Only thing *could* stop it. But y'know, you don't catch me out there now, any night without I got the door open behind me – and then no further than the terrace."

"Isn't it just dangerous," said Ernestine cautiously, "on nights of the full moon?"

"Nah," said Nancy. "It sure ain't, here. That thing with Donald – wasn't even a moon that I recall." She looked straight at Ernestine. "This thing plainly ain't normal. Not even for something that ain't normal *anyhow*. It comes and goes as it wants. And, I tell you, there's been nothing like this until now, not since that stuff thirteen years back. Something's stirred the critter up."

And this said, Nancy swept on. Leaving Ernestine to stand there and think, with a strange inappropriate modesty, *Am I the one who's done that?*

She lay in the bed, under the satin comforter, and she murmured to the night, to the gleam of the glassy moon beneath her blind, "Why do you want me? Is it me that you want? Do you want to tear me apart and gobble me up? Surely you can see, I'm Granny not Little Red Riding-Hood? Not very toothsome anymore, I'm afraid. Or - am I just a crazy old woman, like the writer said?"

Through the water of the night, something – *something* – glimmering over the wall... not a shadow now, unless the palest shadow made of darkest light.

And then, for one split second, a face looked down at her.

She lay, gazing back up at it, even after it had vanished.

Silver-grey in silver, not quite substantial – for through the pewter eyes that were now like blue moon-rays on leaden crystal – she saw the shapes of things, the armoire, the bureau... Of course, it was not solid, how else did it come and go straight through the closed pane of the window, posing as a shadow itself, even by day?

All over it, the thick electric smoulder of hair, over its face, its head, the great whitish mane that circled its neck, almost amusingly copying the stiffly-starched and lacy ruff of an Elizabethan gentleman. But for its pelt, it was naked. And she could see that it was, as she was, old. It was old, and there, where its heart must be, something like – the flicker of a winter star – the bullet which had killed it?

"Now, Ernestine, what was it that you wanted?"

"I think I may have left my eye-glass case out on the terrace."

"Or Findlay did. Are your glasses in it?"

"No. I have them here."

"Well, the case won't come to much harm. Fetch it in the morning maybe."

"I'd rather fetch it now. I don't want to damage them."

"Then I'll go get it for you..."

"I don't want to put you to the trouble."

"No trouble. I have the key right here."

It was Ernestine rattling on the door which had alerted the keepers. (Ernestine felt, as soon as she found the doors to the terrace and the grounds had been nocturnally locked, that this was now less school than jail.)

She watched as the woman undid the glass door, closed it again from outside, and soon located the 'lost' article, which Ernestine had carefully left on the pavement by a pot of feverish flowers.

"Here it is, Ernestine."

"Thank you."

Why had she wanted to go out anyway? What was wrong with her? Had she planned to take a tumble down the steps and end up like poor old Donald? Or to meet the werewolf in the woods?

Yes, that was it. After all, it came inside the house to call on her, and had done her no harm. Lulling and luring her? Oh really, what *had* she planned? Wandering away from the terraces and closely-cropped lawns, the roses and syringa organised in beds, and tidy urns of camellias or French geraniums. Out to the woods. To wildness and lawlessness. To the boundary of grim reality and the fancifully imagined.

For none of this could possibly be true. Either she was, despite her clean medical profile, going mad, or hallucinating, perhaps in the onset of some unpleasant disease – or else she was merely fooling herself, letting daydreams and night fantasies become too real.

She had been like that when she was a girl. Even about love. All the boys she had refused to even date, gently but firmly. "Ernestine is waiting for the Prince," friends mocked her. "Young women don't *do* that anymore." No, she thought, like now they live alone, or they end up with a Not-the-Prince, some man who is mean and jealous or downright evil, who ignores them, uses them, grows bored with and cheats on them, hates and beats up on them. When she was twenty-six, still daydreaming, Ernestine's Prince had arrived for her one blue morning, on a horse even, riding up through town towards the mountains: Jim.

Ernestine never would settle for second best. Never.

And in the end, she had found the Best. But now she had settled for – the worst. She had let herself come *here* – not because her daughter Lois was a simpleton and Lois's husband Greg was a bully – but because Ernestine herself had been too – *chicken* to stay and command her own life, in that house which had been theirs, hers and Jim's. Just because there was a storm and a bit of roof went and she needed two little stitches in her leg. Lord's sakes, she *deserved* Gracious

Pines.

Unless... there truly was a werewolf. Since to face that, to meet with *that*, would take less courage than to go on with all of this.

Deep among the pine trees, it was possible to lose sight of the house, and so pretend it did not exist. You needed to be vigilant, however, to successfully keep this up.

Ernestine walked slowly, the late westering sun sending copper tines between the straight boles of the trees. There was little undergrowth, only the powdery debris of shed needles, occasional stones and small pieces of bark. Sometimes a squirrel would fly by overhead from sunny bough to shadow bough, or a rustling around the claws of the trees indicate the passage of a mouse.

There were no tracks of a wolf, no hints of one. But Ernestine had not thought there would be. Not even of a wolf which was also a man. And what she was looking for was perhaps more elusive even than that – his grave.

She had come out this morning, before breakfast, to the startlement of two of the patrol-men, who were standing under the lowest terrace, smoking and talking about girls, and who looked bemused when they saw her.

"Morning, Ma'am. Where are you off to? It isn't even six yet."

"I like to be about early," she had said, winsome and guileless, cursing them, wondering if they would try to return her indoors. But no, they were quite young, and wrapped up in their own affairs, like everybody else.

"You take care now," they said, and forgot her, as she ambled apparently docilely off around the garden's edge, now and then sniffing flowers. The sun was up. They probably thought, if they considered anything peculiar went on at all, that it was a night business, and after sunrise everything was safe.

She had wondered too, slipping off, once out of their sight, into the pines, why the werewolf had no interest in these men, for they, or others of their kind, supposedly patrolled the grounds regularly through the night. Perhaps they just never did, or only those areas nearest the house. But then, Donald had been very near the house...

So you don't intentionally kill? she thought. *No? Well presumably, you can't, not now. How can you? You're not what you were, not flesh and blood anymore. Now you're the ghost of a werewolf. Your only violent power is fear.*

What would the patrol-men do if they met this being? Not believe their eyes, or else take it for an intruder in a fur-coat and Halloween mask. If they fired at it – the bullets would hardly do any harm. Not

327

under the circumstances nor ever. They were not silver.

She went back dutifully, (cautiously), for breakfast and for lunch. And she would have to go back again soon, for the too-early 6.30 dinner, after which they would lock the doors.

The sun was going now anyway. Did she really want to be out here after dark? She was alone now. No Jim to reassure her about the glowing eyes beyond the campfire. No Jim to reassure her about anything.

Besides, she had about completed her circuit of these woods, and found nothing. Really it *was* crazy to think she could find anything. If it were true, they would hardly have marked the spot: *Hic jacet Werewolf – which we recently shot; do not disturb.*

Then, between one pine trunk and another, she found the grave.

The light, fluctuating, fading, had made her strain her eyes to see, and so she did see. A glint of grey stone under scattered soil. Some animal had been digging there, she thought.

Ernestine knelt stiffly. She brushed some of the dirt away, and saw a piece of the stone, artificially smoothed, placed flat, and with a little shape cut into it. The shape was a cross.

That was all.

She stared, then drifted the soil back over.

Poor thing, she thought.

"Hi, Ernestine," said Greg the Gruesome. "How you doing? Sure is a swell place, this. You don't know your luck. I wouldn't mind all this, put my feet up, waited on by comely slaves."

Lois scowled. "That woman is much too big, Greg."

"Nah, just right. I like the fat ones, baby. Y'know I do."

Lois, thin and withering before her time, childless but for one truly awful son of nineteen, a more scholarly, know-all replica of Greg (Gruesome Jnr?) turned her eyes from Nancy, who had served the tea. As if by ignoring it all, it would go away. Which, of course, it never had.

Greg himself was quite big, not fat exactly, but large. Baseball had been his game when younger, and even now, overweight, overbearing and in his forties, he still had the confidence of a golden, well-built youth. That was no doubt how he saw himself – a young man, only slightly his son's elder, but with distinguished grey in his thick wiry hair that, Ernestine regretted, he would probably never lose. Lois had been reduced, you could clearly see, to the role of mother to both of them, a skinny nag, who must be loftily tolerated because she did the chores, or saw that others did them, and nervily tried to put the comforts of her ungrateful menfolk first.

Where on earth had she learnt that? Ernestine guiltily suspected it had come from Lois's growing up in the shadow of a happy, perfect relationship, which had also not really needed her. Had Jim and she shut Lois out, despite their best efforts not to? Or was it only Lois too had been looking for a Prince, and incredibly thought, (temporarily blinded by Greg's youth and baseball honours), that Greg was he?

"Well, Ernestine," yodelled Greg, "this is real nice."

He was stingy, too. Other in-laws bore their relative off for the day to the city, at least to the malls of Lake Tarho. But Greg kept rich by giving little and taking as much as he could. The tea and cakes here would show on Ernestine's monthly account, not his billfold. Did he realise that she did not mind so much, because the thought of being 'treated' by Greg would have been far, far more revolting?

"Is it OK, Mom?" Lois asked her, as opposed to telling her it was, when Greg had gone off in pursuit of Nancy and/or another cigarette.

"It's fine, honey," said Ernestine, trying to inject a little mild enthusiasm.

"You're not unhappy? You look well…"

"I am well. I'm not unhappy. And it is very good to see you. If rather a surprise."

"Well – well they called us," Lois blurted.

"Who called, dear?"

"I probably shouldn't – Greg said we shouldn't…"

"Damn Greg, he's an asshole," said Ernestine precisely. Lois blinked. But she had seen her mother's battle flag go up before, not often, but enough times to recognise. "*What* shouldn't you?"

Lois looked flustered. Staring at her unfinished blueberry muffin, she told Ernestine how Gracious Pines had called up to tell them Ernestine had been acting a little strangely. "Wandering about the grounds in the dark," said Lois, watery-eyed with nerves.

"*Wandering* in the *dark* – the chance would be pleasant. They've started to lock up after 6 o'clock. Oh, once – *once* – I came back just after 6. I'd been for a walk – which is healthy, so they should have been delighted. But they'd already locked the doors, so there was a scene. You'd think I'd tried to escape."

Lois stared. "Oh Mom. You make it sound like…"

"Alcatraz?" Ernestine bit back her anger. "I'm sorry, Lois. I'm only a little – well, offended by their whining to you. Scaring you, too, I can see. I suppose Greg wanted to come see me to gloat – but as you see, I'm not *acting strange*. I'm not going nuts. Everything is fine and dandy."

Greg was returning, smiling a fat secretive smile. As if he had done something sexy and clandestine behind Mom-Lois's back.

"Don't say I told you, Mom."

"You're afraid of him."

"No – no, of course I'm not. It's just…"

"…you're afraid of him."

"Afraid?" said Greg. "Who's afraid?"

"Of the big bad wolf," said Ernestine.

Greg boomed with laughter and many heads turned.

"That Nancy sure as hell ain't," said Greg.

They stayed on for dinner. This was allowed, occasionally, to the residents – unfortunately.

Greg put on his usual performance, grinning around, complimenting everyone on the great 'home-cooking', (but then he had requested and received the pan-fried chicken that the inmates seldom attempted. For reasons of cholesterol it was strictly rationed.)

Sometimes, he made comments on the others, too, in a loudish low voice. "That old charmer sure has some hot rocks there."

"That's Coral. Her husband left her a pearl and diamond collection when he died," said Ernestine in, she thought herself, far too poisonous a widow-making voice. But Greg never noticed.

Or did he? He came back at once.

"Shame Jim couldn't help you out that way, Ma." (He called her *Ma* only at optimum.)

She refused to show how she hated it. "Jim left me some memories I wouldn't trade for diamonds."

"Sure he did. What was that dumb thing you did back then? Hey – you went to a medium, right, Ma? I mean, when he died."

"Yes. "

Lois said, "Greg, honey, let's not…"

"Ernestine doesn't mind, do you, Ma? And this woman told you – what was it?"

Rather than let him see visibly how much pain he must know he was causing her, Ernestine asked levelly, "She told me Jim was doing well, but he had reincarnated."

"That's the one! Yeah, that's the one. What a prime bitch. There you go, Jim gone only two – three years, and you want her to say 'Oh, he's waiting for you, baby, in the sweet by-and-by'. And the witch tells you No, he's back already, couldn't even wait up there a few years."

"Yes, Greg," said Ernestine. "But why should I be greedy? I had him a long time. If it's true, now someone else will have him, and he'll be young and fit again."

"You believe that crap?"

"It's better than some of the other crap," said Ernestine.

Greg gave another of his laughs. He signalled to Nancy across the room, as if he were in a bar someplace. Somehow, Nancy did not see.

Lois said, "Mom, Greg doesn't mean…"

"It's all right," said Ernestine.

She wanted to cry. Just like a girl. Like she had that day when she lost him, and she was only a girl of sixty-three, not a girl of seventy-six.

We don't change inside. The pain doesn't. Nothing does.

Having scored his hit, (he knew he had, he had fed on it, like the chicken and potatoes, apple donut and whipped cream), Greg belched softly and said he would take a stroll outside to smoke a couple of cigarettes.

As Nancy cleared the table, Lois said diffidently, unlikingly, "Thank you *so* much. My husband *did* enjoy his meal."

"Keeps up that kinda eating," said Nancy, "he ain't gonna enjoy too many more."

Lois's mouth fell open. Ernestine stared.

Lois said, marshalling herself, "How dare you say…"

"I say as I find," said Nancy.

She walked off.

"I shall make a complaint about that," said Lois. "The darn cheek…"

"No," said Ernestine. She broke out laughing. Could not help herself.

Lois glared at her, then she too began to laugh. Suddenly tears were running down her face, there in the middle of the public dining-room.

"Oh Mom – oh Mom…"

"I know. Can't you…"

"No. What'd I do if I left him? I just have to hope he won't throw *me* out. I don't have a cent – he's made sure of that. Where'd I go?"

And Ernestine thought bitterly, *You could have come to me, if I'd kept the house. Oh damn, damn.*

She took a Kleenex and mopped Lois's face gently, mothering her, praying Greg would not come back yet. It must be soon. Though they would have allowed him, a visitor, to go outside – especially with another frowned-on cigarette – there was not much to *keep* him out there. Unless Nancy, as he had seemed to imply, might choose to join him. But it seemed Nancy had indicated her preferences.

"Oh, making a fool of myself in here with everyone looking," said

Lois, blowing her nose. No good denying that, they all were. The eyes of Coral and Findlay were almost out on stalks.

"They'll think I'm a cruel bitch of a mother who's made you cry."

"Then they'd be wrong," said Lois. "You were the best kind of mother to me. God, Mom. The times I've wished I had that back. The way we were then."

"Oh, darling." Ernestine knew she too would cry now, helplessly, and he would come in and see it... "Nancy!"

Nancy answered the call at once. "You gals OK?" Nancy looked concerned. A first.

"Just remembering old times – we've gotten sentimental. Do you think we could have a couple of vodka tonics – large ones?"

"Sure thing," said Nancy. "Bar's probably closed. Don't matter. Rocks and an olive?"

Let the bastard come back now and see them drinking, Ernestine thought, and no third glass.

But the vodkas had come and slowly, steadily gone down, and they were eating the olives last of all, and it was an hour later. And Greg had not actually marched in to catch them, either in tears or in their cups.

"I wonder where... if he's OK?" said Lois. She sounded relaxed and indifferent.

"Perhaps he went to look at the car – check the gas," said Ernestine. "I guess you'll have to be on the road soon."

"Yes. It's a two hour drive."

They went into the lounge however, for coffee, later than everybody. It *was* late. Only Findlay was still there, watching a TV programme on famous fantasy writers of the '80's, which did not include Findlay Finn, cussing occasionally.

"I think I'd better go find him," said Lois, standing up.

"Sure, darling."

"I'll come say goodbye before we leave. I promise I'll visit, somehow – Greyhound, if I have to."

Ernestine sat alone. The TV programme ended. It was 10 pm – the final hour favoured for the residents to make for their rooms and bed.

Findlay got up. "That fat jackass gone?"

"My son-in-law? Yes, I think he must have done."

Fat jackass, she thought, warming slightly to Findlay. Evidently the jackass had not allowed Lois to come back in for any goodbyes.

"Care to join me in my room?" said Findlay.

"I think I'm a bit too crazy, for you, Mr Finn."

Chuckling, he went out, and passed Lois in the doorway coming back in.

She was flustered again, anxious. Greg could always do that for her. But then she said loudly to Ernestine, "He's disappeared, Mom. Greg's just vanished. No one's seen him. Those police guys here, the patrol – they're going out to look. With guns. Oh God, Mom, what's happened?"

And Ernestine, who thought she knew, with a clutch at her heart that might be terror or joy or simply the vodka not digesting, got to her feet and said, "It's OK, honey. It'll be OK."

They found Greg in the end near morning, at the edge of the woods. He had had a heart-attack and was immensely dead. Although, (like Donald) recent routine medical checks had revealed no problem, he was an ideal candidate for a coronary, of course. He was in the right age group, smoked heavily, over-ate consistently, and had for years been friendly with most available women not his wife. There were no marks on his body to suggest anything else. Nothing, it seemed, had even wanted to nibble him.

Because of the situation, the scenario of investigation was, however, complex and somewhat drawn-out; exhausting and somehow unsavoury. Like everything to do with Greg. Except possibly his funeral.

How curious, Ernestine thought, standing above the grave of Greg the Gruesome, *here I am at almost seventy-seven, and there he is at forty-three*.

It was no use pretending to be sorry. She contented herself with being serenely non-committal. She did not want to hurt or confuse Lois any more than Greg had already managed.

As for Gruesome Jnr, he came to the funeral with a couth and pretty college girl, who seemed to have the upper hand. He was not nearly so graceless, and when the girl spoke, he listened, not interrupting. Even when Lois spoke, he did not interrupt – something that had probably not happened for ten years.

When Lois spoke to Ernestine, it was Ernestine who interrupted.

"No, Lois, it isn't I don't want to, I'll be happy to stay until you feel more yourself. But live with you? No. We have our own lives."

To her gratification, Lois nodded. Ernestine had feared Lois, used by now to martyrdom, would put up a fight to keep her martyr's crown intact – chained to an elderly mother if not a bullying spouse.

"Let's try this, then," said Lois. "Greg left me loaded. You do know that? OK. How about we put you back in your house. Get it fixed up and safe first, so it won't be a worry."

"But, Lois, I sold it to the developers…"

"No, Mom. I'm sorry, but you sold it to Greg. You just – didn't know you had. He said he did it that way to help you get an easy sale."

"Sweet of him."

"Well, it's going to make things simple now. Say yes. We'll only be half an hour away from each other by car. So long as that's enough space to preserve your style I mustn't cramp?"

The shadows had gone. They never came into the room now. Nothing leaned over to look at her, nothing ran across the distant view of lawn and pines. She thought of the starry flicker where its heart was, (had been?), the scar-memory of the silver bullet. Was that why it killed *that* way now, instead of how it must have done, once, with fangs and claws?

She visited the place with the stone again, in daylight. She knew where it was. She had seen with Jim how things could be refound in a forest, let alone in the narrow woodland of Gracious Pines. But the marker was no longer there. At least, she thought it probably *was* there, but he had hidden it deeper. Hidden it with his old grey talons, where she could not see, and was not meant to search.

Ernestine wondered if Louisa too had been shown this, and she wondered also what Donald had done to Louisa, unguessed by anyone, that had made him a candidate for the actions of the werewolf's ghost.

School, she thought. Well, she had learned something here. Quite what it was, Ernestine was not certain. The werewolf was old, and its concerns were with the old, but perhaps it was also learning, paying some of its karmic debt of personalised wanton murders, by judicial murders, that gave back freedom – an extraordinary, crazy and fanciful notion. It had died – perhaps – about the time that Jim had died. But any fears on that score were irrelevant. She had been told, Jim was now a baby in a city in India. If she could really believe it. But why not, if she believed in a werewolf – the *ghost* of a werewolf.

Lois came to drive her back home in the fall.

Ernestine saw her daughter, for the first time in fifteen years, looking attractive and well, in light make-up, cobalt-blue jeans and high-heeled boots. Her hair was blonde, and Nancy and Findlay Finn both whistled her as she helped take Ernestine's things to the car.

"Look what Nancy gave me for dessert tonight," said Ernestine, showing the bottle of vodka, garlanded by a pink ribbon. "I thought for a moment she might break it over me, launch me like a ship."

Then they drove out of the gates of Gracious Pines. Every amber, red and marigold colour was in the trees, and for a second, swifter than a thought, something bounded across the road, was gone.

"What the heck was that?"

"Oh," said Ernestine, "a wolf."

Blood Chess

Winter and the Sorian Approach

A crumbling stone staircase leads down the mountain-hill from the castle. About a mile above the valley, there is a walled terrace, and here the gigantic chessboard is laid out. It is old and faded, the black squares grey, the blood-red squares a lifeless pink. As she crosses the chessboard, each square taking a full three steps, Ismira glances down at it, at the cracks in its paving where wild flowers push up in spring, and where, now winter is approaching, they die.

She is not a vampire, but the people in the valley are afraid of her, thinking she must be. Her brother is the vampire. In the valley they call him the Sorian. He comes from the land of Soriath, over the mountains, so the name is not inappropriate – but really they are trying to distance him in the only way they can. They are aware of his true name, which is Yane, and never use it.

Ismira knows her brother will return during the night. By going down to the village, she is also warning them.

There is an afternoon frost. When she reaches the village street, the tall trees by the well are clouded with cold. Icicles thin as needles spike the roofs. Already the ball of the sun is rolling off the sky. Before, she would often come here in full daylight, striving to convince them she was only herself, had no fear of sunlight, and did not require blood. But when she saw this did no good, she did not do it anymore.

All the doors are shut and the street and alleys empty. Somewhere a dog howls and is struck – she hears the blow – to silence it.

Ismira stops in the centre of the street, by the well. In her long black garments, her long black hair curling down like a fleece to her shoulder-blades, she is only what they must expect.

As she stands waiting, the sun too runs away, afraid she will see its redness and desire its blood.

Yane, the Sorian, once said to her, in one of his intermittent fevers: "The sun – give me the sun to drink – it's *full* as a wineskin..."

After a time of merely standing there, Ismira sees a door is being eased open in the side of the big house, the one with the carvings that pretend to the decoration of the castle on the mountain-hill.

336

Something is thrust out. It drops and lies motionless on the street.

Ismira goes over to this object, which turns out to be a young woman of about sixteen, clothed in white, and with her fair hair washed and braided. She is not unconscious, as sometimes they are. She stares up at Ismira from the dirt.

"Don't make me, lady – let me go..."

"I can't. Get up and come with me."

Shaking and temporally past tears, the girl does so. She will probably walk meekly behind Ismira all the way back up the mountain. Now and then, one of them will dash off, and never be seen by Ismira again. She suspects the village pursues and murders them.

Ismira herself has done what she must. She has procured the sacrifice for her brother's needs, and also warned the village by her presence, that he is imminent.

The sky burns crimson.

Ismira and the sacrifice plod doggedly up the terrible, ruinous stair.

"Look," says Ismira, encouragingly, as the epic bulk of the castle looms over them, touched with ruby by the falling sun they have, through climbing, managed to keep sight of. Now the girl starts to cry.

Ismira hardens her heart, at which act she has, over the fifteen years since her tenth birthday, become adept. Why attempt reassurance? These ones the village select by unlucky lot. Each of them knows what will happen.

They pass the chessboard. The weeping girl takes no notice of it. All the flowers have been abruptly frost-bitten to death, and above, in the castle garden, scarcely any leaves remain on the tangled trees, and those that do are like silver daggers.

The Return of Yane

The girl's name is Thental. She sits crying on and on.

Once it begins to be very dark, Ismira walks about the castle, the rooms, passages and annexes, lighting a few lamps and enormous candles. She wonders if the girl would be more comfortable in the great hall. But the kitchen, with its huge fire, will be much warmer.

Coming back into the kitchen, there is Thental, still crying. Ismira has given her white bread and an apple, and wine for courage, none of which has Thental tried.

How dismal it all is, Ismira thinks, lighting another candle on the branch above the hearth. She hopes Yane will soon arrive.

As if reading her mind, Thental checks her sobs. "Does he fly here, on his bat wings?" she asks.

Ismira senses an unpleasant pettiness in the question. Thental knows she is being given to a monster, the monster must therefore live up to his legends. "No, in fact he'll ride across the pass."

"Some demon will have told you he's near."

"Also no. Common sense, and memory. Snow will soon fall and close all the passes. It's always on this night Yane comes back. Have none of you realised?"

The girl shudders. Her head darts up and her shining hair, loosened by now, flutters candlelit round her head like a bridal veil. "Is that a clatter of wings?"

Ismira says nothing. She can hear it too, and quite obviously the noise is that of hoofs clattering into the yard outside.

Yane will stable his horse in the stall Ismira has prepared, before he enters the kitchen; they have no servants, of course. But the girl springs up and falls now on her knees, tightly shutting her eyes, and praying.

Ismira feels sorry for her, but also it is all so tiresome, this. "*Shush!*" she exclaims sharply, and Thental becomes quiet as the grave.

It will be useless to try to reason with her. Ismira, long since, additionally gave that up with the sacrifices who accompany her to the castle, their names written helpfully on little scraps of book paper and wrapped round their wrists.

They pose there then, in stasis, Ismira seated on the wooden chair, Thental kneeling abject on the stone-flagged floor.

Outside now a sound of boots, then the door is pushed wide. Yane strides in out of the night, bringing the night in with him, cold and mysterious, across cloak and hair.

Ismira sees, as so often, Thental stare, then avert her gaze.

Yane is very handsome. His blue-black hair falls to his waist, he is tall and straight, his body hard and fined from constant journeys, his large dark eyes full of a luminous introspection fatal to most women.

Ismira gets up. She takes him a cup of wine.

Yane thanks her. He drinks the wine. Then he glances at the girl kneeling on the floor, staring at him between fingers she has clamped over her eyes. "Is she for me?"

"Who else?"

"Dear God," says Yane. He sighs, perhaps an affectation. He walks across and sits in the wooden chair, and looks at Thental.

Thental does not look back, but nor does she cry any more.

"Well," says Yane, "good evening. Isn't the floor rather hard on your knees?"

Thental blinks. She puts down her hands. "Don't kill me," she says quietly, "don't damn my soul."

"I'm not interested in your soul. Keep it."

Thental grunts. She lowers her head, desolate now.

Yane stands up, frowning with irritation and tiredness.

Ismira has drawn a bath for him, across the passage, with extra water heating on the fire there. He goes out to this, and Ismira moves around the kitchen, seeing to the supper, constantly detouring past Thental kneeling on the floor.

An Evening at Home

When Yane enters again he is more relaxed, wrapped in a dressing-robe of scarlet, black and gold. He goes to Thental at once and lifts her off the floor, and sits her at the table in a chair adjacent to his own.

She is evidently exhausted by her fright, far worse than Yane from his travels. He takes advantage of that, feeding her scraps of meat and cheese, and making her sip the wine. Her head droops on to his shoulder. He kisses her hair absently,

Ismira watches all this from the other end of the table. It has ceased to offend, puzzle or upset her.

She thinks back to the day the horsemen came to her father's house in another country, not this one, and not Soriath either. That was the day of her tenth birthday. While her proud father sat in talk with the riders, Ismira's chilly mother took her aside. "Listen to me, Ismira. Today you're to go away to another place. We've never treated you as we do our other children, and this is because, you must now understand, you're no child of ours at all. You are the cuckoo's egg left to hatch in this house. We bore it because we must, and we've done you no harm. You've been raised nobly, as our true children have, although without our love. Under the circumstances, you'll agree, you could hardly expect any."

Astounded, shocked beyond reason, Ismira stood listening. Her mother – who was not – told her she was the child of an ancient and corrupt family who exerted much power in this region and elsewhere. The Scaratha, they were called. Due to their way of living, which was that of vampires, blood-drinkers and creatures of darkness and horror, they kept no children of their own in their domiciles before the age of ten. At that age, they would send for and claim them, whether the vampire strain was prevalent or not. "You have been closely observed, more for our sakes than yours," said Ismira's unmother, with great distaste. "You show no symptoms of any of that. Even so you are a fiend, the child of fiends. It's made me sick to have you in this house. I have seldom touched you and won't now. Get out and go to your own, you foul abomination."

"What are you brooding on, Ismi?" asks Yane from along the table. The girl from the village has fallen asleep against him, soothed by his glamorous kindness and the Eastern incense he has rubbed into his hair.

"The past," says Ismira.

"Oh, that. Don't think of that. Let me tell you what I saw on my way here – something better than the Eastern markets, for all their glitter and show. Better even than the moon-and-star night over the City of Rome."

"What?" inquires Ismira. She knows what he will say.

"I saw the sun."

"Which will make you ill. It always does."

"Yes, it always does, but this was three days ago. And you see, I'm cool and well. Perhaps I'm growing used to the sun, or it to me."

"The wineskin full of blood," says Ismira. She becomes angry with him, because, in his fevers she must nurse him, and she hates the chore, and also is infuriated to see him suffer so stupidly by his own lack of control. He is addicted to the sun, she sometimes thinks, worse than blood.

But Yane boasts, "I crept out of my deep hiding cave, and I beheld a sunrise in the mountains. The sky was redder than any blood. I'm cool and hale, Ismi. Can't you see? Perhaps, in a day or so, I can try again."

"The sun isn't for you."

"But you can see it every day. Don't you know how jealous I am of you, Ismi?"

She too frowns. She considers how Yane rides about the world, journeying to lands she has never, will never, see. How she remains at home, tending the castle, alone, save for the winter months when Yane comes back, often flaming with sun-fever, crazy and devilish, and girls must be collected from the village, one every thirty days, for Yane's pleasure.

I'm his skivvy, Ismira thinks. And *he* is *jealous*?

In her childhood, once only, she saw one of the Scaratha kin brought to the castle after the sun had caught him, not for a few minutes at sunrise or set, but at the height of noon. He had burned alive and screaming for many hours before he died.

This is why they value those of their kind who are not vampiric. They take them in and load them with codes of honour and high dreams of loyalty, and make them into useful servants of the house.

Ismira can hear Yane talking endlessly, in raptures about the sun. She pretends – she is quite clever at pretence that she attends to him. She loves him, admires him, but resents him. They may have two hundred years more like this, for, left to themselves, the Scaratha are all long-lived. The rest of the castle inhabitants perished in a war with other Scaratha ten years ago. But other castles and fortresses exist, still well-stocked with their kind. Sometimes, Yane promises to take her visiting. He never does, and doubtless never will.

She considers leaving him and going off on her own. Wherever she went – on foot, alone, unsafe ways for a woman, even – *especially* – a Scaratha woman to travel – she would in the end fetch up with the Scaratha. She would have no other place to go. And then her life would be the same as it is here, save with more to do, more persons to love, admire and tend - the higher echelons of the practicing vampires.

Now Yane is speaking to Thental, the flower-like sacrifice. "Time for bed, sweetheart."

There was something too he had put in the wine. The girl stirs and smiles at him, sleepy and adoring, ready as a summer peach on the vine.

He half carries this now-willing and pliable companion – perhaps she thinks this is her wedding-night? – away along the passage, and up the steps of a tower to the bedroom Yane has there. Ismira has put fresh embroidered sheets on the bed, sprinkled lavender and other herbs. Scented lamps burn, and the window is heavily shuttered against sunrise, and locked – Ismira keeps the key.

Up there, Yane the Sorian will make love to the girl, exquisitely, and also he will drink her blood, with passionate discretion. It will do her no harm whatsoever. He is wholesome, his teeth clean and flawless. Even the marks on her throat will fade when, after seven or so nights, he turns her out of bed, with enough money and jewels to make her rich beyond her most avaricious dreams. He will also escort her – by night – along the valley. That is Yane's gallantry. He knows about women travelling on their own, particularly with wealth about them. He will make sure she reaches some sort of safety, for the Scaratha are careful with the goods they handle. After a certain point, however, once he has discharged his duty to *her*, or his payment for her services, Yane will leave the girl. If something happens to Thental then – or has happened in the past to any of the countless others – that will not be Yane's fault.

Ismira tidies the table. She hauls a pitcher of cold water and adds it to a wooden tub of hot, and rinses the platters and knives. The precious cups of emerald crystal, rimmed and stemmed with gold, she replaces on the stone top of the hearth, among the candles, vases of dead flowers, iron keys, onions, and other things.

Outside the wind is rising. It howls like the dog in the village they had struck to make it silent. Who will strike the wind?

The villagers naturally believe all who are brought here die, drained like bottles. Or else they are turned into undead devils, and subsequently roam the countryside, preying on the sheep, or small unguarded children, which in fact lammergeyers or starving wolves have picked off. One day perhaps, the village may rebel against the castle. But probably they will not, for Scaratha power, though so isolate and scattered, is yet omnipresent and much dreaded.

Ismira blows out the kitchen candles. She takes one with her, and goes about the castle again, replenishing the lights. Later, when her brother has had tonight's fill of the girl, he will ramble through the passages, enter the great hall, take down old swords, and musical instruments to play. The castle is a rare treat for Yane – how not, when he is hardly ever here.

As she retires to her room beyond the kitchen, Ismira hopes the sun will not have made him ill, and that he has enjoyed Thental. But when she falls asleep, Ismira dreams of herself riding his horse away and away, her own black hair and cloak rippling in the race of their speed. Dimly in the distance she thinks she sees the acres of a sea, the domes of the East, the moonlit columns of Rome. *I am Ismira,* she sings in her sleep, *nor was I born in Soriath...*

The Chess-Game

It was how the Scaratha taught their young the rules of existence – that is, the *vampiric,* more-valued young, although the others, the lesser, but so-useful breed, they were allowed to stand by and watch. In this way Ismira had been part of the audience at the chess-games, played out on the huge board halfway down the mountain-hill.

They commenced at dusk, often not concluding until midnight, all by torchlight – and in the village below, no doubt, the people covered their heads in fear. This was before the war among the Scaratha had wiped away all but two of the castle's indigenous population.

Scaratha chess was not like humanly-employed chess, of course.

There were no pawns, for humanity was all made up of pawns, as far as the Scaratha were concerned. Here, the Scaratha hunted each *other* over the squares, which then were kept vivid with paint. A knight might take a queen, a queen a priest, as they pleased. Physical figures performed these actions. Deliberately, always, the *wrong* moves were educated into the Scaratha young, so they should learn to break all the other rules of the world.

Only at the very end would the victors fasten on their conquered own. This was not like a war. None died. They milked their victims, in mutual delight, of blood. Tokens, *love* tokens, which still meant someone had won. Blood to the Scaratha was not a food, but a covenant. From human things they took it as of right, from their own they took it as the sigil of conquest. And life was all a game, like chess. The spilled blood had dripped, during these playings, through the paint into the chessboard, then coloured red for blood and black for night. Because of the nourishment of those libations, when finally allowed by neglect, flowers came to break cracks in the squares. The flowers were very strong, tougher from being kept down, from fighting back. Only harsh frost could kill them now, and in the spring others would come, rising from death as gods and vampires allegedly did.

How Fair the Day

Waking early as always, Ismira gets up. She sets about the business of the morning, equably, quietly. She anticipates nothing of it, but it has a surprise for her after all.

She is in the great hall, clearing up the mess of spent candles and replacing them with fresh, when Thental steals in like a slim white ray around the door.

Sometimes these girls do venture down, while Yane lies sleeping in the dark. Then, by now besotted with the vampire from Soriath, they talk on and on of his virtues to Ismira. It is her task too, to give them food and drink, to keep them healthy, bathed and appealing, for her brother.

When she turns to Thental, however, Ismira is briefly bemused. It seems to her the girl has impudently put on Yane's dressing-robe of chessboard red and black, edged with gold.

But no. The gold is Thental's dishevelled hair, and the white her own skin, some of it. The red and black, which are thick on her naked body, are rich red blood and skeins of black hair, which seems to have been torn out at the roots.

Thental lifts her head and smiles at Ismira.

"How fair the day. I've done what I came for. Just as I swore I would, I did it. He had my sister a year back. I never forgot, never. I can cry always just thinking of her. I told them this time, let it be me, I'll go. And so they let me. See this? My little dagger, razor sharp. The hilt's silver, that helps with killing a demon-thing. I bartered for it off a pedlar. He fucked me for it. Sensible trade, worth every jolt." Thental raises the dagger high. If it was ever silver, now it is not. It is blood-red, like most of the rest of her. "What a lot he had in him," Thental remarks of this blood, conversational, moving nearer. "Some of it after all was mine. What he drank from me last night. I stabbed him through as he slept. Then I hacked off his head – quite a job I had of that, but I managed. It's how you must do it with that kind – *your* kind – I'll do it for you..." She runs headlong at Ismira.

Ismira, Scaratha though not vampire, kills the girl instantly with one swift sidelong blow that breaks her neck.

Then Ismira stands there, staring at the wreckage, thinking about the other wreckage, which will be all that is left of Yane in the tower.

Presently, Ismira sits down.

She considers graves, digging them, which is easy, she has dug a couple, if some years ago. She thinks of her glorious brother, she thinks of the human heritage she has never had, the vampire Scaratha heritage she has also, being second rate, never had.

Yane's horse is in the stable. The snows have not yet begun. The sun, for Ismira, provides no difficulty – though later, she can always make believe it does...

Ismira goes over to Thental, the fragile white flower which grew strong enough to crack the paving of the chessboard, but which the frost of Ismira's hand then finished. Human flowers do not recover from that, nor vampire flowers, so Ismira has discovered.

Ismira dips her finger in the still-wet blood Thental has thoughtfully brought with her, Yane's blood. Ismira licks the finger. It means nothing to her, nothing at all. But, as with the sun of this fair day, she can always *pretend.*

Midnight

Above the glittering ballroom, the gilded clock hung like a baleful planet. The hands on the face of it showed ten minutes to midnight.

Only ten minutes more. Then, she must be gone. But the girl – how could she bear to leave? She looked away from the clock, back at the face of the young prince who was dancing with her, over the marble floor.

They fitted together like hand and glove. Both so young, so beautiful, and so wonderfully dressed. For not only the prince was clad as one would expect, in garments of silk and velvet, so was the girl. She too looked like royalty.

How strange it had been. The old woman the girl had sometimes helped, giving her scraps from the kitchen, nice things when possible, though the girl herself got little enough. Then suddenly, this very night, when the evil, tyrannical women of the house had flounced away to the ball, the old woman entered – not by the door, but out of the *fireplace* – shedding her rags, her old age, becoming a shining creature. "Bathe yourself," the being had said to the astonished girl, "wash the soot from your hair. Then you will find there are garments for you, and everything else, to show your beauty as it truly is."

Bemused, indeed under a *spell*, the girl obeyed. Stepping from the tub, she found herself at once both dry and scented, and she was next instant dressed, in the whitest silks, whiter than new-polished stars – her hair plaited with diamonds. And on her feet two shoes of such lovely peculiarity, she stood gazing at them.

Then the being was beside her again. "They are not made of glass – you will be well-able to dance in them."

The girl saw then the shoes were only stitched over, each of them, with a hundred or so tiny sparkling crystals. And taking a step, found she was already gliding – dancing – as if in a dream.

"Outside," said her benefactor, "a carriage awaits you. I made it..." – a little, perhaps boastful, laugh – "from a pumpkin – but now it is formed of gold. The six white horses are mice, but no one will know – not even they. Go to the palace, and win the heart of the handsome prince. You will find it quite easy, as now you are."

The girl - who in her recent awful years of ill-treated slavery, had been called in mockery, *Ashy* – murmured, "But these are faery gifts.

They will vanish away at morning. "

"True. The very first moment of morning, which comes when night turns back to day – at midnight. Thus, before the fatal hour strikes, you must depart – or be seen in rags and ruin."

"But then," whispered Ashy, turning ashen under all her beauty, "what use is any of this?"

"He will love you. You must trust in that. Love is *never* blind. He will find you, even after midnight has struck. Do you understand?"

"No, Lady," said Ashy. But her own real name came back to her at that second. It was Elvira. She bowed to the one who had been an old beggar woman, and who could walk out of a fire. "But I thank you. Even if this night ends for me in tragedy, to taste the joy of it will be worth any later pain."

Then Elvira went out and found the incredible golden carriage and the white horses, and stepping inside the vehicle, was carried faster almost than light – which she now resembled – to the palace of the prince.

Through all the crowds, he saw her at once. As she saw him.

Like two magnets, one of stellar silver, one of flame-lit steel, they flew together.

"I thought the moon had fallen on the terrace," he said, as he led her out across the gleaming floor. "But it was you."

What had they said to each other, after that? Beginning with courtly phrases, presently the passionate desire, the deep tenderness each had at once conceived for the other, spangled in their brains, more vital than champagne, and sprang from their lips like arrows. There among the host of other dancers, they spoke of love – shameless, precipitous, sincere.

But, for all their bond of truth, Elvira told him nothing of who she was, of what had happened to her, the jealous wickedness of false family. Nothing of her station now in life, that of a girl smudged with filth and living among grey cinders.

She could not bring herself to do it. She was afraid. Love is *never* blind? Yet he saw her now in a gown of moonlight, with diamonds in her hair and shoes that seemed magically made of glass. He thought her the daughter of a king, just as he was the son of a king.

And so she had arrived with him at ten minutes to midnight.

Yet now – oh now – the hands of the gilded clock had leapt forward impossibly. Eight minutes were *gone*. Only two minutes were left. She must fly – she must run away for her very life.

Let me stay one minute more. Only one...

For after this – no, he would never find her. How could he? She would be hidden again in darkness. And then he would forget her completely. Or else his heart would break as her heart already broke, thinking of the empty desert of despair beyond this night.

A single minute now, all that was left. How slowly the hands of the clock crept – how swiftly.

If only Elvira might freeze time. One *half* minute – all that remained – to make that half minute last another night – another hour – at least... at least another ten minutes...

"My love," Elvira said to the prince. There on the gleaming floor, among the crowds, they ceased to dance. Seeing this, the other dancers also stopped dancing. The orchestra fell silent in a sudden phantasmal flowing away of sound.

"My love – I must..."

The clock *struck*. The first stroke of the terrible twelve – an axe-blade that cracked asunder the pane of night.

Elvira stared up into the face of her lover. She saw how his laughing delight was altering to bewilderment – dismay.

She drew her hand from his. She drew away from him.

The clock *struck*. The second stroke. Already smashed, the night scattered in bits like black and golden snow.

"I..." she said.

"Never leave me," he said.

"I..."

The clock *struck*. The third stroke. The palace and the city reeled.

Elvira's feet in the shoes of glass – were lead. She must gather up her glimmer of skirts and run – *run* – before the glory of the spell of illusion deserted her.

Four, struck the clock, five, six, *seven*...

Like a statue, Elvira. Turned to stone.

Already it was too late.

The crashing axe-blows had become a thin honed sword, which sliced away the imagery of enchantment. Eviscerated, the white gown, foaming up like feathers, *melted* – the diamonds, shed like rain, *dried* – even the peerless shoes – for how could they remain, when all else that was sorcerous vanished? The shoes were two puddles of mirror. Then a mirror's double shadow. Then – nothing at all.

Eight, nine, ten, eleven.

Twelve, roared the clock, the voice of judgement: *Twelve-twelve-twelve*. The echo continued forever... But after forever, silence returned.

Elvira had not run away. She stood there in the midst of strangers, three of whom – though she could not see them – she knew to be the enemies from her own house. These people had not lost their finery.

They bloomed in it, and bloomed also with eyes stretched wide with shock, disgust – or fear.

And there before her, he – her lover, her prince, also changed at last to expressionless pale stone.

The girl wore only her dirty shift. Her hair hung down her back, thick with kitchen grease and cinders. She smelled no more of flowers and essences, but of sweat and toil, ash and agony.

Love is not blind. No, love sees too much. Love sees and becomes a whip with thorns in it. Oh, she had already learned as much, when her stepmother and stepsisters first turned upon her like starving rats.

Elvira waited, her head still raised, too shamed to be ashamed, her tears now the only jewels she wore.

And he, the prince, stretched out one hand, as if to push her away.

Instead, his hand clasped hers. He looked into her face, and suddenly the sun rose behind his eyes. He smiled at her gravely. "Now I understand," he said.

"But," she faltered, "do you still know me – even *now?*"

"Just as I knew you at first sight," he said. "It is still you. And how courageous you are, to have stayed. How you must love me, Elvira – perhaps even as much as I love you. Ladies and gentlemen," said the prince, turning to his astounded court, Elvira's dirt-blackened hand clasped firmly in his own, "Here is my future wife."

Arthur's Lion

That year I had some business to see to in Kent, and it wasn't long after arranging this that I received the letter from my uncle. It came as a surprise; at first I hadn't the faintest idea who was writing to me so familiarly. When I realised, I was in two minds. But curiosity got the upper hand.

I had better explain that I was nephew only to one uncle, Arthur, the brother of my by then deceased male parent. Arthur had made a lot of money in the north of England, as my mother had been wont to say: "By exploiting the workers and putting them into marmalade." This had always been the joke, that Uncle Arthur had made a fortune in marmalade, some exotic variety which, I'm pretty certain, never appeared on our table. Frankly, once I'd grown up and moved into my own life, I may well, here and there, have eaten the fabulous spread – and not known it. Basically, Arthur had removed himself from the family early on, and never afterwards himself maintained any contact. My father had seen his brother last in childhood. "I was only five when he took himself off. But I always remember, he was a funny chap," said my father. "Peculiar things stick in your mind, even when you can't recall what they were all about."

The peculiar Arthurian thing which had stuck, apparently, concerned an Arthur then sixteen years of age, letting out a loud cry and promptly fainting to the ground.

"We were in some sort of park – I think it was a park. We were going somewhere, but there was such a fuss, we didn't go. I've no memory as to where. All I recollect is Arthur yelling at the top of his lungs and sprawling on the gravel path."

"Perhaps," postulated my mother, "it was the first time making a fortune in marmalade occurred to him."

In fact, though Arthur did become extremely rich, it formed a dark mark on his escutcheon that none of this wealth was ever put in the way either of my grandparents, or my father's family, of which it seemed Arthur had been told.

Arthur's contemporary letter, however, when it reached me, was friendly and warm in tone. He said that he had come across my name in a promotion in the local newspapers, relating to the theatrical performance, because of which I was going down to Kent. Since our name is rather unusual, he had decided it must be me, and an inquiry at a London theatre provided him my address. The substance of his letter was to invite me to stay with him at his house. This was, he assured me, only three miles from my business venue, and his chauffeur would, of course, drive me in each day and retrieve me in the evening. Arthur was sure, besides, I would appreciate the comforts of a house over an 'inn', and added that he sincerely hoped I would visit him; we had been 'estranged' too long.

Initially I tossed the letter in the waste-paper bin. But then, as I say, curiosity won me round. By that era of my life, I was involved in work I found both fascinating and highly remunerative, so Arthur's fortune had no allure. But I'd heard of the house, which I will call Blue Firs, a place, it seemed, of luxury. And I confess I wondered very much what Arthur would be like – and if at all like my father, or even myself.

I therefore rescued his letter, and replied in the affirmative. The next morning, I travelled down to Kent.

It was a mild October afternoon when I arrived at Kesslington Station. Arthur's huge shining car, complete with respectful driver, picked me up and bore me away down autumnal lanes thick with yellow foliage and cows peering across gates.

Blue Firs was a large house, if by no means a mansion. It had been built in the 1800s for someone or other's mistress. Enormous trees framed the views as we drove up through the grounds, and there gradually appeared a cream and rose facade with pillarings and tall windows. Long roofs, with sun-gilded red tiles, had put up the periscopes of rather charming ornamental chimneys, modelled on an earlier design. I could imagine my mother saying, "Ah, the house built of marmalade."

When I'd got inside, I found myself in one of those polished echoing halls, whose acoustics are normally so bad for actors – a whisper carries like an unintelligible roar, and a roar like a rumble.

I asked the housekeeper if my uncle was about. She told me he was lying down but would meet me at the drinks hour. I went to unpack. It seemed Arthur hadn't after all lost his social gracelessness, at least where it could be applied to relatives.

But my room was large and airy, with a fire laid ready for later, and the great bed comfortable, and the bathroom well-appointed. Someone had also supplied gin, whisky and soda, and a bowl of hot-house oranges. Not so bad.

When I went down at six, a butler showed me at once into the long, narrow, drawing-room that looked out across the lawn. No one else was there.

"Is my uncle coming down?" I asked, rather impatiently.

"Yes, sir. He'll be here directly."

"Are there other guests for dinner?"

"No, sir."

Left alone, I sat by the fireside, watching the brown shadows gather over the room, and the bluer ones fill in the sweep of grass and trees outside.

I felt – and now for the first I admitted it – distinctly uneasy. Was I worried then, to be confronting my 'peculiar' uncle? Or was it the big quaint house? I thought not. Already, once or twice, I had stayed with various theatrical royalty, and been in buildings far more eccentric and grandly expanded. Besides, I have never been the nervous type. Even First Nights move me only to extra diligence. A cool head: I've been mocked for it.

The shadows thickened. I got up and switched on a pair of lamps, and turning again, saw the light reflecting on a short stocky man, formally dressed for dinner, standing in the wide doorway, and staring at me with enormous eyes. It struck me, extraordinarily, he was most like a child, an *anxious* child. I had the urge to put him at his ease. And too the wild notion he *was* truly frightened, scared at meeting at last this alien nephew, son to a brother he had barely troubled to know.

What did I call him?

I decided on mundane family courtesy.

"Uncle Arthur?"

"Oh," he said, "Arthur. We're both past the age of needing 'uncle' shoved in. And you must be..." He named me.

And I found myself saying kindly, "Oh, please call me Jack. It's what I generally answer to with friends."

"I hope we shall be," he said.

"I hope so too."

He stole forward – no other way to describe it. We shook hands. His was warm enough, but slightly stiff and swiftly withdrawn. He then came to the fire and stood there, lit by the flames and the lamps, his melancholy gaze now on the hearth and now, in fleeting glimpses, on me. Neither of us sat down.

Finally, he glanced at the drink in my hand, but didn't seem to want one for himself. Suddenly he said, "You must think it odd, my contacting you like that, out of the blue."

"It was a pleasant surprise."

He looked away from me then, discounting, I thought, the shallowness of my reply. He looked instead at the dark lawn beyond the window, and the trees heavy with a new night.

"Don't you think," he said, "this lighted room is like a camp in some jungle place, or on some open plain. A fire, a pair of lamps. Anything might be there," he said, strangely, "beyond the light."

"Do you mean in your grounds? I suppose..."

"No, not in the grounds. Nothing's there."

Somewhere from the depths of the house there came at that moment a long, indefinite sound. It was, I thought, the timbers shifting at the chill of evening. But Arthur looked round now at it, scanning the doorway, as if he expected someone – something – to appear. He seemed less startled, though a little startled, than apprehensively resigned.

At that second moment too, something did move into or over the doorway. It was a large bulky shadow, reeling across the duller lighting of the hall. And it was instantly followed by its cause. The butler filled the doorframe.

"Have you locked up?" asked Arthur, rather breathlessly, I thought.

"Yes, sir. All but the usual door."

"Good. That's good."

The butler then spoke about the dinner arrangements, which sounded ordinary enough that a report seemed unnecessary. Arthur must be a very pedantic and unsettled man. I pondered also why the house had been locked so early, and why the 'usual door' was not. Perhaps to let particular servants, who didn't sleep over at the house, return to the village?

When the butler again went out, he left the drawing room door wide open. Looking after him quite idly, I saw that flowing shadow veer again along the hallway. This time it seemed not to match his movements, nor that of anything in the room. But firelight can play tricks.

In any case, Arthur now sat down, and I with him. He helped himself to a drink and me to another. And then at last, in the expected way of relatives, he began to question me about my father and mother, our past life, my present one, and so on, until a maid came to call us to dine.

The meal was very good, with local fish and roast, and a wonderful sugary dessert concocted by Arthur's cook. All through the courses he seemed fairly relaxed, and only once got the jitters, for some reason I couldn't fathom at all. But he swallowed another glass of wine and cheered up again.

We went into an old-fashioned smoking-room after dinner, with the brandy and cigarettes – it was a tradition of Arthur's, because smoking otherwise was permitted everywhere about the house.

The velvet curtains were drawn, and another fire sparkled. Everything all told was very appealing and comfortable, had it not been for the constant sense of unease and alertness – most like a vague, almost undetectable smell – that also hung over virtually every instant. Even Arthur's relaxed periods had begun to seem forced. What was bothering him? I had come to the conclusion, whatever it was, it would be the very same matter that had prompted him to invite me to his home. I'm afraid I felt quite irritable at this. Once tomorrow dawned, I would have my hands full with the theatrical event in the town, and little time for sudden extra dramas.

Throughout dinner, we'd spoken only of trivial things, mostly to do with the family. Arthur had remarked that I resembled my grandfather, when young, which I valued. In him, although I didn't say so, I could see no likeness to any of our tribe.

Once in the smoking-room, a silence drifted down. We sat in armchairs, and Arthur stared long into the fire. And I thought, by now highly apprehensive myself, any minute and he'll come out with it. Whatever the hell it is. And then let's hope it can be put right very simply. Otherwise it must wait until the play is done.

Arthur said, again, "Yes, I can see my father in you. My brother must have grown to be a strong, well set-up young man. I know he can have been afraid of absolutely nothing. As a little child, even, he was fearless. I remember his nanny, the very woman who had terrified me as a child with her ghost stories, having no effect on him whatsoever."

I said, "Yes, he was a brave man. I've seen as much myself from his war record."

"Indeed. But I suppose," said Arthur softly, "we are all of us, in the end, afraid of something. Otherwise, could we be human?"

"Certainly, I'm terrified of several things. The British tax system for one thing. Oh, and I admit, a certain well-known actress who shall be nameless."

Arthur smiled, but the smile slipped off like water.

His face was closed-in, bent to the fire, his eyes viewing, it seemed, only that.

"Yes, but there are other fears, aren't there. Inner fears. Fears located – how do they say it now – within the Id. "

I said nothing. This promised to be more weird and much more time-consuming than I'd supposed.

Arthur stirred the fire slowly with a poker. Then he sat there, holding the poker loosely in his hand.

"Since I was a boy," he said, "since then, about six years of age. Something. I saw it first in a book, one of those stupid, highly-coloured old illustrated books for children. Though I'd guess now it was meant for a much older child than I then was. It was on a low table, in the library. Thinking back, I believe it must have been my father's property, when he was little. Had it terrified him? Apparently not. And why, anyway, was it lying out open where I could find it? I've often wondered that. I'd think, really, almost any child might have been frightened by it. The drawn picture – was very crude, all reds, yellows, blacks – horrible..." He raised his eyes straight up to mine. And they were full of utter terror that glowed like tears. "I know now it was a book about Ancient Rome. And this picture concerned the Emperor Nero's habit of having Christians thrown into the arena, and savage hungry animals let loose on them. An awful subject to illustrate. Probably meant to be improving. But me it did *not* improve. I rather think," he lowered the poker slowly back into its place, "it ruined me."

I was then, and am, no psychiatrist. I said, no doubt with inappropriate foolishness, "Of course, as a child, you might be afraid at it. But – how can it have ruined you?"

"I'd been quite a bold little boy. Always in scrapes. Brave. I used to lead a little local gang. We had some piratical name. But after I saw in that book – after I saw that picture – a change came over me. I used to dream, you see. I used to dream over and over about the picture."

"The Christians being killed in the arena by the animals."

"Killed, and devoured. Yes. They were..." He hesitated, and the oddest small twist of a smile distorted his lips. "They were lions," he said. And then again, "Lions." As if to repeat the name took a great effort of will, which he *must* exert.

Something in how he had stirred the fire had upset the logs. It sank and darkened, and the room seemed to darken too, despite the electric lamps.

I said, encouragingly, "Well, what you describe could be enough to give any kid nightmares."

"Perhaps. But I must explain. My dreams were very specific. *I* was in the arena, you see. I, as a child. And I was alone. Alone that was, but for a huge, formless, faceless crowd shouting and baying all around me from the seats. And I would stand there on the sand, naked, shivering and afraid – sickeningly afraid – and then a kind of black hole would come in the side of the arena, and a lion would come out. Only one, you see. Only one." Arthur stopped. He put his head into his hands, but not before I'd seen his face was now almost green.

"Don't go on if it distresses..."

"I *must* go on," he said. He lifted his head and brought his brandy to his mouth and gulped the lot. "One lion," he said. "I know him so well. A huge ochre beast, with a vast black-ruffed head. There were bloody welts on his side – they must have whipped him up from the cages below – that filthy book showed all that too... Each of his eyes were like yellow-red coals. He stank. I could smell him. He stank of butcher's meat. And then he ran towards me – right at me – and I stood there screaming – and as he leapt his great claws flashed like silver hooks – and I woke – always I woke – just before his weight could come down and his talons and teeth could go into me. Always. And always, screaming. It happened every night, yet only ever once – once every night. It happened once every night for a whole year. I was afraid to go to bed. I would make myself keep awake, sitting up in the darkness – but in the end always I fell asleep. And then I'd be in the arena, alone but for the crowd, and he would come, the lion. And he would run and leap and in that split second, with the rush of his stinking flesh and his claws already felt like a boiling wind across my body – I'd wake up. I would *escape* him."

"My God," I said. Finally, I thought, the elements of his fear had truly communicated themselves to me. As with a powerful acting performance, the catharsis of empathically induced emotion. I was shaken.

"Well," Arthur said presently. "I must tell you why the dreams stopped. First my parents tried to laugh and tease me out of them. Then they tried to bully me out. You perhaps have wondered why I've been a stranger to my own family all these years. Partly it began there. I never forgave them for it, their crass lack of understanding. And though in later years I could grasp almost perfectly that it came not from cruelty, but from a genuine, if entirely misplaced, conception of how best to deal with me – the rift had widened and was too enormous to heal. However, long before that, when I was seven years old, I met a gypsy in our garden. He'd just walked in at the gate, and was going round to the back of the house with some tinker's stuff he'd got for the kitchen. But seeing me, he pulled a face, and then called to me, quite politely and gently. *Come here, young master.* That was what he said. And for some reason, to him I went. I was by then a thin, pale-faced child, with rings under my eyes from never sleeping well. I must have looked haunted enough; our doctor had already apparently warned my father I might be in the early stages of some incurable malady – which idea alarmed mother, but my father scoffed at it, saying I was just in a silly mood, trying still to be a baby, and waking everyone by yelling every night.

But the gypsy man stared into my face, and then he said, 'I can make him go away. One day he will come back. But you'll be a man then, and perhaps a man will have the strength to turn him off for good.'

I gaped at him, and because I'd been brought up a certain way, I feebly said to him, 'What do you mean?'

'Hush now,' he answered. Then he put his hand on my head. It felt scalding hot, his hand, and he breathed in my face, and his breath was bad, because I suppose, poor fellow, his teeth weren't up to much. But somehow that didn't repulse me. When he lifted his hand away, I felt something go with it. He said, 'Done now. Not till you're a man will it come back. Go and tell the cook you took a toy off me from my sack, and I'm owed half a shilling.'

I did what he said, and later I received a smacking from my father, who told me off for making the cook pay for a paltry toy for me. He asked where the toy was. I said it had broken, and my father said that served me right. He would have broken it if I had not. That night I crept up to bed, and sat there in the dark as usual, my back sore from the blows, and biting my hand to keep awake, But I kept thinking of the gypsy, too. And in the end I let go. I let go and I slept. I slept right through. It was the first night in a year I didn't have the dream. But after that, night followed night without it. Gradually then my general health improved. I was soon at school, and began to lead my own boy's life again. Although I was never as I had been before I saw the book. I hadn't the stamina I had had, even though I'd grown older and bigger. I tended to weight rather than muscle. I had headaches, and once or twice fainted, if I was too hot or cold, and sometimes in church. But the dream was entirely gone. Gone till I should *be a man* and have the strength to face it once more, and then be able to send it away, to *turn it off for good.* Nevertheless – I could never be reconciled to that word, that name, or if I saw any picture of them, even a fine painting. Or if it was in a lesson. In Latin, for example. I even fainted then, too. Something in Suetonius, I think it was, about the Roman Circus."

The fire was dying. I took it on myself to poke at the logs and drop on another one. Arthur poured us more brandy but said nothing. His face was less pallid, but had the greasy look of light sweating.

When I straightened up I said, "What happened then, when you were sixteen?"

"Oh," said Arthur, "your father remembered that, did he? Yes. It was nothing really. Nothing for them. We were to visit a garden. A zoological garden. By that time, I'd got much better at suppressing my fear. Or I told myself I had. I'd been nerving myself to the excursion, thinking it might be a test I could overcome. But then – I heard them roaring, you see. In the distance. Over the trees. Lions. I knew instantly what the noise was. I screamed, as I had in my nightmares, and screaming is all I recollect after this, until I found myself at home again. I left my father's house as soon as I was well enough to do so. I led then a quite unadventurous life. I won't bore you with the details. They bore me, too, you see. Until that piece of luck with the recipe, the marmalade – more an orange jam, you understand. An old Scottish formula. Pure luck. Idiotic. But it made us rich, my partners and I. I can assure you, however, such good fortune doesn't hold off loneliness. I have always found it awkward to mix with people, to find companions. And so I have been a lonely man. Unmarried – childless – I can't imagine such things as wedlock or paternity, for myself. Even so, I have got by. I have lived. And now," he said. Arthur leant back in his chair as I sat down again in mine. "And now," he repeated.

Though never having myself walked out on the boards, save in the most administrative capacity, I found myself responding as if we two, he and I, were spotlit now at the centre of a stage. Faultless on my cue I announced, "And now it has returned."

Arthur met my eyes. His had changed to flat dark stones. "Yes. It has come back."

"As the gypsy said it would."

"As he said."

"Do you know why?"

"Oh yes. Something very ordinary."

I leant forward. "Which is?"

"I saw the damnable picture again."

"Good lord – where? Where did you see it?"

"Oh, not in that vile little book. No, it was reproduced in a catalogue. It seems the ghastly work is now something of an antique, and this illustration, the particular one, the one I think was fashioned in Hell, for me alone, that picture had been reproduced in the brightest, gaudiest detail. Leafing carelessly through the catalogue in the house of a business associate, suddenly it was all before me again. I had to leave the house immediately, making some incredible excuse, I can't remember what. That night I tried to reason with myself. But it was no use whatsoever. I found myself at 2 a.m., wandering about with the whisky decanter. Afraid to go to bed, just as I had been, night after night, when a child. In the end, of course, adult common sense propelled me to my room. I downed a final glass of whisky and fell instantly asleep. Half an hour later I woke half the servants with my shrieks. My poor housekeeper believed criminals had broken in and were murdering me. It might have been amusing, if this state of affairs hadn't, then, continued for six further months. Yes, naturally, my doctor, and then several specialists, were summoned. They could do nothing, only drug me to a deathly moribund slumber from which – despite all the muck I had swallowed – I still woke once a night screaming in terror. The lion..." Arthur spoke the name now in a loud clear stroke, like the movement of a surgeon's knife. "...the *lion* came for me. As he always had. Out of the dark hole in the arena wall, over the dirty sand, leaping, his claws raking the air, just missing me as I sprang awake."

I too lifted my glass and drained it.

"But," I said, "six further months, I heard you say. Do you mean you found a way again to stop the dreams?"

"In a manner of speaking." Arthur stared downwards into nothingness. "A last specialist arrived here two months ago. In his demeanour he reminded me once more of my father, though he was younger than I am now. A strong-minded, bullying man, himself brave as – I was going to say, brave as a lion. He told me roundly I was a nervous wreck, and that the fault lay only with me. I had let this literary phantasm prey on me, and had offered no resistance. To drug myself with morphine or liquor was past the point. I must instead lie down to sleep and face the beast, in the knowledge that it was *nothing*. Nothing at all. It was only, he told me sternly, *my own fear*, which had birthed, and subsequently sustained, the nightmare. Forgivable, he admitted, in a very young child, but in a grown man nauseating and absurd. 'It is your cowardice,' he bluntly said, 'which is destroying your sleep, your health and your life. You and you alone can be rid of it. You must cast it out. Then you will be free.' When he'd quite done with me, I was trembling like a boy. But I could see, as I can see now, that he was fundamentally in the right. *My* terrors had formed this curse. I must turn my back on them. And so I ate a light supper, had a couple of drinks, and went to bed. I stayed awake about half an hour, during which time I refused myself a single thought of the nightmare, and fell asleep abruptly. I dreamed of nothing at all. Since then too, the dream hasn't plagued me once. Indeed, I can sleep at any hour of day or night without any inconvenience."

I sat looking at him. His hands were folded down, one on each arm of his chair. He stared on into the abyss, invisible to me, which opened at his feet.

Arthur said, "I think you'll be both too mature and too young to know the fears and nervousness, in their way not unlike those of infancy, which can come on with increasing age. I suspect, too, being so like my own father in appearance, that you yourself may never succumb to this form of trepidation, even in old age. Death may never tap *you* on the shoulder to expound his prologue. You may never think about it. Your kind, and please do not think I insult you, I am only very jealous, can stay impervious to most horrors and frights. Your nerve holds in battle, and if there are ever such things as ghosts or demons, you would confront them, face them down. Or produce a revolver and shoot them, perhaps, back to mortal life."

Embarrassed by his accuracy, I too lowered my gaze. Where my glance fell then, I saw, across the fine Aubusson carpet, a curious baroque shadow, thick and black, lying oddly sidelong from the lamps. What was it? Puzzled, I turned my head and looked straight up into the corner of the room. There was a slice of darkness there also, and in the dark, something – no, two things – glittered in a sudden crushed flicker of brilliancy, now yellowish, now red.

"Ah," he said, in a quiet, cracked little voice, almost sarcastic, almost biter. "Is it there? Can you see it?"

I turned back and glared at Arthur. "See what, precisely?"

"Don't you know?"

"No, frankly. Of course I'm sympathetic to what's happened to you. But even you yourself are now calling it a form of neurasthenia. So what is there to gain from dramatising any of it further?"

"I can't help myself, it seems. When that clever specialist rehearsed my case before me, he mercilessly showed me exactly what I had most to fear: my own fear itself. My terrors, whether real or groundless, are my worst enemies. But I have to tell you, for such a person as myself, terror is now basic to my personality. And by refusing to let it visit me in sleep, it seems – it seems – I've let it out into the concrete world, at last. Where, having had me consistently elude it for so long, it has always yearned to follow me. My nightmare – has become a reality, and my terror feeds it every hour. Perhaps not even only terror, either. My *accustomedness*."

"Rubbish," I said. "Utter rot."

Behind me, some entity stirred, a velvet sound, edged with something rasping and barbed. Like the noise of a cat, amplified.

I stood up and looked round again. Something was there. No doubt of it. In deep shadow, between the top of a wooden cupboard and the cornice of the ceiling. It looked most like a large full trunk. It hadn't, I thought, been there previously.

My conclusion was that my Uncle Arthur had become insane, and was playing some type of bizarre, possibly dangerous, trick on me. I've had dealings with the unstable before – the profession on whose perimeter I work has presented to me some fine examples. To humour Arthur therefore seemed the best course.

Reluctant to stay with my back to whatever it was that had manifested in the corner, I moved my chair to a different angle, before sitting back down.

"Very well," I said. "But you've got your answer to it, haven't you? Cast out fear. Then it will go."

"I try," he said. "I try. It's a war that never stops. That gypsy man who helped me in my childhood, he thought I might eventually prove the stronger, and the victory be mine. Or maybe that was only his pretence, because he could foresee what was more likely. I try and try, and try. But the fear never goes. How can it? The evidence of what there is to fear is frequently in front of me. Besides, by now, I believe it is less fear – than how mighty that fear it has already fed on has made the – creature. How else has it done what it has? Perversely, at last, it's only in sleep I ever evade it. Others here," he said, with a weary, flat, matter-of-factness, "see the thing too. Oh yes, that's how actual, despite my resistance, it has become. They see it. As you just did over there, up by the ceiling. And look now, the shadow on the carpet moving, the tail of it wagging slowly to and fro."

I stared resolutely into the fire. Behind me, far off, vague, I heard a kind of soft grumbling guttural, that might only be some freak sound of the autumn wind in the chimneys.

"You should pack up and leave this house," I said, lighting another cigarette.

"It would go with me," he said. "By now, it goes with me always. Sometimes it disappears, as if it has other little tasks it likes to see to about the place. Then it's there again. My housekeeper has seen it. You can ask her. She's decided it's the ghost of a dog that once lived here. And my butler. The cook and maids somehow generally refuse to see it. Those who do sometimes complain of a large cat that has got into the main house from the kitchen."

There was a long, slipping, heavy noise.

Arthur's eyes went over above me. I saw him watch something move quickly across the upper air. His face was green again, but again he smiled. He nodded. He said, "It's gone for the moment. I could see them then, the welts on its side. Poor thing. It must suffer. Poor damnable thing."

I'd had enough. I got up again and said, "Sir, I have a very busy schedule, which begins quite early tomorrow. I understood you were aware of that when you invited me here. This matter, whatever it is, is beyond me. I don't know what you expect me to do."

"Only to listen. What else is feasible? I'd ask you to shoot it, if that were any good. But how could it be? It came out of the dark inside me. The dark where we go in dreams. It wants to take me back there, to keep me, to play with perhaps, or only to fulfil its function. Rend me. Devour me. Like the hapless Christians in the book."

"You'll have to excuse me," I said. "It's midnight. Perhaps I could ring for your man... Do you have any opiates to help you sleep?"

"Yes, go to bed," Arthur replied. His face was icy with disgust.

I stood in the doorway of the smoking-room. The hall outside was rosily low-lit from a single lamp standing on a table. At the curve of the staircase, one of the maids was crossing, with an armful of what looked like table linen, to the baize door giving on the servants' area. I looked at her, her trim brisk figure, and how, just before she reached the baize, something loped across her path, from shade to shadow, and she hesitated, as if to check the fall of one of the pile of linens she held, which were not slipping at all.

I saw its eyes gleam, fitfully. It glanced at me, indifferent. In its half-seen, solid shape was all the intangible presence of the night. But as he had said, it was an indoor beast, a beast of locked houses that left only one door open for it, in the frantic hope it might go out and lose itself. A beast too of the indoors of the brain, the psyche. A beast of the indoors of the human soul.

Like a scene from a play, I saw it, his dream, and how the beast leapt at him, missed him, always missing, as he fled outward to the world. And then his fear coming out of him, rejected, but still inextricably attached. Externalised.

The lion had gone around the corner and the maid passed through the servants' door and the hall was empty.

I walked back into the smoking-room. He was sitting quietly crying, poor old child, with the welts of horror blistering on his side.

"All right, old chap," I said. "All right."

"I don't," he said, apologetically, "want to be alone.

"Then you shan't be. Hang the theatre. I'll deal with it tomorrow."

After a while, we went upstairs, and along one of the corridors to his room. Nothing was about, all was silence and, in the cracks of windows, where curtains didn't quite meet, a low moon floated on a cloud.

We had another brandy, and he went to bed, or at least lay down with the coverlet over him. His round fallen face on the pillows stared at me.

"Nothing can be done. I know that," he said. "When it comes back..."

"I'll wake you," I said. "Sleep for now."

I'd asked myself if it *could* come in when he slept, but of course it could, that was the whole point to it now. It was in the world, and outside of him. And his former fear of meeting it in his mind had been replaced, not unreasonably, by the fear it would eventually seize him while he slept.

The electric light on the upper floors was dimmer. I sat in an armchair in this duller glow, and midnight passed into one, and so on through two. I smoked, and watched the clock, and wished I'd thought to bring some coffee upstairs. But even so, I was wide awake. Arthur slept, deep and dumb. He might have been dead, I couldn't help thinking that. I had no inspiration of what I could do. Keep the creature off him, then in the morning drive him somewhere, look up any one of a number of people who dealt in fractured minds and hallucinations – God knows. The brain ticks away in its backrooms often, and we're unaware of its secret progress. I sincerely hoped it might offer me a plan, but hadn't much faith it could.

For I knew too, of course I did, this now was more than a dream or mirage. I'd seen it. I'm prosaic enough, and it was merely pragmatic now to *admit* to having seen it. To deny the situation further would be to enter myself the lists of the fanciful or mad.

It returned when the clock said a quarter past three.

It came up through the floor.

That was like a stage effect, something clever with traps and levers, but involving no dry ice to mask it.

Arrived, it shook itself. The housekeeper had convinced herself it was a phantom dog, and there was something doglike about it certainly, as there often is with the big cats; tigers, panthers, and the rest. But its face was savage and evil, its eyes two mindless sumps of decayed fire that seemed to have given off the smoke of its mane. It did faintly stink, as he'd said. How had he known, as a child, what it might smell of? But perhaps lions don't smell of meat, it was only something he'd heard and so made this one do it. For it was all his own work – his, and that of the artist who first so luridly depicted it and its kind, in the arena of Nero.

I'd promised him I would wake him when it came back. I called his name sharply, and Arthur opened his eyes, instantly fully conscious. "Is it there?"

"Across the room by the window."

The moon had gone, but the low-burning electric light illustrated the lion as accurately as its initial paint.

It did not look at him or me. It looked about itself at the massively-furnished room. Then it padded away, across the floor, and nudging open the bathroom door, went inside.

In the total noiselessness of the night, Arthur and I listened as it drank from some trickle of water, real or etheric, issuing from the taps of the bath.

When it had finished, it returned, not through the door, but simply out of the wall. It stood, its heavy head lowered, its tail swinging.

Something struck me then. I couldn't have described it. But abruptly I saw the cruelty in its face was only instinct, and perhaps the pain from the stripes on its side, which anyway looked partly cured. It was an animal of sorts, at least. It was hungry, and had been thirsty, and chose sometimes to use a door rather than pass through a blank floor or wall.

So then I spoke to it, by its name.

"Lion."

It made a snorting noise, and turned, and looked at me, that terrible look, the hellish eyes that were really only reflecting light.

"There he is," I said to it. "There. Look *there*."

And the head again turned, as if it grasped my meaning. And I saw Arthur brace himself. I said to Arthur then, "It's yours. You made it. You gave it life. You're – you're like a father to the damn thing, Arthur. Stop resisting it, do you hear? It's your belonging now, whatever it was to start with. It doesn't want to drag you back into the shadows – if it did, it would lose all this new territory you've given it. I'm fairly sure it knows that, or it would have done it by now. After all, it's had a couple of months to try. First you gave it the Roman arena to play in. But now it's got a whole house – and anything outside it fancies too. Why do you think it goes off and leaves you? It goes exploring like a bloody cat. And why do you think it follows you, comes back to you? If it isn't for violence, it must be something else. Maybe that's where it *is* like a dog. It knows, if you don't, it belongs to you."

The lion, with no warning, sprang. It was too quick for Arthur even to cry out, even to register his fear. It landed, and balanced on his bed, at the foot of it, gazing at him, breathing.

I crossed the room in three strides and pushed it hard in its unmarked side – except there was nothing, nothing substantial to push – but with a grunt it dropped, and flopped down. It lay there sprawled. It blinked at me, growling. "Be quiet," I said. "You must do as you're told. If you want to stay, you must behave yourself." The growl changed to a yawn.

We remained watching it, Arthur bolt upright on the pillows, I standing at the bedside, and after a while it lowered its head on to the coverlet. The horror of its eyes shut.

After that, we kept vigil till first light, talking slowly and methodically, discussing it, over its sleeping form, Arthur not moving an inch, I static in a chair. When dawn began to seep in, the lion woke and rose. It kicked its paws and jumped off the bed – and vanished.

At ten to seven some tea was brought up by a maid, and I went down to telephone the town, reporting my absence as due to food-poisoning.

The lion was standing in the echoing hallway when I turned, looking off along a corridor to a narrow, opened door. The morning smelled enticingly there, of trees and mist, and bonfires. While the open door, since the lion could utilise blank walls for exits and entrances, was presumably an aesthetic choice. Outside lay the grounds, with plenty of game – mice and squirrels, birds, rabbits and hares. Any big animal could hunt for itself if it wanted, although I doubted any of the hunted things would suffer much worse than a nasty shock. The lion, though it was visible and could create smell and sound, had no actual substance. But, like the bath-taps, which didn't leak but had provided water, an idea was conceivably enough for it to feed from. A beast of imagination in more than one way. Arthur's beast, very apparently. Even as I watched, it made a decision and bounded off along the corridor and out of the open door. Hungry – well, it had had to wait several decades for a meal.

Needless to say, I recounted nothing of any of this when I reached the theatre the next day. My assistant had managed pretty ably without me, and all was soon put in order. I meanwhile secured myself a room in the local hotel.

Arthur survived another twenty-five years, and died without warning, but peacefully, during a fishing holiday in Scotland with one of his partners in the marmalade venture. There had been some talk of a large ghost dog, I believe, being seen often about Blue Firs, and also in other houses where Arthur visited. A slight mythology had connected itself to my uncle, who, apparently, was once or twice spotted, as witnesses thought, throwing sticks for some large hound, in a selection of rural retreats. In Scotland, years before he died, there was a strange story of something lying on the foot of his bed, purring – but it had disappeared by the time others came to investigate. After

Arthur's death, the beast vanished completely, at least according to his housekeeper. Blue Firs is now, I rather ashamedly admit, mine, but I am seldom there. Nevertheless, those who rent the property relate nothing either of dogs, cats or lions.

From Arthur, in the years before his death, I heard very little of anything, and less of his creature. With his renewed sense of safety, our 'estrangement' had recurred, which seemed to suit us both. Only a postscript appeared now and then to a rare letter: *The lion is in good spirits.* Anyone reading this correspondence might take it that Arthur referred sportively to himself. People told me afterwards my solitary visit had done him a power of good. He had thrown off at once his old timidity and depression, and the recent bad nerves. Instead, he took to long hale walks, and large cuts of meat served almost raw at dinner – though these were barely touched. Sometimes, when alone, he would, it seems, laugh aloud. He informed anybody who asked him, it was at something he had read in a newspaper.

Naturally I have no knowledge of where either of them is now. For myself, I assume life ends with the body. But then again, perhaps there are some mind-fashioned heavens in which certain mentally creative people continue to exist. If so, I don't think for a moment Arthur and his lion are now locked back in any Roman arena. He freed the lion, and ultimately was set free by it. Trite in the paucity of my own imaginative knack, I see them bounding along a seaside, Arthur a gleeful kid of seven, wiry, healthy and tough, and with a great, black-maned dog, scarred a little on one flank, whose claws flash like silver hooks, and leave starry markers on the clean unearthly sand of the shore.

Sold

The woman climbed the stairs to her apartment. She was about forty-five, but looked very much older. A medication she had to consume daily had made her – ironically? – forty-five pounds overweight. The medication helped keep off her life-threatening condition, but didn't help her *other* condition, which was arthritis. Haggard though fat, her hair thin as if eaten away, she dragged herself over the last step and, turning the key with difficulty, went into her room.

It was a grey room, of course. Anything she'd ever owned worth anything had been sold off long ago. Just the elderly word-processor sat there, a machine which often now went wrong, and for which spare parts were fast becoming unobtainable. A computer she couldn't afford. Realistically this hardly mattered. Nobody had wanted to publish her stories for at least twenty years, nor play the music she had composed on the old piano which, before she sold it too, her neighbours had complained about so regularly.

The place was filthy. She couldn't clean, though such amounts of dirt annoyed her – her hands and joints...

She opened a window to let in the icy night-time river fog. It was better than the reek of dust, rats and damp.

Today she had lost her job. That was inevitable. She could no longer sort the files nor operate the machines. Besides, as they had pointed out, she had often been away sick.

The woman – her name was Judith – now opened the cupboard. It wasn't quite bare. She took out the hoarded small packet of good coffee and, being very careful with her disobedient, wooden hands, made herself a single mug.

Then she switched on the side lamp and sat down at the table.

On the table was quite a paraphernalia. It involved, among other items, candles and brown bones, certain plants, utensils of various metals, resins, spices, powders and chalk.

Judith, the woman, sat considering these as she drank the bitter coffee.

She had no one to consult. Family, lovers, friends, they had all been lost, some to death, and some to their own exasperated boredom and creeping empathic fear at her condition.

She peered about at the array on the table. She herself was frightened. No, she was terrified at what she might find out tonight.

Terrified.

The woman Judith drank down the bitter dregs.

Damn it, she thought. She smiled. Yes, *damn* it all.

For seven whole months she had studied, in books loaned from libraries, or unearthed from eldritch stores for a few dollars. More than this, she had gone back into her own more esoteric memories, when she had had wise teachers and enjoyed her education, the time when she had been young and able, and had thought she might stand a chance in the world. Judith then had learned a lot. Now she learned and re-learned more.

She put down her mug. She stared at it as if she had put down something vital, fearsome. Then she rose and left the table, and went into her tiny shower-room to begin the meticulous process of her preparation.

By the hour it happened, probably near to three in the winter morning, Judith was beyond exhaustion, quite numb.

All of her, that was, except for her mind.

That kept working. It had had to. What she had been doing, or attempting to do, demanded complete concentration and unfettered readiness. And, at least for the duration, no shred of doubt.

Then it – *he* – came.

Up from the floor maybe, or out of a wall – it was difficult to tell. There was no flash of fire, no theatrical smoke-and-trapdoor effect. Just a kind of hole punched in reality, and out of this a glittering golden horror *swarmed,* dull-burning like a dead sun, or some other insane contradiction.

Having entered, he stayed positioned, an inch or so above the mg.

Judith bowed low from within the chalk and salt and other essence-sprinkled circle. She wasn't safe there, she knew, and this was only etiquette. But she had gathered that if she stringently observed the courtesies, so might... *they.*

He spoke.

The room turned to gelatine and rhythmically shook, but she understood not one word.

He seemed to grasp this and to find it amusing.

Then he did – *something* – and suddenly she heard and knew.

The exquisite music of his voice was unbearable – and disgusting. Exactly as the look of him was beautiful and glamorous beyond all things, yet nauseating almost to the point of agony – no, in fact *to* that point.

Despite all this, she now heard him speak, as others had claimed to, more or less in her own language and in a format she could recognise. It was actually, she thought, less that she understood his meaning – than that they had somehow had at least this part of the conversation before.

"You have called. What is it you want?"

Judith cleared her dry throat. "What humans always want of you, great lord."

"I see. You wish to sell... something."

Judith felt a rush of elation so intense she must curb herself. It was like a mixture of alcohols – champagne perhaps and vodka – things she hadn't tasted for a decade. But no, really it was *much* more than that. It was as if someone had suddenly gently melted off her ruined back, and replaced it with two silvery wings that worked.

"I've read," she quietly answered, "that if you come, I may offer my soul to your great lordship's mightiest lord, in exchange for... certain benefits."

He smiled.

The smile laved then eviscerated the room, disembowelled it and left it bleeding all around her.

Judith ignored that.

"You are correct," said the Demon. "My Master, that your kind term, inaccurately, Satanus, or the Devil, will honour such a bargain. We will accept your soul in exchange for your heart's desire. What would you like?"

Judith's wild joy now almost swamped her. She must exert over it the iron will she otherwise used only to tap the keys on her machine, or climb the stairs, or rise in the morning from bed. This though had tempered it sufficiently. Iron it was. Even so, the kindled pure *glee* inside her found one outlet – she grinned.

In return apparently the Demon grimaced. This was less painful than his smile.

"Well, lord, what'll he give me?"

"Say what you will have."

"Oh," said Judith consideringly, as if she hadn't considered it over and over and *over.* "Beauty, vast beauty. And youth. About eighteen, shall we say – permanently. And dress-size eight?" The Demon regarded her, and for a second she thought she saw the same type of repulsed boredom she had noted on the faces of erstwhile friends, when she'd mentioned hospital appointments and debts. Poor Demon. He must have heard this or similar demands so often. From Faustus onward. Or from long *before* Faust, if it came to that. From the days of the earliest so-called enlightenments. Beauty and youth, and next riches and powers... "And riches," Judith stated, "and power, of course."

"Of course."

"And a very long life to relish it all," said Judith. "How long a life can I have, by the way?"

He looked her over. She sensed, and perhaps she was right, the computers of Hell were performing a rapid check on her physical credentials and other applicable data.

"Three hundred years," finally announced the Demon, emissary of Lucifer.

Judith pretended to faint shock. "Can't I have a bit longer?"

"Oh." Now he laughed: the bleeding minced bits of the room seemed to fly apart screaming. "At your age, and working from the original basis of your current ill health, only three hundred years are possible."

"I'd hoped for much more."

"Then you should have called us sooner."

Judith lowered her head meekly. Her joy was now so insane and shining she felt she might burst. She wanted to kiss the tattered rug and laugh-riven walls. She restrained herself.

"I suppose," she said, "beauty and power and so on, for three hundred years, is a pretty good deal. I mean, I've never had any of them. Oh, did I mention complete healing and thereafter enduring good health? I wouldn't like to be lovely, wealthy and powerful – and sick all the time."

"Naturally," he said. "This is usual. It goes without saying."

"So really," she said, "your terms are more than generous. They're – bountiful. And so... I'm puzzled," she went on hesitantly. "All *you* ask for all *that* is – my soul?"

"Your soul," he agreed.

"And what happens to my – er, soul, then, after the three hundred years of the good life are up?"

"After the three hundred years, your soul becomes forfeit to us. My Master receives your soul."

"And?"

"And," he said.

In his eyes that weren't quite eyes she saw the answer more vividly than even the single contemptuous word had conveyed. The answer involved complex excruciation and nightmare from which there was no relief and no waking up. Ever.

"I see," she said. "And all the extraordinary gifts you'll give me while I live are worth that to you? I mean, simply so you can have my soul, and torture it forever? It *is* for forever?"

Tanith Lee

"It is forever, yes," he said. "Yes."

Yeesss said the dying room, crashing through space with its hands over its ears.

Yyeeessss said the city, the landscape, continent – world? – trying not to listen.

"Why?" asked Judith.

The Demon half turned. Through his profile and armoured musculature she glimpsed swamps of acid and fire and monsters that had teeth for eyes.

"Because your soul," he said, more softly than she or anyone could, "is *your soul.*"

"So precious?"

"So precious."

"Thank you," breathed Judith. "Oh – thank you."

"If you are ready then," said the Demon, turning back like some gothic Santa, "just a few drops of your blood and..."

"Thank you," repeated Judith. She straightened. "But no thanks."

A crack appeared in the ethos of the apartment, of what was left of the apartment.

A kind of day-night-day rushed through the fabric of all things.

"What did you say?" he whispered, with the silent sound of a million, million stars exploding – silently.

"I said, thank you so much, but I think I'll leave it."

The room, which was whirling, settled with a sudden ghastly crunch. Nothing structural happened. It was all in the psyche.

"You have summoned me, by the prescribed formulae. I have arrived. You have required, through me, the cognisance of my Master, Lord of the Abyss, in the matter of the Eternal Bargain. You cannot now say No."

"I can. And if I say No, No it is. You can't have my soul unless willingly I agree and sign it away in my own blood."

Judith watched the Demon foam and fleer before her. She was utterly afraid, but no more than she'd been afraid of all the other life-threatening shit that had webbed in her over-threatened life.

"Let me explain," Judith said at last, with the slightest trace of temerity. "Until tonight, I couldn't be sure I had one – I mean a soul. Actually, calling you up this evening, I was so scared you wouldn't come – scared you were a myth, and so scared because of that – because then it really did mean the soul didn't exist. Which meant this – this physical disaster was all there was to me. But your, if I may say, very kindly *advent* here, and your preparedness to adhere to the antique bargain and reward me for it so extravagantly, have proved to me that

370

a soul I do truly have. More. Even assuming I had – *have* a soul, how could I be sure it wasn't already doomed to Hell? I've not led a very exemplary life – I haven't had much chance to, with the crap I've had to contend with. But it seems, despite that, I'm not doomed or damned, or you'd hardly have travelled such a way and been so eager to buy my soul when you got here, would you? Last but not least, if your sort exist then patently so does God, in whatever curious, marvellous, abstruse form He, She, They or It employ. And that therefore means there *is* Eternity too – which, if I avoid you and your organisation, will be an Eternity of bliss. Well, come now. What's three hundred niggling little good years to blissful eternity? What's three hundred years to eternal life as my very own healed and healthy, beautiful, powerful – and for all I know rich in unimaginable ways – perfect and *precious* soul? The flesh really *doesn't* mean a thing. And that being the case, I can, sure as Hell, put up with *this* a bit longer. Frankly, the physical state I'm in, I'll probably be dead in a couple of years anyhow. And then – well. The *other* world's going to be my oyster, isn't it?"

Darkness and great Nothing sank through the apartment, which only groaned now, beyond anything stronger.

He said, "You have toyed with the aristocracy of Hell. For this you must hereafter expect, while alive, inimitable horror and immeasurable torment..."

"I've known plenty of those, Sunshine. Oh, sure, I'm certain you people can do it much better. But so what? If you tear me in pieces, you'll only kill me quicker. I can promise you, the mess my body's already in, I can't stand up to much. Hurt and harrow me, I'll die at a rate of knots. And if that happens, surely you'll be turning me into a kind of martyr? Which will fast-track my entry to Heaven. That's fine by me. I mean it. Please. Be my guest."

The Demon turned his back.

In his back was Emptiness.

The room too was empty. The world.

Judith stood alone, trembling with mad happiness. Her apartment stank of brimstone.

Presently she stepped out of the circle.

For a second she waited, wondering if imps would hail immediately upon her. Unfortunately, she thought, they almost certainly wouldn't demean themselves any further. She'd be left alone to drag out the rest of her short but awful life in the normal human way.

Judith returned to the window. Looking up through fog, she saw the moon drift in cloud, pale as an angel. It was years since she had noticed the beauty of the moon. Or of anything much. Perhaps her concluding time on earth could be used to do just that.

"I have one," Judith murmured, "I have a soul. *Why sell* it if I *have* it? Why give up eternity for a few hundred, a few thousand years? No sale," said the woman. "*Souled.*"

The Heart of Ice

A casual but fine piece of artwork by a friend, the very portrait of the beauty described at the tale's beginning, caused this story to evolve. Though unluckily the art couldn't be used as an illo in the black-and-white-only magazine that first published it. In a very odd way, I myself detect the influence of Hans Andersen, too. Less through the icy cruelty of his Snow Queen, than his crystalline snowscapes, the sense of otherwhere inextricably tangled in the everyday, and if loneliness – also self-collection.

Oh, the Ice Maiden. He has been hearing of her since he can remember. Her dark and coiling hair with the gleam in it of blue-green coal, her jewellery of icicles, her eyes that are like frost on lapis lazuli. But her skin is warm, the colour of honey, which from a distance can make her for an instant seem almost human. She dresses in the pale furs of winter beasts which she charms from their backs, leaving them naked but for shivery flesh and bones in the bitter cold. And then she clothes them instead in ice and they become ice-creatures, and her servants.

Nirsen worked in the town. He had been apprenticed at five years of age to the Kuldhoddr, who with his boys bought the unwanted things of the townspeople and hauled them to his yard, where they were sorted and turned into other things – such as broken pots into filling for wall-building, or spoilt furniture into firewood, or old garments into rags – and resold. Nirsen was by now nineteen and this was all the life he knew, the town life of buying, sorting, smashing, chopping, tearing, and so on. He knew the shabby house of the Kuldhoddr, where he slept in a shed off the yard with the other once-boy, now twenty, Jert. This one did not like Nirsen, had bullied him when they were children, and currently sneered and played adult tricks on him. The Kuldhoddr was himself a villain, and his wife a sow. The house, the work, the bad food, the winding narrow self-centred town, the whole of existence, were foul to Nirsen. Even the red-cheeked girls that Jert leered after did not entice him.

Yet beyond the town lay the fields that in summer turned yellow, and in the winter black then white. Out there too lay the stretches of the river that were not choked with muck, but flowed in summer like, ale with strawberry fish in it that in winter froze themselves to pewter. Beyond, the great forest began, ash and birch and pine, and this ran all the way to the distant mountains, far as outer space. And the summer woods were green and the mountains lavender, but in winter both were white and the home of the Ice Maiden.

Where had he heard of her first? Nirsen could not recall, but he must have been a baby then, for it was before the Kuldhoddr bought him (one more thrown-out thing) and clobbered and smashed and thrashed him into a new, more useful article.

Even in the house of the Kuldhoddr, however, the Ice Maiden was spoken of, as a sort of curse – "May the Ysenmaddn take him and hang his skin on her trees!" Or whispered to by the wife as she stirred her filthy soups on the fire: "Don't you be harming my poor fingers, Lady Ice." For it was a fact the wife had had a finger bitten off by the frost one year, and everyone knew the Ice Maiden made the frost. It spun from her blue eyes and dropped from her mouth in her cold sweet breath, but changed to needles and knives in the air. It would paint the round windows prettily over, but if ever the Ysenmaddn caught you out of doors and you could not get away, she kissed you and froze you, and then her frost filmed over your eyes like the windows and blinded or crippled, or you were dead.

Amulets were put up to placate her on half the houses, though it was supposedly a Godly town. These were in the form of little man dolls all in a white spindly mummy-wrapping, like the rime, or they were polished awls, or the long teeth of wolves or foxes or the skull of a white cat or a white owl. She liked white animals best (if she took their coats she made them new ice ones that were whiter.)

Offerings, such as dead hares and round cakes were slung by the forest's edges or along the inner tracks, by hunters and wood-cutters. But few ventured into the trees once snow was down.

And now it was.

The russet town was muddy white, but the fields and forests and the mountains and the sky were whiter, like scrubbed china. And as they ran from smoky hot brazier to brazier at the corners of the streets, the children sang this rhyme:

> *Leave on our hands, Queen of Ice.*
> *Leave on our feet, Queen of Ice.*
> *Leave on our noses, Queen of Ice.*
> *Yet take it all and leave us life –*
> *Such a small price, such a small price.*

One freezing night Nirsen went to the tavern on Killfox Street and drank a couple of cups. He spoke to no one, liking no one. As for the tavern girls, he turned his face away, and then they called him names – High Nose, Little Cockerel. He had never been with any of them. They loathed him like an alien, as if he had two horns growing out of his head. But the drink was comforting.

When he got back he entered the yard beside the Kuldhoddr's house. The Kuldhoddr was away at the other end of the town, bargaining and drinking with some merchants. In the kitchen window smeared a tiny orange chink of light. Nirsen rapped softly on the door. The idea of the fire's embers appealed before he slunk to the shed.

When no one answered, he slipped the latch.

Inside the kitchen, ah now. The sow wife was riding with Jert, and each of them grunted and moaned in pleasure. Nirsen felt sick, for he hated them both as they him, yet too they broke his heart, poor things, trying to find joy in the glacial heart of winter and unkindness. He would have gone away and said nothing.

But Jert on some sudden impulse turned from his work and learned he and the wife had been seen.

He shambled up, pulling his clothes together, his face already a clenched fist.

"You," was all he said. But the single word was a malediction.

Then he sprang and Nirsen fell back on the stone floor under the weight of him.

There they struggled, and in the background the dishevelled, nine-fingered woman babbled, and then she grew utterly quiet and a shadow splayed over the fighters which smelled of ale and said, "What's this?"

Both Jert and Nirsen were bloody but Nirsen had perhaps had the worst of it. He was lighter, and anyway Jert was accustomed to fighting.

It was Jert who rose and, with the wife whimpering behind him, he exclaimed, "She screamed out so I come running. He was at her, had her down, and Mrs trying to beat him off and calling for you. Hadn't I come in he'd have done her, your wife."

Nirsen lay stupidly marvelling at Jert's ingenuity, and heard the woman say, "It's true. Ruined I'd have been, you off at your business. But Jert was our friend and saved me."

After which the Kuldhoddr leaned right the way down to the kitchen floor, and he lifted Nirsen up from it with a curious sort of tenderness, all the time peering into his face. The Kuldhoddr did not ask what Nirsen had to say on any of this. Nor did the Kuldhoddr pass any comment. About a minute after he slammed his fist twice into Nirsen, at the heart and at the jaw, and everything collapsed in a storm of black pain and roaring.

When he came to, Nirsen did not know immediately where he was. He had been somewhere similar during the summer, for occasionally in the long fine evenings he would walk out to the edges of the fields, sit on the grass of the pasture and watch the fringes of the forest, where rabbits and squirrels and birds darted in the last westered sunlight. But he had never been out here in winter. Few ever were. It was another country now.

And in the land of full winter, here he lay, and much closer to the wood indeed. Over his very head arched the first deep ranks of the trees, the ash and birch with thick foliage of white snow, and the tall pines and firs beyond, crystallised. Glass beads and pipes and strands of ice had spun all the trees together too. The forest hung now inside the web of some giant ice-spider. Darkness was coming, the sky cold lead, and a thin wind whistled through the forest's avenues.

Nirsen understood well enough what had happened while he was helpless. He had been cast out for his supposed crime of attempted rape. There were stories of such punishments as this. No one would have minded. Why harbour the wicked when the winter would see to him?

He found they had bound his hands and his feet in case he should wake and struggle with them, but he had not woken till now. He shifted round to see and one of the cords on his wrists snapped. His hands were not well tied, both Jert and the Kuldhoddr would have been drunk. Besides, the cold made such cheap rope brittle.

Quite soon Nirsen was free. Then he stood up and looked back from the forest towards the town.

How small and murky it was under its huddle of dirty snow and smokes. The bleak fields between, white as starched tablecloths in rich houses, showed only the trample of the two men's feet and the snake-track of Nirsen's body as they had dragged him.

Without warning Nirsen found he had fallen down again. It came to him how hurt he was, also that he must have lain here most of one night and a day unconscious, for it had been before midnight when he reached the yard and now a second night was just starting.

Surely he should be dead? Perhaps he was. His face ached and gnawed where it was struck and his heart felt sometimes as if it stumbled. His hands were almost numb, the fingers too pale, threatening the awful frostbite. He could feel nothing of his feet –

partly the reason he fell. He wore his outdoor clothes but they were not of course of the best. His head was uncovered.

He sat on the white earth under the white trees and the web of the giant spider, and knew if not yet dead still shortly he must be. But he could not go back to the town. Only the forest seemed to offer any shelter. At least it was a better place to perish, cleaner and far more beautiful.

Once again he rose and stamped about until, though no feeling came, yet his balance re-established. Presently he moved forward in among the trees.

Night arrived. The forest sank to dark silver.

As he trudged drearily onward, Nirsen heard the sound of darkness begin, the night chorus of owls and foxes, and once maybe a wolf, for in such weather wolf packs might well run this way. But there were stranger sounds also. He started to hear them and put them down to the sudden cracks of branches broken under the snow's weight; frozen streams that had fissured in the greater tepidity of day and now were sealing shut again; the wind, breathing. But really he knew what they were.

He was entering the kingdom of the Ice Maiden.

Those splinterings were the noise of her mirrors smashing; those murmurs like sealing ice were the resonance of draperies drifting over floors of snow. The clink and hush of the wind was an echo of some music played for her. And there! That sheer light platinum note – oh, that was the Maiden's laughter. Something had amused her tonight. Maybe it was the thought of one more lost outcast stumbling through her world, with Death treading close behind.

Nirsen continued until he could go no further. He was aware that to stop now meant that he must stop living. But finally another footstep became impossible. He took it but never moved. So then he slid down and leaned against the silver stalk of a tree, and watched the forest glowing though no moon had risen, shining from its own deathly whiteness, so the black sky changed to tin threaded with the blue sequins of stars.

But the blue stars were the eyes of the Ysenmaddn. Pitilessly they gazed at him, and yet it was not truly pitiless. How could one like she comprehend that his wretched little existence had been precious to him, or that to lose it was, for him, his greatest tragedy? Go to sleep, he imagined that she whispered through the snow-leaves. Go to sleep like a good child. And only a slight impatient indifference was in her voice. Nothing sinister or cruel. For she had no heart to be heartless with, the Ice Maiden.

An animal crouched over him. This now was what woke him up. He took it for a wolf – perhaps the very beast he had heard earlier in the night. But then his sore eyes, caked with rime, widened and Nirsen saw it was one of her creatures. It was a wolf of ice.

Whiter than any whiteness of the woods, it gleamed with the sleek pure sheen of steel. Every tuft of its pelt was sculpted from ice. Its mask-like face was ice, yet had both expression and potential ferocity, and the profound, solemn wolfish eyes gazed through, the unexpected colour of gold. And then it licked out across its glacial meltless mouth with a living tongue, and he saw its ivory teeth – all that, inside the skin of ice the Ysenmaddn had given it.

The beast will kill me, he thought. He woodenly composed himself, half dead as already he must be, to endure this finish as best he could

But the wolf only touched his cheek with its rock-hard freeze of muzzle, then raised its head. The howl raked the forest, the sky. The stars shook but did not fall.

Then the others drew near. Nirsen, in his deathly trance, watched. Not for an instant did he reckon he dreamed any of this. There were the two ermines, now ice-clad, their black markings caught perfect in the white slippery glitter of their coats. There was the albino bear, its thick fur all ice and ruffling and combing back and forth as it moved. Some ice-foxes came and played savagely before him as if to demonstrate that even when nipped or scratched their icy overlay was not disturbed. Ice-rats bustled from between the claws of tree roots and stared with chestnut eyes. Last the white owl floated down, silent as a single white feather, and settled on his boot, regarding him from its own round eyes which, in that moment, reminded him oddly of the pale lemon faces of two clocks that showed time had ceased.

Maybe he lapsed; it was like sleep but was it only death? Yet then once more he was woken and he was being dragged again, as his two human enemies had dragged him from the town. Now it was the wolf and the bear that pulled him, their taloned nails, their teeth, fastened in his clothing. The foxes pushed at him. The rats ran by and across him like overseers, and the ermines padded like bodyguards at his sides. The owl flew above them. He observed its metallic solidity passing along weightless just below the web of white quartz branches. Its wings hypnotised him: every feather chiselled from ice –

Nirsen sensed the earth under his body turning toward morning. He did not grasp what that could be, for he had had no education and did not know it was the earth which turned, as he had never seen that, only the sun rising or going down.

The bear it was who alone hauled him the last distance, bundling him across huge roots that slammed his spine like hammers, so this beating seemed far more brutal than anything Jert or the Kuldhoddr had done to him.

By then a sort of mist or smoke was lifting from the ground. It was like breath on a mirror, and through it the embroidered boughs of the great trees had been unstitched. A view opened. A lake spread before him. It was frozen to alabaster, save now and then you saw thinner places that dully glimmed. In the middle of the lake something rose up.

The bear dropped Nirsen. From behind, the wolf now was pushing at him. He found he had sat up.

The mist rippled and somewhere near a flower-pink stain was seeping: dawn sharpened the scene of the frozen lake, and so Nirsen saw the palace of the Ice Maiden standing at the lake's centre.

It was like a vast crystal goblet, and filled with a fizzing champagne light.

He thought, flatly, Well, I have seen it. It exists. Hadn't I come here I should have missed it. At least this I've done.

But then he glimpsed the sled of ice that had appeared on the lid of the lake, and how by itself it glided to the shore. The bear with a grumbling curdle of a growl rolled him over on to the sled. How cold the sled was, far colder than the snow. It seared him and he did not care. He would be dead before he reached the palace. Good, good, that was good.

There are chimes all through the house of the Ice Maiden. They depend from all the high, high walls under the wide sky, for here there is no roof. The snow never falls here, or if it does it becomes simply part of everything else – a curtain, a screen, a mosaic. But the chimes chime with a fearful tinsel deliciousness. It is like sucking raw icing-sugar to hear them. They please, but they sting.

There are no windows. The entire edifice is transparent. Any who are inside can always see out. Yet from the outside nothing can be seen within but for the lumination of the enormous chandeliers. These stretch from the roofless spaces above until they reach the floors that are perhaps a quarter of a mile below. Prisms and slender opal pillars comprise the chandeliers, and they convey a candleshine that has no candles, nor, night or day, do they go out.

These floors of the Ice Maiden are laid with circular tiles, each of which is the top of a human skull, remorselessly waxed and rubbed so slim it has become impervious and will magically carry any weight. Who – what – then rubbed them? The refining winter wind, who is never afraid of the prolonged harsh work of brooming, beating, scouring.

There are ice cisterns set in the bone floors where fish, scaled in ice, swim and frisk over little pebbles like polished zircons, which possibly they are.

Then the Ice Maiden comes in.

She is attended by invisible or partly visible beings that are wind-spirits, frothy flurries of light snow, or beasts which have died and become themselves bones, but that still want to remain with her nevertheless.

She is as they say she is. Her skin is like honey, and from a reasonable way off she looks almost like a young mortal woman. Her hair is wavy and darkest blue – that might also seem pale black until you look carefully. She is crowned with a diadem of ice. Her garments are white fur. But her ears are like the ears of no human thing, more dainty, pointed, and she wears in them jewels of ice.

Her eyes. Her eyes define and defy everything ever said of them. You believe they may be dark until she looks at you. Then they are blue as lapis, just as all the legends tell, lapis lazuli behind sparkled casements of frost. And they are terrible. For they have no wickedness in them and know no malignity and no wish to deliver pain. But they know nothing of need, nothing of empathy, nothing of the merest momentary kindness, nothing like that. And they never will.

Nirsen has stood up on the floor of impervious skulls. Thinking he is dead now he feels strong and not unwell.

He bows to the Ice Maiden because he knows one must, with royalty, or they will be angry. But too he senses she feels no anger either. To bow is foolish, but he does.

She says nothing to him. Although he has been shown her eyes, if she even really glances at him he is unsure.

Does she credit he is here? Will it matter to her?

A boar that is made of bones nuzzles at her hand. She does nothing, does not respond, yet a mild flame runs through the skeleton of the beast. It is plainly happy and canters round and about, and all its vertebrae twinkle. Each of the others wants to touch her then, and she seems to allow this, for it happens.

Nirsen though would never dare attempt it.

He stands there and stares and listens to the chimes. Is he now her slave? He supposes she does not require slaves, requires nothing.

Even the furs she steals he now suspects are not stolen. Probably they spontaneously fly off to adorn her and then she sighs her fragrant breath and never notices the animals reclad in living ice.

However, since she is there looking at him – or not – and being himself human and a man, in the end he speaks.

"What am I to do, Lady?"

The Ice Maiden answers.

Nirsen lowers his head.

Of course she has replied in her own language. He tries at once to retain and analyse what the words were like. Mostly, he thinks, like the sound of the chimes. He could not and does not understand and doubts he will ever have the means to learn.

Again he speaks. "I'm lost then."

At this, strangely, the faintest glint of something crosses through her gem-stone eyes. But she has no humour, he believes, as no cruelty or compassion. Surely, despite his notion in the forest, she could not be amused.

Besides anyway, this is when she moves on over the long floor between the stalagmite-stalactite chandeliers, her crowd of insubstantial attendants furling round her like a fog. She vanishes somewhere amid the curtains of frost.

Just then Nirsen realises he has regained total feeling in his feet and hands and ears. His throat is moist and does not hurt, the ache in his face has gone. He has, apparently, eaten and drunk, and he is warm. This must be because he is dead, then. But no. Strong and bravely now his heart is beating in his chest.

He goes to the curving side of the glass of the palace and stares out. He sees the long lake and the tangle of the archetypal forest all around. The sky is golden as the eyes of the ice-wolf. When he puts one finger to the palace glass it gives off a delicate note, as a refined goblet would if tapped, say, with a priceless ring.

There is no way out – or in – that he can detect.

If he is a prisoner he doubts, but nor does he have liberty. He checks every so often to be sure he has not become all bones, or is sheathed in ice, like the animals here. But he is only as he always was, there in his growing beard, and his poor clothes that do not suit the palace (as his beard does not) and his whole skin with his heart thumping rudely and healthily away.

After some hours during which he wanders through the veils and partitions of the seemingly endless chambers, he sits again on the skull floor to look out of the window which is wall. Time does seem to have passed in the normal manner, for now it is evening. A flight of winter swans flies over, real birds whose white is plumage not ice.

The sun sets like a red wound, except now he knows it does not set at all. Instead the earth turns backward, away from it. In the cisterns the glistening fish weave patterns and at last he sees they do not swim in water but in liquid silver. Now this scarcely matters. Night enters the palace and the chandeliers burn no more brightly. Spirits appear to shimmer through the air. An owl of flesh and feathers perches high up on the rim of the tall goblet and calls once in its voice like a ghost, before flying away. Can Nirsen sleep? He will try. Ah yes, thank God, he can.

How often does he see the Ice Maiden after that? Does he count? Yes, but then forgets. He forgets.

How can you remember anyway such a visitation? It would be as if a man said I will count up every occasion I see that star appear in the sky.

Sometimes she does seem to pause, and to examine Nirsen for a while. Then, as the days and nights continue, he wonders if he can ask her for something, as in stories the woebegone man does ask the supernatural being to grant his heart's desire. But Nirsen has been trained only in sorting and demolishing rubbish into greater dross. He has learned to have no heart's desire, cannot imagine one. Or else he has simply been too wise to harbour dreams.

Only one more time does he try to talk to her. He says, tentative, "Here then am I, but why then I, not others?"

And as before she seems to reply. But in her own language like chimes and little bells, and ice that deliberately splinters.

Besides, he knows he is alive. His body works almost completely, breathing and letting him see and think and walk or sit, and even sleep. He needs no food or drink, and therefore the other accessory functions to do with digestion do not trouble him either. He is warm. Really it would be an imposition to petition the Ice Maiden for any other thing, particularly an explanation. So then he asks no more, only bows to her and steps aside if she enters a part of her palace where he has taken himself. But frequently, too, she passes high up in the air, moving some way off over the floorless space between the upper tines of the chandeliers, the snow and spirits and skeletal animals dancing round her, affectionate and undemanding.

It reminds him a little of some priest's view of God's Heaven. He had never credited that; it had sounded also boring to Nirsen, for he was used to having to work despite the low and ugly nature of his labour. He is not bored in the palace, however, though he has nothing to do. Indeed he does do something, which is that he goes from area to area of it, and he watches the world outside, that is the abbreviated region of lake and encircling forest, and the sky.

In these he finds astonishing constant metamorphoses. They are like books he can read. He studies all the ways that snow comes, and slight thaws, and dawn and day and sunfall, dusk and night, and clouds, and all the stars and planets, and the moon and sun. The lives of the outer animals that survive he is a student of, and also he sees how two die, one a deer and one a hare, there by the lake's margin. But a while after he notices that the blithe and lively skeletons of a deer and a hare have added themselves to the Ice Maiden's entourage. This puzzles him slightly. So many creatures die in winter, seen or unseen, surely there should be more about her. But then it occurs to him not all the dead would want to come to her. Then the other persistent riddle is sharpened, as to how it is he is here alive. Again, despite all evidence, he wonders if he is.

Whatever else Nirsen, doubting or indifferent, goes on with his scrutiny of the outer world. On certain nights he is so immersed in it he forgets to sleep.

But then there is a night when he does slumber and at daybreak he is wakened by a dreadful noise.

He starts up thinking that at last his heart has cracked in two pieces. But it is the lake that has cracked in twain. Black water bubbles up.

Nirsen notices how the edges of the forest are dripping white, cool tears.

In a day or so colossal ledges of snow slide crashing from the trees. Through a shallow place in the lake he catches sight of iceless bluish fish, swimming and rising to a narrow slot where all the frozen lid has gone. On the boughs above, a fearful reddish glint begins to show like fire during the afternoons. Spring is returning.

That evening a bird of bone, perhaps once a sparrow, flies down through the air layers of the Ice Maiden's palace, and sitting on Nirsen's shoulder it twitters in the startling bird-language of the outer world. Is it warning him? He thinks that it is.

Had he a bag he would pack it. He would be ready. He longs to see her one further time, but she does not appear, and by the hour the moon – no longer white, but having a brazen face – crests the trees, the sparrow has flown away. Not upward among the chandeliers, but out through a tiny flaw in the goblet of the palace.

Nirsen does not risk sleep.

He waits, standing on the floor of skulls.

When the wild crunching and crackling begins he is not surprised. It is grief he feels. As if he must truly die now, or worse, for a fact, be born.

As the walls liquefy and pour in the melting lake, sailing from him in rafts like narrow pearl, the sled is there and he steps on it. It draws him away and away towards the shore.

He stares back. Every bit of the towering crystal of the palace has disappeared.

Of course, where could she go in spring?

Only slowly, as he nears the forest edge, does Nirsen recall the sparrow and wonder if, in the warm weather, the Ice Maiden emerges on to the earth in a different form.

Who then, what then, is she? Is she spring now? Summer next? He cannot understand. Landing on the muddy shore he observes the sled dissolve. The trees are flitting with birds and somewhere in the forest a stag bellows. Like beads small flowers decorate the ground.

Nirsen went away from the lake and, although he did not properly comprehend it, towards the town from which he had been cast out.

He knew no other place to go. It was instinct, or thoughtlessness.

As he trekked through the green lace architraves of the forest, he wondered where the ice-creatures took themselves in warmer weather. Did their pelts thaw too, and proper pelt grow back? Or did they melt altogether, and were there unseen streams of fox and bear, wolf, rat, weasel, owl, under his weary boots?

He hoped not to see their animal masks when he caught his own image in some puddle, nor did he. He looked as ever, but he had never had much interest in himself. The springing leaves spoke in a foreign tongue. Already they discussed him, whispering.

He dreamed of her when he sheltered by night. When he slept between the paws of tree roots or in skull caves beneath canopies of spreading fern. He saw again her amber skin and her icicle eyes. He was no longer frightened of her, if ever he had been. He felt a sort of cold love, but it was not entirely cold, nor love: it had no name.

Six days, five nights before he reached the fields where they were now sowing, and beyond them the huddle-muddle of the town.

How warm the spring was; the fields steamed. As if under the winter smoke the town was shrouded by vapour. He felt time had played tricks on him. He debated whether, as in old tales, he would find the town a hundred years younger than he had left it – or aged five hundred years into a future he could not know.

But reality is sometimes more unusual than myth.

Once in the town, considering events with greater prudence, he was wary, expecting threats or even a further assault. But those that looked at him seemed only suspicious. This struck him more and more as peculiar. They would, reasonably, reckon him dead.

Then a carter halted his load and strode over. "What you at here, stranger?"

Nirsen recalled him. The Kuldhoddr had several times bought things off the man with Nirsen waiting by. The town was not large. Everyone knew everyone to some extent. But not, it seemed, any longer Nirsen. For having muttered something appeasing to the carter and gone on, other similar inquiries came Nirsen's way.

At length, driven, he even sought the gate by the Kuldhoddr's yard – then shrank back as Jert burst suddenly out. But Jert glanced at and passed Nirsen with just a contemptuous thrust and cursing, "Get from the way!"

Nirsen had seen himself in water on the wet earth, and since entering the town in a window or two. He looked as he had always done.

He wandered through the town and out its other side.

On the track beyond he hesitated, considering. The sun punched down a furnace heat yet he did not sweat. The town too had been like a furnace. The breath of the people there had spooled like fog and had smelled of boiling water or cooking meat to him. Here on the track Nirsen found too something had burnt him on the arm. Lifting back his sleeve he saw a great blistering welt as if from a scorch or scald. It was where Jert's hand had pushed him.

There was pasture ahead with some goats.

As Nirsen travelled on, the animals turned one and all to watch him by. Even from the goats waves of heat emanated, and the tang of smouldering grass.

He trudged all day, away from the town and up into some low hills where the ringing hammer blows of the sun on his head were less bearable, but the landscape was empty of human habitation, and therefore of human incandescence.

When night fell he hoped for coolness, but there was not much difference. A full moon rose yellow and blazing, and he sheltered from its fire.

Through the soles of his boots the ground, in sunlight or darkness, flamed against his feet. If he should brush against a tree or shrub, he felt a surge as if warm steam pressed through his clothing. But when after some further days he went by a single hillside cottage, the heat that gushed from it was like dragon's breath. He had to know, and so set one finger's tip to the wall. It did not blister his skin as Jert's touch had done, yet it burned. It was like a pan just off the stove.

For days and nights again Nirsen went on. The spring was flowering into early summer. The heat of the sun and of most things reached a powerful crescendo, extreme and omnipresent. He could not bear it, but then he could. As with so many bad conditions, he grew used to it. Yet where able, he touched nothing with his unprotected skin. Even the coldest streams that ran down from the circling mountains, still fretted by the recent memory of snow, were tepid if he tried them. But he never drank from them, he did not feel thirsty ever, never hungry. He walked, and studied the book of the world. He was not distressed. Nor in any way exalted. In his life always it had been that he had little or less and must additionally put up with diverse troubles. Nothing had altered for him in that way then, though everything else had changed utterly.

Inevitably he was drawn back sooner or later to the forests. The far-as-space mountains were all that lay beyond and he sensed they, though not of man's making, would be torrid as the lava that once had seethed inside them. They were nearer to God too, presumably, being higher up, and certainly nearer the sun. These features must ensure they were, for Nirsen, killing hot.

Deep in the summer woods he discovered a rock cave. Chill moss smoked with warmth above an icy little stream softly warm as a bath. Here Nirsen took up residence.

Throughout the season he observed the plants and animals. He would sit all day, all night, as he had done on the skull floor of the Ysenmaddn, reading from the forest's pages.

Autumn-fall transmuted the metal of the woods to copper and bronze, and then the cold blew in wild sweet breaths. As the pines put on their white armour, of course he thought of the wide table of the lake. He thought of the palace of glass. He would never seek it save in his mind. He could no more return there than into yesterday.

But as the winter gathered, for Nirsen true spring had come, the time of plenty and of ease.

There in his hollow Nirsen lived a long, long life. He seldom stirred from his place, not needing to. Perhaps instead the beasts of the forest, undisturbed by his immobility, carried on their own existences not an arm's reach from him. Perhaps in the core of winter even the ice-beasts came, her creatures, to prowl around the cave, to lick his fingers with pliable cold tongues, to show him things or tell him things, for maybe he learned their language after all of necessity, just as he had, that way, once learned his own. Did the skeleton sparrow sit on a bough, or on his shoulder, and twitter to him and teach him also the secret tongue of birds and bones?

For sure, he never saw her again, the Ice Maiden, save in dreams and thoughts.

But two others saw her once, for the briefest moment, many decades later, and that was because of Nirsen.

It was summer by then, yet some hundred years or more from Nirsen's youth. The two fellows who forged through the forest were not oppressed by the sun at all; they liked it and boasted of it, as if they themselves had invented it, lit it and hung it up on a string to please the world.

But it was a hot enough day, and coming to a shady spot where a stream trickled from a cave, they sat down to eat their midday snack.

"That tree there," said one, pointing with his knife, "that we'll have over for the merchant's fancy door."

They were wood-cutters, sizing up the woods to choose things to slaughter for the use of their town.

The other grunted. But then he said, "That cave-hole there, that's gloomy-chill enough. We might find some rare, tasty fungus along in there for the stew."

So when they had eaten, they got up and went over the bank and stood gawping in at the cave.

Cold enough? Oh yes. The cave was very cold. It was a hole back into winter, black and shining with the mail-coat of ancient ice, and spears and daggers of ice pointing downward from its ceiling, dense as iron. Even the stream was frozen over, only thawing once it had escaped the cave.

"I never saw summer such like that," said the older woodsman, "in all my born days."

"Look there," said the other hoarsely, "what's that?"

The bolder older man went in. He leaned forward and beheld a heap of human bones and a human skull sat on top of them. He was not afraid of the dead. He did not understand what dead was, and that it might affect him ever seemed unlikely. And so peering shamelessly through the bones he saw another thing, and, curious, he bent to pick it up. "See here this lying in the middle. It's a chunk of slate, and a picture on it."

But the other would not go in, and then the old man drew the lump of slate from among the toppled bones and brought it outside, into the sunshine.

That way both men saw the picture fashioned on the slate. This was of a beautiful young woman with dark, bluish-greenish locks of hair, and a honey skin, and azure lips, and eyes like the blue icy shadows that gleam behind the face of the winter moon. By this era the stories of an Ice Maiden had been forgotten, or had chameleonised into some other legend, and the wood-cutters did not know what they saw. And it was only for a second anyway that they had the chance to look at it. For abruptly the old wood-cutter let out a yelp and dropped the slate, on which the image of the Ice Maiden was imprinted, down on the earth, where it shattered in a thousand fragments. "So cold – cold as the frost and ice it burnt me…"

And muttering oaths and prayers they hurried away, even sparing the tree they had meant to fell. The older man's hand would carry the scar to the day of his death. But the shattered slate had not been slate.

It was Nirsen's heart.

Magpied

(Translated from the Germanic-Alurguric Poem of the Same Name)

His clothes were those of the magpie –
Black and white.
He entered the town with the brown sky
Of first night.

The traveller, in garments of white and black, enters the elegant and stone-built town at evening, but discovers the streets are full of rowdy youths and children, running and shrieking, drinking alcohol copiously, and doing battle with each other. Unable to pass through the pack, and sometimes receiving blows, he stands staring:

Like casques and masks, lacking all mind,
Their faces.
So much red-pride-flushed and drunk-gushed blind.
No traces

Were there, of care, or sanity,
Living shells -
Unlike births of Man, humanity;
These - From hells.

A man then rushes out of a house, and drags the traveller back inside with him, locking the door once they are within. He warns the traveller that these young persons rule the town after sunset, breaking into stores for purposes of robbery, hunting for stray older people in order to attack them; vomiting on the roadway:

You, stranger, such danger were in
On the street,
The hordes of these young - you among - spin
And retreat!
Beware of their arrogant slights,
Dirty words,
Their scuffles, each trick, broadcast sick, fights,
Scattered turds.

Tanith Lee

The traveller remains that night in the comparative safety of the man's house, whose windows – as are all those in the town – are shuttered up after dark.

Sleep though is constantly disturbed by the screams and yowls of the young outside. And once some of the creatures get up on the roof, hurling first stones, then faeces down the chimney – a regular urban occurrence, his host assures the traveller.

The next morning:

> *When pale the sail of the dawn rose,*
> *Fair and gold,*
> *They broke the first fast, tumult passed; close*
> *The host told,*
>
> *In low tones, slow, how the anthem*
> *To loved boys*
> *And girls - as if royal - did so spoil them*
> *They to noise*
>
> *Went, vile deeds, while – in enough time –*
> *They ruled all,*
> *And nightmared each night, till new light climb*
> *The day's wall.*

By day the young, it seems, sleep off their excesses in various purloined roosts. None go home, for which their former parents and guardians are very grateful. A modicum of business and normal life resumes in the town daily, but interrupted always by the necessity of cleaning the streets and byways of the stinking mess in which the town's children nightly have left them.

At the traveller's request, his host then takes him to the house of the Mayor. This fellow, to begin with, makes excuses, but in the end breaks down and weeps. Hundreds of adults gather, also in tears. From adoring them, the townsfolk have come to hate, loathe, dread and be terrified of their young. They have been driven half mad and have no idea any more what to do.

The traveller then, flexing the snow and ebony magpie wings of his sleeves, makes the Mayor and the townspeople an offer.

He can play upon a magical pipe and:

> *This reed with speed, such is its sway,*
> *Will subdue,*

And mesh in a net like a debt they
That harm you.

To wit, each chit and child uncouth,
Snared in steel,
And locked as in jail, each most bale youth,
Till earth reel.

For some subsequent hours the town debates with itself a dilemma many parents must perhaps, now and then, acknowledge, whether they wish their offspring good or ill – or elsewhere entirely, and forever.

But eventually the sun tilts towards the west, the sky flames, and bothering sounds once more start to filter up from round about, reminiscent of wild beasts waking. Although it is a fact *no* beast, however maddened or savage, can approach – let alone surpass – the sometime evils of mankind.

Then the townsfolk hurry to the magpie traveller and entreat him, giving over everything into his hands – before once again dashing into their homes, putting the boards and shutters up at their windows, and bolting fast their doors.

Left alone upon the thoroughfare the piper, standing then in the evening's final rays, seems not quite as he has been. He is taller, perhaps, and his face less evident, and his garments both blacker and more white, while in his hand, the pipe he has spoken of gleams with a thin and silvery sheen, though it was surely only of wood, and nothing at all special in its looks:

Then lout and loutess, ever quick,
In a crowd,
Come armed with their flasks and dark tasks sick,
Laughing loud.

Nevertheless, immediately, before even the road is properly filled up by the horde, a peculiar music commences:

So soft that often, sure, none hears,
Faint as sighs,
Yet thundered like drums, still it comes; ears
Burn – and eyes.

Each walk all talk has lost; all sound

Now quite done.
A massive full tide, vast miles wide, ground
And air – one.

Those that squint through shutter-cracks or keyholes *hear* and *see* a miraculous gleaming, which accumulates. And they see too, how the demonic young are instantly snared inside it – as promised – and made and *kept* dumb. There they stand, unvocal and motionless, unprotesting, gazing and gaping like things mesmerised by the glare of a colossal snake, or some unthinkable sorcerous spell, which supposedly it *is*.

And when the magpie traveller, the piper piping on, moves off and up the street, the horde parts to let him by, as never would they, or have they for years, any creature other than themselves. And when he *has* passed by, stupefied as somnambulists, they troop after him. They do not speak or call, they do not screech or fight or throw up their drink. There is no upheaval. Only the flagons and bottles fall from their hands and bleed stolen liquor on the lane.

So, as the shadings of night begin to seal the avenues, the town's children ebb away after the piper, away through the town and out of it, up into the high hills beyond:

The skies, their size with darkness lave,
Fill the jar
Of town, closing black, front to back, save
Just one star.

Void is all this, and no last noise,
Single form,
No roaring girls reign, no profane boys.
Speechless storm.

The troublesome young are never seen again. Never heard of. They have vanished, like dried rain, or blown dust. Not even a chip of bone, not a footprint, to mark their passing, or their *being*. Only the dropped flasks for a while spilling wine.

Perhaps there are maybe one, or three, nine or thirteen children left, sons, daughters. But these are those who never went out to join the nasty revels. *These* would drink socially among their own families, indoors, and sing there, or read, or discuss proper matters, properly; unusual children, old beyond their years and having, perhaps, parents more than usually loveable.

After the filthy sea of the miscreants is gone, these few thirteen or so children and young people are respected and reverenced in lieu of the rest. They are held up as examples, and accept this modestly, and kindly.

As for any of the adults who thereafter pine again to produce offspring, they guard sternly against the desire, saying it is a brutish one, and they are not "mere" animals, and will resist. Which they do. Instead they breed and adopt intelligent and pretty rats, whose playfulness, geniality, and warm fur entirely satisfy any parental urge:

> *With red and bred black coats, or white,*
> *They give joy,*
> *And yearning hearts fill through furred skill, bright*
> *Rat-girl, – boy.*

As for the Magpie, the traveller, the piper, he too is never heard nor seen there again. Except in legend, or the mind's eye. *Yet....*

> *Well hid; where did he send clod, bitch,*
> *To their doom?*
> *To some cliffs high brink? The sea's sink? Which*
> *Unworld tomb?*

Or to a new world, tolerant
Of vile youth.
To hearts, much too wise more to prize rant –
Than love truth.

> *For where – foul, fair – is childhood lured,*
> *By what? – Fuss?*
> *Or pipe's shadow sob, perhaps obscured:*
> *Jealous, us?*

Centuries after, it seems, when taxed by other communities on the disappearance of its children, the town lied, and blamed an itinerant, magpied piper, who – they said – had spirited the perfect youth of the place away, from sheer meanness.

But it is a fact, they still love their rats the best.

The Waters of Sorrow

(Parallel Earth: Age of Steam)

The dead live in the trees. But in winter, when the trees are bare, the dead go down after the fallen leaves, into the waters, and hide there, in the glowing dark.

The dead are cruel. They have reasons to be.

And they dance.

Back in the old days, when some of us were children, and some, of course, not yet born, the only boats on the River were the kind with paddle and sail. But for a while now we have had the levisteamers, which travel two or three feet above the River's surface, with only their steel 'sippers' trailing down in it to suck up wet fuel for the fired pod. And the long trails of white steam go fluffing out behind them, like the feathers of a swan in moult.

When the first few of these craft appeared, they were a marvel. Folk would take a special journey to the shore to watch them go by. Some still swear the wide River grew wider, and its water grew darker green, because of the constant churning. Others tell you they have eaten fresh, hot steam-cooked fish straight from the water. Certainly, the birds that use the riverbank roost higher up. But in half a dozen years anyway, we had a handful of steam-chariots too on the inland tracks, and now and then a pretty coloured balloon-pod would sail across the sky.

It was about then that the levisteam showboat came down the River.

She was a lovely sight, the boat, green and gold and polished up like a medal. No matter she had an unlucky name.

The *Vilya* she was called. After all those girls who die of broken hearts, when their lovers betray or abandon them, those dead girls who live in the trees or the waters, and come out on certain nights of the year to catch men – any man – since to any vilya, by that hour of their living hating death, any man may have been a traitor to all or any woman. And they lure him, with their weird dead beauty, to dance, until his own heart, or his lungs, go out and he dies. Or else they cast him under the River. There were and are stories even now of a particular lady, daughter of a rich businessman in the steam-power trade. Her name was Myrra, for that Biblical ointment of mourning. He gave her the name as an ignorant fancy, it would seem, but it turned out a prophecy too, because her lover jilted her two days before their wedding, and she broke her own heart – by driving a dagger through it. Five or fifteen years after, depending on who tells the tale, the wrongdoer strayed back to his former haunts. And one midnight, as he smoked his cigar in the woods, she found him, Myrra. Beautiful and unhuman and terrible she must have seemed to him, with her long, uncombed hair and flimsy garment, and her skin, white as the live-dead ancient moon, staring at him from them. She made him dance too, dance till he fell into the River, where she and her fellow vilyas drowned him, but very slowly, they say, very, very slowly.

Even today you can find entirely blameless men who will refuse to leave their homes, be they mansion or hut; they will not set one foot out of doors on such nights when the moon is full. But nowadays they are generally old men, who remember when the River was empty of steam traffic, and only horse-carts and carriages on the roads, and birds to cross the sky.

It was becoming respectable for women to go the theatre without male escort, providing they did not go singly. So Ghisla slipped on to the showboat with a bevy of other young women, as if she were part of their group. They were strangers though and she quite alone. She was nervous, yet eager. She had heard of the play from her mother's customers at the haberdashery shop in the town. Due to the shop as well, Ghisla had been able to kit herself out quite nicely, in a plain white gown, hair combs and proper gloves. It was a warm night, and all along the track to the River, the crickets were tuning up like tiny violins. Set up by the *Vilya's* stage hands, coloured lanterns lit the trees.

"Such an exotic name for the boat," the gossips had cried. "*Vilya!* My goodness. But *he* is exotic, everyone knows that, the *Prince*."

As she wrapped their ribbons and stockings, Ghisla had listened. She was sixteen, quite tall, and slender as a reed, graceful too, which she somehow realised without naming it to herself, let alone ever having had anyone tell her. Her mother certainly never told Ghisla such things. What Ghisla must aim for, her mother always said, was to be virtuous, polite, modest, and hardworking. She must help her mother, who herself had toiled so ceaselessly she had aged in looks, voice and personality to an embittered crone of sixty by the time she was thirty-three. But the mother's husband had died of coughing fits when Ghisla was only seven years old. Another betrayer, Ghisla's father, heartlessly running off with death like that, and leaving the pair of them to cope as best they could.

Ghisla's hair was very black and silky. She had put it up on her head with the four green combs to support it. Her eyes were that kind of brown that looks like jet at dusk or by moonlight, but under sun or a lamp go the colour of Amontillado sherry with a dash of gold in it.

The exhausted mother was already in her bed by the time Ghisla left their little apartment behind the shop. But light lingered in the sky, it was not yet nine o'clock and the show began late. When Ghisla reached the River and went up the broad gang-plank just behind the other girls, the air and the water were like pale amber. But on the boat, and seated in the gilded gallery's front row, only the steam lamps shone, and outside darkness fell swiftly. It was like being in a cradle too. The boat, now grounded on water, rocked softly at her moorings. Which made Ghisla a little giddy, but she did not mind.

Then the lights went down, and the stage burned up, and out he came, to great applause, the actor-manager they called the 'Prince'. His name in fact was Lutz Alvarek. His hair was long, ice-blond-white, and his eyes were of a clear, gleaming glacial blue, like a blue topaz. Tanned by the summer, and accented by his stage make-up, he was fit to knock anyone else's eyes quite out. He stood there in his elegant costume and welcomed his audience, and they clapped and cheered, and the women sighed. The drama was to be a play known as *To Hunt the Hidden Sword*. But the showboat had brought to it one further startling element. The main female character, a *femme fatale* of enormous beauty and treachery, Bithida, was played in this version by a steam mannequin, a life-size doll run on fire, water and clockwork. It was able to move and to make a variety of gesturings, although an actress must supply the voice from the wings.

The novelty of the doll was what had brought Ghisla to the boat. She was yet child enough, you see, and had possessed no doll since her father's death. For the past week, she had offered extra assistance to customers – sewing on lace, replacing buttons – and kept back the payment for her ticket. True, she had felt guilty about this, but only in a vague and childish way, which now she put aside. She had had great practice in doing so, since her mother had always made a point of ensuring Ghisla would suffer guilt whenever possible.

When Prince Lutz appeared and then went away again, Ghisla still longed to see the moving doll. But also, with a peremptory and sore desire, to see again Prince Lutz. Unlike guilt, in her deprived existence, she had never before experienced such a feeling.

Perhaps you will believe that, even when he instantly appeared once more in the thick of the play, and her heart leapt up as if it had caught fire, even then she did not realise she had fallen in love at first sight with him. She had never seen a man like him, obviously, had no chance to. And he was very wonderful to behold, Prince Lutz Alvarek, anyone will tell you that.

The play went on, with some intervals, quite a time. But it was full of sensation – poisonings, stabbings, the lurid uncovering of secrets – only its high moral tone had made permissible giving it a public airing at all.

Perhaps Ghisla was bemused. Or did she properly notice the dramatic events? Bithida the doll was herself very captivating, though in the end rather disappointing. Not least because clouds of steam tended to furl out of her whenever movement was required. Beyond the doll's initial entrance, and one subsequent exit, her motion was soon limited to slow turns of the head, wafting gestures of the hands, and the occasional blink of two cobalt eyes.

The audience thrilled to everything, however. The atmosphere buzzed and sparkled, cheers, groans and involuntary oaths scorched to the roof, and echoed out into the riverine night, where the lanterns by now guttered, and only golden and crimson fireflies spangled the trees.

But in the end the play finished, as all plays, and all things, eventually do.

By then, you might imagine, Ghisla was wrung out, in a sort of trance or dream. Not *wanting* the play to have ended, of course, for then he too would vanish from the stage and from the world. Without thought even, she grew aware that then – now – this inexplicable joy, somehow caused only by him, would leave her with him. Surely, surely, she did now grasp that what she felt was love – or was this fact unavailable to her, poor girl? Had it not seemed to her that, during the concluding act, he had looked up into her eyes very often, held her gaze which, in any case, could not look away from his, even if his eyes were blue lightning, or shards of silver glass... But all her usual dreary and meaningless existence was crowding back to her, smoking over her heart and mind, as she sat alone on the gilt gallery, and the mass of other theatre-goers ebbed, like the dry ice and steam, away into the bar, and so into the firefly dark, returning to all their own realities, arduous or horrible or sweet. And when the last of them had gone, and the last internal lamp was fading, as if fading too, still Ghisla sat there. She must have forgotten how to stand up and independently move. Or, like steam-driven Bithida, was restricted from anything more than the slow turn of her head, meaningless flick of her hand, the infrequent blinking of her eyes.

Prince Lutz turned himself to find Heine in the doorway of the dressing-cabin.

"They say there's a young woman sitting up in the gallery still."

To Heine's curiosity, Lutz Alvarek, who had sloughed his make-up, paled. "*Where* on the gallery?"

"At the very front... that pretty one with dark hair and the white dress. Maybe you noted her. Oh, no doubt you did, Lutz, knowing you."

"You know nothing about me, Heine," said Lutz, in the cold and arrogant manner he could suddenly adopt, often taking his fellow actors by surprise. Though they failed to like these turns in him, they checked at the signal, for he was not only their star but their banker, and mostly they had no wish to anger him.

"I meant no offence, Prince."

"Good. Then tell me why she's there."

"Ermelind says she thinks the girl may be unwell..."

"In God's name..." said Lutz. Next moment he was out of the cabin and running up the ladder to the higher decks. Doing that, he heard the low thrum of the boat's pod, and too the whispery drinking of its sipper-tube, working now in the black River below. But reaching the upper levels, where such noises were less, they were with him still. He knew then it was the tension in him. For he had indeed noted the girl on the gallery. Once or twice during the performance, he had looked steadily straight into her eyes. It was not the first time, naturally, he had ever done such a thing. Maybe seldom with such purpose. But she was so young. So fragile. What had befallen her?

By now it was well after midnight, nearer one in the morning. The smoke-cloud of her mean life had completed its re-conquest of Ghisla.

She had stood up, bemused and uncertain still, but able to move, able to leave the boat with the strange unlucky name, to pick her way back along the black, wooded bank, to reach the town streets and the loveless apartment behind her mother's shop, slip into her cramped and loveless bed, into her loveless and unlovely place in the real world.

As she went up the gallery towards the exit, a man's tall figure abruptly filled the doorway.

Ghisla stopped. She felt a little sad twinge of fear. She had stayed too long, was in the wrong, as always, and would now be scolded and abused. Perhaps even she had broken the law...

"My God," he said, "in this dark you seem... Are you a ghost?"

For a second, she did not know who spoke to her. Or she did, surely? Yes, she must have done, that marvellous voice of his that had filled her ears for three hours and more.

She became less fearful. More terrified. She said nothing. Was afraid to speak.

And then he stood directly in front of her, so much taller than she, and still in the flamboyant clothes he had worn for the play. He carried a scent too of the stage – the steamy footlights, the metal doll, the grease-paint and candlewax, sawdust and fire.

She looked up into his face and his pale gem-stone eyes burned out of it, as they had from the flamelit stage.

"Oh," she said. "It's you." Mundane words, such as might be spoken by handmaidens, when a dead god rose and appeared before them, and was known.

"Yes. And it is *you*. Are you well?"

"Oh, yes... no..."

And what indeed was she, this young girl, that no one had ever spoken to in such a caressive, meaning-filled way, that nobody ever asked of whether she was well or not, or if she was a ghost, that nobody had ever greeted with such evident ardour:

It is *you*. *You*.

Prince Lutz led her quietly out, across the darkened and vacant bar. Elsewhere, the other actors, the stage-hands and boatmen, held their own follies, a dim rumble of noises, chink of bottles; while the sipper sipped the River, and the River rocked the boat gently, so he caught the girl's arm to steady her. And as they moved on across the scene-shifting half-light, under the beam of a single lamp on deck, he saw her face, her neck and shoulders, her piled-up hair with its River-green combs, her eyes now cool black, now the warm of copper and bronze. He halted her there, in that soft beam, and said, so softly to her, "How beautiful you are. More beautiful even than I thought you from the stage. I've been waiting for you a long while. Did you know that? No? Well, my love, now you do."

And now she did.

The dead live in the trees, or in the waters. No doubt they watch the final scene of this First Act.

It occurs about three in the morning, there in the darkness of the wooded bank, some way upstream from where the golden showboat *Vilya* is anchored.

There is a rustling and snapping to begin with, a sound of torn cloth and small tearing branches, undergrowth that is trampled, however lightly. And breathing, fast respiratory stabs.

And then the white figure appears, with a flurry of combless undone hair, like new tearings from the material of the night. Straight to the brink of the bank, the brink of the River she runs, the young woman in her torn white dress. And then she stands quite motionless as if, all over again, she has forgotten movement, even – now – how to flex her wrists or turn her head.

Tears stream from her eyes.

She stands there on the brink, holding her hands like frozen steel against her breasts, weeping, her emotion so colossal it seems she smiles or laughs. And then a spasm of movement after all quakes all through her, and her eyes shut. Weightless as a swan's feather, she drifts over from the bank and falls floatingly into the dark below. Which opens like many pale arms, unearthly out of the black, receiving her, drawing her in and down to sanctuary and oblivion.

They know. Those ones who have dropped down here before. The girls betrayed, the girls like Myrra, they know how the heart breaks, and the taste of deep water.

Only ripples then, only silence then. It never changes, in the end, the way we mislay things in the dark.

Lutz Alvarek came back to the town and to the River five years later. He travelled firstly down to the city in his big steamwheeler car, that had once been painted and trimmed, green and gold, like the *Vilya*, but which by now was plain black and chrome. At the city, he stabled the 'wheeler and, with just twenty others, boarded the steambus, that old panting rattler only some of us anymore remember; she was nicknamed Puffing Pankra.

Alvarek did all that to avoid too much notice in the town. Then it was a small place still, and quiet.

Probably some of us did recall Prince Lutz. No doubt a number of the women did, would you say, those who watched him on the showboat. But by then too *Vilya* was long gone with Alvarek's former employee, Heine. Some people said that Heine was gifted the *Vilya* by Lutz, to keep Heine dumb about something or other, though this gossip had never come so far as the town. In any event, even without his boat, Lutz had kept his career all glowing bright. He had stayed a success, a great actor many claimed, and he was as handsome as he ever had been, they said too, even the ones who reckoned he had committed some crime. But we need to remember anyway, he was only twenty-two years of age on his earlier visit. And now he was only twenty-seven.

It seemed he went first of all to the registrar's office, but why and for what nobody guessed. And then, very oddly, he turned down one of the town's curling streets and fetched up by, of all unlikely spots, a haberdashery.

"I was never so astonished," said the lady who now ruled the shop. She had had to explain to Prince Lutz also that the former owner had sold up and gone away five years before. "I said, it was after her daughter died so young, poor little Ghisla who fell in the River and was drowned." But Prince Lutz had brushed that aside, rather callously, the present shop owner decided: "which was peculiar, since until then he was the perfect gentleman. A lovely handsome man he was, though," she added. "And he was nicer again presently, and asked me a question or two. I confess, I watched him as he strode off up the street."

It was a fact Ghisla's mother had sold this woman the shop. Ghisla's mother had been mourning the loss of her bond-slave Ghisla, without whom she could not, she said repeatedly and bitterly, manage. No one knew where Ghisla's mother had since taken herself, and perhaps nobody cared.

Lutz spent little more time in the town. He went off into the country land beyond. The ones who had identified him wondered why he had come back, and hoped he might be going to stage another drama there. But he never did that. It was the last any of them saw of him.

There had been a scene with Heine, however, all those long short five years before.

It happened on the night following the night already described – that night when Prince Lutz and Ghisla met in the theatrical afterdark.

The next evening's performance was once more done, but it had ended earlier on this second night, around eleven, owing to a mechanical failure of the steam doll Bithida, which had needed improvising over.

Everything settled, and the patrons having left, most of them not realising they had missed anything much – the actors sat about the public bar to toast their genius on pulling the occasion through. And it was then that Ermelind gave up her news. Did they know, she asked, a town girl had gone missing, that very pretty one who had lingered on the gallery after yesterday night's show? It seemed her name was Ghisla. At which, another of the players cried did *Ermelind* not know the poor girl's body had been found this evening, in the River further upstream. She was drowned dead as a stone.

Possibly, Heine glanced round at that point, to see if the Prince reacted at all. If so, Heine was rewarded. For Lutz, even *under* his make-up now, had gone white as a cleaned bone. Then, getting up without a word, Lutz walked quickly from the bar.

Until then, he had been his usual self, better than ever maybe. But most of them were trained to his sudden moods, as mentioned. Heine as well, but this time he too rose, and went to see where the Prince was heading, and what the Prince might do there.

Heine found him soon enough. Lutz had reached the ladder to the underdecks but not got on to it. Instead he lay, slumped against the inner ribs of the boat. He was, Heine said, out cold, in a faint like death.

It seemed Heine waited, but next Ermelind bustled up, and perhaps at that Lutz stirred, and uttered some moaning noise, and then sat up, his eyes half-shuttered and swimming still, staring at them as if he had no idea in the world who they were, or who he *himself* was, come to that.

Well, Heine could not resist, he later reportedly said. He bent down and murmured like a lover into Lutz's ear. "Must have been a shock to you, Prince," murmured Heine, "her being found so soon after you had her, and then killed her and threw her in the River."

But it was Heine who got the proper shock. For instantly, like one more doll set going by clockwork and steam, the recumbent Lutz sprang off the deck, and getting hold of Heine, shook him. "His eyes had gone red as rubies," Heine reportedly said. But they were the last things Heine saw for a while, because Lutz then clouted Heine such a blow on the jaw it knocked him clear across the space and down the ladder to the deck beneath. Unlike the Prince, Heine did not recover his wits for forty minutes, and beside bruises he had three teeth loose for a week.

She was not in the cemetery. Five years on, the registrar had informed Lutz of that. There had been – how should he say? – some slight difficulty about her death. It appeared she must have gone mad, wandering alone about the woods by the night River, in clothes purloined from her own mother's shop. One drew the reluctant conclusion she threw herself at length into the water to drown. Suicide. What a waste of a young working life, of a body fit to bear children. It seemed some doctor had protested, but nobody took any notice of his ramblings. He had attended the young woman's father apparently, and was now entirely out of touch with modern life. The mother? Oh, the registrar could not recollect, but the haberdashery was still there, a silly little shop, catering to the vanities of women...

The registrar afterwards, when gossiping about this, said that the man who had wanted to know these matters had seemed eccentric. Although the registrar had initially credited the fellow's tale that he was a relative, subsequently the registrar thought he might have been lying. At no juncture did the registrar mention the generous tip Lutz had bribed him with. Also, the registrar never detected who Lutz might really be. Famous actors of quality were beneath the interest of the registrar.

But the woman in the shop helped Lutz. She had heard the girl was buried on a hillside above the River, about a mile from the town. This was a vernal and mostly unvisited place, rising up in the midst of the trees. It had not cost much to have a grave dug there. A stone had been set on the grave, but marked only with the young girl's given name, though written in full: *Ghisella*. "I said I couldn't swear to it, of course. But he thanked me again, in such a gentlemanly way. It was like talking to royalty. But then, didn't they call him 'the Prince'?"

No one, aside from the creatures of the woods, the birds, the trees themselves, the wide River below and sky above, saw him climb up to her grave. By then it was far on in the afternoon, and the sun over to the west. Shadows divided the ground with their long, dark rulings. It was a glade artificially and incidentally fashioned by men, for many of the trees there had been lopped for timber. Those that remained stood forlornly, as if in unease. When would death come back for them?

Without some attention, it must have been easy to miss the spot. Lutz Alvarek took care not to. He parted the tall grasses with their spurs of hard, dying flowers. The mound was overgrown by briars and tufts, and a young birch had rooted in it, speckled yet ivory white, with thin sprays of greenery that glittered against the sinking day.

Lutz knelt down by the grave.

He put his right hand on the stone, and then, leaning forward, laid his head against it. The angle and the gathering mass of shadows hid his face. He made no sound and did not again move.

All light drained from the sky. The birch turned grey then wan, the sky wan then deepest grey. A star, pink as watered blood, soaked slowly through the darkness.

Lutz had not, did not, move. He too might have been shaped from stone.

What did the trees think of it? Perhaps only that the most horrible guilt can take the strangest forms.

But it was too as if he were waiting. For what?

Other than vilyas, sometimes they are known as rusalki, those ones who inhabit the trees or the water. They may be beautiful to see, or vile as the nightmare, but they bring retribution always; there is, the stories tell us, no alternative subject between them, these long-haired female shades, and human men, their partners in that dance of death. They are cruel as the moon, which on nights of its fullness is itself like a deathly marble stone, rounded yet incised with skull-like cavities, lit by a transient golden sheen, which allows it, thing of night and underworld that it is, to pass for a shining lamp.

On these nights that are given to them, the dead girls rise from their living tombs of bark or water, they stretch out their long pale arms, and the skull-moon gilds them also, making their skin gleam silk-bright, and their eyes dark emerald as leaves and rivers, and the knotted wildwood of their hair into spider webs of spun silver.

Fair or hideous, they are irresistible, the rusalki, the vilyas, and they glide weightless over the earth with their arms holding up the air, and the hungry tides of black fire already dancing in their eyes.

Very probably it was the blinding moonlight that roused Lutz.

It was not that he had been sleeping, but he had been in a sort of hypnotised state. He wanted nothing else but to lean his body and his head against the stone marker, his eyes shut, lost in the slow, dull, black dungeon-vault of some inner room that might have been his brain.

But the moon now would not allow this.

It speared in through his eyelids. The rays stuck and stayed like javelins, bisecting his interior prison.

He had no choice but to look, and to come out.

An actor, even in everyday life it would often be quite difficult to tell what really he thought or felt. Even the old fool of a registrar was mostly reacting to Lutz's wealth, manner, good clothes and powerful, graceful bearing, when deeming this stranger 'eccentric'. Jealousy can nearly always brush up its syntax.

Besides, Prince Lutz was accustomed to an audience.

Standing up with the ease of a trained and still quite youthful physique, he glanced around. Did he smile or bow?

Perhaps not. Conceivably he judged at once *this* audience would be hard to win. He raised his brows in a voiceless question, that was all.

None answered.

But the one he faced when he did this seemed to be their leader. Yes, without doubt, she was the feline ruler of the she- pack. All were women, were girls, some extremely young, fourteen or thirteen years he might have guessed, while certain others were much older – that one there a mature woman in her forties... But they were, everyone, most beautiful. And each of them – his blood ran colder. Again, he turned around and looked about the circle of female beings that enclosed him. How long their hair in every case, some all frosted over silver, all tangled with reeds and weeds – hair like steam and cobwebs... They were white as the best paper otherwise, both their skins and their indecipherable garments. And their eyes were after all not dark, but like pale green pearls. Looking at them, he began to see too that while dissimilar, they were each alike, and the *most* alike of all was the one who led them. There was a green moss in her hair, he saw now, and a flicker of black in her cream-green eyes. But next they all had this moss, this black sparkle, taking their cue from *her*. He had heard the legends of the riverbank, of course he had. He had named his showboat for them, *Vilya*.

Therefore, Lutz did give a short little bow to their queen. "Ill-met by moonlight," drawled Lutz, "proud Myrra."

But Myrra, if so it was her, and like enough it was, gave no answer again.

Then he shrugged. "Since you exist, do what you want. It seems to me, even if I never believed in you for a single minute, I may still have come back to find you. No doubt it's the only method for me now. I've never been free of it, of *her*. I never will be free of her. All the brilliant moves I've made for myself, all the cunning escapes I've tried to effect – giving the boat and the business to Heine, running off to the theatre-temples of the cities, hiding in those roles of other men – *Ulysses, Doctor Mirabilis, Hamlet* – all useless to hide me from *myself*. My life ended five years ago. So then. Here I am, and you exist. Better do what they say you do. I won't deny you. Exit. Curtain. No applause necessary, no encore."

They do not require his permission to begin. Does he feel he has to do it, to be sure they are properly riled, sufficiently aggravated to attack him at once? Or does he, educated, urban sophisticate, yet partly believe he imagines or is dreaming them?

And does he wonder anyway why Ghisla – or Ghisella, as her tomb has it – is not with them, the horde of vilyas. Should she not be here?

Above the glade, a smoky cloud shawls up the moon. There is a low quivering susurrus, a dry crepitation sounding like crickets, where no crickets are; also there is a vague persistent rumble under the earth, thunder underground, continuous – drums, where drums too are not.

The vilyas have begun their dance.

Slow and rhythmic as the winding of a serpent, they moved about him, anti-clockwise it goes nearly without saying, as they tell us the dead must, opposite always when passing in again through the mirror of life. They were so beautiful as they danced, they dazzled him, even in his hell of misery they *seduced* him, but now and then, like a sudden flash of lightning on a dark pool, he saw straight through the shimmer of their charms, and beheld plainly they were also foul, things like decaying carrion, with long yellowish hooked teeth and nails, and their eyes only holes, gleaming up opaque white or hollowing to black, with nothing behind or inside, but a malice so mindless it was an idiocy, yet a killing one nonetheless.

He had started to feel how they touched him, on the face, on the body. Each tiny small little touch went straight through like pins. He felt his skeleton twist, and his muscles displace and cramp, and his blood, so cold, went thin as ice-water.

He began after that to turn irresistibly with them, round and round, but not now of his own volition. He turned like a wine cork in a tidal pool. Slow even so, slow as slow can be. But his entire framework had commenced to resist, as he did not, to crank and to lock and to *hurt*. Yes, he hurt, like an old man with aching bones. But very much worse.

And then inevitably the tempo of the dance, and the turning, increased. He was drifting, then walking, then trotting, and now he ran. He was sprinting, spinning, he had no say in any of it, could not have stopped himself, could not try.

They were laughing, he thought distractedly. Either they laughed – or uncontrollably wept – faces in a rictus of anguish or overwhelming pleasure, either or both, resembling the throes of physical love...

Overhead, over the tree tops, the moon spun too, bowling along like a smoky mechanical wheel.

And now Lutz became the moon's marionette. It had somehow attached to him invisible wires, and jerked irregularly and brutally at his arms and legs, feet and hands, his neck and head and spine.

All of his body, outside and in, was spasming, jumping, leaping. His arms and fists made the violent gestures of a drunken prize-fighter, his legs thrashed, as if to kick at objects or lurch him over fences. His head darted and shook, snapping on its cord.

Lutz was in sheer agony now. As the seizures of the wild dance convulsed him, he cried out at the excruciation, the tearing and pulling of sinews, his vertebrae crushed and crunching.

He thought the moon above him changed to black-green, like a malachite.

Lutz Alvarek soon lay on the ground. Still striking out and kicking as the convulsions dictated, he had stopped screaming, no longer able to make much sound.

This, the true nature of the 'dance' the vilyas award to men. The dance of death.

But they themselves, with an odd feral innocence, went on, effortlessly twining and circling. Where they dance, the stories stress, the grass grows up rich and deep, corn or barley rises thick, trees put on ripe fruit. Or else, the other stories warn, the ground there goes black and the grass perishes and the trees fall down.

Lutz stayed conscious. The dance did not permit full loss of awareness. He lay contorted and insanely writhing, and above him, against the malachite moon, he could just make out the crown of the birch tree that grew from Ghisla's grave.

In that way, senselessly, he noticed that something was rising up from the tree, like pale steam. It was meaningless in his pain, only pain had meaning. Yet the paleness gained shape, the paleness had become a girl – a galvanic wrench of his torso flung him over on his face. For that reason, he could not witness how next the girl stood in the top of the tree, and then stepped off on to the air, and came walking quietly and simply down it, as if on a stairway.

She had finally come out to view the evening's drama, a neighbour woken by noise in the street. Ghisla, still sixteen years old, her black hair loose and pouring round her, her white dress torn, her drinkable sherry eyes stern and intent.

And some ten feet from the earth, above all the measures of the dance, she paused immobile on the air, and gazed down at her lover, at Prince Lutz, as he grew ready to die.

How much was left of Mrrya, ruler of the vilyas? Maybe only an impulse, still clad in partially human form. Why anyway was she queen of these revenants? Could it be only she had made herself so because, when alive, she had had status, the rich man's daughter?

We must never doubt this, they never 'speak', these creatures. Even so, like other elements that appear not to converse, yet do, the earthly-lingering dead have a language, and use it.

Myrra demanded of Ghisla why she stood by, balanced on darkness.

Come down, said Myrra. *Join us at our game. Watch him snuffed out like a match.*

Ghisla spoke.

She said softly, "I'm here to say you must leave him alone."

Did she absolutely say that, that shy and ill-treated girl, and only a ghost now? In life, she had been unable – taught in her first years by that harsh mother – to stand up for the rights of anything, let alone herself. And now she stands up on the air, you see, and tells the ghoul-queen of the damned and murderous dead that they must let go.

Never, presumably Myrra replies.

"At once," says Ghisla, with a peculiar glint of asperity, obviously ironically learned too from her mother.

The drums and rattling whispering of the dance-music have gone. The night is deaf with noiselessness. Not a leaf stirs, or dares to.

Ghisla speaks again, "He isn't for you. You have nothing to do with him. You must let him live, and I will heal him."

You! Myrra will be amazed – does so much intelligence remain to her undead state? – *You died through him and what he did to you.*

"Yes," Ghisla responds, "but you know nothing about it. You have no power to harm him. Only I have power over him. You must give way."

In the deaf and awful noiselessness, Ghisla, fragile as a moth, undoes one page of darkness and of time, as is the talent of ghosts. This is like that contemporary phenomenon we have seen so recently, the moving steam-flickers, those cinematic images that can be thrown on a screen, and then perform there a drama. And from the tunnel of the past, this living movie glides out, reborn on the screen of darkness: that night five years before, when Lutz had met her on the gallery of the showboat, and said to her, "I have been waiting for you... did you know?... My love, now you do."

Leaving the showboat, they had walked out into the woods that overhung the River.

His arm had been about her. She could feel nothing else, but also strangely was aware of everything else, every leaf that brushed another, the grass under their feet growing, the flavour of the dark. No night had ever been so liquid black, but the River shone jade. Fireflies or stars sometimes washed through the trees. Somewhere, he turned her to him, and kissed her, mildly, then deeply. And Ghisla had become all the night, full of a power like flight. She had held him, and taken his kisses like the feast they were, a banquet after starvation, and also *familiar*, *known* to her, as if they had kissed like this forever – somewhere, in some other region or condition, and as if now, here again they came home to each other, he and she.

After a while, he spoke to her very seriously. "You won't believe me; please try, my darling. Listen. I'm older than you, and no boy. I've had – forgive me – many love affairs."

At this gently she shook her head, smiling. Of course, what else, for a man so beautiful and fine? It did not matter.

He held her closer, he said, "There was never one like you. This is a *cliché*, and very trite, but I've no other phrase to explain it. The instant I saw you – did you feel this too?"

"Yes," she answered.

"Then you'll understand me," he said. "I want you and will have you," he said, "providing always that you'll agree not to be my sudden companion as suddenly given up. I want you with me, my love. I want you with me until I die, which event I intend not to let happen less than a hundred years in the future."

She laughed at this, not in silly amusement or mockery. She laughed because she thought, that moment, it was possible, and that she too, now he had found her, would also live another hundred years.

"So," he said, "our best course is to marry. Do you think so?" he asked.

She had gained such confidence. She had become another person, or perhaps become herself, opening like a flower. But she only nodded again.

He, trained in words and their delivery, was the one who said, "We are already married, I think, elsewhere. We've only to formalise the state. Oh, Ghisla..." – by then he knew her name – "we will be so happy."

And after that they had made their plans, or he had outlined *his* plan, which was both bold and sensible enough. He explained that he had noted something was going awry with the mechanical doll from the play, and so tomorrow he would need to get that taken care of, and, should the doll be beyond help, coach the rest of the company on how to nurse the play to its end without overly disappointing their audience. After the performance, it would be too late to go calling. But the day *after* tomorrow he would arrive at her mother's shop at noon. He would sweep the mother off her feet, being able, too, financially to sort out her overworked situation. He was completely confident the mother would not stand in their way. He had always been lucky, he said, and tonight was the proof of that for he had found Ghisla, had he not?

So, they were to part, and one whole night, and then another day and night must go by until that third day, the noon when he would come to claim her. Would she wait for him? he asked her, smiling. She said she would. Otherwise Ghisla's Prince did nothing to endanger or offend. His passionate and prolonged kisses, which had so thrilled and re-formed Ghisla, had not in any way infringed what her mother might have called Ghisla's 'chastity'. There had been no rabid seduction, no betrayal. And there would never have been any betrayal, not by him, her lover, Prince Lutz Alvarek. When he spoke of loving her, he spoke sincerely and from the deep of a heart and mind equally clever, fly and genuine. Every word uttered to her was truth. He had 'loved' often, but never *loved*. Now he did. And maybe it might even have lasted a lifetime, even a lifetime of one hundred and twenty-two years. Maybe, as he had felt also, blindly, sublimely, their love had begun in another time, on another planet perhaps, an elsewhere as real or more real than mortal life.

He intended to escort her home, but Ghisla refused this. She assured him the woods thereabouts were safe, and she had only a brief journey. She told him too she would need to compose herself, and although by now the spectre of her mother had shrunk very small, Ghisla did not want to alarm or shock her. Ghisla had, during this magical interlude, learned to pity her mother greatly.

Their last embrace, meant only to be a promise, continued for hours and was over in a split second. But she took down her hair for him so he could kiss that too, and gave him her green combs to keep, when he asked for them.

She went away through the trees like the white ghost she already seemed. He watched until she vanished, then walked back to the boat. The *Vilya*. As in all his endeavours, or most of them, Lutz had known success. Only his professionalism had made him prepared to organise the business of the faulty doll. Otherwise he would never have wasted a single day.

He woke and slept and woke that night, in the inebriation of new love. And saw to business all the next day, and in the second night, lounging vainglorious with the other actors, after they had – by sheer ingenuity, and most of that his – saved the play despite failed Bithida, the doll, he had drunk his fill in a sweet, blurred triumph of anticipation. Thinking of the day after, of noon, of claiming her, his love. And then he heard about the drowned girl, the pretty one in the white dress, who had lingered on the gallery. Ghisla. Ghisla drowned. Ghisla dead and lost and gone, and his life with her, all the burning one hundred years of it.

What then, in God's good name, had happened?

That Lutz had not, at the time, tried to discover the true cause of her death – well, who can say why not? The shock had assailed him too terribly, perhaps. And perhaps too, despite the vaunted luck of most of his life, in the past had there been other strokes, which had robbed and hurt him, as if to balance the rest? That he went at once away is strange, yet imaginable.

410

That he remained haunted, also.

But she – what, in the name of Hell – what, *what?*

She had felt, the young girl, so filled by rushing delight, remade, reborn, she knew she could not yet go back to the cramped stale little apartment. So, she ran, childlike, to the River's edge, and her dress was torn, but without fear she thought: He'll pay for it, he's so kind, and she won't be cross.

Her head sang and her heart beat crazily, and she stood – there on the brink of the dark and she began to weep – not from pain or horror or – from pure joy. Joy infused her, set her alight, joy brimmed her over, not knowing, as how could such a lambent thing as joy ever know, that though Ghisla's soul was well able to encompass it, her young, fragile body – *could not.* Her father's doctor had guessed and tried to tell them, you will recall, what might have killed her, other than insanity and water. For Ghisla's father had died, not of a cough, but since his weak heart could not withstand the barrage of coughing. This weakness in the heart had passed, unknown, to Ghisla. And never before had it been so taxed. The joy, the bliss of love, the wonder to come, the *rescue* – they filled her physical heart, and her heart – broke. It broke, like the clockwork of the doll. And being human, Ghisla was not reparable. A single moment, as if the earth cracked end to end, and then the unfelt drifting fall, like a dying leaf, down into the waters of sorrow, the River made of tears. She was dead before the leaf of her body clove its surface.

The flicker-movie is over. *They* have watched and seen all, the vilya horde. And Ghisla they see too, her phantom, seated now on the ground beside Lutz, passing her quiet compassionate ghost hands through and through him, healing, as she said she could, every injury the dance of the damned has caused. And as she does this, also, she has found her four green combs, wrapped up in a piece of clean linen, and lying over his heart. *His* heart that is strong. He will live.

When she lifts her head at last, the finishing shreds of the vilyas, Myrra with them, are fluttering, like skeletal butterflies, away into an eternal shadow. What happens here is, and has been proven, none of their concern. And now they are gone.

Near sunrise he wakes up, battered and sore, as if he has been beaten, but not so very badly, and he sees her looking down at him, his lover, the true love of his life. Her face, framed by the dark river of her hair, her soft breasts that he has *never*, Prince that he is, ever touched, her mouth that he has kissed and longs to kiss again, but which he knows cannot anymore be kissed. He is dreaming her, naturally. Ghosts, superstitious though he may be, are only for the plays.

Nevertheless, he says, "No chance for us, then."

"No, my love," she answers, or something lays the words inside his mind.

"Next time we meet, perhaps," he says. But he is aware it was a miracle they had met *here*. Why should they have the fortune to manage that miracle again when, with all things seemingly on their side, they had failed to capitalise upon it now?

Yet, "Oh, yes," she answers. And she smiles. "One day it will happen."

The dawn is coming, that must be the unforgiveable glare that blazes along the hem of the earth, its rays smoking through her, pink as pearl, cruel as knives.

"I believe it will," he staunchly says. "Till then, my darling girl."

Already in front of him he beholds himself, trudging off from the River, avoiding the town. The steambus met at some other halt, the return to the cities and the glass-paste theatres And the unreal acted lives. And the dawn smoke turns black and clouds him through.

Despite the fact of impossibility, she leans to him and kisses him on the lips. He feels nothing of the kiss.

He says again, "Until then, my love."

And as she fades into the light, she answers, "Till then."

Author's Note:

The story on which this is based, (and which provided the plot-line of Adolphe Adam's ballet, *Giselle*), seems to derive from Slavic Russian and/or German roots, and the legends of the Rusalka, Wili, Vili or Vila. But for reasons that may be obvious of possible mispronunciation, I've spelled 'vila' phonetically throughout – Vil*y*a.

About the Author

Tanith Lee (1947-2015) was born in London. Because her parents were professional dancers (ballroom, Latin American) and had to live where the work was, she attended a number of truly terrible schools, and didn't learn to read – she was also dyslectic – until almost age 8. And then only because her father taught her. This opened the world of books to her, and by 9 she was writing. After much better education at a grammar school, she went on to work in a library. This was followed by various other jobs – shop assistant, waitress, clerk – plus a year at art college when she was 25-26. In 1974, her career as a writer was launched, when DAW Books of America, under the leadership of Donald A. Wollheim, bought and published *The Birthgrave*, and thereafter 26 of her novels and collections.

Tanith was presented with a Lifetime Achievement Award in 2013, at World Fantasycon in Brighton. During her lifetime, she also received the World Horror Convention Grand Master Award, as well as the August Derleth Award and the World Fantasy Award for short fiction (twice).

In 1992, she married the writer-artist-photographer John Kaiine, her partner since 1987. They lived on the Sussex Weald, near the sea, in a house full of books and plants, and never without feline companions. She died at home in May 2015, after a long illness, continuing to work until a couple of weeks before her death.

Throughout her life, Tanith wrote around 100 books, and over 300 short stories. 4 of her radio plays were broadcast by the BBC; she also wrote 2 episodes (*Sarcophagus* and *Sand*) for the TV series *Blake's 7*. Her stories were read regularly on Radio 4 Extra. She was an inspiration to a generation of writers and her work was enormously influential within genre fiction – as it continues to be. She wrote in many styles, within and across many genres, including Horror, SF and Fantasy, Historical, Detective, Contemporary-Psychological, Children and Young Adult. Her preoccupation, though, was always people.

Publishing History of the Stories

Taken from *Daughter of the Night, An Annotated Tanith Lee Bibliography*,
compiled and maintained by Allison Rich
http://www.daughterofthenight.com/

Antonius Bequeathed:
  Weird Tales No. 306, (Vol 54 No 1), Spring 1993
  Weird Tales 305-6 (Winter 1992-Spring 1993). Wildside Press, 2003
  Hunting the Shadows: The Selected Stories of Tanith Lee Vol 2, Wildside Press
  2009

Arthur's Lion:
  Weird Tales. No 340 (Vol 61 No 3), May-June 2006
  Tails of Wonder and Imagination. Ed. By Ellen Datlow, Night Shade Books,
  2010

Blood Chess
  Weird Tales. No 331 (Vol 59 No 3), Spring 2003
  Vampires: Classic Tales, ed. by Mike Ashley, Dover Publications, 2011
  Blood 20: Tales of Vampire Horror, Telos Publishing, 2015

Death Dances
  Weird Tales. No 290 (Vol 50 No 1), Spring 1988
  Best of Weird Tales, ed. By John Betancourt, Barnes & Noble, 1995
  Dancing Through the Fire, Fantastic Books, 2015

Flicker of a Winter Star
  Weird Tales. No 327 (Vol 58 No 3), Spring 2002

Flower Water
  Weird Tales. No 313 (Vol 55 No 1), Summer 1998
  Weird Tales 313-316 (Summer 1998-Summer 1999), Wildside Press, 2003
  Hunting the Shadows: The Selected Stories of Tanith Lee Volume Two, Wildside
  Press, 2009

Girls in Green Dresses
  Weird Tales. No 321 (Vol 57, No 1), Fall 2000
  Octocon: The National Irish Science Fiction Convention Program. Octocon 2004
  Legenda Maris. Immanion Press, 2015

The Heart of Ice
  Weird Tales. No 349 (Vol 63 No 2), March/April 2008
  Cold Grey Stones, NewCon Press, 2012

Colder Greyer Stones, NewCon Press, 2013

An Iron Bride
Weird Tales. No 318 (Vol 56, No 2), Winter 1999-2000

The Kingdoms of the Air
Weird Tales. No 291 (Vol 50 No 2), Summer 1988
Chronicles of The Holy Grail, ed. By Mike Ashley, Carrol & Graf, 1996
Tempting the Gods: The Selected Stories of Tanith Lee Vol. One, Wildside Press, 2009

The Lily Garden
Weird Tales. No 304 (Vol 53 No 3), Spring 1992
Weird Tales: Seven Decades of Terror, ed. By John Betancourt & Robert Weinberg, Barnes & Noble, 1997

Magpied
Weird Tales. No. 361 (Vol 67 No 1), Summer 2013

Midnight
Weird Tales. No 335 (Vol 60 No 3), March-April 2004

Mirror, Mirror
Weird Tales. No 308 (Vol 54 No 3), Spring 1994
Weird Tales 307-8 (Summer 1993-Spring 1994), Wildside Press, 2003
Blood 20: Tales of Vampire Horror, Telos Publishing, 2015

One for Sorrow
Weird Tales. No 308 (Vol 54 No 3), Spring 1994
Weird Tales 307-8 (Summer 1993/Spring 1994), Wildside Press, 2003
Hunting the Shadows: The Selected Stories of Tanith Lee Vol. Two. Wildside Press, 2009

The Persecution Machine
Weird Tales. No 308 (Vol 54 No 3), Spring 1994
Weird Tales 307-8 (Summer 1993/Spring 1994), Wildside Press, 2003.
Hunting the Shadows: The Selected Stories Of Tanith Lee Vol. Two, Wildside Press, 2009
Steampunk II: Steampunk Reloaded, ed. by Ann and Jeff Vandermeer, Tachyyon Publications, 2010

Scarlet and Gold
Weird Tales. No 316 (Vol 55 No 4), Summer 1999
Weird Tales 309-312 (Summer 1994-Summer 1996), Wildside Press, 2003

Tanith Lee

The Sea Was in Her Eyes
Weird Tales. No 322 (Vol 57, No 2), Winter 2000/2001
Octocon: The National Irish Science Fiction Convention Program. Octocon 2004
Legenda Maris, Immanion Press, 2015

Sold
Weird Tales. No 346 (Vol 62 No 4), September-October 2007
Dancing Through the Fire: A Collection of Stories in Five Moves, Fantastic Books, 2015

The Sombrus Tower
Weird Tales #2, ed. By Lin Carter, Zebra Books, 1981
Weird Tales: The Magazine That Never Dies. Doubleday Book and Music Clubs, Inc, 1988

Stars Above, Stars Below
Weird Tales. No 314 (Vol 55 No 2), Fall 1998
Weird Tales 313-316 (Summer 1998-Summer 1999), Wildside Press, 2003

La Vampiresse
Interzone. No 154, April 2000
Weird Tales. No 324 (Vol 57, No 4), Summer 2001
Vampires: The Recent Undead, Ed. By Paula Guran, Prime Books, 2011
Blood 20: Tales of Vampire Horror, Telos Publishing, 2015

Unlocking the Golden Cage
Weird Tales. No 315 (Vol 55 No 3), Spring 1999
Weird Tales 313-316 (Summer 1998-Summer 1999), Wildside Press, 2003
Hunting the Shadows: The Selected Stories of Tanith Lee Vol. Two, Wildside Press, 2009

The Unrequited Glove
Weird Tales. No 291 (Vol 50 No 2), Summer 1988
Women as Demons: The Male Perception of Women Through Space and Time, The Women's Press, 1989

The Waters of Sorrow
Weird Tales, Nth Media, electronic preview story for World Fantasycon 2011
Red as Blood, Or, Tales from The Sisters Grimmer (Expanded edition), Wildside Press, 2014

When the Clock Strikes
Weird Tales #1, ed. By Lin Carter, Zebra Books, 1981
Year's Best Fantasy Stories: 8, ed. By Arthur W. Saha, DAW Books, 1982

Red as Blood, or Tales from the Sisters Grimmer, DAW Books, 1983

Red as Blood, Or, Tales from The Sisters Grimmer (Expanded edition), Wildside Press, 2014

Masterpieces of Terror and The Supernatural, Science Fiction Book Club, 1985

Dreams of Dark and Light: the Great Short Fiction of Tanith Lee, Arkham House, 1986

Spells of Enchantment: The Wondrous Fairy Tales of Western Culture, ed. By Jack Zipes, Viking, 1991

Writing and Reading Across the Curriculum, ed. By Laurence Behrens and Leonard J. Rosen Harper Collins, 1994

Where All Things Perish

Weird Tales. No 325 (Vol 58. No 1), Fall 2001

The Mammoth Book of Best New Horror 13, Ed. By Stephen Jones, Constable Robinson, 2002

Sounds and Furies: Seven Faces of Darkness, Norilana Books, 2010

Weird Fiction Review. January 11, 2012

The Winter Ghosts

Weird Tales. No 303 (Vol 53 No 2), Winter 1991/92

100 Fiendish Little Frightmares, Ed by Stefan Dziemianowicz, Robert Weinberg & Martin H. Greenberg Barnes & Noble, 1997

Ghosteria Volume One: The Stories. Immanion Press, 2014

IMMANION PRESS
Purveyors of Speculative Fiction

The Lightbearer by Alan Richardson (May 2017)

Michael Horsett parachutes into Occupied France before the D-Day Invasion. He is dropped in the wrong place, miles from the action, badly injured, and totally alone. He falls prey to two Thelemist women who have awaited the Hawk God's coming, attracts a group of First World War veterans who rally to what they imagine is his cause, is hunted by a troop of German Field Police who are desperate to find him, and has a climactic encounter with a mutilated priest who believes that Lucifer Incarnate has arrived...

The Lightbearer is a unique gnostic thriller, dealing with the themes of Light and Darkness, Good and Evil, Matter and Spirit.

"The Lightbearer is another shining example of Alan Richardson's talent as a story-teller. He uses his wide esoteric knowledge to produce a story that thrills, chills and startles the reader as it radiates pure magical energy. An unusual and gripping war story with more facets than a star sapphire." – Mélusine Draco, author of "Aubry's Dog" and "Black Horse, White Horse". ISBN: 978-1-907737-63-3 £11.99 $18.99

Dark in the Day, Ed. by Storm Constantine & Paul Houghton

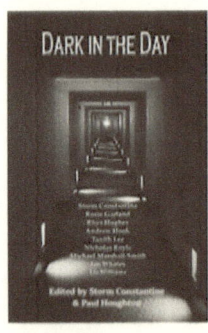

Weirdness lurks beyond the margins of the mundane, emerging to dismantle our assumptions of reality. Dark in the Day is an anthology of weird fiction, penned by established writers and also those new to the genre – the latter being authors who are, or were, students of Creative Writing at Staffordshire University, where editor Storm Constantine occasionally delivers guest lectures. Her co-editor, Paul Houghton, is the senior lecturer in Creative Writing at the university.

Contributors include: Martina Bellovičová, J. E. Bryant, Glynis Charlton, Storm Constantine, Louise Coquio, Elizabeth Counihan, Krishan Coupland, Elizabeth Davidson, Siân Davies, Paul Finch, Rosie Garland, Rhys Hughes, Kerry Fender, Andrew Hook, Paul Houghton, Tanith Lee, Tim Pratt, Nicholas Royle, Michael Marshall Smith, Paula Wakefield, Ian Whates and Liz Williams. ISBN: 978-1-907737-74-9 £11.99, $18.99

Blood, the Phoenix and a Rose by Storm Constantine

Wraeththu, a race of androgynous beings, have arisen from the ashes of human civilisation. Like the mythical rebis, the divine hermaphrodite, they represent the pinnacle of human evolution. But Wraeththu – or hara – were forged in the crucible of destruction and emerged from a new Dark Age. They have yet to realise their full potential and come to terms with the most blighted aspects of their past. Blood, the Phoenix and a Rose begins with an enigma: Gavensel, a har who appears unearthly and has a shrouded history. He has been hidden away in the house of Sallow Gandaloi by Melisander, an alchemist, but is this seclusion to protect Gavensel from the world or the world from him? As his story unfolds, the shadow of the dark fortress Fulminir falls over him, and memories of his past slowly return. The only way to find the truth is to go back through the layers of time, to when the blood was fresh. ISBN: 978-1-907737-75-6 £11.99, $18.99

Animate Objects by Tanith Lee

There is no such thing as an inanimate object… And how could that be? Because, simply, everything is formed from matter, and basically, at *root*, the matter that makes up everything in the physical world – the Universe – is of the same substance. Which means, on that basic level, we – you, me, and that power station over there – are all the exact riotous, chaotic, amorphous *same*. Here is an assortment of Lee takes on the nature, and perhaps intentions, of so-called non-sentient things. And you're quite safe. This is only a book. An inanimate object.

From the Introduction by Tanith Lee

The original hardback of this collection, of which there were only 35 copies, was published by Immanion Press in 2013, to commemorate Tanith Lee receiving the Lifetime Achievement Award at World Fantasycon. It included 5 previously unpublished pieces. This new release includes a further 2 stories, co-written by Tanith Lee and John Kaiine, and new interior illustrations by Jarod Mills. ISBN: 978-1-907737-73-2, £11.99 $18.99

Immanion Press
http://www.immanion-press.com
info@immanion-press.com

NEWCON PRESS

http://newconpress.co.uk/

The very best in fantasy, science fiction, and horror

The Ion Raider by Ian Whates

As Corbin Drake receives his most unusual assignment for First Solar yet – one which he suspects is a trap but knows he can't refuse – his former crew, the notorious brigands known as the Dark Angels, are being hunted down one by one and murdered. Determined to find those responsible before they find her, Leesa teams up with Jen, another former Dark Angel, and together they set out to thwart the mysterious organization known as Saflik, little dreaming where that path will lead them.

ISBN: 978-1-910935-38-5 £12.99 paperback (Also in signed limited edition hardback)

Entropic Angel by Gareth L Powell

Award-winning science fiction writer Gareth L. Powell delivers his first collection in nearly a decade. Gathering together twenty stories, including four that are previously unpublished as well as some of the author's best-loved tales, the content provides highlights from across twelve years of his career, delivering a powerful collection that is both entertaining and thought-provoking.

ISBN: 978-1-910935-42-2 paperback £12.99 (Also in signed limited edition hardback)